gift

D1168294

UNTIMELY DEATH

A NOVEL

FRED YAGER
AND
JAN YAGER

Hannacroix Creek Books

Copyright © 1998 by Fred Yager and Jan Yager

Manufactured in the United States of America.

Library of Congress Catalogue Card Number: 96-94539

Publisher's Cataloging in Publication
(Prepared by Quality Books, Inc.)

Yager, Fred, 1946 -
   Untimely Death : a novel / Fred Yager, Jan Yager.
   p. cm.
   ISBN: 1-889262-01-3

   I. Yager, Jan, 1948- II. Title.

PS3575.A447U67 1997   813'.54
                                                 QBI96-40052

Published by:
HANNACROIX CREEK BOOKS, INC.
1127 High Ridge Road, #110
Stamford, Connecticut 06905 U.S.A.
(203) 321-8674 Fax (203) 968-0193
e-mail: Hannacroix@aol.com
on the web: http://www.HannacroixCreekBooks.com

For Scott and Jeffrey

CHAPTER ONE

"It's a simple combination of leverage, speed and being able to use the attacker's weight for momentum. Now let's try it again, okay? Who's ready? Professor Stone. How 'bout it? Want to give it a try?"

Professor Kimberly Stone looked at the instructor when she heard her name, but she had no idea what he was talking about. Her mind and attention had left the building and it was all Joan Walsh's fault. Ever since her best friend had told her that today was going to be the day her boyfriend would propose, Kimberly had felt a growing pang of impending abandonment. Maybe she was over-reacting. Their friendship would withstand the strain of marital commitments. Or would it?

"Professor?"

Kimberly could feel eight pairs of eyes staring at her as she remembered where she was. The weekly self-defense class had been Joan's idea, but had Joan made even one class? No. And was she here today? No. What was her excuse this time? She had to finish correcting term papers before her special lunch with Bill. But here you are, a 37-year-old criminology professor, about to get your ass kicked by a macho Chuck Norris-wannabe who thinks he's God's gift to martial arts.

"You're gonna have to do this sooner or later Dr. Stone," said Richie Tucker, a third-degree black belt in karate and a first-degree black belt in bullshit. Richie held out his hand, but Kimberly pushed up from the mat, unassisted.

"That's the spirit," he said, grinning.

While the other women remained sitting in a semi-circle around the outside of the two-inch thick blue mat, Kimberly walked to the center. So far, every other woman in the class had humiliated herself at the hands of this bully who obviously enjoyed flipping helpless females over his back and pinning them into submission under the guise of teaching them how to avoid such situations.

"The Professor here has been working out," Richie addressed the sitting women. "I've seen her pumping those Nautilus machines, toning up those triceps and biceps. She sure looks good don't she?"

Kimberly felt the blush in her cheeks. Step a little closer Richie. Let me see how far I can bench-press your testicles.

Richie tightened the cinch on the black web belt that held his white karate robe together and walked behind Kimberly, who, like the rest of the students, was wearing black leotards and spandex.

"Let's see if Professor Stone has been paying attention. Remember what I said. Leverage, speed and momentum. Ready Professor?"

"I supp ..."

But before Kimberly could finish, Richie grabbed her from behind with a choke hold, his forearm cutting off her windpipe.

Kimberly dropped to her knees and tried to flip Richie over her shoulder but he wouldn't budge. Instead, he grabbed the back of her head and slammed her back into the mat, then straddled her chest with his fist pointing down at her neck in striking position.

"You need more practice, Professor. Next."

Inside her Greenwich Village apartment, Joan Walsh stepped out of the shower and began to dry off. She looked at the clock. Nine-thirty. That gave her two and a half hours to grade forty Introduction to Criminology term papers before catching a cab to mid-town and lunch at Lutece with Bill Gardner. It was the choice of restaurants

2

that gave him away. It was the first restaurant he'd taken her to, and she remembered telling him what a special place it was. He'd responded by saying he only went there on special occasions. They'd been dating for three months now. If he didn't ask her to marry him at lunch, she was ready to propose to him.

Joan continued drying as she walked to the kitchen for a cup of expresso. Looking out the open window over the sink, she could see that it was going to one of those beautiful spring mornings. The trees that lined Sullivan Street had started to blossom and turn green. The air smelled crisp and clean. And here she was, trapped inside. It wasn't fair. Unfortunately, this was the only time left to read the midterms. The grades had to be turned in tomorrow.

Wrapping the towel around her, she started to carry the cup into the living room when she heard the door buzzer. She wasn't expecting anyone. It was probably Mr. Fontes, the building's superintendent, who just happened to stop by whenever he heard her shower running, hoping to catch a glimpse of her semi-naked, towel-clad body. Not this time old man.

Joan removed the towel and slipped on her bathrobe. Pulling the robe tight and cinching the belt, she walked toward the front door, resentment building with every step. She didn't have time for unnecessary intrusions and was ready to tell him so when she looked through the peephole.

"Well, this is a surprise," she said, smiling when she recognized her visitor.

Joan quickly unlocked the three deadbolts and door-club she had installed to keep out the army of weirdness and insanity that patrolled the Village at night. Pulling open the heavy door, she thought of polite ways to keep the visit short but sweet.

"Is this a bad time?" asked the visitor, noticing Joan's frizzy red hair was still damp from a recent shower and that she smelled of scented soap.

"Actually, it is," said Joan. "I have to correct some papers. And the place is a mess. But you're here. So come in. You can't stay very long though."

"I understand. I thought I might have left something behind the last time I was here. Mind if I look around?"

"Go ahead. Want some coffee?"

3

"No thanks. Maybe some water?"

"I'll just be a second."

The visitor watched as Joan walked into her small kitchen, barely the size of a narrow hallway. She turned on the water faucet and reached into a cupboard for a glass. She seemed different this morning. Had something changed? No make-up. That must be it. But even without her normal beige foundation and eye shadow, Joan Walsh had a natural attractiveness, with her red hair pulled up into a pony tail and her cheeks colored by blotches of freckles. And although Joan had recently turned 35, this morning she looked ten years younger, with an innocence that nearly broke her visitor's heart.

Joan returned to the living room with a glass of water and an awkward smile.

"Did you find what you were looking for?"

"Not yet," said the visitor taking the glass and then taking a drink.

"Why don't you keep looking while I get dressed?"

It was then that Joan realized her visitor was staring at a small framed photograph, one of many pictures lining the dark mahogany mantel over the fireplace.

The visitor then reached over and picked up a picture of Joan with a man in a ski suit. They were standing in front of a ski lodge.

"Who's this?"

"Just a friend." But as soon as she said the words, Joan sensed a subtle shift in the air that sent a shiver of fear down the back of her neck.

"A friend," said the visitor. "I thought *I* was your friend."

"You are," said Joan. "Come on. Don't get like that. Especially about Roy. He's just an old friend I ran into last year at my fifteen-year high school reunion."

Joan took the picture from her visitor and set it back down on the mantel.

"You don't have a picture of me."

"Why would I need a picture when I have the real thing?"

The temperature in the apartment suddenly seemed colder. The air thickened with static electricity. When Joan reached out and touched her visitor's arm a tiny spark shocked her finger.

"Look, I don't have to start grading papers right away."

4

"We have to talk about it," said the visitor.

"There's nothing more to say," smiled Joan. "Besides, I had a more non-verbal type of communication in mind."

The visitor stepped back. "What can I do to change your mind?"

"Nothing. Now stop bringing it up, okay."

She started to let her bathrobe fall open.

"Why don't we just ...."

The blow came fast and furious, a full fist in the face. It crushed her nose and knocked her back.

Feeling as if she was about to fall, Joan reached out to grab something, but two powerful arms spun her around and held her from behind.

Her eyes widened as she tried to comprehend what was happening. It was then that she felt the belt of her bathrobe being torn from its loops. She opened her mouth to scream, but a hand muffled the sound while the other hand bound her wrists with the terry cloth belt. She opened her mouth wider until she could feel the fingers and knuckles beneath her teeth. She bit down as hard as she could.

"Aggghhh!" the attacker screamed, pulling the hand from her mouth.

Joan tasted bile in her throat and felt a trickle of blood running from her nose into her mouth. A feeling of rage soared through her body as anger replaced the fear that had filled her moments before. She started to scream again but this time the sound was muffled by a piece of terry cloth torn from the pocket of her bathrobe. She thought she would gag as the attacker pushed the wad of fabric to the back of her throat.

The attacker blew on the bitten fingers and then backhanded Joan across her face. A blinding pain from her already broken nose caused her eyes to fill with involuntary tears. The room became blurry and for a moment she felt as if she would pass out from the pain. But then she felt the attacker pull the cloth belt tighter, burning the skin around her wrists and the anger returned briefly. She kicked out but all she hit was air.

She tried again to scream but what came out was a gurgling sound and even that seemed to fade into the wet cloth that filled her mouth. She tried again to kick, but the attacker grabbed her leg, spun her around and punched her in the lower back, knocking her to the

5

floor. The assailant then held her down by putting a foot in the center of her chest.

It was then that she had the most terrifying thought. "I'm going to die."

Joan's eyes bulged as she gasped for breath. She saw a running shoe pushing down on her chest. She tried to breathe, to fill her lungs, but the foot pressed down harder. There was something on the running shoe that caught her eye, but everything was starting to blur. She tried to focus, to see what was on the shoe, but the light was starting to fade, as if a cloud had moved across the sun. Just as she thought she would pass out, the shoe lifted. In the brief moment of relief, she saw the object on the running shoe. It was a daisy. Someone had sewn a daisy onto the side of the running shoe. Joan took in a deep breath as she watched the running shoe walk across the floor.

"This isn't happening," thought Joan. "Maybe I'm not going to die. I can't die. I've got all these mid-terms to grade. I've got commitments. I have to get the laundry. I've got school tomorrow. I have that research to complete."

Joan tried to free her hands when the attacker returned holding something. It looked heavy, whatever it was. Where's that breeze coming from, thought Joan, just before she heard the whooshing sound.

It was the last sound Joan heard as the marble horse-shaped bookend slammed into the left side of her head, leaving a crease from the corner of her left eye to the edge of her ear.

Joan blinked and the world went black. Then, a light returned with a searing pain. It was a white hot light, blinding and burning and for a second that would last an eternity, she tried to rise up from the blackness, but she couldn't feel anything. Where were her legs? She couldn't feel her legs. What just happened? Her fingers started to twitch as the attacker untied her hands. Eventually, the finger tremors ceased and darkness filled her mind as she entered a dream she knew would never end.

The attacker knelt down and looked closely for signs of life. A small puddle had formed on the floor between her legs. Sniff. Urine. The killer removed the gag from Joan's mouth and then took off her bathrobe.

With trembling hands, the assailant reached out and touched her right breast, cupping it fully, then moving the index finger in a circular motion around the nipple. No response. Fingers checked for a pulse. Nothing.

The killer wondered if she was really dead. How would you know for sure? What were the signs? She wasn't breathing. No pulse. Was that it? Was that what dead was? No heart beat. No breath. Did that equal no life?

"I didn't want to kill you. I really didn't. I just want you to know that. But you gave me no choice. Your mind was made up and nothing I said seemed to matter."

Joan stared up through glaring lifeless eyes, an expression of rage frozen on her angelic face. Even in death, her beauty was apparent, despite the misshapen upper left side of her face, which had started to turn a bluish purple around the unnatural crevice that ran across the cheekbone, connecting her natural red hairline to the left eye.

A hand reached out and yanked a thin gold necklace from around Joan's neck.

"You won't be needing this anymore, right?"

Another hand placed a small plastic flower, a daisy, into the opening of Joan's right ear. The artificial flower with its yellow center and white petals fit perfectly, just covering the hole to the eardrum, as if that was where it always belonged, resting in the curve of the ear's opening.

The killer then stood up and looked around the tastefully-furnished apartment one last time before starting to leave. That was when the phone beeped its audible intrusion. The killer stared at the off-white phone as if it were alive. On the third series of beeps, an answering machine clicked on and the voice of the dead filled the silent room.

"This is Joan Walsh. I can't come to the phone right now but if you leave a message, I'll return your call as soon as possible. Wait for the beep. Beep!"

Another woman's voice followed.

"Hey babe. It's just me. I called to say hi and wish you luck. Just remember. Our bet's still on. He pops the question, then you buy me dinner. If he doesn't, I'll grade the rest of your term papers. Then I'll

7

kill the bastard. And don't worry, okay? Your secret's safe with me. Catch you later." Click!

The killer stared at the phone machine with its red light now blinking, then walked over to the phone machine, reached down and hit the "erase message" button. The red light stopped blinking.

"Your secret's safe with me?" Did she really say that? Could somebody else know, Joannie? Did you lie to me? You said it was just between us. Our secret. You told somebody, didn't you? Do you have any idea what this means? The position this puts me in? I mean, it's not like I can't take care of it, right? Because now we both know I can."

CHAPTER TWO

By the time Kimberly returned to her apartment, she didn't know what bothered her more, the pain from Richie pulling her hair, or the embarrassment of letting the pompous ass get the better of her. It did get her mind off Joan and the prospect of having to find a new best friend and for that she was grateful. Kimberly didn't make friends easily, which made the close relationship she had with Joan even more valuable and special.

She tossed her gym bag on the floor and settled down onto the over-stuffed sofa in the living room and closed her eyes. Come on. You've got to get on with your own life. You also have to grade thirty-five mid-term papers written by members of your Juvenile Justice class.

Kimberly wiped her eyes and looked at the stack of papers. One student had actually submitted two papers, apparently hoping the two half-hearted attempts would add up to one passing grade.

She opened the first paper and immediately recognized the language. It was from a paper submitted two semesters earlier. The current student had purchased the report either directly from the upper classmate or indirectly from an underground supplier of "b" or better papers. The practice was a problem that plagued nearly every campus in the country. Unfortunately for the student, Kimberly tended to remember the better papers. She stapled together the two papers the student had submitted and scribbled "Zero plus zero still equals zero. Try again."

Before reaching for the next paper, she stood up from the sofa and stretched her five-foot, seven-inch well-proportioned figure, pushing her arms out to the side as far as they would reach, then overhead and finally down to the floor, feeling the muscles pull in the calves and thighs of her long athletic legs, developed from intensive ballet and modern dance instruction between the ages of six and sixteen. She then kicked out, bending at the waist, pretending to connect with Richie's face.

"Take that you Tae Kwan *dork,*" she muttered to herself.

Letting out a deep sigh, Kimberly walked over to one of the two front French door windows and looked down at her tree-lined block on Sullivan Street, midway between Bleecker and West Third Street and two blocks south of Joan Walsh's apartment building.

She breathed in the scent of fresh roasted coffee from an Italian restaurant three floors below. Every morning, she awoke to the rich aroma of newly-ground expresso wafting in through her bedroom window like a morning spirit lover draped in a blanket of caffinated scent.

As she stared out the window, Kimberly remembered when she first told her parents she was getting an apartment in the Village. Her father told her she was crazy. "The Village? Isn't that where all those gay people and drug addicts live? Why do you want to live there?" But when she showed them the old-fashioned railroad flat with the charming bathtub sitting atop four ornate brass feet in the over-sized kitchen surrounded by turn of the century townhouses, even her parents were impressed.

She needed her father's approval along with his financial help. Even though she was a candidate to become a full tenured professor at Ferguson College in suburban New Jersey, near Princeton, academic salaries had yet to catch up with Manhattan real estate. Her father reluctantly provided the down payment and even paid for the extensive renovations, which seemed to be taking forever.

The first thing to go was the charming tub in the kitchen, which became less charming once you tried to explain to guests the usefulness of being able to bathe where you ate. An interior decorator who had also designed Joan's apartment recommended that one of the bedrooms be cut in half to make room for a small office and a bathroom large enough to hold a Jacuzzi.

The decorator managed to convince Kimberly, and her father since he had to pay for it, that the tub and Jacuzzi added another $30,000 to the value of the co-op and should therefore be seen more as an investment rather than an elaborate and unnecessary luxurious altar of hedonism, as her father had called it.

Once installed, the bathroom with its pink ceramic tile, gold trim and floor-to-ceiling mirrors, became her favorite room. It was here where she felt most at home in the warmth of the Jacuzzi's pulsating water. There was something secure about the solid marble floor and steps, or as her father had put it, something to help her get away from the dirt and depravity that walked the streets just three floors below.

The Village itself offered another escape from both the formal atmosphere of academia and the authoritarian world within the criminal justice system where she served as a consultant to various divisions in need of her expertise as a criminologist. For Kimberly, the Village represented a creative bohemian world of endless possibilities, where people expressed a freedom of arts and attitudes without care or recrimination.

Spanning the island of Manhattan between Fourteenth Street to the north and Houston Street to the south, the Village contained perhaps the most diverse group of people found anywhere on the planet, where brokers and bankers shared apartment buildings with artists and actors.

To the people who lived in the Village, there were actually two Villages: the one that existed during the day, populated by residents, tradesmen and students at NYU or The New School, and the Village that came alive at night when the bridge-and-tunnel crowd seized control. Invading armies of young men and women poured in on search and destroy missions from places on Long Island like Hempstead and Syosset, from Bayside, Queens and Bay Ridge, Brooklyn as well as Bayonne in New Jersey and every other Jersey hamlet along a bus or train line into Manhattan. They drove down from Rockland and Westchester Counties or took the Metro North train in from Connecticut.

They came searching for excitement, some for adventure, some for sex and drugs, and some came because that's where you went to be cool. Some just came to get lost among the maze of streets that seemed to follow no logical pattern. Occasionally, streets would change names from one block to another while others twisted around like snakes, or went off at improbable angles and eventually disappeared.

What Kimberly liked most about the Village was that it was always full of surprises and situations and people were often far from what they seemed. Her father would joke and say, "You've become Dorothy in the land of odds." And she would smile and say "No, I'm the wizard."

Today was one of the two days a week when she did not have to make the seventy-five minute trek from Manhattan to Ferguson College, a commute she shared with Joan, her best friend and colleague. Together, they were two-thirds of the school's criminology department.

Kimberly returned to the blue-and-white stripped sofa and spent the rest of the morning grading term papers, occasionally drifting in and out of a half sleep depending on the boredom factor of the paper in hand. She had just finished an A-minus opus and was enthralled by the student's writing about a homicide she had witnessed when her cordless telephone rang. She looked at the wall clock. It was a quarter to one in the afternoon. Time flies when you're not reading drek.

She grabbed the phone on the second ring. "You have reached Kimberly Stone. This is not a recording. This is the real person. If I sound a little zany, it's because I've been up all night grading term papers and I'm late for an appointment. So if you're not conducting some ridiculous survey or trying to sell me something I don't need, starting speaking at the beep. Beep."

"Kimberly?" said a loud, strong male voice. "Is that you?"

"Yes," she said, only it sounded like a question.

"It's Bill. Bill Gardner. Is Joan there?"

"Ah ... no. I thought she was having lunch with you."

"So did I," said Bill. "She never showed."

She could picture Bill Gardner on the other end of the phone —
his flattened nose, broken since childhood, that gave him a pugilistic
appearance. Actually, any fighting in which Bill Gardner ever really
engaged was in a courtroom where he could rant and vent his rage on
behalf of clients who often became more frightened of him than the
opposing attorney or the jury's decision. It was his thick, bushy,
teddy-bear eyebrows that women found most attractive; they softened
his rough and ruddy face and offset an overly aggressive and often
antagonistic manner.

"Maybe she lost track of the time," said Kimberly. "This is term
paper season. Hell, I can't even remember what day it is when I'm
reading these things. We're under a lot of pressure to get the grades in
before spring break."

"I know. I called her. But she's not home. She's not at the
women's shelter. I don't know where she is and I sorta planned a surprise for her."

"You mean like a proposal?"

"So much for surprises. How did —"

"Bill. She's my best friend. She tells me everything."

"Do you think she's okay? What could have happened? Maybe I
should go over there."

"You mean just barge in unannounced? That's probably not a
good idea."

"Why not? Is she seeing somebody else?"

"No. Why would you even think such a thing?"

"So why shouldn't I go over there?"

"Because it looks so desperate and needy, not to mention a violation of Joan's privacy."

"Violation of privacy? We were supposed to have lunch for
God's sake."

"Look, Bill. How do I explain it? I've seen this happen before,
okay."

"What?"

"Maybe things were moving too fast. Be patient with her."

"Patient? Do me a favor. When you talk to her, tell her I don't
like being stood up."

"Bill ... " Kimberly stopped talking as soon as she realized he
had already hung up.

13

She put the phone down and let out a deep sigh. She looked at the term paper opened in her lap and then closed it. Something Bill Gardner had said was bouncing around the canyons of her mind. What was it? She wasn't really worried about Joan. The last time someone was close to asking Joan for a serious commitment, she disappeared for a week. The fact that she didn't make it to the lunch actually made Kimberly smile. But then she shook her head. Think. Focus. What had he said that was gnawing away at her subconscious? Was it a word? A place. Yes. That's it. What had he said? The shelter. The woman's shelter. Kimberly jumped from the sofa and looked at the clock. Oh no. She grabbed the phone and punched in a number.

"Saint Catherine's," said the voice on the phone.

"This is Dr. Kimberly Stone. I'm running a little late. I had an appointment to interview some of the residents starting about an hour ago. Just tell them I'm on my way and that I'm sorry. But I'll get there as soon as I can."

She looked at the remaining pile of term papers and estimated she was about halfway done. She looked at the clock again and checked herself in the hall mirror. Even in sweatshirt and jeans, she didn't look half bad. She knew others thought her attractive, but Kimberly downplayed her physical appearance, afraid that it would detract from her intelligence and prevent people from taking her seriously. How come Joan was able to get away with it? She knew the answer. Joan simply took it all for granted. Her good looks. Her intelligence. Her desires. Her personality. She never felt the need to apologize for it. Why couldn't Kimberly be like that?

She ran to the bedroom and pulled off the jeans and sweatshirt, then opened her walk-in closet and switched on the light. What image did she want to project? Professional? Academic? Somber? All of the above. She decided on one of the conservative classic dark suits she usually taught in, along with a high-necked beige silk blouse.

Five minutes later, Kimberly was walking down the tree-lined street, past the row of specialty shops that came and went with every trend. This week it was "art jewelry" and "fancy balloons." Last week it had been roller-blades and exotic teas.

She headed down Sullivan toward Houston Street and past the Church of St. Anthony, where she started waving for a taxi.

In front of the church was a glass-enclosed billboard announcing the day's sermon: "God Wants Great Men Small Enough to Be Used."

Kimberly stared at the sermon until she realized a taxi had stopped. "So that's what God wants," she thought, getting into the cab that reeked of pastrami and mustard. She checked the seat before getting in to make sure she wasn't about to sit on something disgusting. Once seated she saw the source of the aroma, a half-eaten sandwich wedged into a space on the dashboard between a contraption for holding pencils and receipts and a cup-holder. She gave the driver her destination and then opened the nearest window as far as it would go.

It took about forty minutes in heavy traffic to make the trip uptown to the battered women's shelter on West 90th Street. It should have taken half that time, but the taxi driver decided it would be shorter to cut through Central Park and took her about two miles out of her way. She decided it wasn't worth the protest, so she paid her fare and got out of the cab. She was just about to close the door when the driver complained about not getting a tip.

Kimberly smiled and said, "You want a tip? How about two? Don't screw your customers. And eat your lunch on your own time, not on mine."

With that, she slammed the door, and the taxi driver shouted out what sounded like a profanity in a language she had never heard before. You'd think he'd at least learn how to curse in English, she thought angrily.

Kimberly waited for the light and then crossed the street to a three-story brownstone on the corner. A small sign next to the door said "St. Catherine's Women's Shelter."

She and Joan had been visiting shelters in New York and New Jersey, interviewing the residents for the last three months as part of a study about why women left abusive relationships *before* violence became the only solution. She straightened her suit jacket and rang the bell.

A few seconds later, a petite twenty-five-year-old woman with mousy brown hair and a perpetual smile answered the door and gave Kimberly the once-over. The woman wore black slacks, a white blouse buttoned to the collar, and a red sweater that was starting to fray at the sleeves.

15

"Can I help you?"

"I'm Dr. Kimberly Stone. From Ferguson College. My colleague, Dr. Joan Walsh, usually interviewed the women at this center, but she couldn't make it today. We're both working on the same study, so I'll be picking up where she left off the last time she was here."

"Of course. Melanie Kinser. Assistant director. Come in. We didn't think anyone was coming," she said, still smiling but with an edge of annoyance to her voice.

"Sorry I'm late. I called. Did someone give you my message? I was grading term papers and lost track of time."

"Yes. Term papers." The tone of her voice made Kimberly feel like crawling in a hole. These women have been disappointed enough she thought as she followed the woman into the shelter. Once inside, Melanie locked three dead bolts and a long metal rod that wedged against the inner door. There were two peepholes in the door. One at the top for adults and one lower down for children.

"Can't be too careful," Melanie said. "Our biggest problem is keeping out the husbands and boyfriends."

"I can imagine."

"Some of them just want to talk, but a few actually want to kill or at least maim their partner for running away."

"That's precisely what we're studying," Kimberly said. "Why some women leave before it's too late."

"Cup of coffee?" Melanie asked.

"No thanks. I'd better get to work."

"Follow me," said Melanie as she led Kimberly into a large living room with faded yellow walls where several women, some still in bathrobes, sat reading, watching television, or nursing babies.

They looked up as the two women entered the room. A wave of anxiety seemed to wash across their faces. Melanie noticed that Kimberly was aware of the change.

"They think you're with some social service agency. It's the suit. Dr. Walsh usually wears a T-shirt and jeans. Puts the women at ease. They don't feel like you're talking down to them."

"Sorry," said Kimberly. "I should've checked."

"I'll get your first subject."

The next forty-five minutes went by quickly as Kimberly interviewed four women who seemed too frightened to provide any helpful

16

data for the study. She was about to give up on this shelter and move on to the next when she started talking to Maria, a striking, dark-haired twenty-two-year-old Hispanic woman with four children under the age of five.

"I leave after he tried to hit me with a hammer. I moved. He bashed the refrigerator," Maria told Kimberly.

"When did he first hit you?"

"When I was pregnant. The first time. Seven months. He kicked me in the stomach. He said, 'I hope you and the baby die.' I know I should have left then."

"Did you tell anyone?"

"Who? I just have one sister here. And she and I are never close. She would say "I warned you.' No. I could not tell her. Everyone else in Puerto Rico."

"What about friends?"

"My husband say he cut out my tongue if I tell anyone. Besides, I don't have time for friends. Anyway, he's too jealous to let me have an *amiga*. He would get angry if I ever left the house without telling him. First thing he does when he comes home, he feels the hood of the car to see if it's warm. One time, he forget he let his cousin borrow the car and when he felt the hood, he just went crazy. He started to punch me in the stomach, in my back. I thought he was gonna kill me. I finally screamed out 'your cousin' and he stopped. But I couldn't get up after that."

"You were pregnant when this happened?"

"*Si'*."

"Was the baby hurt?"

"I go to the emergency room. I told them I fall down the stairs. They say the baby okay."

"Did he ever hit your children?"

"*Si'*," whispered Maria and lowered her head.

"What happened?" asked Kimberly.

"He slapped Teresa. My third. You could see his hand on her face for hours. Then he pick up the hammer. We leave that night."

"Have you seen your husband since then?"

"No."

"When was that?"

"Four months ago."

"What are you going to do now?" Kimberly asked more out of concern for Maria than as a necessary question for her study.

"I stay here as long as I can. I learn to do cleaning. Senorita Melanie say I should go back to school and learn computer. Maybe I get an apartment with a woman I met here."

Kimberly cleared her throat. "Maria, I'm going to have to ask you a few questions that might upset you but I have to ask these questions. Your answers are very important. They'll help me and others who care about battered women get a better understanding of how we can be more helpful to you."

She paused, waiting to see if Maria would nod that she understood. As soon as she did, she continued.

"Did anyone at home ever hit you or touch your private parts when you were growing up?"

Maria shifted in her seat, uncomfortably.

"I'm sorry but I have to ask." It was this question that distinguished their study of battered women from all the previous ones.

"What do you mean?"

"Did your father or a brother or a cousin hit you or do anything sexual to you when you were a child or a teenager?"

"My cousin used to touch me here and here," she said, pointing to her breasts and between her legs.

"How about your father?"

"My father tried to rape me once," she said almost matter-of-factly. "But I hit him in the back with a bat. He never tried again. He wasn't really my father. He was my sister's father. I don't know who my real father is."

Kimberly looked at the woman and felt an overwhelming sadness as well as a new respect for her ability to survive such treatment.

"Thank you, Maria," she said.

"Is that all?"

"I may want to talk to you again. Would that be okay?"

"I don't know," said Maria. "These questions. They bother me. You going to put this in a book or something?"

"I'm not sure yet. We're still doing the research. It could lead to a journal article or a book."

"What if my family reads it, or my husband? He'll kill me!"

"I would never use your real name or the name of the shelter."

18

"But they could know it's me, just from the story."

"Trust me, Maria. I doubt if anybody in your family reads the kind of scholarly journal that would publish our sociological study about the prevalence of childhood sexual abuse among battered women. I'll change your name and disguise your appearance, make you fat instead of thin, taller. That sort of thing. Your husband doesn't know you're here, does he?"

"I don't know. You don't know my husband. He won't stop until he finds me. He's very ... he can be cruel. Mean. You gotta warn that other lady who comes here."

"You mean Dr. Walsh?"

"*Sí*. She's the one who got me to come to the shelter. I think she might be in danger," said Maria.

"Danger? What kind of danger?"

"My husband. Just before the last time he beat me, the police had me talk to Dr. Walsh. She tried to get me to go to a shelter then, but I was still too scared. So she gave me her card in case I changed my mind. Anyway, Luis found it. It was her business card from some college. It didn't have this address on it, but he might try to get to her, you know, to get her to tell him where I am. So if you see her, just tell her to watch out for Luis. He can get crazy sometimes."

"I'll give her the message. Thanks, Maria. Don't worry. Nothing's going to happen."

"Oh you don't know Luis, Dr. Stone. He thinks when I leave, I take his machismo. His manhood. He won't stop until he finds me. So don't say nothing's going to happen. Something is definitely going to happen."

Maria stood and left the room. Kimberly looked down at her notes and for a brief moment felt a ripple of the kind of fear that the women in this shelter had to live with everyday. That poor woman, thought Kimberly. She made a few more notes and was about to leave the shelter when she got out her cellular phone and punched in Joan's number again. The answering machine picked up.

"It's me again. I'm just leaving the shelter and wanted to catch you before I went out for the night. One of the women here, Maria, says her husband found your business card and might try to contact you as a way of finding out where she is now. I don't want to scare you, but this guy sounds like trouble, Joannie. Keep your eyes open

19

and watch your back. See you tomorrow. And don't be an asshole. Call Bill and apologize."

Kimberly gathered her papers together and left the shelter. As the thick door closed behind her, she could hear the deadbolts click back into place. She suddenly felt vulnerable, as she stepped out onto the sidewalk.

The sun was starting to go down. Some of the street lights near the taller buildings were already on. The evening air was damp and getting colder. She started to walk toward the street to flag down a taxi when she felt someone was watching her. She looked around, but no one seemed to be paying any attention to her.

Two taxis sped by without stopping, so she stood out in the street and nearly body-blocked the next cab with its availability indicator light on. As she climbed in the back of the cab, she still had a sense that someone was watching her. She scanned the sidewalk and doorways as the cab pulled away. She saw several people, but no one seemed to be staring at her.

Dusk had settled fully over Sullivan Street by the time Kimberly returned to her block. The last rays of a setting sun glistened like gold off the upper floors and windows of the taller apartment buildings. It was going to be a perfect spring evening in the Village. Not too warm and not too cold. And tonight she had a date, her first in three months. Dinner and dancing with David Ross, a thirty-two-year-old jeweler she had met two weeks ago at her cousin's wedding. Okay, so he was a couple of years younger. He wasn't really Kimberly's type, and he wasn't much of a conversationalist. So what? He seemed like a nice guy, at least for one date. As a single unattached woman living alone, it seemed important to stay as socially active as possible, even if a date wasn't "the one."

She felt as if her body and heart were slowly becoming disconnected. She needed this date if only to remember what it felt like to be in someone's company for no other reason than to have fun. Her work was becoming too much of her life; teaching, preparing lectures, conducting original research and keeping ahead of the "publish or perish" criteria which had become an ever-growing part of academic survival. Her twenties had raced by because of studying and finishing her degree. Now the same thing was happening to her thirties. It was starting to scare her as she realized she was getting closer to 40 than she was to 30.

At school, a few of the married professors had said they envied her single life in the "big city." If they only knew how rare it was for her to even go out on a date, or how hard it was for her to manage matters of the heart. The analytical world of the criminologist left little room for emotional entanglements, and while she was a scholar in many areas, she had never been an expert in love.

Kimberly looked at her watch as she walked toward the lobby of her building. Six-thirty. Just enough time to relax in her Jacuzzi for a few minutes and then change. She was about to open the door when she noticed Hal, the part-time doorman, chaining down the bushes in front of the building.

"What are you doing?" she asked.

"Saving you a maintenance upgrade," said Hal, who was about fifty years old, stocky and spoke with an East European accent. "We've replaced these bushes four times already. Kids pull them up and sell 'em on Twenty-sixth Street to a fence in the flower district."

"How much could they get?"

"Enough for crack, or heroin, or whatever they're taking these days. I say we shoot 'em all. Save a lot of money. You steal, you get shot. In some countries, they cut off your hand if you steal. But here, it's too easy. Most of the time, nothing happens."

Kimberly quickly decided that she was too tired to get into a debate with her doorman over the merits of the American criminal justice system so she just smiled and unlocked her mail box. She scanned the bundle of envelopes and dropped the assortment of bills, flyers, and magazines into her canvas tote bag.

As she started toward the elevator, Hal called out.

"I almost forgot. I let your carpenter in a couple of hours ago. He showed me your note saying it was okay. I think he's still up there."

"Thanks, Hal."

She stepped off the elevator and found the door to her apartment open and a pile of lumber lining the hallway next to the entrance. It was partly her fault that the renovation was taking so long. She had told the carpenter she needed a break from the sawdust. So they made up a schedule that spaced out the work on the bookcases and platform bed to just two days a week which now meant he had to fit her in between his other jobs.

This was George Stewhalf's third visit to her apartment in the last two weeks. He had just about finished her custom-built king size platform bed with enormous over-sized storage drawers, but he still needed one more part that was on special order. In the meantime, he was working on the wall of oak bookcases that he was building in the living room. It would house her cherished collection of more than two-thousand reference books, novels and poetry collections that she had been moving around for the past 15 years, from her parents' house, to college and graduate school, to storage and finally to this apartment on Sullivan Street. Besides Joan, these were her friends. Old friends such as Dostoyevsky, Edna St. Vincent Millay, Shakespeare, and Guy De Maupassant, as well as new friends like Elmore Leonard, Ed McBain, Mary Higgins Clark and Patricia Cornwell.

"Hello, George," Kimberly said as she stepped over the pile of lumber and entered the construction site that had once been her apartment.

George was checking the level on the bottom shelf of the bookcase when he turned around and smiled. Dressed in a blue denim work shirt, torn at the elbows, George looked like a young James Dean, with a boyish, handsome face, light brown hair combed to the side so that it would fall over his right eye whenever he looked down.

"Dr. Stone. How's it goin?"

"A little crazed, George."

"You work too hard, Professor."

"You're starting to sound like my mother."

"You hungry? I stopped by that bakery you like and got a couple coffees and that special cheese Danish they make."

"That's really sweet, but I'm gonna pass. I forgot you were even coming today and I'm expecting company. Are you going to be much longer?"

"Actually, I'm almost finished with this section. I can come back Saturday, around three-thirty," George said as he loaded up his tool box and grabbed his jacket.

"Saturday? I think that'll be fine."

"Be seein ya, professor," he said smiling, as he left the apartment.

22

Kimberly closed the front door and wondered if maybe she was dragging out the renovation just to keep George around. He sure was nice to look at and she had been fantasizing about him lately. Let's get it together. You've only got twenty-five minutes before your date arrives. Forget that you want to crawl into bed and hide. It's just anxiety. There's nothing to worry about. How bad could it be? It's just a date. You go to dinner. Do some dancing. You come home. Life goes on. So why is it all so terrifying?

David Ross arrived at 7:04 p.m. carrying two dozen red roses.

"They're beautiful," said Kimberly, taking the flowers out of his sweaty hands. "I'll put these in a vase." She carried the flowers into the kitchen as David looked around the apartment.

"I made dinner reservations at the Plaza," he said blushing and trying to appear taller than his five-foot, six-inch frame. With her heels, she was now a good two inches taller than he was.

"Would you like something to drink first? Some wine?" she asked.

"Well, actually, we should probably get going. The reservations are for seven-thirty and I think they're strict about holding them."

"Let's go then," she smiled and led their way out of the maze of lumber and building supplies.

As they left her apartment, Kimberly had an overwhelming pang of regret about this date. In the cab ride to the Plaza, she continued taking an inventory of her companion: on the minus side—three gold chains and two rings. Remember your rule: never date men who wear more jewelry than you do. On the plus side—he brought flowers. How often does that happen? Also, he's kind of cute. Except for that hairpiece. It almost looks real, except when the cab stops for lights and it slides down his forehead. Also, he's nearly as tall as I am. I shouldn't have worn heels. Okay. It's a wash. Save the grades for the term papers. Try to loosen up and have some fun. Now if only he'd just stop rubbing his knee against my thigh like an anxious puppy.

The Plaza Hotel's Oak Room was an old-fashioned wood-paneled restaurant, with dim lighting and a lot of atmosphere. They were studying the expensive menu when David looked up sheepishly.

"I just realized something," he said with an embarrassed look on his almost handsome face. "I think those flowers pushed me over the limit on my credit card. But I may have enough cash."

"We can use my card if you don't," she said, suddenly feeling sorry for the guy and repulsed at the same time.

"We could? That's great. Next one's on me. Promise."

Kimberly looked back down at the menu and quickly switched her choice from a full dinner of salad, filet mignon, a glass of Chablis and dessert to the cheapest thing on the menu, plain chicken breast. Forget the wine. Forget dessert or the dancing. Besides, this is a school night. Now you'll get home in time and with a clear enough head to finish grading the rest of those term papers. Isn't life great?

CHAPTER THREE

There was a chill in the air at 6:37 a.m. as Kimberly stepped out of her building. Shivering from the cold, she now wished she'd worn a spring coat or at least a heavier wool suit. It was too late to go back and change now because she was already running about ten minutes late.

She walked to the curb trying to think up some excuse for her tardiness when she looked up and realized Joan wasn't there. Normally, she would have been sitting in her eight-year-old Buick Skylark in the "No Parking" zone in front of Kimberly's building. But this morning the space was empty.

Kimberly looked up and down the street but there was no sign of Joan's car. She shifted her briefcase and tote bag full of term papers and began walking up Sullivan Street toward Joan's building, which was just two blocks north.

On the next block, she picked up her pace as she hurried by the supermarket and the playhouse where *The Fantasticks*, New York's longest-running play, was still being performed

Today was Kimberly's heaviest course load for the week. In addition to three sections of Introduction to Sociology and Juvenile Justice, she taught a once-a-week, three-hour seminar, Introduction to Criminology. She had become notorious on campus for the last project of the semester, where each student was assigned an actual unsolved homicide so they could help the police in their search for the killer. She got the idea from the television docu-drama, *America's Most_Wanted*. So far, none of her students had actually cracked a case, but at least they were learning how a bona fide criminal investigation was carried out.

As she got closer to Joan's building, Kimberly felt a sense of uneasiness. Joan had never been late. She reached her friend's building and rang the buzzer next to the name *Walsh*.

As she waited for a response, she thought about what she'd heard at the shelter. She imagined Maria's husband trying to find his wife through Joan.

She rang Joan's buzzer again.

After buzzing for a few more moments, she rang the superintendent's buzzer instead.

"Who's there?" responded a sleepy male voice.

"Mister Fontes. It's Kimberly Stone. I'm a friend of Joan Walsh. Apartment Ten B?"

"Yeah? Whachu want?"

"I think she overslept and we're late for work."

"Whachu want me to do?"

"Could you please buzz me in?"

There was a long pause.

"Mister Fontes. We've met several times before. I teach with Dr. Walsh. Remember?"

"You that other professor?"

"That's right."

"Okay," he mumbled. Kimberly heard the door buzzed open.

She pushed her way inside and walked down a narrow hallway to the rear of the first floor where a tiny elevator that could barely hold two people waited for its next passenger. Kimberly got in and pressed the button for the tenth floor. The elevator seemed to take forever to reach its destination and once it did, it took another eternity for the elevator door to open.

As soon as the door opened, Kimberly rushed into the hallway and walked quickly toward apartment B. She pushed the buzzer next to the door.

No response. She buzzed again and then knocked on the door hard.

The force of the knock caused the door to open slightly. Immediately, Kimberly knew something wasn't right as she felt a tingling sensation ripple down her back. Everything she had ever learned in criminal justice training told her to never enter an unlocked door that should be locked. The rule was stay outside, call the police. Never enter an open apartment. You could be walking in on a burglary. Or worse.

But this was her best friend. What are the rules for a best friend? There are no rules. She had to enter. Emotion overruled logic. Kimberly pushed the door open and went inside.

"Joan? Joan?" Kimberly called out as she walked into her friend's dark and still hallway. She turned on the light. The hallway was empty. The air was stale.

"Joan, are you here?"

She went through the living room strewn with term papers, into the kitchen and then into the bathroom. The sound of her footsteps on the hardwood floor echoed through the otherwise silent apartment.

"Anybody home?"

As she started to walk toward the bedroom, she stopped. There was a scent in the air. She knew this smell from her days of visiting crime scenes. She looked around the living room until she saw an outstretched hand lying still on the floor on the far side of the living room, behind a leather recliner.

Moving slowly, her heart fluttering, Kimberly approached the chair, following the hand with her eyes until she found the rest of the still, nude body of her best friend, Joan Walsh.

"Oh my God!" Kimberly felt a scream rise in her throat, but no sound came out as she covered her mouth. Bile was rising in her throat and had her stomach not been empty, its contents would have splattered onto the floor.

Instead she dry-heaved and gagged, then doubled over and leaned against a wall. A wave of nausea nearly knocked her over, but she gripped the wall and refused to fall. A cold sweat erupted all over her body. Her neck and shoulders locked up and she suddenly felt numb all over. This wasn't happening. I'm going to wake up from this nightmare soon, she thought. She took a deep breath and dared to raise her head. It was still there. The body. Joan's body. She had to go to her.

She pushed away from the wall and staggered over to Joan's body. As she got closer, she noticed Joan's skin and features had taken on an unreal quality, like that of a wax figure. Kimberly slowly knelt down beside the still body and gently touched Joan's face. "Oh my God!" she cried. She ran her finger down Joan's cheek and was amazed at how cold her friend's skin felt and how her once vibrant pink complexion now looked blue-gray.

A burning sob caught in Kimberly's throat as her eyes filled with tears. Oh Joan. Dear Joan. What's happened to you?

Immediately, Kimberly pulled her hand away from Joan's face. Her criminologist's mind took over. This was no longer her friend's apartment, it was a crime scene and her mere presence might already be contaminating evidence that could lead police to whoever ended Joan's life. Don't touch my friend? How can I stop myself? I want to hug you. I want to tickle you until you laugh. I want to breathe life back into you. I don't want you to be dead. Joan. Poor Joan. How? How could this happen?

Suddenly, feeling the presence of someone else in the room, Kimberly looked up and froze. A man was staring at her from across the living room. Her knees started to shake. Then she realized it was Mr. Fontes, the building superintendent.

"She's dead," said Kimberly, a burning bubble of pain filling the back of her mouth. She wanted to scream, to cry out, to make a sound. But when she opened her mouth again, nothing came out.

Fontes stood silently, staring at Joan's naked body. "*Dios mio.*" Then he made the sign of the cross and started to sit in a nearby armchair.

"No!" shouted Kimberly in a cracked, parched voice. "Don't sit down. We can't touch anything," she explained, as she led the shaken fifty-four year old superintendent back out of the apartment.

Once in the chilly hallway, Kimberly pulled out her cellular phone and dialed 911 to report her friend's death and give the address.

For the next few minutes, until the police arrived, all time seemed to stop. Kimberly let herself slide down the wall of the hallway outside Joan's apartment until she hit the tiled floor, her back firmly braced against the wall. She looked back into the apartment, through the small hallway leading to the living room where she could still see her friend's lifeless hand. She stared at the hand and felt as if a part of herself had died. Kimberly then had a magical thought. Maybe if she stayed real still and quiet, Joan's spirit would talk to her from the other side, like in that movie *Ghost,* with Demi Moore. If you're here Joannie, talk to me. Let me hear your voice one more time.

Officer John Murphy and his partner, Officer Michael Doherty, were two blocks away when the call came in. They arrived at the Sullivan Street address four minutes later. Mr. Fontes, still wearing a sleeveless T-shirt and pajama bottoms, met the patrol unit officers at the front door and escorted them to the tenth floor.

They found Kimberly sitting in the hallway, staring into the open doorway of the victim's apartment and writing in a paisley cloth-covered notebook.

As Officer Murphy, who had nearly twenty years on the force, approached her, Kimberly looked up, and for a flash, saw her father in a blue uniform. What was her father doing in uniform? He wasn't even a policeman. But as the figure came closer, she realized the face was not her father's. With graying brown hair and tired blue eyes, Officer Murphy looked older than his forty-two years. She noticed he had a tiny but distinctive scar across his right cheek. She wondered how he got it.

She then noticed the second policeman, twenty-five-year-old Officer Doherty, whose career, she imagined, was preordained by generations of Irish ancestors that preceded him through the army of blue. Studying his bulky, 5' 9" physique, Kimberly concluded that

Doherty had to work hard to keep his weight within the department's limits.

She quickly closed her notebook and stood up.

"In here," said Kimberly, as she re-entered the apartment. They followed her back to the living room and to Joan's body. Kimberly's first impulse was to cover her friend's nakedness, to offer some kind of protection. But she pushed those feelings aside and tried to think of the nude corpse lying at their feet as merely the shell of a passing spirit that had once been Joan Walsh. As hard as she tried, she still could not suppress the pain burning through her heart. Looking down, she felt her eyes fill again, blurring away the face that stared back up at her with blue green eyes that still held an allure of mystery.

"Is this how she was found?" asked the older officer.

"Yes," said Kimberly. She stared down again as she wiped her eyes. This time she forced herself to study her friend's still attractive but lifeless face. It almost looked like a mask, an exact replica of Joan Walsh, a once-living, caring friend and colleague, struck down in the prime of her life.

"Miss, I'm Police Officer John Murphy. This is Officer Doherty. Is the deceased a relative?"

"A relative? No. She's my best friend," Kimberly said, her chin quivering.

"I'm afraid you're gonna have to wait in the hallway. We need to seal off the area to conduct our investigation. A crime may have occurred here, Ma'am."

Officer Murphy extended his hand, which Kimberly accepted as he started to escort her out of the room. She looked back at Joan's still body on the floor. An involuntary smile came to her lips and she saw Officer Murphy staring at her.

"I'm sorry," she said. "I was thinking of something Joan used to say whenever we saw a body or took the class to the morgue. She would put a serious look on her face and say, 'Class, we are now about to have a near-death experience.'"

Officer Murphy looked perplexed.

"I guess you had to be there," said Kimberly, slowly becoming aware of the inappropriateness of her remark but not knowing how to take it back.

30

"Right," said Murphy. "I'm gonna want a statement so maybe you could wait out in the hallway there. We'll try to find you a chair. We're also gonna need a set of prints since you probably touched some stuff while you were here."

Kimberly nodded and walked into the living room still feeling, still hoping, that this was all just a horrible nightmare. As she stepped out of the apartment and into the hallway, Joan's apartment quickly filled up as more police officers, a police photographer, and forensic specialists arrived. She watched them begin their work as someone brought her a chair. A few minutes later she realized the chair was for sitting and so she sat.

Murphy supervised the posting of the yellow crime scene tape with the words "Do Not Cross" stenciled in black every few inches across the entrance to the apartment. There was another sign that read:

CRIME SCENE SEARCH AREA
STOP!
NO ADMITTANCE
BEYOND THIS POINT UNTIL SEARCH IS COMPLETED
BY ORDER OF POLICE COMMISSIONER

Kimberly watched as crime scene signs were strung with thick cord across the open front door of the apartment. She watched transfixed as more police officers were posted in the hallway. They were advised to keep out all unauthorized persons and to make sure only those who actually lived on the floor were allowed to enter. She saw the photographer videotape the entire living room, Joan's body and then every other room in the apartment. After the taping, he took out a still camera and using a flash, took at least twenty photographs of Joan's body from every imaginable angle.

Officer Doherty took Mr. Fontes down the hallway and started asking him questions that Kimberly couldn't hear. She was staring at them when she looked up and saw Officer Murphy looking down at her.

"Miss, I have to ask you some questions."

Kimberly stood up and let out a deep breath.

"Could I have your name?" asked Murphy.

"Kimberly Stone."

"Are you a resident of the building?"

"No. I live down the street."

"You said you were a friend of the victim."

"Yes. We, ah, also work together. Criminal justice professors at Ferguson College."

"Where would that be, ma'am? Ferguson College?"

"Brighton, New Jersey. Near Princeton."

"I see. When was the last time you saw the deceased alive?"

"Monday, when she dropped me off from school. Around three o'clock. We drive there together three days a week. Monday, Wednesday, and Friday. Joan has a car. I pay for gas and tolls. We were supposed to go there this morning, and when she didn't pick me up, I came here. I figured she must have overslept or something."

"Did she do that a lot?"

"Do what?"

"Oversleep."

"Never. She was always on time."

"So you didn't see her since Monday, when she dropped you off. What time did you say?"

"Around three o'clock."

"Do you know anything about her whereabouts from that time until when you found her?"

"We spoke on the phone at around eight o'clock Monday evening. Everything seemed fine. She called back later that night and left a message on my machine."

"What did the message say?"

"She just wanted me to call her."

"Did you?"

"The next day. Yesterday. I called her but I got her machine."

"What time was that?"

"I don't know. I called a couple of times."

"In the morning? Afternoon?"

"Both. Her boyfriend called me and said Joan hadn't shown up for their lunch date. I told him not to worry. That she probably ... Oh God," said Kimberly, suddenly looking pale and feeling nauseated.

"What is it?"

"She might have still been alive. Maybe I could have saved her." Tears refilled Kimberly's eyes and Officer Murphy looked down, feeling helpless. She wiped her eyes, already smeared with mascara, and looked out a window to the street below just as a small dark van arrived with the word "Morgue" written on the side. She lowered her head and let the tears flow. When she looked back up, morgue attendants were getting out of the elevator carrying pink plastic nose plugs that swimmers use. The dispatcher had only said "Dead body in apartment on Sullivan Street" without giving them an indication if it was recent or a five-day stinker.

One of them carried a stretcher with a black body bag tied to the side. Murphy greeted the morgue orderlies.

"Sorry, boys. Can't have this one yet. We're still waiting for the medical examiner, a warrant to search, as well as someone from the homicide unit. Go out for coffee and a doughnut or something. I figure we'll need at least another hour."

While Murphy talked to the morgue attendants, Kimberly dried her tears. Feelings of guilt flooded her body and made her tremble. Was it possible she could have saved her friend? Why hadn't she gotten worried when Bill Gardner called? Why had she been so sure she had it all figured out? What was the matter with her? Was she jealous that Joan had somebody and she didn't? Was that it? Oh Joan, please forgive me, she begged to herself.

From where she sat, Kimberly could see inside Joan's elegant but simply decorated apartment. She tried to determine if anything was missing. Could she have been the victim of a burglary? So far, everything seemed intact. Stereo. Color TV. Were Joan's laptop computer and laser printer still in the bedroom? What about her jewelry box? Kimberly hadn't noticed and would probably not be allowed back into the apartment once the search for evidence began. She began to make mental notes when Officer Murphy returned.

"Feeling better?"

"A little. Thank you."

"Good. I just have a few more questions. I'm afraid when the detective arrives, he'll probably have some more."

"I understand."

33

"That's right. You're a criminal justice professor. You ever teach at John Jay?"

"Two semesters, about six years ago. I was still in graduate school then."

"I went there nights," said Officer Murphy. "I dropped out. Anyway. Would you know where the deceased parents live? If it's within the metropolitan area, we'd like to send a police team out there to tell them in person."

"Maplewood, New Jersey. Near Newark."

"Thanks," said Murphy giving Kimberly a reassuring pat on her shoulder as he walked toward the phone to call in the information.

As she sat on the chair in the hall, she thought about the last conversation she had had with Joan. It was in the car coming home from school Monday. They were stuck in traffic in Jersey City at the approach to the Lincoln Tunnel.

"Either I get married by the end of the year or we become roommates," Joan said. "It's that simple. I'm tired of living alone, Kim. Don't you ever get tired of coming home to an empty apartment every night? Climbing in between cold sheets with nothing but a pillow between your legs?"

"Do you really love this man?"

"Love? How's that song go? What's love got to do with it? I'm thirty-five years old. I want a husband. A family. A house in the country. A couple of kids. I want the dream. Is there anything wrong with that?"

Kimberly now remembered how Joan's comment had surprised her. She thought that of the two of them, Joan was the happier one. She stared through the doorway and into the living room, at the framed photographs on the fireplace mantel and remembered how she and Joan had planned to go shopping for new curtains for Kimberly's living room. Kimberly hated shopping and so did Joan. It helped if they did it together. "Who'll go shopping with me now?" she thought. She suddenly realized the time and that she was never going to make it to her first class. She also realized that she didn't care, but then thought about the classroom full of students and pulled out her cellular phone.

As Kimberly made her call, Officer Murphy gave Doherty some more instructions.

"How come we need a search warrant?" asked Doherty.

"Because," Officer Murphy explained, "the person in control of this location is dead and refuses to sign a consent-to-search form. It's on the way, so stop bitchin'. Our job is to secure the area, take statements, and try not to fuck up the evidence. We got a body here. Cause of death appears to be a blow to the head. But we don't know if it was from a fall, an accident, or if something else caused the death."

"I got the super's statement," smiled Doherty.

"Good. Now why don't you start down the hall there and knock on some doors? See if anybody saw or heard anything."

The killer watched as more police cars pulled up and double-parked in front of Joan's building.

Aren't you the popular one today? They all came to see you. They're all here to see Joannie. Phonie Joannie. Joannie Baloney. They're gonna find out all about you. What you're really like. And then it's gonna be in all the newspapers. Who you really are. What you really are. They're gonna pick your life apart like birds eating road kill. Look at all the people that's gonna be hurt by all this. Your family. Your friends. All the people who trusted you. Who thought they knew you. It's all gonna come out. And to think it's just the beginning. Because of you and your big mouth, others will have to die.

CHAPTER FOUR

Detective Alan Blake was about to ask another question when he felt the vibration against his waist. He unclipped the beeper from his belt and looked at the familiar number.

"If you'll just excuse me?" he asked the couple who owned the Horatio Street townhouse where he was close to wrapping up the initial questioning of an investigation into the shooting death of their two-year-old child.

Blake walked across the living room, took out his cellular phone and called the number on the beeper's small screen.

"Blake."

"Possible homicide at the corner of Sullivan and Fourth. Can you respond?" asked the voice of Detective Agnes O'Toole, the administrative officer for the homicide unit.

"I should be able to handle it. I'm almost finished here," said Blake as he looked across the antique-filled living room at the child's body.

After two decades of dealing with the darkest side of humanity, Blake's face had taken on an expression of perpetually sadness.

"What's the situation there?" he asked.

"Thirty-five year old woman. Appears to have been dead at least twenty-four hours from an apparent blow to the head. Officer Murphy and Doherty from the patrol unit are on the scene."

"Have you called the M.E.?"

"Coroner's just arrived."

"Case closed. No coroner has ever beaten the investigating detective to a homicide scene in this city. He must be the killer," said Blake, grinning.

"It's Clayborne," said Agnes. "He lives in the area."

"Tell them I'll be there in ten minutes." Blake ended the call, put away his phone and returned to the bedroom where Alice and Byron Bender waited in silence. They were the parents of two-year-old Megan, who had been shot and killed by her seven-year-old brother, Ian, with their father's target pistol.

"Tell me again where you kept the gun," said the detective.

"In the back of my bedroom closet," replied Byron Bender, without emotion.

"Where did you keep the bullets?"

"In my dresser drawer."

"Separate from the gun?"

The father nodded yes.

"Did your son know the bullets were there?"

"I didn't think so," Bender replied, clutching his distraught wife's hand.

"How did he get the bullets?"

"I don't know."

"I'd like to talk to him," said Blake.

"Shouldn't I have my lawyer here?"

"That's up to you Mr. Bender. "I'm just trying to gather information. No charges have been filed yet. Since your son is a minor, both you and Mrs. Bender would .... "

"I'd still like to talk to my lawyer first."

Blake nodded, flipped the mustard-colored cover of his notebook closed and put his pad and pencil into the pocket of his sports jacket.

"That's it then?" asked Mr. Bender.

"For now. Talk to your lawyer. Then let me know when I can talk to your son. The sooner the better," said Blake. "While it's fresh in his mind. Right now, I have to respond to another call."

"What's going to happen to my boy?" asked Mr. Bender.

"I don't know," said Blake.

"He thought it was a toy," said Alice Bender. "He didn't mean to hurt her."

Detective Blake gave the Benders his card and left their town-house just as the morgue van arrived. He walked across the street and got into his four-year-old black unmarked Oldsmobile.

It took Blake longer than usual to strap the seat belt across his six-foot-four, two-hundred-forty pound frame. He was beginning to feel the extra weight that his large frame managed to conceal. He reached out to put the key in the ignition and realized his arms seemed disconnected from his body. This last case had shut him down. Dead children. They were the hardest cases to investigate.

He looked up and saw his reflection in the rearview mirror. Was that another worry line? His high cheekbones made him look slightly Indian, although his ancestors were mostly English and Irish.

Blake felt a tingling sensation in his legs as he pushed down on the accelerator. He turned on the ignition and gunned the engine until the whole car shook. He then slipped a Phil Collins tape into the cassette player. Not too loud, so he couldn't hear the police calls, but loud enough to mask his anguished roar.

Who was he really angry at? The boy who killed his sister? Or the father who kept a gun in the house just waiting for disaster to strike? Or to the city for filling people like the Benders with so much fear that they felt the need to keep a gun in their home? He thought of all the women he had trained in self-defense classes, who showed up at the target range with a cocked, loaded handgun in their shoulder bags with no knowledge of what to do next. All of them, accidents waiting to happen.

He turned down the music and headed for the next death scene. If the coroner so rules, it would be the seventh homicide in the city in twenty-four hours.

Last week, Blake remembered reading in one of the tabloids that there had been twelve killings in one twenty-four hour period. The headline read: "City at War?"

But wasn't the overall body count actually falling? Didn't the last report say the numbers were down? Only one thousand killings in the city last year. Fewer than in the last twenty years. But even Blake knew that one thousand unnecessary deaths was one thousand too many.

As he drove, Blake felt like a lonely soldier driving from one battlefield to another, counting the bodies, filing the reports, entering the numbers that became statistics, which were then used in reports by politicians, social workers, criminologists, and editorial writers about how outnumbered the police were in the never-ending war on crime. The difference was that none of them ever had to look into the eyes of dead babies, wipe the blood off a young mother's corpse to find the entrance wound, or arrest a ten-year-old mugger who didn't mean to shoot and kill his victim.

None of them had to touch the dead and the dying that they talked or wrote about. Maybe that's what Blake felt so angry about as he pulled up in front of the apartment building on Sullivan Street. He looked up and down the peaceful residential street on this otherwise glorious spring day and shook his head as he entered the building.

It was Officer Murphy who first noticed Blake standing in the doorway of Joan Walsh's apartment watching the uniformed officers and forensics men.

In his street attire of a navy blue sports jacket, white shirt, striped tie, and dark pants, Blake looked like any other civilian stopping by to take a peek at a possible murder scene. Murphy was about to tell him to beat it when Blake took out his gold shield and slipped the leather backing into the breast pocket of his sport coat, with the shield out.

Officer Murphy walked across the room.

"Detective Blake?" Murphy inquired.

"That's me."

"We thought we lost ya."

"Sorry. I was on another call when this came in. You find the body?"

"She did," said Murphy, nodding toward Kimberly who was still sitting in the chair in the hallway. "Says she's a friend of the deceased. Dr. Kimberly Stone."

"Doctor?"

"P-h-d doctor. She and the deceased are criminology professors at some college out in Jersey." Officer Murphy looked at his notes. "Here it is. Ferguson College in Brighton. They were supposed to drive there this morning and when her friend didn't show, she came by, found the body, and dialed 911."

"What's your take? Blake asked.

"My take? Like is she a suspect?" asked Murphy.

"Like how did she act when you arrived?"

"She seemed pretty shaken up. But that don't mean she couldn't a done it, right?"

"How'd she get into the apartment?"

"Super buzzed her into the building. She said the door to the apartment was unlocked. Closed but unlocked."

"Anything missing?"

"We're still checking. But doesn't seem so."

"Let's have a look," said Blake, pulling on thin off-white plastic gloves.

"Body's in the living room," said Murphy, leading the way.

"Did anyone hear or see anything?"

"No."

"Who lives next door?"

"A ninety-year-old woman who's almost deaf," said Murphy.

"Anyone talk to her yet?"

"Officer Doherty questioned her. He said she told him she didn't hear or see anything."

"What about the super?"

"He claims he was at another building yesterday for most of the day, four blocks away doing repairs. Spent the night at home with his wife and children."

"Can anyone back that up?" Blake asked.

"He was with his assistant yesterday. A guy who's worked with him for the last twenty years. His wife said he was home all night."

"Anyone check either one of these guys out?" Blake asked.

"Both family men. No arrests. No evidence of any criminal activity."

"Did you talk to the assistant?"

"He's pretty broken up about what happened. Seems he really liked the victim. He'd talk to her when she did her laundry in the basement laundry room."

"Maybe he wanted to do more than talk."

"We'll keep an eye on him."

As Blake walked into the room where Joan's body lay, he got the rush. It was the same rush he always felt when he was near a homicide victim. It was not a good rush. It was more like a breathlessness, like he was gasping for air. But he had to proceed. This was his job. He had chosen this line of work. He could have gone to law school after he graduated in the top of his class from the University of Pennsylvania, but he didn't want any kind of a desk job. He wanted to be out in the world. He wanted an exciting job that totally consumed him. Dead bodies were a basic part of his work. Of course, there was a good feeling when he solved a crime and got a killer off the street. Especially if it was a killer who had seemed certain to strike again.

Blake looked across the room and saw a man in a white smock with big letters on the back that said *Medical Examiner* leaning over the body. Dr. Milton Clayborne was in his early sixties but no one knew his exact age. He was heavy-set and balding, with a perpetual pout. He looked up as Blake approached.

"Well, well. Detective Blake."

"Doctor Clayborne. What? No golf game today?"

"The day is young," quipped Clayborne. "How come you catch all the pretty ones?"

"Seniority," said Blake. "What have we got?"

"Nude, thirty-five year old, well-nourished white female, dead 24-to-48 hours, in full rigor. Postmortem lividity indicates this is where she died. No obvious signs of sexual intercourse. Which means we didn't find any seminal fluids or marks around the pubic area. But she was wiped down pretty well. We'll know for sure when we run her under the lights."

"Cause of death?"

Dr. Clayborne turned Joan's head to the side, exposing a two inch indentation on the right side of her forehead. The area around the imprint had turned a bluish green. The skin was broken but there

41

wasn't much blood. The side of Joan's face beneath the wound was swollen and had turned a dark purple.

"Fracture of the left temporal fossa where the coronal suture crosses the superior temporal ridge or stephanion. This is where the parietal, the frontal, the squamous and the greater wing of the sphenoid meet. I won't know for sure until I open the cranial cavity, but I'd say a blunt force trauma strong enough to do this much exterior damage probably splintered one of the temporal bones and punctured the parietal lobe, causing death."

"Weapon?" asked Blake.

"Something with an edge. Something heavy."

"Like a brick?"

"A brick would have left particles. Something real solid. Dense, like wood, or metal."

Blake rubbed his hand across the corner of an end table.

"No chance she could have fallen, I suppose. Hit her head on the edge here?"

"Not unless she got up and did it twice. We found two wounds. They're right next to each other and hard to see. Whoever did this wanted to make sure she was dead. Plus, I did find some bruises and wrist burns indicating there was a struggle and that she was tied up. There were bruises and contusions around the mouth, which means she was probably gagged."

"Any prints? Fibers?" asked Blake.

"Nothing so far. We scraped her nails and bagged her hands but I couldn't see anything. See this little mark here?"

Blake bent down as Clayborne put the light back on the neck. A jagged line inside the other darker marks on the throat was barely visible.

"What's that? asked Blake.

"I think she might have been wearing a necklace," said Dr. Clayborne.

"A robbery gone sour," said Blake, looking up at Murphy. "Any signs of a break-in?"

"No sir."

Blake turned back to the body and carefully studied the wound on the side of Joan's head. He leaned in closer, putting his nose close to the wound and sniffed.

Murphy gave Clayborne a look and the M.E. just shrugged.

Blake stood up and took in another deep breath as he looked around the room, studying every object until his head stopped turning.

"What is it?" asked Murphy.

But Blake was already walking across the room to the wall unit that contained a few shelves of bric-a-brac, some compact music discs, and several books. At one side of the books, holding them upright was a marble bookend in the shape of a horse's head. Blake stepped in front of the bookend and stared at it. He then leaned in and took in a deep breath, like a bloodhound trying to pick up a scent. Officer Murphy was standing right behind him with his mouth open.

Blake turned around and looked at Murphy, who stepped back. "Sorry."

"No, come here. Smell it."

"Smell what, sir?"

"The bookend."

Murphy leaned in and took a deep breath.

"Did you smell it?"

"I'm not sure, sir. What was I supposed to smell?"

"Shampoo."

Blake took out a pen flashlight and pointed it at the bookend. In the circle of the beam of yellow light was a brownish red blotch. "Does that look like blood to you, Officer Murphy?"

Murphy's eyes widened as he looked at the beam of light.

"Holy shit," said the uniformed officer. "Get forensics in here."

Blake walked back to the body as Clayborne looked up.

"I can see the headlines now. The cop with the psychic nose."

"Lucky hunch," said Blake as he knelt back down next to the body. Blake focused his attention to the side of Joan's face and that's when he saw it. Something in her ear.

"What's this?" asked Blake as he turned Joan's head to the side. Dr. Clayborne pulled tweezers out of his jacket pocket and carefully extracted the tiny plastic daisy.

"A flower?" asked Blake, perplexed.

"A plastic daisy," added Dr. Clayborne, holding it up so they could both study it.

The doctor put the flower in a plastic evidence bag.

"Let's keep the flower quiet, okay?" said Blake.

"You're the boss."

As Blake walked back across the living room, he looked out the front door and saw Kimberly in the hallway writing in her notebook. He walked over to her.

"Professor Stone?"

Kimberly looked up at Blake.

"Detective Blake. Homicide. I have to ask you a few questions."

"Do you have a cigarette?" she asked.

"No. I quit."

"Me too," said Kimberly. "I just really feel like having a cigarette right now."

"I understand you and the deceased ..."

"Her name was Joan. Joan Walsh."

"Joan Walsh," said Blake. "I'm sorry. I understand you and Joan were close."

"Best friends. She knew her killer, didn't she?"

Blake looked up from his notebook and stared at Kimberly.

"What makes you say that?"

"No signs of forced entry. No broken windows. No cracks around the door. Whoever did it just walked in. Invited."

"How do you know she didn't just slip on a wet floor?

"Didn't you just see the body?" asked Kimberly. "If she slipped, she would have reached out to block her fall. Yet, when I found her body, her hands were by her side, not out in front to blunt a fall. Plus there are red marks on her wrists. I think she was tied up and that she fought with her attacker. Anyway, I've been thinking about this for the past half hour and came up with a couple of possibilities."

"A couple?"

"Joan and I have been working with this battered women's shelter on the Upper West Side. One of the women told me yesterday that she was afraid her husband might try to get to her through Joan."

"How would he do that?"

"He had Joan's business card."

"Do you have a name?"

"Luis Alvarez, I believe. At least that's his wife's last name. Alvarez."

"You said a couple."

"There was a student. But I don't think ..."

"A student?"

"We laughed about it at first," said Kimberly. "This sort of thing happens every semester."

"What sort of thing?"

"Students falling in love with you. But Joan said it was starting to get out of hand."

"What did she mean by that?"

"He wouldn't stop sending her letters. Love letters mostly, some poems. But then they started getting explicit. Sexual. That sort of thing."

"Did this student ever threaten her?"

"If he did, she never told me about it."

"What's the student's name?"

"Wayne Clark. He's in Joan's criminology class."

"He sent her letters and poems? Is that it?"

"And flowers."

"What kind of flowers?"

"I don't know. Why?"

"Just curious. Go on."

"I can't imagine Wayne Clark doing this. He's afraid of his own shadow. Joan tried to talk to him once and he just ran away."

Officer Murphy appeared and tapped Blake on the shoulder. "Detective. One of the forensics boys found these in the trash can in the bedroom."

Murphy handed Blake crumpled pieces of stationary paper. Blake smoothed out one of the pages and read aloud: "My head, my heart. You gave my life a start."

"No wonder she threw it away," Blake lowered the paper and looked at Kimberly. "Signed, Love, Wayne."

"That's him," said Kimberly.

Detective Blake made a note to call Ferguson College and get Wayne Clark's home phone number. As he looked up from his pad, he saw Kimberly watching him. It was then, in that moment, that he felt the connection. It was as if they had touched. But they hadn't. It was something in her eyes that seemed to connect to Blake's. He suddenly felt very protective and wanted to shield her from the terror

45

that occupied these walls, this space where everyone's worst fear had been realized.

The silence became awkward and Blake looked down at his notes.

"Anybody else?"

"Not that I'm aware of," said Kimberly feeling her eyes filling with water.

"Did the ...."

"Joan."

"Did Joan have a boyfriend?"

"Yes."

"His name?"

"Bill Gardner."

"Was it serious?"

"They'd been dating for several months. I'd say it was serious. Joan thought he was getting ready to propose."

"Were they having any problems?"

"Not that I know of." Kimberly paused and looked around.

"What is it?" asked Blake.

"Joan had some expensive things in her bedroom. A jewelry box, a laptop computer and a laser printer. I was too upset before to look and see if it's still there."

"Thanks. We'll check. Anything else of value?"

"I noticed her stereo and color TV are still here."

Blake took a few moments to look around Joan's living room, studying the art work on the walls and the new furniture.

"I'm kind of curious, Professor Stone. How could she afford a place like this, on a college teacher's salary?"

"Joan's an only child," said Kimberly. "Her parents subsidize her rent and paid for the renovations."

"That's very generous of them."

"They're very generous people."

"Can you tell me a little more about your friend?" Blake asked.

"Like what?"

"Like what was she like?"

"Outgoing. Friendly. Smart. Neat," Kimberly said, almost laughing as she looked around the living room floor, covered with

dozens of term papers. "Well, most of the time. She was very consci-
entious."

"How would she spend a typical day off?"

"Joan was an early riser. I bet she was down in the laundry room
the minute it opened. Then she might put in some time at the library."

"Which one?"

"Research branch of the Forty-second Street. She was working
on a paper about teens who kill."

"What else?"

"She liked to hang out in coffee shops, especially the Cafe Paris
on Bleecker Street."

"You said she was friendly," said Blake trying to maintain a
completely blank expression.

But Kimberly noticed his eyebrows rose, ever so slightly, in a
somewhat judgmental way. So she worded what she said next very
carefully. She didn't want Detective Blake to take it the wrong way.

"She was friendly and she talked to strangers. But Joan was also
very selective about who she got close to, and she never gave out
personal information that might put her in jeopardy. She wasn't like
what you're thinking."

"What am I thinking?"

"She wasn't foolish," said Kimberly. "She was as afraid of crime
as anyone. But she wasn't going to let it stop her from being friendly
either."

"How about neighbors?" Blake asked, changing the subject.

"What about them?"

"She ever talk about them?"

"There were one or two she was fairly close with. Have a cup of
coffee. That sorta thing."

"Any hobbies?"

"She liked to go to art auctions and museums. The Metropolitan.
Museum of Modern Art. And the Museum of Natural History with
her boyfriend and his five-year-old son."

Detective Blake closed his notebook.

"Is that it?" asked Kimberly.

"For now. Here's my card," said Blake. "I'll probably want to
talk to you again, but you can call if you think of anything."

"If I didn't have three classes waiting on me, I'd stay here and help, but I'm sure everything is in your capable hands, Detective Blake."

As Kimberly saw the morgue attendants carrying the black bag out of the apartment, she let out a sigh, then picked up her attaché case and straightened her skirt.

"Officer Murphy will escort you to the elevator," Blake said.

"That won't be necessary," said Kimberly as she slowly walked down the hallway.

Officer Murphy gave Blake a look.

"What's on your mind, Murphy?"

"Nothing, Detective."

"I'm gonna take another look around," said Blake. "Why don't you help Doherty question some more neighbors. Anyone who's home."

"I'll get right on it," said Murphy.

Blake started walking through the rooms, hoping to get a sense of how the victim had lived and died. He walked into the kitchen first. It was white oak, galley-style, and meticulous. Not a dish in the white ceramic sink. The counter top was bare.

Next he entered a separate dining area and looked over the walls. One entire wall was covered with floor-to-ceiling mirrors to make the small, square area appear larger than it really was. On the other walls were carefully framed original art works, collages, pastels, and oil paintings. Nothing by a master or probably even worth a lot of money, but colorful, nicely crafted, and in good taste. The ceiling of the dining room was covered with a delicate traditional nineteenth-century print in a lightweight fabric. This woman cared about her surroundings, Blake thought.

He then entered a red marble bathroom. It was not like the typical rental bathrooms where almost everyone was reluctant to spend any money decorating because they were unsure they would get back their investment. This had been completely redone.

From there, Blake examined the walk-in closet in Joan's bedroom. There was an extra pole across the right side of the closet where blouses and other tops were hung in a double row. The closet was color-coordinated and separated by season.

In the middle drawer of the bedroom wall unit, Blake found a week-at-a-time appointment book with a black leather cover. "Grade papers" was entered for Tuesday morning, then "Noon, lunch with Bill." Every Monday, Wednesday, and Friday Joan had drawn an arrow from 8 a.m. to 3 p.m. and had written the word "teach" in large block capital letters.

There were several appointments entered for the week before. "Painter." "Wayne Clark." "Dean Putnam." "Plumber."

Blake noticed at least half-a-dozen additional appointments for the rest of the week. "Decorator, Dee Porter." "Lunch, Bill." "Dinner-Kimberly." "Interviews for study" was entered for the following Tuesday for the hours of two to four. "Term paper grades to department secretary."

Blake looked at the telephone number and address section in the back of Joan's appointment book, full of names and addresses, from A, Priscilla Alberto, to Z, Anna Zorn, with Robert Birnbaum, Chris Morris, Todd Stern, and dozens of others in between.

"The boyfriend," Blake said to himself as he searched the addresses until he came to the "G's." His finger followed the names until he came to Bill Gardner. Blake quickly wrote Gardner's address and numbers for both work and home. He should pay Mr. Gardner a visit as soon as possible.

Blake closed the book, looked around the room, and felt the rush again. Someone had suffered an untimely death. Now it was up to Blake to figure how that death occurred, who or what was responsible, and then gather evidence to get a conviction if someone was arrested. He looked around and thought that as battlefields go, this one wasn't half bad. Then, he reopened the address book and leafed through pages until he came to the page with the letter "S." There he found Kimberly Stone's name and address. As he wrote down the information, he realized how much he was looking forward to seeing her again.

CHAPTER FIVE

Kimberly stepped out of Joan's building and into the bright glare of sunlight. Shielding her eyes, she turned around and looked at the doorway of the building where her friend used to live. Her eyes moved to the list of tenant names next to little buttons; when she came to *Walsh*, her shoulders slumped. She put down her attaché case and tote bag full of papers. A new wave of grief rippled through her heart as she reached out and touched the name, feeling the cold, cracked plastic ribbon of raised letters. She pulled her hand away as a jolt of anger quickly replaced the grief. Unable to control herself, she began to pound on the side of the building with her fists.

"No! Not Joan."

People walking by gave her wide berth. After a full minute of punching and kicking, Kimberly let out a deep sigh and lowered her arms. Her knuckles were bleeding, but she felt no pain. She looked up and realized people were staring at her. She didn't care. At that moment, she didn't care about anything.

Kimberly reached down slowly, picked up her attaché case and tote bag full of term papers and started to walk down the street. As she walked along, she had the feeling someone was watching her, but when she stopped and looked back, no one appeared to be paying any attention to her, so she continued on. As she walked by, she didn't notice the young man sitting behind the wheel of a black Saab with tinted glass.

When Kimberly reached the corner of Sullivan and Sixth Avenue, the driver of the Saab turned on the engine and waited. He wiped tears from his eyes as he watched Kimberly stop and flag down a taxi. After she got in and the taxi headed uptown, the young man put the Saab in gear, pulled away from the curb, and followed the taxi.

In the taxi, Kimberly pushed her body as far back into the rear seat as it would go, hoping this would stop the shaking. She reached out and pressed one hand against each door and tried to watch the city pass by. But everywhere she looked, she saw reminders of Joan and all the places they used to go together and her eyes filled with tears again. She didn't even try to hold back this time as she began to cry, softly at first, and then deep, wrenching sobs.

The driver looked in his rearview mirror and wished he had taken his lunch break instead of stopping for this fare.

"Are you all right back there?"

Kimberly ignored the question and continued crying. The cab driver shook his head and kept driving.

When the taxi arrived at Penn Station, Kimberly just sat, staring at the back of the front seat, until the driver tapped on the thick plastic partition.

"You okay, lady?" said the cabby.

Kimberly looked up and saw the driver staring at her. She wiped her eyes, blew her nose, and gave the driver a ten-dollar bill.

She got her change and grabbed onto the taxi door to pull herself out of the cab. Her legs felt like gelatin. Taking in a deep breath, she entered the terminal without noticing the black Saab that had pulled up behind her taxi and idled there until she was inside. The driver of the Saab then gunned the engine and pulled away.

Kimberly found an empty window seat on the train to Brighton, New Jersey. She sat down and leaned against the glass, staring out at the darkness of the terminal as the train pulled out of the station and into the tunnel that ran beneath the Hudson River. As the train rumbled underground, Kimberly stared at her own reflection and wondered what she was overlooking. Who could have done this? Had Maria Alvarez's husband somehow talked his way into Joan's apartment? Despite what she told Detective Blake, Kimberly didn't really believe Wayne Clark was capable of murder, but then how well did she really know the student? Maybe he went crazy and killed Joan because she refused to get involved with him outside the classroom. And what about Bill Gardner? Could he have used the lunch as an alibi? Maybe Joan changed her mind about marriage? Could this have angered him enough to kill her, then go to the restaurant and pretend to wait for her to show up?

These questions went unanswered as the train rose up out of the underground on the New Jersey side of the river. Kimberly's reflection was replaced by many of the familiar scenes she used to see while riding to school in Joan's car. As the train moved through the Meadowlands, the oil refineries, and then the New Jersey countryside, Kimberly let her mind drift back to memories of her friend and happier times.

Joan had been such a large part of her life. It just didn't seem possible she was gone. All those nights of laughter and tears. The battles they waged together at Ferguson to improve the curriculum. They were a team. Joan and Kim. A force to reckon with.

An enormous wave of emptiness swept over her, washing away latent tremors of fear. Was this how it was going to be? Fear or sadness. Anger or sorrow. Would she ever smile again? It was the same feeling she had after her grandmother died. It was from the realization that someone very special had gone out of her life forever, and it would take time and luck to replace that feeling.

Kimberly had had a very unique relationship with her grandmother, who lived a quarter of a mile away from her first home in the little town of Monroe, Pennsylvania. It was to her grandmother's home where she would run or bike when she was old enough to go there on her own. Her mother didn't mind. She was glad to get Kimberly out of the house. She and her mother never got along. Her sister, Anne, was the favored of the two daughters but her older brother David was the most favored of all three. There was always more tension between her mother and father whenever Kimberly was around.

But at her grandmother's, she felt safe and accepted unconditionally. Her grandmother made her feel she could do no wrong and called her "Little Grandma" because she and her grandmother were so close. Her grandmother taught her how to bake, how to sew, how to fold towels, and how to set the table. These were skills in which her mother took no interest. In fact, she resented them, thinking they were beneath her. But Kimberly wanted to know about such things so she could do them too.

When her grandmother died, she was angry and sad that she could not make others in her life feel toward her the way her grandmother had naturally felt. It was a special bond. She had the same connection to Joan, an unconditional, loving relationship. Their friendship was deeper and stronger than any she had ever experienced and now it was gone forever.

Kimberly got off the train in Brighton and quickly grabbed one of the local taxis that waited at the station. Five minutes later, she was looking up at the ivy-covered front of the Old Main building at Ferguson College, a small, quaint college of less than three thousand students set on several sprawling acres of what used to be farm land. It reminded Kimberly of the Pennsylvania countryside where she had grown up.

As she started to go inside, she felt an aching in her fingers and toes and wondered if the pain in her heart had moved to the very tips of her extremities. She looked at her watch. She had already missed her first class and the next one was to begin in three minutes. Grabbing her bulging tote bag and attaché case, she entered the building.

Kimberly made it to the classroom with a minute to spare. She put her bags on the desk and watched as students filed through the door. How was she going to get through the next forty-five minutes, let alone the rest of the day? She was about to close the door when Charlotte Katz, an associate criminal justice professor in her mid-forties, entered the classroom.

"I just heard about Joan," said Charlotte, who was slightly overweight but had a warm and pretty face.

Charlotte gave Kimberly a long hug that helped her feel human again.

"You poor thing. Do they know who did it?" Charlotte asked.

"No."

"It's that damn city. You gotta get outta there, honey."

"Joan knew the person who killed her," said Kimberly.

"She did? I thought you said the police didn't know," said Charlotte looking around the classroom suspiciously.

"They don't. But whoever killed her was let into Joan's apartment."

"Oh dear. Have you told Dean Putnam?" Charlotte asked.

"Haven't had a chance to talk to him. I barely made it to class. But I'm sure he knows by now."

"What do you think? A student?"

"Why do you say that?" Kimberly asked.

"I don't know. I just get the feeling half my students want to kill me." Charlotte scanned the classroom again.

"Do you have Wayne Clark in any of your classes?" asked Kimberly.

"I do," Charlotte answered. "Why? Do you think he did it?"

"He was writing Joan love poems."

"Spare me."

"She told him she was going to tell the dean if he didn't stop."

"You *do* think he did it."

"I didn't say that. I don't know."

"Wayne Clark," Charlotte continued. "That boy gives me the creeps, I'll tell you that. Sits in the back of the class with those weird expressions on his face, undressing me with those fishy eyes."

While Kimberly and Charlotte were talking, the black Saab that had followed Kimberly to Penn Station pulled into the student section of the Ferguson College parking lot and stopped. The door opened and Wayne Clark, a young man with a stocky build and a boyish face, stepped out. He gathered his books and papers together and walked toward a class building. His eyes were red from crying.

Two hours later, Kimberly had finished her second class and was walking down the hallway when something caught her eye. It was a

54

notice posted on the outside of one of the classrooms. It read, "Professor Walsh's classes have been reassigned."

It then listed those classes underneath.

Kimberly looked again and moved in closer when she saw some handwriting toward the bottom of the notice. Someone had crossed out the word "Criminal Justice" and had written the word *"Murder"* over it so that one of the classes now read: "Introduction to *Murder*."

Word of Joan's death had spread fast, and Kimberly was saddened and angered by the student prank.

She continued walking down the hall and was about to enter the faculty lounge when she felt someone staring at her.

Kimberly turned around and saw Wayne Clark across the hallway. His eyes were bloodshot, and he had a pained look on his face. Kimberly tried to think of something to say, but when she opened her mouth to speak, Wayne ran down the stairs and out of sight. She opened the faculty door and entered with an uneasy feeling.

Inside the small lounge, a meeting was in progress.

"Well, have you hired extra security?" asked Charlotte Katz.

"Is that really necessary?" said Dean Putnam, head of the criminology and sociology departments and Dean of Student Affairs. Dean Putnam looked the part, with his neatly trimmed beard and tweed jacket.

"What if the killer is here, on campus?" said Charlotte.

"That's exactly the kind of irresponsible talk we have to avoid," snapped Putnam. "Do you realize what something like that can do to a school like Ferguson?"

"I'd feel better if you hired a few more guards," said Charlotte.

"Professor Walsh died in Manhattan," said Putnam. "Her death is still under investigation. So until I know more, I will not alarm my students with the presence of more guards. Our student population is down twelve percent already because of the new state school."

"What if the killer is a student?" said Kimberly.

"Not you too, Professor Stone," said Putnam with disgust. "This has got to stop. If we start spreading stories about a campus killer, you can all just kiss your jobs good-bye, because this place will be closed down."

"There was a note saying Joan's classes were being reassigned," said Kimberly.

"Until we can hire a replacement, we'll just have to divide them up among the rest of us," said Putnam.

Putnam looked around the room and saw sad and frightened faces staring back at him. His eyes stopped when he came to Kimberly.

"We are all deeply saddened by this tragedy," he continued. "Joan Walsh was a special member of this faculty. We're arranging a memorial service following the funeral and we're also discussing the possibility of establishing a Joan Walsh Scholarship. But most importantly, for now, let's not forget our responsibilities to our students. They need us to be strong and calm. A detective from New York will be coming out and he'll want to talk to some of you. We want to do everything we can to accommodate him. So, if there are no other questions, let's get back to work."

CHAPTER SIX

Back in Manhattan, Detective Blake was battling traffic on the uptown side of the FDR Drive. He was on his way to see Joan Walsh's boyfriend, Bill Gardner, who, according to his office, had gone home for the day after hearing about Joan's death.

Blake had asked Gardner's secretary if she knew how he found out and she said he received a call from Joan's parents.

After twenty minutes of navigating the never-ending construction on the FDR Drive, Blake got off at Sixty-second Street and turned right on York Avenue. He drove up York to Sixty-eighth Street and turned left.

According to Joan Walsh's address book, Gardner lived on the corner of Sixty-eighth and Second Avenue. Blake pulled up in front of an exclusive apartment building and stopped in a "No Parking" zone in front of an awning that extended to the curb from an ornate front door.

An elderly doorman dressed in a black-and-white uniform was about to tell Blake to move his car when the detective got out and flashed his shield. "I'm here to see a William Gardner," said Blake.

"Penthouse-E," said the doorman, who happened to be a retired police officer and knew the drill. "Have to take the elevator in the rear."

Blake let his eyes roam over the white marble floor, dark mahogany walls and ornate ceiling moldings as he walked through the lobby to the elevator. Old money. He came to an elevator, with an operator who seemed even older than the relic at the front door. Blake entered the ancient elevator and the old man pulled an elaborate brass lever, shutting the door.

"Penthouse E," said Blake. An arthritic finger pushed "P" and the elevator made its slow creaking ascent. When it finally reached the top floor, the operator pulled the brass lever and the door opened, not to a hallway, but to another door.

Blake was about to knock when the door opened. A tall, burly man wearing dark blue, tailor-made suit stood in the doorway holding a glass filled with a clear liquid.

"Detective Blake I presume. Bill Gardner. My office said you were on your way. Come on in."

As Blake entered the apartment, the opulence nearly overwhelmed him. Another reason he hated lawyers. They all made ten times more money than he did for ten times less work.

A center staircase wound up to the second floor while the main floor was designed for entertaining. A large, ballroom-sized living room was to the left, a mammoth library was to the right, and this was where Gardner was headed. Blake followed behind, looking at the room filled with thousands of books in sturdy walnut bookcases. A ladder on rollers gave access to the top shelves of the eleven-foot floor-to-ceiling bookcases. Blake noticed one entire wall was law books.

"May I get you something?" asked Gardner.

"No, thank you."

The room was quiet except for a Brandenburg Concerto softly piped in through built-in speakers that were barely noticeable on two sides of the bookcase.

Blake stood next to the burgundy leather sofa and matching leather reading chairs. Out the window, he saw a magnificent view of Manhattan's East Side and the East River, visible all the way down to the Brooklyn Bridge.

"Why don't we sit over here?" Gardner led them to a sofa, loveseat and chair arrangement around clear glass coffee table. Blake took the loveseat, while Gardner sat in the chair.

"I'm sorry about your loss," said Blake.

"Hey," said Gardner, taking a drink. "We all have to go sometime, right?"

"Ah ... yeah."

"It could have been worse, you know."

"I'm not sure I understand," said Blake.

"I mean what if this happened after we were married? My son is still getting over his mother leaving us, and that was five years ago. She took off the day Peter was born. Left him right there in the hospital. I had to cancel a business trip to come back and get him. Ah, what the hell."

Gardner took another drink.

"I need to ask you some questions," said Blake, taking out his notebook.

"Of course," said Gardner.

"How long have you known Miss Walsh?"

"Three months, give or take a day."

"How would you describe your relationship?"

"Let's see. How would I describe our relationship? I was going to marry her. So, I guess I'd have to say our relationship was pretty damned good, wouldn't you?"

Blake wondered how much of Gardner's sarcastic tone was real and how much was the booze talking.

"Was Miss Walsh seeing anyone else?"

Blake noticed that Gardner's face turned a dark shade of red.

"Someone else? You mean romantically? Not that I know of. We sorta agreed to stop dating other people. Why? Do you know something I don't?"

"No sir. I'm just trying to learn as much as I can about the victim."

"Right."

"When was the last time you saw Miss Walsh?"

"Sunday night. We had dinner. The three of us. Peter, my son, Joan and I. We went to a restaurant on First. The Manhattan Bistro. They have great crab cakes. Then we came back here for awhile. I

59

took Joan home around ten. It was a school night, and she didn't like to stay out late when she had to teach the next day."

"Could you tell me what you were doing yesterday morning between the hours of nine a.m. and one p.m.?"

"Why? Is that when it happened?"

"Could you just answer the question, Mr. Gardner?"

"We were supposed to have lunch. I waited at Lutece for over an hour."

"What about before then?"

"You mean in the morning. Let me think. I'm a suspect, aren't I? I'm the boyfriend, so of course I'm a suspect. I didn't kill her."

"If you could just tell me your whereabouts Tuesday morning."

"I left here at around nine-thirty and arrived at my office at around ten thirty. I decided to walk. It was such a lovely day. I stopped along the way for a croissant and coffee. A place a few blocks from my office. Then I worked till eleven-forty-five, when I left for my lunch date with Joan. Like I said, I waited for her from noon until one-thirty."

"Did anyone see you?"

"My secretary. At the coffee shop, I guess there must be someone who would recognize me. Then, at the restaurant, the maitre d' and the waiter."

"Were you and Joan having any problems?"

"No. We were very happy. I told you. I was going to ask her to marry me."

"Do you have any idea who might have killed her?"

"No!"

"Was anything troubling her?"

"Like what?"

"I don't know. Did she ever complain about anyone bothering her?"

"You mean that student? That pathetic poet. Poor bastard. Why? Do you think he did it?"

"You knew about him."

"He's a joke. Joan and I would read his poems and laugh ourselves silly. I caught him hanging around her street once and chased him away. I don't think the kid would have the balls to do something like this, if you want my honest opinion."

60

"Anybody else?"

"That's the only one I can think of. You might want to talk to Joan's friend. Kimberly Stone. If anyone would know, she would."

Blake closed his notebook and stood up.

"Thank you for your time, Mr. Gardner. Here's my card, if you think of anything that might be helpful."

"You can be sure of that detective. Here's my card as well. Please let me know when you catch the bastard."

"I will."

As Blake returned to his car he was convinced that Gardner was hiding something. It was more in the way he acted than what he said or didn't say. His body language had told Blake he was covering something up, in the way he looked away while answering a question, or how he occasionally put his hand over his mouth when he talked. It was as if he had something else to say, but couldn't bring himself to say it.

Blake got into his Oldsmobile and checked his notebook. He looked at his watch. It was two p.m. and he had missed lunch. He bought two hot dogs with everything on them from a street vendor at the corner of Fifth and Sixty-eighth and then headed for the Lincoln Tunnel, eating while he drove.

Barring any unforeseen traffic tie-ups, he should be in Brighton, New Jersey in about seventy-five minutes. On the way there, he called in and got an address for Wayne Clark. He also ran a check on Luis Alvarez and found there were thirty-seven Luis Alvarezes in Manhattan, fifty-four in the Bronx, another twenty-three in Brooklyn and seventeen in Queens. There were also eighteen *Luiz* Alverezes.

As he entered the tunnel to New Jersey, he made a mental note to check in with the women's shelter and talk to the battered wife. She should be able help him locate the right Luis Alvarez.

Ironically, Blake had passed within twenty yards of Luis Alvarez, who was having a heated discussion with Silvio Martinez in their clubhouse next to a fruit stand on Ninth Avenue and the Thirty-sixth Street entrance to the Lincoln Tunnel.

"I'm gonna rip her fucking heart out is what I'm gonna do," said Luis, wearing a black tank top, and oversized dark green pants, with suspenders. At twenty-eight, Luis Alvarez stood five-feet, five and half inches tall, and weighed a muscular one-hundred fifty seven pounds. His nearly handsome face would have been more appealing had it not been for the distinctive two-inch scar on his right cheek, a souvenir from an old street fight that ended in the death of Luis's opponent.

"What about the kids, man?"

"Fuck the kids," blurted Luis. "I never wanted any kids. I tole her. Take the fuckin pill. 'But it's a sin,' she'd say. The church says 'no pill.' Well the hell with the church. You know what she expects me to do?"

"What?"

"Pull out."

"Pull out?"

"Yeah. Pull out. You believe that, man? When I'm comin she thinks I gonna pull out? I mean. Is that natural? To do such a thing, man? It ain't natural. I go deeper. I fucking ram my cock up to her eyeball. Pull out. Shit. That bitch is gonna die."

"Luis, come on. Forget about her. You can get all the *putant* you want, man."

"I can't forget about it. I gotta teach her a lesson. I know where she is now. I just need a plan. Some way to get inside. A disguise or something."

"What kinda disguise?"

"I donno. I'll think of something."

CHAPTER SEVEN

As soon as the maid left to pick up the dry cleaning, Rebecca Clark decided to make sure she was alone before returning to her son's room.

"Wayne? Wayne, are you here?" Mrs. Clark called out into the impeccably-decorated ten-room center hall Colonial.

Set in the center of a four-acre plot of prime New Jersey real estate, the Clark residence made an impressive statement. The white house with green trim and shutters was located at the end of a long private road that became a circular driveway in front of the structure's six-column entranceway. Mr. Clark had once remarked that when it came to homes, you could never have too many columns.

Rebecca Clark pressed a button on the intercom next to the front door that would transmit her voice to all ten rooms. "Wayne, are you home?" asked the thin woman with velvety skin who was still very appealing at sixty-two.

No answer. He must be at school. Still, she checked the kitchen, a guest room and bathroom as she slowly made her way to Wayne's bedroom and knocked on the door, just in case.

"Wayne. Are you in there?" Again. No response. She carefully opened the door, went inside and looked over the bookcases that covered one entire wall of his room. There were dozens of hardcover and paperback books about homicide, serial killers, the criminal justice system, and the criminal mind.

She found back issues of *Soldiers of Fortune* magazine strewn on the bed and issues of *Playboy* stashed underneath. As she stared at the bookcases, she saw an envelope lying across the top of some criminology text books. Oh dear, she thought. Another one. Memorizing exactly where she had found the letter, Mrs. Clark slowly removed it from the shelf. She read the name on the envelope: Professor Joan Walsh. She pulled the letter from the open envelope and started to read:

Dear Joan,
May I call you Joan? You seem more like a girl I could be
dating than a professor of mine. You are so beautiful.
You know that I think about you day and night. I may
flunk your criminology class on purpose just so I can take
it again. (Ha! Ha!) Only kidding. I remember that red
suit you wore last week. My favorite color is red. Did you
know that? I spent the whole class thinking about your
breasts. Until the next time.
                  Yours forever,
                  Wayne

Then on the bottom of the letter, written in long-hand in red ink was the following:

Wayne, please stop writing me letters. This will be your
last warning. If I receive another one, I will refer the
matter to the Dean of Students for disciplinary action.
Joan Walsh, Ph.D.

Mrs. Clark carefully folded the letter exactly the way she had found it and replaced it on the shelf. Then she returned to her master bedroom suite, closed the door, and sat down on her pink satin chaise lounge. Several moments later, the phone rang. She waited until the third ring to answer just in case the maid had returned to the house.

"Hello."

"Is Wayne Clark there?"

"Who may I say is calling?" Mrs. Clark asked.

"This is Detective Blake with the New York Police Department. Are you Wayne's mother?"

"Yes. Wayne's not in right now," Mrs. Clark said. "Is Wayne in some kind of trouble?"

"No, ma'am. I'd just like to talk to him about one of his professors, Joan Walsh."

Rebecca Clark suddenly felt a tightness in her throat.

"Professor Walsh? Is this about the letters?" she asked.

"I'm afraid Professor Walsh has been murdered."

Mrs. Clark gasped, grabbing the telephone cord. "Oh dear. Oh no. Wayne wouldn't ... No, you're making a mistake."

"Mrs. Clark. I just want to talk to Wayne."

"He would never ..."

"I'm on my way out there now, Mrs. Clark, and I thought I'd stop by and see Wayne."

"But he's not here."

"When do you expect him?" asked Blake.

"It's hard to say. He sorta just comes and goes. But he's usually here for supper."

"I should be there in about an hour."

"Suit yourself," said Rebecca Clark. She set the phone down and closed her eyes.

Was is it all starting again? How many years had she lived with the fear that Wayne would have another "accident" like the one that happened to Lisa Murphy? How that lovely young girl's face had haunted Rebecca Clark. Wayne had maintained it was an accident and Rebecca had tried to convince herself that he was telling the truth. Even the authorities believed it was a tragic car accident. Why couldn't she?

Now there's been another killing, and again it was someone with whom Wayne seemed infatuated. Was it all starting again?

Rebecca felt very tired. She turned on CNN and listened to the news. But it all seemed so irrelevant. She started to flip through the channels with her remote. But even that became too tiring, so she turned off the sound and thought about her change-of-life son. Wayne had been an unexpected addition to the Clark home.

Born ten years after his closest sibling, a sister who was now married and a mother of two, Wayne was raised more by his two brothers and sister than his middle-aged parents. His oldest brother was graduating from college the day Wayne was born and was forever resentful that neither parent could attend this milestone. In fact, most of Wayne's three siblings resented the burden this newborn caused in the Clark house.

With both parents working, it was up to the brothers and sister to take care of little Wayne, and Wayne was not an easy baby. Demanding, constantly whining, tantrums day and night, the infant craved attention and if he couldn't get it one way, he'd try another. He was unrelenting until one day, the middle brother, tired of Wayne's crying, put the child in a closet and left him there all day until Rebecca returned home from work. From then on, Wayne acted like a different child. Instead of throwing tantrums, he was quiet and withdrawn, always compliant and always depressed. Missing were his tantrums, but so were his smiles.

As Wayne grew older, he also grew more distant from his siblings and parents. He had no friends or visitors and spent most of his time alone, reading some macho survivalist magazine or watching television. He developed an addiction to police stories and programs. Crime and punishment became his passion. He slowly began to come out of his shell and some of the old, demanding Wayne began to re-emerge. He quickly realized that with a little whining and a lot of moaning, he could get his parents to do anything, just to shut him up. Once out of college he planned to apply to the police academy and then maybe even law school, although neither his college boards nor his grades at Ferguson offered much hope for acceptance.

Rebecca Clark felt her eyes grow heavy as the fatigue pulled her into a restless sleep. She didn't hear Wayne arrive fifteen minutes later when he parked his black Saab in his parents' four-car garage. The only other car in the garage was his father's 1963 mint-condition red Cadillac. Rebecca's Acura was having its bi-monthly service and she had a loaner parked in the driveway.

Dressed in worn denim overalls, his greasy brown hair pulled back in a pony tail, Wayne retreated to his private quarters on the lower level. He picked up a term paper that was due for Dr. Walsh's criminology class the next day. It was on capital punishment and Wayne was supposed to take both sides, for and against. He researched and wrote the "against" side in just two days, but the "pro" side eluded him.

The subject had even invaded his haunted sleep. In one nightmare, Wayne was on death row. He was the wrong man, but the only person who knew he was innocent had been run over by a truck on his way to tell the judge. In his sleep, Wayne screamed out his innocence as they strapped him in a chair and prepared the deadly injection. As the needle penetrated his skin, he'd wake up screaming.

Wayne looked at the report, and then hurled it across the room. He looked around his bedroom and felt all alone. Maybe it was time to move out. Wayne was still living at home even though he was twenty-two. His father had offered to pay for an apartment, but Wayne liked living at home. He liked the way his mother waited on him now that she had retired from her job. But most of all he liked having his parents all to himself now that his two older brothers and sister had left the house.

But how would he be able to explain Joan? He could almost see his mother's eyes, questioning, convicting. Another Lisa Murphy? Wayne opened a drawer and took out a sheet of stickers. This was how he was buying his LSD lately. The street term was "blotter acid" and it came in sheets of harmless looking stickers, each one soaked in a solution containing the powerful hallucinogen. He put one of the stickers on his tongue and crawled into bed.

He closed his eyes and remembered the day he tried to offer Lisa Murphy a ride. She was one of the most attractive girls in school, but she wouldn't give Wayne the time of day. Wayne fantasized obsessively about Lisa, hoping against hope that she would drop her basketball hero boyfriend and date him instead. One day, just before the end of their senior year, Lisa was walking along the back road and Wayne was driving to the pool hall. He asked her if she wanted a ride, but she threw her nose into the air so high she almost tripped.

That cunt. Something snapped in Wayne. He turned his car around and started chasing her. She ran across the field with Wayne's car right behind her. She ran faster, but was no match for Wayne's car as it sped after her, tearing up the field, bumping up and down.

"Run, you bitch. Run faster." Wayne still didn't know exactly what had happened. Either she slipped and fell or he purposely knocked her down. It happened so fast he couldn't remember.

They found her mangled body under his car. Because he had not run away from the scene of the accident, everyone believed it was unintentional, a stupid teenage game of chicken gone wrong. But Wayne knew his mother always suspected Lisa's death was not an accident. He could tell just by the way she looked at him, the way the pupils in her eyes grew smaller as if she was closing herself off to him, shutting him out.

For Wayne, that was far worse than the mild punishment he received, which was a year's suspension of his driver's license and a court order to see a psychotherapist for two years. Wayne never revealed the truth to his therapist. And in time, Wayne had even convinced himself it was an accident, that he had never meant to hurt Lisa, only to scare her.

Now Joan was dead. But this was different. This was a whole lot different, thought Wayne. He just wished he could remember what had happened. The acid had really messed things up. He made a pact with himself that if things turned out okay, he'd give up LSD forever. That was a promise. He'd even check himself into one of those Betty Ford-type clinics. Get the shit out of his system. He loved Joan. She was just starting to notice him. But she was dead. He saw her lying there. His Joan. Dead. Maybe he was dreaming. He had a hard time telling lately when his dreams ended and the real world began. Still, he remembered her eyes. Joan's eyes. Staring up at him. Lifeless. She was gone. Gone forever.

Rebecca Clark opened her eyes and looked at the clock. Was that the alarm clock? A chime. Someone was at the front door. She got off the bed and made her way downstairs. She could hear music coming from Wayne's room. He must have arrived home while she was asleep. She rubbed her eyes as she walked to the door. The chime rang again.

"Hold on. I'm coming," she said.

She opened the front door and saw a man with a sad look on his face standing on the other side of the screen.

"Mrs. Clark?"

"Yes," she answered.

"Detective Blake, NYPD. I called about your son," he said showing her his identification card and shield.

"Please come in," she said, opening the door.

"This is a beautiful home," said Blake, as he stepped inside. He was truly impressed by the spacious estate with its Roman columns surrounded by well-cared-for grounds adorned with flowering shrubs and bushes, daffodils and pansies. This was a far cry from the tenements and rundown apartment houses he usually had to visit when investigating homicides in the city.

"Thank you," said Mrs. Clark. "Wayne must have come home while I was napping. I haven't had a chance to talk to him."

"Actually, that's probably good," said Blake.

"Why don't you wait in here while I go get him?" said Mrs. Clark as she led the detective into an elegant living room that overlooked an Olympic-sized swimming pool still covered with green canvas for the winter.

Mrs. Clark walked down a long hallway and then down a staircase to the somewhat musty lower basement level. She knocked loudly on a door.

"What do you want?" came a response.

"There's a policeman here to talk to you. He's from New York."

Wayne opened the door and glared at his mother. "Tell him I'm not home."

"I already told him you were."

"Goddamnit, Mom. What's he want?"

"I think you know what he wants."

"What's that supposed to mean?" demanded Wayne.

"Don't act like you don't know what I'm talking about."

"Give me a couple minutes."

Wayne closed the door and took a deep breath. Oh, man. I'm fucked. Someone must have seen me. Fingerprints. They've got my fingerprints. I gotta be cool."

Wayne splashed some cold water on his face and looked at himself in the mirror. "You didn't do anything wrong," he told his reflection. "Hell. You loved her."

Detective Blake stood up when Rebecca Clark entered the living room.

"He'll be right up," said Rebecca. "Can I get you something to drink? A coffee, or tea perhaps."

"No thanks," said Blake.

Just then Wayne strolled into the living room.

"You're here because of Dr. Walsh, right?" said Wayne cutting right to it.

"As a matter of fact," said Blake, "I'd like to ask you a couple of questions, if you don't mind?"

"Why should I mind? Mom, could you get me a soda? Would you like something, Detective .... ah ...."

"Blake. No thanks. Why don't we get started? Where were you yesterday morning?"

"I was ... let me think. Yesterday morning? I was in English Comp."

"What time was that?"

"Let's see. That would have been from eight to eight-fifty. She has us sign in. You can check that out."

"Where'd you go after that?"

"Went to the library to study."

"For how long?"

"An hour or so."

"Did anyone see you there?"

"I'm not sure. I went up to the fourth floor and got one of those cubicles. I can't study out in the open. Too distracting. I'm not sure if anyone saw me. Maybe."

"Then what'd you do?"

"I took a drive."

"A drive. Where'd you go?

"Around."

"You didn't happen to drive into Manhattan by any chance?"

"Actually, I did."

"Where in Manhattan?"

"Uptown, downtown."

"The Village?"

"Probably."

"Sullivan Street?"

"I did not kill Joan Walsh."

"I'm not saying you did."

"I don't know who did."

"When was the last time you saw Professor Walsh?"

"In class, Monday."

"You didn't stop in and see her on your drive into Manhattan?"

"No."

"You liked Professor Walsh, didn't you?

"Sure."

"You were sending her love letters and poems."

"Is there a crime against that?"

"How did she react to your letters Wayne?"

"What do you mean?"

"Didn't she tell you to stop?"

"Well, she might have, but I think she really liked them. She was just embarrassed you know. Around the other professors. Like she had to put up a front."

"A front."

"Pretend she didn't like them. They were just jealous. Nobody was writing love poems to them."

"Who's them?"

"Those other professors. Stone and Katz. They all work together. Joan's the best, though. I still can't believe she's dead. If I ever get my hands on whoever killed her, I'll rip out their heart and stuff it down their throat. Any other questions, Detective?"

"Have you ever been in Professor Walsh's apartment?"

Wayne's reaction was subtle but Blake saw it. The shift in his eyes. A hesitation.

"Yes."

"When?"

"Couple of months ago."

"What were you doing there?"

"Picking up some of my letters."

"Why was that?"

"Ah ... Prof ... Joan said she didn't want them."

"Why didn't she just mail them back? Or give them to you at school?"

"Well I just happened to be in the neighborhood, when I stopped by."

"I see. You were there uninvited then?"

"No. She invited me in."

"To give you the letters?"

"Right."

"How did you feel about that?"

"About what?"

"Getting your letters back. Didn't that upset you?"

"A little. But I understood. She was under a lot of pressure. She had this dork boy friend."

"Bill Gardner."

"Is that his name? It doesn't matter. She didn't love him."

"How do you know?"

"I could just tell. Instinct. A feeling. You know. You're a detective. You know how to read people. Well, I could read Joan about whatshisname."

"How did she feel about you?"

"Confused. I think I confused her."

"Did you know that she threw all of your precious poems in the wastebasket?" Blake said hoping to get a reaction.

"She wouldn't do that."

"I'm afraid she did, Wayne. I found them. All crumpled up. Tossed away. Rejected. I don't think she liked them."

"You don't know shit, detective."

"Wayne!" shouted Rebecca. "You apologize to Detective Blake."

"Shut up, Mom. I know what he's trying to do. It's not going to work."

"What do you think I'm trying to do, Wayne?"

"They don't teach this stuff in criminology one-oh-one, but I've watched enough true crime shows to know when somebody's trying to set me up. You don't have enough evidence to charge me with anything so you're hoping I'll do something stupid like take a swing at you so you can bring me in."

"I think you've been watching too much television, Wayne."

"Yeah? Well I think this interview is over. How about that, Detective Blake. I've got homework to do."

Wayne started to leave the room.

"Wayne," said Blake.

Wayne stopped and turned.

"I may need to ask you some more questions, so if you don't mind, I'd appreciate it if you'd stay in the area."

"What if I don't?"

"Are you planning any trips?"

"No. I just don't like the idea that I have to be at your beck and call."

"Let me put it this way, Wayne. Right now you're a material witness in a homicide investigation. I can have you detained for up to 48 hours and placed in protective custody if I have to, but I'd rather not. Now, if anything changes whereby your status is elevated to primary suspect, then we will return with a warrant for your arrest. As a criminal justice student you must be aware of how it can be for someone once they've entered the system. If you've got nothing to worry about, all I ask is that you be available for further questioning. If that's a problem, you can come with me right now and that way I'll be sure you'll be around when I want to question you."

"I'm not going anywhere," snapped Wayne as he stormed off to his room.

Rebecca Clark let out a deep sigh and turned toward Blake. "Wayne's got his troubles, and sometimes he gets in these moods, but he worshipped that professor."

"Mrs. Clark," said Blake. "I'm just gathering information. I'm talking to everyone who knew her."

"Should we get a lawyer?"

"That's up to you. At this point, I think a lawyer would probably do more harm than good."

"Why is that?"

"Like I told Wayne: Right now, we consider him a material witness. But if you brought in a lawyer who advised Wayne to stop being cooperative, then we might have to bring him in and book him on suspicion of murder. As of now, we have no reason to do that."

"But that doesn't mean you won't."

"Let's take it one step at a time. Just tell Wayne that it's in his best interest to cooperate and to be as helpful as possible. Especially if he knows anything that might shed some light on the murder."

"I will," said Mrs. Clark. "And thank you."

As Blake left the Clark house, he was troubled by his exchange with Wayne Clark. Something was definitely not right about this kid. Both Kimberly Stone and Bill Gardner had described Wayne as a frightened boy, afraid of his own shadow. Only the Wayne Clark he had just questioned did not fit that profile. Maybe he had a split personality. Something had boosted his confidence. He made a note to question Wayne Clark again, but at a different location. He wanted to see how he acted in an interrogation room. Blake was sure the student knew more than he was telling.

It took Blake ten minutes to drive from the Clark's home to Ferguson College. He parked in front of the red brick Old Main building and asked a student for directions to Dean Putnam's office.

Putnam was talking on the phone to the parents of a prospective student when Blake appeared in his doorway.

"We are fully accredited, Mr. Perkins," said Putnam. "We may not have the high profile of some of the ivy league schools, but our graduates are ranked among the top twenty academically in every major we offer. Yes, sir. I will, sir. Good-bye."

Dean Putman stood up, "Can I help you?"

"Detective Alan Blake, NYPD."

"Ah, yes. Please, come in. Take a seat. Some coffee? A piece of homemade corn bread?"

"Coffee would be nice," said Blake, starting to feel weary.

While Putnam poured, Blake opened his notebook.

"I'd like to ask you some questions about Professor Joan Walsh."

"It's just shocking. We're just .... What can I tell you? This ... We're all just devastated. She was one of our family."

"Did Professor Walsh tell you about anything or anyone who might have been bothering her lately?"

"No. Why?"

"A student?"

"A student. You think a student killed her? Oh God. Do you realize what that would do to the reputation of this school?"

"We're looking into all possibilities. When did you last see Professor Walsh?"

"Monday, I think. She had three classes."

"Did she seem upset about anything?"

"Not that I'm aware of."

"What did you think of her?"

"Joan? Professor Walsh was one of our most admired teachers. Everyone liked her, detective."

"Well. Not everyone," Blake said dryly. "I'd like to talk to her students and any other teacher she spent time with. So I'll need a class list."

"She was killed in her apartment. Shouldn't you be focusing your investigation in Manhattan?"

"Like I said. We're looking at all angles. Here's my card. Call me if you think of anything."

"I will," said Putnam, thinking that the sooner this terrible murder was solved, the better. In fact, maybe he should start to organize the memorial or the scholarship fund. That always looked good and the school might even receive some sizable alumni donations pondered the dean as he walked toward the door.

"I'll also need to see Professor Walsh's office," said Blake.

"Of course," said Putnam as he reached for a key ring. "It's right down the hall here."

Putnam unlocked the door to the tiny office and Blake went inside. He didn't hear Putnam let out a deep sigh as his worst fears were about to come true. A homicide detective was going to be prowling around the school asking questions, interviewing students and generating fear in the hearts of everyone connected with Ferguson College. It was going to be a public relations nightmare.

I have to be careful thought the killer. *Especially if I have to eliminate anyone who could know. Is that going to be possible? Do I have a choice?*

CHAPTER EIGHT

Kimberly looked at the clock in the back of the classroom. Just one more class to go. God help me get through this last class, she prayed.

She looked out at the students and saw the fear in their faces. This was Joan Walsh's Introduction to Criminology class and she was filling in, but she felt like an interloper. It wasn't right. Dean Putnam should have canceled this class as he had with the earlier ones. But no, he wanted to put things back to normal as fast as he could, to make it all go away, like it never happened.

Kimberly fought a wave of nausea and fatigue. She could almost feel Joan's presence in the room, like a phantom shadow looking over her shoulder. What would Joan do in this situation? She'd pull herself together and get on with it.

She realized the students were staring at her so she stared right back, scanning each row, looking each student in the eye, trying to make a connection with each one, to show that she shared their fear and sorrow. As she looked across the third row she came to an empty seat, paused a moment, and then continued on until she had looked at each student.

"Before we begin, I think we should have a minute of silence to mourn the death of Professor Walsh."

Kimberly lowered her head, and the young men and women followed her lead. After some time had passed, she looked up and saw the class was again staring at her.

"For those of you who don't know me, I'm Professor Kimberly Stone. I'll be taking over Professor Walsh's Introduction to Criminology class until a replacement is found. I know we're all in a state of shock, so instead of me trying to come up with some lame lecture, why don't we just talk about the only crime that matters right now. The murder of Professor Joan Walsh. I need to tell you that Professor Walsh was more than my colleague, she was my friend."

A petite female student in a tight sweater raised her hand.

"Yes," said Kimberly.

"Do the police have any suspects?"

"Not that I'm aware of."

"We heard you found the body," asked a young man in the front row.

"I did," she said, looking down, thinking that maybe this was a mistake. She then looked up and at the empty chair and then back at the student who asked the last question. Time to change the subject.

"Who's missing?"

The question made several students squirm in their seats and Kimberly knew whose seat it was even before a young man in the rear spoke up.

"That's where Wayne Clark usually sits."

"Does anyone know where Mr. Clark is?" she asked.

"No," said another student, "but he must be pretty messed up about what happened."

"Why do you say that?" asked Kimberly.

"Because this is the first time he's ever missed this class," said the student.

"I saw him earlier today," said another student. "We have statistics together. I think he went home. He didn't look too good."

Kimberly thought about what she just heard when she looked out a classroom window and saw Detective Blake. He was in a window of the Old Main building where the faculty had their offices. Isn't that the window to Joan's office? She could see Blake talking to Dean Putnam. Maybe she should tell the detective what she had just heard about Wayne Clark. Blake reached for his hip and lifted something to his face. A beeper? It was too far away to know for sure. He said something to Putnam and disappeared from sight. A moment later, Blake stepped out the front door of the administration building and walked toward the parking lot. Kimberly was wondering what he might have found in Joan's office when a student broke through her reverie.

"Professor Stone?"

She turned from the window to see a young woman in the front row waving her hand.

"Yes?"

"I don't know if this applies here, but just last week Professor Walsh was just teaching us about some psychiatrist's theory on murderers."

"David Abrahamsen?" questioned Kimberly.

"That's the one," said the student. "He thinks that all acts of murder are about the killer's rage at their mother. He said that in their unconscious, murderers are really killing their mother but since they can't bring ourselves to kill their actual mothers, they kill someone else."

"A mother substitute," said Kimberly.

"So all we have to do is find out who considered Professor Walsh a mother substitute and we catch the killer, right, Professor Stone?"

"Good theory, but I'm afraid it's a little more complicated than that," said Kimberly. "Besides, wouldn't that make most of you suspects?"

The question had the desired affect. The room turned completely quiet. Several eager hands that had been raised, suddenly came down.

"Why don't we end early today?" said Kimberly, as she gathered her books and notes together and left the classroom.

In the hallway, she let out a deep sigh and started walking toward her office, which was next to Joan's. She was about to unlock her door when she noticed that the door to Joan's office was slightly ajar. Putnam apparently had forgotten to lock it after Blake had left.

She pushed open the door and went inside. The office was similar to hers with a large wooden desk, bookshelves, coffee table, sofa and two visitors' chairs, and diplomas on the wall. However, unlike Kimberly's cluttered and chaotic workspace, everything here was in its place, even down to the paper clips and rubber bands.

Kimberly closed and locked the door behind her and then sat behind the old and oversized wooden desk. She smiled at the contrast as she gazed around at the bookshelves that covered three of the four walls and held hundreds of books, organized by subject and author, fiction and non-fiction. Many were about crime and crime detection. She wasn't surprised to see she and Joan shared many of the same books. There was a separate shelf for video tapes of true and fictional crime movies and a section labeled Court TV.

Like the rest of the office, everything about the desk seemed to be in perfect order. Pencils and pens filled a green felt cup. There was even a tray for bottles of correction fluid next to an old Smith Corona typewriter. She thought about how Joan preferred to type short notes on a typewriter instead of booting up her computer.

She gave the center drawer a slight tug and it opened. Inside, the desk was as organized as the top. There were slots for big paper clips, little paper clips, medium sized clips, staples, stamps, keys, scissors, a sterling silver letter opener, and napkins.

Kimberly shook her head at the neatness. She then opened the side drawers where Joan kept her student files, all in alphabetical order, all neatly filed.

"Maybe I shouldn't be doing this," she thought. She could be contaminating evidence and not even know it.

Instead of stopping, she started to pull out the bottom drawer on the left but it wouldn't open. How could one drawer be locked and not the others? No. It was just stuck. She found a ruler and wedged it in the top and pushed down, unhooking whatever was stopping the drawer from opening.

The drawer opened slowly and Kimberly looked down. What was this? Some kind of joke? In the bottom drawer of an otherwise neat and organized desk in an extremely neat and orderly office, was one of the messiest drawers Kimberly had ever seen. It looked like an overstuffed garbage can and smelled just as bad, filled with candy wrappers, chunks of old chewed gum, moldy packets of catsup, old telephone messages, half eaten chocolate bars, a mummified half-eaten peanut butter and jelly sandwich, used tissues, and individual packs of mayonnaise.

Could it be? Did neat, clean, obsessively organized Joan Walsh have a dump drawer?

Using the ruler, Kimberly began to poke through the refuse until she found something beneath a layer of wrappers and decaying food. It was a well-thumbed copy of a paperback book, entitled: *Why Am I Afraid to Tell You Who I Am?*

Inside the book, was a folded piece of paper. She removed the paper and smoothed it out. On the paper was an abstract pencil drawing of a woman. Under the picture were the words: "Take a chance on getting slapped, you might get kissed."

Kimberly placed the paper next to the book and closed her eyes. Take a chance on getting slapped? Is that what you did, Joannie? You took a chance on getting slapped, and got killed instead. Who did you take the chance with?

A sound made Kimberly open her eyes. Someone was coming. She quickly closed the drawer and stood up. She could hear footsteps in the hallway. They were getting closer. She stood inside the closed door. A hand tried the door. Had she locked the door after she entered? She couldn't remember. The knob began to turn slightly and Kimberly held her breath. But then it stopped. The lock prevented the knob from turning enough to allow the door to open. After a couple of more shakes, the person on the other side of the door gave up and walked away.

Kimberly waited another two minutes before opening the door. The hallway was empty. She quickly left Joan's office and entered her own next door.

Classes were over for the day, but there was still administrative work to be done, grades to enter. It was after five when Kimberly finally walked out of the Old Main building. Exhausted and depressed, she headed toward the taxi stand across the street.

Charlotte Katz was just getting into her car when she saw Kimberly.

"Hey. How are you doing?"

"I made it," said Kimberly. "I didn't think I would, but I did."

"If I didn't have someone coming by later, I'd invite you over."

"That's okay, Charlotte. I want to go home. Get into a nice warm bath and pretend today never happened."

Charlotte gave Kimberly a warm prolonged hug and got into her car.

Kimberly arrived at Penn Station an hour later, then took the Seventh Avenue subway to Christopher Street and Sheridan Square. She walked down Bleecker to Sullivan Street, where she looked north and saw that a police car was still in front of Joan's building. She let out a deep breath and headed south to her building on the next block.

As if in a trance, Kimberly meandered into her fourth floor apartment and placed her shoulder bag on the door knob of the hall closet. Walking down the narrow hallway, she passed the framed prints of exhibits she had attended at various museums around the world. She looked at the ornate gold clock on the hand-carved mahogany desk, a gift from her parents when she got her doctorate.

According to the clock, it was 7:24 p.m. She felt as if it should have been a day later, not just twelve hours since she discovered Joan's body.

At that moment, the phone rang, making her jump. She grabbed the phone.

"Yes."

"Kimberly?" The woman's voice was familiar.

"Mrs. Walsh," she said, gripping the phone.

"She was our only child," Mrs. Walsh cried.

"I know," Kimberly answered, her facial muscles twitching from the effort it was taking to control her tears.

"We'll never speak to her again. We'll never be grandparents. There's no one to pass on our family name. We'll bury our child before ourselves. How could it happen, Kimberly?"

"I don't know, Mrs. Walsh."

"My husband and I so looked forward to your weekly visits with Joan. Our Sunday night dinners together had become our favorite day of the week."

She listened to Mrs. Walsh's sobbing as she moved from the bed to her beige cotton reading chair.

"Is there anything I can do?" she asked.

"The police have asked us to go to the morgue to identify her. Would you come with us?"

Kimberly took a deep breath. "Of course," she answered, biting her bottom lip at the thought of seeing Joan's lifeless body once more.

"Thank you," Mrs. Walsh said. "We'll meet you there in an hour."

"We'll find the animal who did this," Kimberly said in a stronger voice.

Mrs. Walsh hung up the phone without any closing words.

Tired and drained, Kimberly climbed into her bed. All she wanted to do was sleep. She set her alarm to wake her up in forty minutes. She was only about ten minutes from the morgue by cab, so that gave her time for a catnap.

She spent the next fifteen minutes drifting in and out of sleep. She dreamt she had a summer job putting formaldehyde on bodies and watching them decay. She wanted to quit. Three others had quit, but she couldn't. She called Joan to brag about her job. Joan then told her that Bill Gardner got the outstanding actor of the year award, but he had to fly to Dallas to accept it. Joan had run into Rock Hudson and bragged to him. He cautioned her, "Watch it, watch it," as if things were going too well.

The dream woke Kimberly up.

She checked the clock. She had about ten minutes left to rest, so she closed her eyes and quickly drifted off again. This time she dreamt of Joan, who was trying to leave, but Kimberly wouldn't let her go. She grabbed Joan by the shoulders and started to shake her. Joan just smiled, pulled Kimberly to her and kissed her softly on the lips. Kimberly could feel Joan's tongue slide into her mouth while Joan's hands slipped under her blouse and cupped the curve of her breasts. But then, something happened. She could no longer feel Joan's hands on her breasts. In the dream, Kimberly opened her eyes and saw Joan's face begin to fade. No. Don't go, Kimberly cried. Not yet. You can't go yet. You might not come back.

She awoke with a jolt. Her eyes were burning and her head ached. Then the tears came, putting out the fire in her eyes and soothing the pain in her head. She quickly dressed in a charcoal gray suit and dark navy blue blouse. She started to apply make up to cover the dark circles under her eyes, but stopped. Who was she trying to impress? She put down the under-the-eye concealer and left the apartment.

At 8:15 p.m., Kimberly arrived at the blue-and-gray building on First Avenue and Twenty-fifth Street. The morgue occupied the bottom floors of the low-rise building; the waiting room was on the first floor. The second through sixth floors were administrative offices, with the morgue museum and library on the top floor.

She had been to that museum a half-dozen times on field trips with her students. It had all seemed so fascinating then. The tools and weapons used to kill people that forensic physicians had put into the morgue museum for educational purposes. Body parts in jars, preserved in formaldehyde. When Kimberly had gone on a tour of the autopsy room, in the basement of the building, several of the medical students on the tour fainted or vomited, but she stood strong throughout the entire autopsy and visit. She had been able to detach herself from what she had seen during those visits, until today.

She walked into the first-floor waiting room. Kimberly had goose bumps on her arms because they kept the place so cold. Suddenly she wondered why she had so magnanimously agreed to accompany her friend's parents to the morgue. What if she lost it? She was starting to feel faint.

Kimberly took in a deep breath and walked over to Mr. and Mrs. Walsh, who were already seated in a row of connected blue metal chairs. They both stood up to embrace her, then sat down in silence and waited.

Mrs. Walsh, a fit and trim sixty-four-year-old retired first grade teacher, was wearing a black dress. Mr. Walsh, a retired salesman, was also dressed in dark colors.

Every few minutes, another name was called out, and one or more persons would file by Kimberly and Joan's parents, and head downstairs. Soon they would hear a scream or two. The family members would come back up the stairs, walking very slowly or running out the door.

"Did Joan tell you about the letters?" Mrs. Walsh suddenly asked Kimberly.

"Yes," Kimberly answered, feeling awkward about how much she should tell Mrs. Walsh without violating Joan's confidence.

"Did she show you any?"

"One or two."

"They were from a student, weren't they?" Mrs. Walsh asked.

"Wayne Clark," Kimberly said.

"She never told us his name," Mrs. Walsh replied. As she made that comment, Kimberly wished she could take back what she had said.

"I bet he did it," Mr. Walsh said, emphatically.

"Brian, you don't know that," Mrs. Walsh answered.

"We shouldn't jump to conclusions," Kimberly said.

The Walshes said nothing more about the letters or Wayne Clark, but Kimberly felt Mr. Walsh was thinking about little else.

"Walsh, Joan," someone called out.

"Yes," Mr. Walsh shouted back.

The orderly in the white coat was tall, black, and husky, with a pleasant mustache and a kind face.

"Come this way," the orderly said.

Mr. and Mrs. Walsh and Kimberly followed him down the stairs. Kimberly noticed how oppressive the stairwell seemed without windows, skylights, or artwork on the walls, how each footstep on the metal stairs echoed their descent into the halls of death.

At the bottom of the staircase, the orderly opened a thick metal door and led them into a cold room filled with rows of stainless steel compartments. This was the temporary rest stop for those who suffered untimely deaths, those who were required by law to have an autopsy, a thorough medical examination that probed all internal as well as external organs, including the inside of the brain, to an analysis of the contents of the stomach, all in an attempt to determine the time of death and cause of each fatality.

The orderly looked down at a form on his clipboard and noted the number at the top. He then walked toward the corresponding number on one of the compartments.

"Number zero-zero-seven-three-six," he said, calmly and clearly.

Mr. and Mrs. Walsh and Kimberly walked slowly together over to the compartment, which like all the others had a metal handle. The orderly grabbed the handle and pulled out a long metal tray. Upon the tray was a nude body under an opaque plastic sheet.

Mrs. Walsh's knees began to buckle, as Kimberly grabbed her to hold her up.

"Are you okay?" asked the orderly, genuine compassion in his voice.

"Yes."

"Are you sure?"

"You can lean on me," Kimberly said to Mrs. Walsh.

"That's okay dear," said Mrs. Walsh who was now holding her husband's hand, trying to look brave while all Kimberly felt was an ocean of guilt and sorrow.

"Just give me a moment to take a breath," Mrs. Walsh said.

"Take your time," the orderly replied.

"Okay, now," Mrs. Walsh said.

With that, the orderly pulled back the plastic cover that had concealed Joan's face. Mrs. Walsh almost passed out at the sight of her daughter now lying still, her skin had already turned an alien, inhuman, gray-blue color. Her face was slightly misshapen by the punch that had broken Joan's nose and the blow to the side of her head.

"Oh, my God," Mrs. Walsh moaned, swooning, digging her nails into her husband's hand. Mr. Walsh had to catch her before she hit the floor.

"Is this Joan Walsh?" the orderly asked Mr. Walsh.

"Yes, this is my daughter," Mr. Walsh replied, his voice cracking, struggling to hold up his wife. "Professor Joan Michelle Walsh."

"I'm going to close the drawer now," the orderly said.

Every part of Kimberly was tingling and numb from the shock of seeing Joan this way. But it was better than the future, where she would never see her again. She looked so young lying there in a never ending sleep, where she would never grow older. No one should die this young, thought Kimberly.

"Sign here," the orderly said, pointing to a line on the form and handing a pen to Mr. Walsh.

Kimberly reached out to take Mrs. Walsh who was leaning against her husband, so he could sign the form. Brian Walsh scribbled his name with a trembling hand.

As the orderly pushed the drawer closed, Mrs. Walsh reached out to touch the cold metal, pressing her hand firmly against the closed compartment.

"Good-bye, baby," she said.

Kimberly felt Mrs. Clark tremble against her as an electric arc of mourning passed through their bodies and she felt her own knees begin to waver. Mr. Clark stepped forward and helped support the two women.

Kimberly's throat burned from half swallowed tears and her face was a grimace of sorrow. She touched her chin and realized it was damp from crying.

She thought of all the autopsies she had witnessed with her students and when she was doing research for her own graduate papers. She remembered the sound of the electric saw, an obnoxious buzz that changed tone as it cut through the skin and skull and eventually the gray matter of the brain. She remembered the sight of body parts, stored in jars, labeled and set aside for further analysis. But none of that had prepared her for the pain and horror of this.

As they began to make their way to the exit, Kimberly shivered and wondered if it was really getting colder, or had she merely felt the coldness that always seemed to surround the dead.

Luis Alvarez stood in the shadow of the building, invisible, waiting. Where was the goddamn truck? He checked his watch, but on second glance, realized it had stopped. Goddamn fucking watch. Luis ripped the 'piece-of-shit' gold fake Rolex off his wrist and hurled it at the sidewalk, then stomped on it with hightop sneakers. He knew the watch wasn't really a Rolex when he bought if off Julio. But it was still supposed to tell time. Goddamn Julio was gonna pay for this man. Now what the fuck time was it? Maybe he missed the delivery. Jesus. The whole world was going to shit and it was all Maria's fault.

He looked around for something to throw. He wanted to break something in the worst way. Rage boiled inside as he rummaged through a nearby garbage can. His hand found an empty whiskey bottle. It would have to do. He gripped the bottle by the neck, reared back, and let it fly. The heavy base of the bottle smashed through the stained glass window on the side of the cathedral.

A light came on in the rectory next door and Luis was about to run off when he heard it. He stopped and looked down the street just as the laundry truck turned the corner and rumbled to a stop.

CHAPTER NINE

Back on the street, Kimberly declined the Walshes offer to drive her home. Instead, she grabbed a taxi to mid-town.

She found Detective Blake at his desk on the second floor of Manhattan South, which housed one of the borough's two major homicide squads. Detectives in these units handled any homicide that had the potential to become a high-profile case. Manhattan South covered major crimes from Fifty-ninth Street to Battery Park, while Manhattan North investigated similar crimes north of Fifty-ninth Street to Washington Heights.

Blake was studying Joan Walsh's appointment book. In fact, he was reading the entry "dinner with Kimberly" on Wednesday, which would have been tonight, when he looked up and saw her standing in his doorway.

"Professor Stone," said Blake, closing the book and wondering if he really was psychic.

"I hope I'm not disturbing you," said Kimberly.

"Not at all," said Blake. "Are you okay? You look a little pale."

"I just left the morgue with the Walshes and feel like someone sucked the life right out of me."

"Have a seat," said Blake nodding toward the only other chair in the office. "Can I get you some coffee or something?"

"No, thanks," said Kimberly, sitting down. She looked at the wall behind Blake and saw two framed certificates: a University of Pennsylvania bachelor of arts diploma and a Police Academy certificate. Nearby, in a wooden frame, was a picture of the Mayor of New York handing Detective Blake a citation.

"How are they doing, the Walshes?" he asked.

"They're devastated. We're all devastated. They lost their only daughter and I feel like someone has ripped out my heart. I keep calling her number just to hear her phone message. I carry on conversations with her as if she's still alive. Does that mean I'm crazy?"

"Only if she talks back," said Blake. "I know some folks who specialize in counseling people who were close to homicide victims. Family, friends, co-workers."

"That's okay. I know plenty of them myself. I appreciate your concern, but that's not why I'm here."

"Okay, then. Why are you here?"

"I was just wondering if you had a chance to follow up on those leads I gave you."

"I interviewed Wayne Clark. I'll probably want to talk to him again. He's a strong possible. But there's no definitive evidence tying him to the scene at the time of the murder. We found some of his prints in her apartment but he claims he's been there on another occasion to pick up his letters."

"You believe him?"

"Until I have reason not to."

"I saw him at school today," said Kimberly. "He ran away when I looked at him."

"You must be a tough teacher," said Blake.

"I'm not here to trade jokes, detective. He also failed to show up for his last class of the day. Introduction to Criminology. Joan's class. But that may not have been his fault. Her earlier classes were canceled, so he might have thought this one was too. Dean Putnam reassigned it to me."

"I met your dean. He seems more concerned with the school's image than anything else."

"You've got that right. What about Maria Alvarez's husband?"

"Haven't been able to locate him. He missed his weekly appointment with his parole officer, so we have an all-points out for him."

"Have you talked to Joan's super, Mr. Fontes?"

"One of the officers did. Why?"

"It's a long shot, but after we talked I remembered Joan told me that she thought he was spying on her."

"Peeping Tom stuff?"

"More or less. It was like every time she had the water running for a shower or a bath, he seemed to show up. She thinks he was trying to catch her naked."

"That sort of behavior doesn't usually lead to murder."

"Not unless she caught him and threatened to tell his wife."

"You're quick."

"I do teach this stuff, detective, remember?"

"Oh yeah. Couple of the guys said they had you at John Jay."

"What did they say?"

"You're tough but fair."

"Who else have you talked to?"

"The boyfriend," said Blake. "Now there's a real pleasant person."

"He have any ideas?"

"If he did, he wasn't sharing them with me."

"You think he's hiding something?"

"Felt that way. How well do you know him?"

"Not very well, I'm afraid."

"Did she love him?"

"She was hoping he'd ask her to marry him."

"That's not what I asked," said Blake. "It doesn't really matter. A lot of people have killed for love. How did they meet?"

"We were stuck in the snow on Canal Street. Just outside the Holland Tunnel. He gave us a push so we could get to school. He also gave Joan his card and a few days later she called him up and he asked her out."

"How about you and Joan?"

"Me and Joan? You mean our friendship?"

"Yeah."

"We met four years ago when we both started teaching at Ferguson. We liked each other from the start. If you knew Joan, you'd know why. She was special. Selfless, sincere. We just connected on so many levels. She was like a sister. But even closer. I mean I've got a sister. But with Joan, I just felt totally accepted. I could say anything and she'd understand. I could do no wrong. Can you imagine how that feels? Total acceptance? That's why this hurts so much."

"I lost a partner once," said Blake. "Second year on the force. I was getting coffee in this diner on Eighth Avenue. When I came out, someone had put a bullet in his forehead as he sat behind the wheel of our blue-and-white. Only then, they were green and black. Seems my partner owed some gambling debts and I didn't even know he had a gambling problem. We never caught the guy."

Kimberly looked at Blake and for the first time she noticed the softness in his eyes.

"I hate to change the subject," said Blake, "but since you're here, could you think back over the last few weeks? Try to remember if Joan said anything, maybe about that Clark kid, or anybody else that might have been bothering her. Anything out of the ordinary."

"I've been asking myself the same thing all day," said Kimberly. "Unfortunately, I haven't come up with any answers."

"What about the neighbors? You were kind of vague before."

"I remember the name of one neighbor Joan used to visit for coffee. Karen Eissler. She lives next door."

"Anything else?"

"I'm afraid not."

Kimberly walked over to the framed diploma.

"My neighbor's older brother graduated from the University of Pennsylvania around the same time as you. Did you know him? Brendan Gilliatt?"

"No, but it was a big school."

"Were you a criminal justice major?"

"Psychology."

"Interesting."

"Fine arts minor."

"You paint?" she asked.

90

"Sculpt. Sandstone."

Kimberly smiled and shook her head, "The hidden talents of a homicide detective." She looked at her watch, "I'd better go."

"Can I give you a lift home?"

"No, thanks," said Kimberly. "I'll grab a cab."

"I understand the Walshes have planned the wake for tomorrow night. I'll probably see you there."

"That's very thoughtful," said Kimberly.

"Actually, the main reason I'm going is to see if anyone looks suspicious. You'd be surprised how often the killer attends these things."

"Good point," said Kimberly, slightly embarrassed that she had misread the detective's motives. "Especially in this case. On the other hand, if someone who Joan knew well doesn't show up, you might also have a lead."

"You think like a cop."

"Actually, I teach cops how to think," said Kimberly.

"So how should I be thinking?" said Blake.

"You have Joan's address book," said Kimberly. "If it's not Luis Alvarez, then chances are the killer's in there somewhere. You know as well as I do that most homicides are committed by someone who knew the victim."

Blake looked down at the black book on his desk.

"We *are* going catch this one," Kimberly said as she walked away.

"We?"

"Don't worry. I'm not trying to do your job. I'm just going to make sure you do it."

Blake stood up as she left. Just what he needed, he thought, pressure from an armchair academic, as if the case wasn't tough enough.

He sat back down and opened the folder on his desk. It was the forensic lab report. So far, all he had to go on were four sets of fingerprints in Joan's bedroom that were not hers. One set belonged to Kimberly Stone, another to Wayne Clark and a third to Bill Gardner. The fourth set had failed to match up with any prints in the computerized system. The report noted two strands of hair, and one fiber on the victim of unknown origin. He also had the marble bookend in the shape of a horse, wiped clean of prints, that seemed to be the murder weapon with only the victim's blood on it.

Blake was still awaiting the final autopsy report, documenting a more precise time of death and any internal seminal fluid or indications that would show whether Joan Walsh had been raped or sexually assaulted.

He opened another envelope marked Crime Scene Photos and removed several eight-by-ten color photographs. Even in death, he could tell Joan Walsh had been an attractive woman. He picked up another photograph and studied the crime scene again, then went back to the photo of Joan. Using a magnifying glass, he could see the marks on her wrists, which could have been caused by rope or cloth. There were similar marks around the corners of her mouth. He tried to imagine her with a gag in her mouth and tied up. He could almost see her struggling to get free, the bindings cutting into her skin.

What kind of a person would tie up the victim and kill her while she was defenseless? Someone with an enormous rage toward, and fear of, women. Like Kimberly, Blake was convinced the killer was someone known to the victim. The only thing missing apparently was a gold necklace worth about two hundred dollars. A burglar would have at least taken the rest of the jewelry. As far as Blake was concerned, the killer took Joan's life for some other reason. Find the motive, thought Blake, and you find the killer.

Blake placed the time of the killing somewhere between 8:45 a.m. and 1:15 p.m. It was unlikely the autopsy report would narrow the time of death down much more than that. The superintendent's assistant had seen Joan doing laundry between 7 and 8:30 a.m., and the clothes had been dried and removed from the dryer. The clean towels and sheets were found on a chair next to Joan's bed, where she probably intended to fold them. Joan's phone machine had a time marker. The messages on the machine began at 12:15 p.m., when the video store called to say that her film transfer order was ready.

The next call was from Bill Gardner, at 12:45, saying he wondered where she was but he would wait another thirty minutes. There were several calls after that, over the next twelve hours, from Bill Gardner again and Kimberly Stone. It's possible that she could have been alive but unable to move when some of the calls came in, especially if she was bound and gagged, as the coroner had noted. But even taking in all the variables, Blake estimated that the time of death was after Joan had returned from the laundry room but before the phone messages from the video store or Bill Gardner, unless she had been screening her calls, or the message timer was wrong. Blake made a note to check the timer to make sure it gave the correct time.

The time of death was a key factor in connecting the killer to the crime. It was now Wednesday night at 9:11. The killer had had more than thirty-six hours to cover any tracks, rationalize what had happened, make up a story, or even to kill again.

Across the street from the police station, the killer stood in the shadows and watched the front entrance of Manhattan South.

Your picture might be speeding across police wires right now. Every patrol car in the city might have your face. And here you are, standing across the street from one of the two major police bureaus in the city. You wanna get caught? This Detective Blake is pretty smart. Maybe you oughta take him out now. Make it look like a mugging or something. Random act of violence. Isn't that what this city's famous for?

CHAPTER TEN

Kimberly stood in front of the precinct and stared out into the brisk night. A west wind was blowing papers and debris across the sidewalk. Someone's discarded wrapper clung to Kimberly's ankle briefly until she kicked it away.

Feeling too wired to go straight home, she started walking east, then south down Second Avenue. Her mind was racing through the faces of all the people who knew Joan. There were so many, Kimberly felt herself getting dizzy. Joan was a popular woman. Maybe she should narrow it down to lovers. At least that was a somewhat more manageable number. But did Kimberly know everyone Joan had ever been with? Besides, why did the killer have to be a lover?

Kimberly walked on, lost in her mental search until she finally looked up and found herself on St. Mark's Place in the East Village. She had walked nearly fifty blocks. Here, the street was teeming with people who lived out their fantasies. You could see it in the clothes they wore and in the way they acted. She loved the East Village and its otherworldly quality, where she could play the stranger in a land of fantasy.

To Kimberly, the East Village was like traveling to a foreign land, where the people looked different, where the air had a fragrance all its own, where even the language was different. As she walked briskly along St. Mark's Place, she saw a young mother with green spiked hair wheeling twins in a specially-designed stroller. For a moment, thoughts about Joan's murder were replaced with another nagging question as she stared at the woman, who was kneeling to retrieve a bottle that one of the infants had dropped. She wondered if one day she would ever be picking up her own baby's bottle.

Then she felt a familiar tug. It was a feeling she and Joan often shared. They called it "the mother force" and a powerful force it was. Kimberly believed it was the main reason Joan was even contemplating marriage to Bill. She wanted a family before the thief of time stole the dream forever.

Another thought suddenly entered her mind. It had something to do with Joan, but she couldn't quite put her finger on it. As she continued to stare at the mother and her twins, an image of something was forming. A feeling without a form or substance. A nagging, tugging feeling. But the harder Kimberly tried to connect the feeling to something concrete, the fainter it became, until it disappeared like a wispy cloud of smoke.

From St. Marks, she walked toward Broadway and then down to Bleecker and over to Sullivan.

By the time Kimberly reached Sullivan Street, she had worked up an appetite. The scent of fresh made pizza made her stop. Across the street she saw the source of the aroma, Sal's Famous Pizza on the corner of Sullivan and Bleecker. She looked at her watch. It was almost midnight, but she didn't have to be anywhere in the morning, so the time was not important. Besides, in a few minutes it would be a new day. And today, black Wednesday would be over. Gone. Dead forever, like her best friend.

She crossed the street and entered the nearly deserted pizza parlor. She walked up to the counter and saw several whole pizzas, still steaming and fresh from giant ovens in the back. She bought one slice and a diet soda, and took them to a table near the window where she could stare out at the night. The streets were now empty, and a wave of loneliness swept over Kimberly.

She looked down at the loose, greasy pizza and suddenly lost her appetite. Instead of eating, she took out her notebook to begin writing down the names of all the faces she could recall and possible suspects. But before she could even think of one, her hand began writing automatically. She looked down at the paper expecting to see a name. What she saw wasn't a name at all.

It was a word. *Pain.* Her hand began writing again as if it belonged to someone else and she just watched as words began to appear in the form of a poem she titled "Pain."

> Pain is watching those you care for ... in pain.
> Pain is wondering why there is so much pain.
> Pain is missing the little girl.
> Pain is leaving friends and pains behind.
> Pain is feeling you will never be fulfilled.
> Pain is feeling loss.
> Pain is feeling
> Pain is.

Kimberly looked down and saw her tears hitting the paper like drops of rain. Stains of pain, they punctuated the poem like bomb craters in a killing zone. She wiped the water from her eyes and stood up. She put her notebook back in her purse, and walked out of the hole-in-the-wall restaurant, leaving behind the uneaten slice of pizza.

Back on the street, Kimberly looked around. It was close to one a.m. and the sidewalks were deserted. She began walking down Sullivan Street toward her apartment, but then stopped and looked across the street at the all-night health club, where she and Joan used to work out and then go to the steam room.

She could almost see the two of them sitting on thick, white, extra-large towels on the hot marble, feeling the steam open their pores. She could see herself and Joan gossiping about all the great-looking bodies on the women who came in and out of the steam room, admiring their well-proportioned curves glistening with sweat. She could see the playful look in Joan's eyes. How she could really get into it.

Joan had once said that if things didn't work out with Bill, she was seriously considering having a long-term relationship with a woman, but then she'd talk about how women can break your heart just as easily as men.

Kimberly looked up at the large windows and saw two men and a woman riding exercise bicycles. Maybe what she needed was a good workout to help her sleep.

That's when she heard the footsteps. She whirled around and looked down the street. Nobody there. She looked all around and into the shadows. Now she was hearing things.

Maybe it was time to go home and to bed. She continued walking down Sullivan Street toward her apartment building two blocks away.

The farther she got away from Bleecker Street, the quieter it became. Soon she realized she was all alone on the street. This was not the best idea, being out alone at one o'clock in the morning. Even Hal, the part-time doorman, would be gone by the time she got to her building.

Suddenly, there was a scraping sound somewhere behind her. A frigid tremor rolled down her spine.

This time she didn't even bother to turn around. Instead, she started to sprint, and then to run full tilt two-hundred yards down the street, then up three steps to the front door of her apartment building, searching for keys, her heart pounding, blocking out any sound of footsteps, finding the keys, searching for the hole, upside down, it wouldn't go in, dropping the keys on the ground, bending down to get them.

A hand reached out, and a scream was about to explode from her mouth when ...

"Let me help you."

"Ahhhh!"

She whirled around and her mouth dropped open.

"Mr. Arnold?"

"I'm sorry," said the elderly man in his seventies, wearing a herringbone jacket, who stood about five-four. "I didn't mean to scare you, Miss Stone."

Catching her breath, Kimberly smiled at one of her neighbors from the building next door.

"No problem, Mr. Arnold. I thought I was being chased."

"You were," he said. "By me. You dropped this."

Mr. Arnold handed Kimberly her notebook.

"I was trying to catch you before you got inside and into your apartment." He peered closely at her. "Is everything okay?"

"Ah ... yes. Yes. Thank you, Mr. Arnold."

She let out a deep sigh and entered her building, locking the door behind.

Back in her apartment, Kimberly sat on a stool at the counter in her kitchen and thought that maybe she should call Dr. Schrieber, her former therapist and get a refresher course on coping. Her life was coming undone. The one person who had helped her keep it all together was gone. Old feelings of anxiety were creeping back, tearing away the fabric, exposing the vulnerable little girl to all the terrors of the world. She knew she had to fight these feelings. The consequences of giving in were no longer acceptable. She'd come too far to let this happen now. She had to stay focused. There was nothing she could do to bring Joan back, but she could at least do everything possible to see that her murder was solved. What wasn't she doing? What do the police do? Photographs. They ask you to look at photographs.

She found the most recent photo album buried under a pile of cookbooks and travel guides in the corner of her living room. She also found numerous envelopes containing photos she hadn't put into the album yet. She looked over the dates on the envelopes and separated them in reverse chronological order. There they were. All the recent photographs she had taken of Joan.

There were a few that Kimberly had taken within the last two weeks, the night she, Joan, and Bill had double-dated. She also took her camera along when she and Joan went to an upstate New York ski resort for a few days over the winter break. Joan met a handsome ski instructor. He seemed especially abrasive when she told him she had a boyfriend and was unavailable. Was the killer in one of these pictures? She poured through dozens of photographs, but after finding nothing that seemed significant, she put the photos and albums away.

What else? Kimberly stood and stretched and then searched through the desk drawer in the wall unit in her bedroom. She was looking for the postcards and notes she had received from Joan over the last year. At the time, the only reason those communications landed in her middle drawer and not the garbage can was that Kimberly shoved everything in there when she didn't have time to figure out where to put things.

She reached way in the back of the drawer and pulled out an unopened roll of wintergreen lifesavers. How appropriate she thought as she opened the roll and slipped two of the round greenish-white candies into her mouth. She then reached back into the drawer and found a handful of slips of paper, some of them stuck in the sides of the drawer. Among the papers were the postcards and notes she was looking for.

"Thanks for the lovely Christmas present," Joan had written in one note. "Have to bring the car in to be serviced. Sorry I can't give you a lift home today," was the phone message Kimberly had written down, dated March 22nd.

"Damn!" she cried out. "Nothing!"

She shoved the papers back in the drawer. She quickly undressed and got into the shower. As she let the water wash away the day, she thought about tomorrow and the wake. It was going to be another emotionally draining time. Being well-rested might help.

She dried off and climbed into bed, setting her alarm for 9 a.m. She was about to turn off the light next to the bed when she sat up and looked at her phone machine. Old messages! Finding that old written phone message had joggled something in her memory. Joan had left a message on her phone machine Monday night. For the last few days Kimberly had been returning home and pressing the "new message" button. That meant the old messages had not been erased, but instead had accumulated on the tape.

She got out of bed, walked over to the phone machine, and hit the "replay" button that would play the new messages as well as the old ones that hadn't been erased.

"You have ten messages," the machine announced. She breathed deeply as it rewound for the next thirty seconds. "One, Sunday, two p.m." "I'll meet you at the squash court at six." That was Susan, a lawyer who lived a block away whom she had befriended at the health club. They played squash and went out for a bite to eat if they both had free time over the weekend.

"Two. Monday, ten p.m." the machine continued. "Kimberly, it's Joan." Her heart pounded at the sound of Joan's distinctive voice. It sounded so alive. "There's something I've been meaning to tell you. But I don't want to say it over your machine. I'm tired and going to bed now so let's talk sometime tomorrow, okay, or in the car on our way out to school. Just don't be mad, okay. I should have said something before, but I couldn't. What the hell. Call me. Love ya."

Kimberly hadn't thought much about the message when she first heard it late Monday night. She didn't think it was that important since Joan had said it could wait. But now she wasn't so sure. What did Joan have to tell her that she didn't want to say on the machine?

It was 2 a.m. when Kimberly finally crawled into bed with her Weston and Wells' *Criminal Investigation* textbook. She had studied the book several times before as an educator. Now she was about to read it again in the hope it would help her solve her best friend's murder.

She turned to the chapter on investigation of criminal homicides and assaults. She was looking for the section on patterns of criminal homicide. She found it on page 273 and began to read. "Among the basic patterns of criminal homicide are the following: the anger killing ... the triangle killing ... revenge or jealousy killing ... killing for profit ... random killing... sex and sadism ... murder-suicide ... and felony murder."

She ruled out murder-suicide, but that still left eight other possibilities. Unfortunately, the nagging feeling she had about Joan's murder didn't connect to any of the patterns, and she didn't feel any closer to an answer. What she did feel was overwhelming exhaustion as she closed her eyes and drifted into a deep sleep.

It was later that night that the killer woke up in a sweat.

You can't put it off forever. It's only a matter of time before they put it together. You have to stop the information flow. Containment. The longer you wait, the more people will know, and the more people know, the harder it's going to be to escape. It may already be too late. They might be coming to get you right now. They could be just outside the door, ready to ram it in. You had an opportunity and you blew it. Opportunity, that motherfucker of invention, only comes every so often. You might not get a second chance.

CHAPTER ELEVEN

Charlotte Katz was wide-awake and glaring at the radio alarm clock next to her bed, watching the numerals on the face flip over as each minute clicked by. Three-nineteen. Three-twenty. Three-twenty-one. With every minute, she dipped her soup spoon into the half-eaten pint of melting chocolate mousse frozen yogurt. With each spoonful, she replayed the message on the answering machine.

"She was supposed to go to her Debtors Anonymous meeting but changed her mind at the last minute. What can I say? She's been acting suspicious lately. I'd better stay home tonight. I'm sorry. I'll try to leave early so we can have some time in the morning. I miss you."

Charlotte looked down and saw she was out of frozen yogurt. She climbed out of her queen-size bed and went to the kitchen, passing the mountain bicycle in the hallway that she used to ride to classes when she first moved into the townhouse on Arbor Lane in Brighton, less than two miles from Ferguson College. She hadn't used the bike in years and had the extra pounds to prove it.

Once a paper-thin anorexic, Charlotte was a size twelve now. While the anorexia had left its emotional scars, her figure had become fuller as she evolved into a more attractive woman with big, dark, almost oriental, eyes and thick, chestnut brown hair. Although she now had a slightly bloated, earth mother quality, some men seemed to find the look appealing.

At least that's what Richard had said, that he liked a woman with heft, with something to hold onto, something to get lost in. At forty-four, Charlotte was feeling that she might never love again. So when she met Richard she rationalized that a married man who provided an outlet for her physical erotic desires, as well as an occasional emotional connection, was better than no man at all.

To supplement her $45,000-a-year salary, she worked as a freelance editor and textbook consultant. That was how she met Richard Meyer, text book salesman for one of the largest national distributors of college textbooks. He told her his marriage had never been happy or filled with passion, that sometimes he felt like running away, changing his name and identity, and starting anew with Charlotte. But she gave him the courage to stay until he could leave the right way, doing whatever he had to do to get a proper divorce and joint custody of his young daughters.

Charlotte had undergone something of an external metamorphosis since meeting Richard. Until then, she had begun to look matronly, letting the gray show in her hair which she wore in an unflattering pageboy along with the same navy blue suit that she wore for teaching practically everyday. Now she dressed in much flashier clothes with brighter colors. She got her hair styled and highlighted, covering the gray, wore attention-getting costume jewelry and even exchanged her flat dull shoes for high-heeled imports.

She dropped the empty yogurt container in the plastic garbage can, opened the refrigerator and took out another container of chocolate fudge frozen yogurt. One more pint should fill the emptiness inside and soothe the burning rage seething in her heart. She closed the door and started walking back to bed, spooning out the rich chocolate along the way, savoring the smooth comfort of the rich dark brown breast-shaped mound as she swallowed it whole.

It was 6:25 a.m., dark and drizzling outside, when Charlotte heard the knock on the door. She rose up and knocked the half-empty yogurt container onto the floor. Splat! She must have fallen asleep while eating it. She didn't remember. She quickly put a towel over the spilled yogurt and pulled on a sexy silk robe. She'd clean it up later.

"Coming," Charlotte said, a lilt in her voice.

She opened the door to find Richard standing in the rain, looking more than a little strained and worried. Richard Meyer was ten years younger than Charlotte, with thinning blond hair and a boyish face. He wore wire-framed glasses for reading, but wasn't wearing them now.

"What's the matter, sweetheart, Mommie wouldn't let you come out to play last night?" she taunted.

"That's not funny," said Richard as he slipped into the hallway, closing the front door behind him. As soon as he was inside, he took Charlotte into his arms and kissed her, long and hard, pushing his tongue into her mouth, filling up every lonely part of her.

"God, I've missed you," she said, pulling him through the foyer into the living room, pulling down the shades with her other hand.

Richard came up behind her, pushing up the silk bathrobe and pressing himself into her buttocks.

"Umm," Charlotte said as his hands started to push her hips and grab inside her robe, taking out her breasts and placing her erect right nipple into his mouth.

"Oh, Richard, Richard," she moaned, overwhelmed by the heat pumping through her body. She let her robe fall to the floor as he took her right breast in his hand while continuing to suck on her left nipple. A wave of warmth rippled down her body, over her stomach and between her legs.

She could barely catch her breath as Richard pulled away and took her hand. She let him lead her into the bedroom. A white satin bedspread covered the queen-size brass bed that almost filled up the room. On top were matching white satin neck rolls, pillows, and shams.

In one swift movement, he flung the bedspread and everything on it onto the floor. Then he threw Charlotte onto the delicately patterned white-and-pink rose bottom sheet. She began undoing Richard's tie, but he stopped her and tugged the now loose tie off himself. Then he wrapped the tie around her left hand and tied it to the brass headboard. He removed his belt and bound her right hand as well.

Charlotte squirmed on the bed and felt the hot wetness between her legs as she watched him remove the rest of his clothes. She rose up, arching her back, trying to reach him with her pelvis. He knelt down between her legs and rubbed her moisture on his chest. Then, draping her legs around his neck, he lowered her, dripping, to his erection. She writhed and bucked like a stallion as he slithered deeper inside her. Her head swiveled back and forth as she tried to loosen her bindings. As he angled deeper inside, he leaned over and took an erect nipple in his mouth. Holding the tip between his teeth and tongue while Charlotte reared up and down on his penis like a super-charged piston moving faster and faster, bucking harder, until she could feel the rush, the tightening, as the muscles in her vagina gripped his exploding penis in a simultaneous orgasm, the like of which neither Charlotte nor Richard had ever experienced with anyone else.

They were sexual soul mates, and Charlotte was trying to resign to herself that this was going to be the extent of their relationship. It was as good as it was going to get.

"That ... was wonderful," Richard said, almost in a whisper.

"Yes, it was," Charlotte confirmed, still tingling from the sensations Richard had awakened in her.

She held him close, flesh to flesh, a comfortable fit, that she wanted to last forever. But after a minute, he pulled away and she felt a rip in her heart.

"I have to go," he announced.

"But my first class isn't till one."

"I have to make a sales call at nine. It's one of my biggest accounts so I can't be late. Sorry," Richard said, regretfully as he pulled on his pants. Charlotte, an ache in her throat, was determined not to show her pain and disappointment as she slowly put on a pink terrycloth bathrobe. She tried to think of something to say to keep him here a minute longer as they walked to her front door. He kissed her on the top of the head. "I'll call you later, sweetheart."

"Wait. I almost forgot," said Charlotte. "Did you hear about Joan Walsh?"

"What about her?" asked Richard.

"She was murdered."

Richard's eyes squinted.

"What do you mean? I just sold her the new Introduction to Criminology textbook. She put in the order Monday."

"She was killed sometime Tuesday morning. Right in her Manhattan apartment. Somebody bashed her head in."

"Did they get whoever did it?"

"No. Kimberly Stone found her. She thinks it might have been a student," said Charlotte.

"A student? Why?"

"They're the enemy. Didn't you have a thing for her once?"

"Who?

"Joan Walsh"

"Who told you that?"

"She did."

"It was a very long time ago," said Richard. "And long before you and I ever met. When I realized you two taught together, I asked her not to say anything."

"Joan never could keep a secret."

"I'd just started selling textbooks at Ferguson. She was very helpful. We went out a couple times, but that was it. I can't believe she's dead."

"So you didn't tie her up too."

"Charlotte," said Richard. "how can I make you believe that no woman has ever made me feel the way you do?"

"Divorce your wife and marry me."

"Charlotte. Come on."

"So you haven't even told her yet, have you?"

"She's going through a difficult time."

"I'm scared, Richard. What if some criminology student is going berserk?"

"You're going to be fine," said Richard. "You know I'd stay here if I could. But I promised Belinda I'd meet her at the doctor's office. This is a tough pregnancy. If I said or did anything now, and something happened to the baby, I'd never be able to live with myself."

"You don't think she knows."

"How could she?"

"Women always know, Richard."

A worried look shadowed Richard's face.

"I've really gotta go," he said, kissing her cheek. "See you later."

Charlotte watched from the doorway as Richard dashed through the rain to his car, got in, and sped away.

She then bent down to get her soggy morning paper. But when she stood up, she had the feeling someone was watching her.

She looked up and down the street but didn't see anyone. But the feeling wouldn't go away. It's probably just a nosy neighbor. Let them look. What did she care? Charlotte closed and locked the door.

CHAPTER TWELVE

The morning rain had turned into a mild drizzle as Kimberly stepped outside her apartment building and felt the damp mist spray her face. She looked north on Sullivan Street and could just barely see the top floors of the building where Joan had lived and died. The police car was no longer parked in front, but looking closely, she could see a yellow flash of police tape tacked across a window on the tenth floor, telling the world that a crime had been committed inside these walls.

On a typical Thursday morning, since Kimberly did not have to teach, she would sleep in, sometimes until ten, and then join Joan at the health club. They'd start off with a series of stretching exercises, ride twenty minutes on the stationary bikes, spend ten minutes or so spotting each other in the free-weight room, then swim twenty-five laps around the pool before hitting the steam room and sauna, followed by freshly-made carrot juice at the health food bar. Not any more.

Kimberly wanted to return to bed and climb beneath a protective quilt, to sleep for a few hundred years. But she had promised Joan's parents she would visit them this morning, so she awoke at 9 and was out the door by 9:30.

The Walshes had said they wanted to spend some time with her alone before the crowds began to arrive for the wake. Kimberly understood the mourning process and the Walshes' need to be with the one person outside their immediate family who had been closest to their daughter.

At the corner of Sullivan and Bleecker, she hailed a taxi and rode in silence through the crowded streets to Penn Station, letting her mind drift, hoping the pain would go away.

Images flashed. The drawer in Joan's office. The dent in the side of Joan's head. Detective Blake. Bill Gardner. A frightened Wayne Clark. She left the taxi and entered the giant cavern beneath Madison Square Garden where thousands of commuters gathered to purchase tickets to Long Island, New Jersey and points south and west.

Kimberly caught the 10:05 a.m. train to Joan's hometown just as it was about to leave. She arrived a half an hour later in the quaint community of Maplewood on the western border of Newark.

By the time she stepped off the train, it had stopped raining but the sky was still dark and gloomy. Kimberly walked slowly from the station to the Walshes' home, three long blocks away.

She noticed that the trees lining the street were just beginning to swell with the berries and buds that would soon become thick leaves. The yellow forsythia were already aflame on some lawns. Bushes that had been completely brown and barren all winter already had a green hue from the tiny shoots.

The Walshes' home was typical of the other gracious and old homes on their street. Built in the 1920s, it was three stories high, with a finished attic, three bedrooms on the second floor, and many nooks and crannies that had served as hiding places throughout Joan's childhood. In the backyard was a fenced-in area of grass, shrubs, and rose bushes.

Kimberly opened a wooden gate and began walking slowly up the cement path from the sidewalk to the house. As she did, she imagined her friend playing hopscotch on that path the way Joan had often described it to her.

She walked up the wide wooden front steps to the porch thinking how reassuring it must have been to grow up in the same neighborhood, and one that never seemed to change. She thought about how different her childhood had been. Kimberly's parents had moved every couple of years. Her father was an engineer and had to follow the work. It seemed every time Kimberly made new friends, they moved to another state. Joan had been her only true friend for any length of time.

She looked at the house Joan had grown up in and envied her stability. The feelings were immediately drowned by a wave of sorrow over the fact that Joan was dead, and all the childhood stability in the world could not change that.

Kimberly thought about the contrast in their lives. Joan had been an only child while Kimberly was the youngest of three. Joan's mother sacrificed her career to raise her daughter. Kimberly's mother always worked, leaving the child-rearing to whatever housekeeper she employed at the time. Joan grew up in a trusting, loving home. Kimberly lived in constant fear, from her older brother and his sexual advances, from her older sister and her resentment over Kimberly's better looks and popularity. Joan grew up loving and trusting everyone she met but now she was dead. Kimberly distrusted almost everyone, but she was still alive.

Kimberly grabbed the oval brass door knocker and hit it hard against the carved mahogany front door. Almost immediately, Mary Walsh opened the door.

"Come in, Kimberly," Mrs. Walsh said, hugging her visitor in the vestibule. Together they stood together for a time, clinging to each other and crying. Kimberly did not care how long it took; she wanted Mrs. Walsh to be the first one to release the hold.

Mrs. Walsh showed her into the elegant wood-trimmed living room right off the front door. It was a room that Kimberly knew Joan had rarely been allowed in when she was a child. Joan had told Kimberly that she spent most of her childhood either doing her homework at a big green Formica table in the kitchen, in her bedroom, or in the den that they used to call the TV room.

"May I get you a cup of coffee?" Mrs. Walsh asked.

"No, thank you. I grabbed a cup on the way."

"Come upstairs with me, dear," Mrs. Walsh suddenly said. "I want to show you something."

Kimberly followed Mrs. Walsh up a steep wooden staircase into Joan's bedroom on the second floor. The pink-and-white room looked as if Joan had just left home, rather than seventeen years before.

Mrs. Walsh opened the door to the one closet in the room. Several stuffed animals fell off the top shelf on to the bedroom floor.

"Joan wouldn't let me get rid of them," said Mrs. Walsh, as she bent down to pick up the childhood toys. "She wanted to give them to her children. She ..."

Mrs. Walsh bent her head down and began to sob, then picked up a small pillow and pressed it to her face to muffle her sobs.

"I don't want Mr. Walsh to hear me," she said in a voice barely above a whisper. "I have to stay strong for him. If I buckle in, where will he get his strength? He had a minor stroke last year, you know. He needs me. And he's all I have now."

Kimberly gave Mrs. Walsh a reassuring hug.

"I feel very alone," Mrs. Walsh.

"I know. So do I," Kimberly replied, her voice cracking as her body felt the anguish that her words expressed..

"I considered Joan a close friend as well as my daughter," Mrs. Walsh said, tears welling up in her eyes again.

Kimberly gave Mrs. Walsh a firm squeeze as she thought how wonderful it was that Joan and her mother had that kind of close relationship.

She looked at the walls of her friend's bedroom. Framed in the same simple sterling silver frame were ten of Joan's school photos, showing Joan every couple of years from kindergarten through her graduation from Rutgers University with a doctorate.

"Joan told me how you used to sneak into her classes at Ferguson to hear her lecture," Kimberly said, smiling. "I was always jealous of that. She told me how good she felt when she'd look out over the sea of heads and see her mother, beaming with pride, and listening to her every word. It filled her up."

"I was so proud of Joan," said Mrs. Walsh.

"She was proud of you too. She said you were her role model."

"I always wanted to be an anthropologist like Margaret Mead. But with a young child and a husband who had to travel a lot for his job, it was unheard of in those days for a woman to go off on field trips and leave her family behind. Joan had the career I never had."

110

Mrs. Walsh looked at the ceramic music box on Joan's dresser. It was a piano player sitting on a piano bench. His hands moved up and down to Scott Joplin's theme song from the movie "The Sting."

"I want you to have this," she said, putting the box into Kimberly's hands.

"Are you sure?"

"Please. It was Joan's favorite."

Kimberly and Mrs. Walsh walked downstairs where Joan's father was waiting. Brian Walsh seemed to be even thinner since Kimberly had seen him just the night before. In the past, he had never looked his age. But now, in the morning gloom, he looked all of his seventy years. His thick, gray hair needed combing, and his good-looking face looked cracked with deep wrinkles of sadness around his eyes and mouth.

"Hello, Mr. Walsh," Kimberly said.

Brian Walsh nodded a silent greeting and then he immediately said, "Kimberly, you and Joan were best friends. Who do you think did this?"

"I wish I knew, Mr. Walsh. Maybe you and Mrs. Walsh can help clear something up. Joan left a message on my phone machine Monday night. She said she had something important to tell me. She sounded excited. Do you have any idea what it could have been?"

Mr. and Mrs. Walsh clutched each other's hands and looked at each other, hoping one of them might have an answer. "Mary?" asked Brian. But Mary shook her head no.

"Sorry," Mr. Walsh said, sadly.

An awkward silence followed.

"I think it was that Wayne Clarkson," Mr. Walsh said, emphatically.

"Wayne Clark," Kimberly responded. "The police interviewed him yesterday."

"Interviewed him? Why didn't they arrest the bastard?"

"They don't have enough evidence to bring charges."

"Evidence. They want evidence. She's dead, for God sakes. How much more evidence do they need?"

"Calm down, Brian. You can't convict that boy because he wrote a few letters to Joan," Mrs. Walsh said.

"Get the letters, Mary."

Mrs. Walsh hesitated but then left the room.

"Have you seen them?" said Mr. Walsh. "The trash he'd write. Did you know he was also stalking her?"

"No."

"Every time she came to visit. He'd sit out there in that black car of his. She used to wait for him to leave before she'd drive back to the city."

"Did you tell the police this?"

"Of course," said Mr. Walsh. "They said there was nothing they could do. It was public street and it seemed harmless. But I know he killed our little girl. I just know it."

Mary Walsh returned with a stack of letters held together with a rubber band.

"Fifty-six letters," said Mr. Walsh. "Fifty-six. One sicker than the other."

"You should give them to the police."

"We want you to do that," said Mr. Walsh.

"I'll take care of it."

"We also want you to do something else," said Mr. Walsh.

"Anything," said Kimberly, as Mr. and Mrs. Walsh exchanged a look.

"We don't want Joan's murder to be swept under the rug because the police are too busy with other cases. To them, she's just another homicide victim. Another statistic. We read the papers. They get a dozen homicides a day in that city. If it happened here in Maplewood people would be talking about it for years. But over there, in a couple of weeks, she'll just be another name on a file folder. We don't want that to happen."

"What can I do?"

"You can make sure they follow every possible lead. You know the system. How it works. Keep after them. Help them get the evidence they need to put that sonofabitch behind bars. You can also make sure we hear about any developments," said Mr. Walsh. "Be an extra pair of hands and eyes."

"I'll do everything I can," Kimberly said.

"Take these letters. Read them before you give them to the police. Maybe there's something there. A threat or something. A clue."

112

Kimberly took the bundle of letters and gave Brian Walsh a reassuring hug. He looked as if a great weight had been lifted.

She realized that this was the real reason they had asked her to visit. They didn't need her help in mourning. They wanted her to make sure justice was served.

But what could Kimberly do? Would her involvement even hinder the process? The criminal justice system had become more complicated in recent years, with more and more laws passed and amended to protect anyone from being unduly prosecuted. District Attorneys were reluctant to go to trial without iron-clad cases. The court calendars were simply too crowded to waste time with anything but rock-solid evidence that could be used to settle the matter through plea bargaining. Police were under constant pressure to get a confession in homicide cases. Anything less proved troublesome for the prosecution and Kimberly was well aware of this. She would have to be careful and make sure any help she offered did not violate proper procedure.

"I'll make sure Detective Blake gets these letters as soon as possible," Kimberly said, preparing to leave.

"Here," Mrs. Walsh said as Kimberly was almost out the front door. "Take these too." She pushed a brown shopping bag into Kimberly's hands.

Kimberly looked into the bag and saw it was filled with Joan's favorite stuffed animals and dolls.

"Joan would have wanted you to have them."

Brian Walsh then took out his checkbook and started to write, but Kimberly put her hand over his. "What are you doing?"

"For your trouble ..."

"No. It's no trouble, Mr. Walsh."

Kimberly kissed Mrs. Walsh on the cheek and stepped outside.

"I'll see you both tonight at the wake," she added before closing the door. Kimberly took a deep breath as she walked down the front path and back toward the train station.

As she was about to turn the corner she saw something out of the corner of her eye that made her stop. She turned just in time to see the black Saab speed off down the street in the opposite direction.

CHAPTER THIRTEEN

By the time Kimberly reached the Maplewood train station, she had made a decision. She took out her cellular phone and punched in the number from the card she held in her other hand. She let the phone ring on, looking at her watch. It was just after 11 a.m. Her headache had returned and her eyes burned in agony. On the tenth ring, a sleepy voice answered the phone.

"Blake."

"I'm sorry. Did I wake you up?"

"Who's this?" grumbled the detective, wiping his eyes and looking at his alarm clock.

"Kimberly Stone. Look. I'm sorry for disturbing you. I'll call back later."

"No no. It's okay. I have to get up anyway. What can I do for you?"

"I'm out in Maplewood, New Jersey, visiting the Walshes, and Wayne Clark just drove off in his car. He must have been sitting outside their house. I think he might have followed me here. In fact, I think he's been following me around Manhattan."

"Maybe I should bring him in," said Blake. "I just don't know how long I can hold him."

"I'm worried about him," said Kimberly. "Not so much as a threat to me, but what Mr. Walsh might do. He's convinced Wayne killed his daughter. He and his wife have read the letters. They also say Wayne used to sit in his car in the street in front of their house whenever Joan visited them. They think he was stalking her."

"But you don't."

"He was smitten with her. He used to follow her around like a puppy. But a stalker? I hardly think so."

"Why do you think he's following you?"

"He knows Joan and I were close. I think he wants to talk to me, but he just hasn't mustered up the courage to approach me directly. So he just follows me around, maybe hoping I'll confront him and he can say his piece. Anyway, I also called to say I've got over fifty more love letters that Wayne sent to Joan. The Walshes think there may be some incriminating evidence in them, so I was hoping I could stop by your office and drop them off."

"Ah, yeah, sure," said Blake. "I'll be there after four. I'm on nights this week, and I was planning on using the afternoon to talk to some of the people Joan spent time with before her death."

"Good idea. Want some help?" asked Kimberly.

"No thank you."

"Who are you seeing first?"

"Some interior decorator named Dee Porter. From your friend's appointment book, she seemed to have had a lot of contact with her over the last few months. You know her?"

"Oh yes. I'm sure you'll find Dee very interesting."

"How so?" asked Blake.

"I'll let you figure that one out," said Kimberly. "See you this afternoon." Kimberly put her phone away smiling to herself at the thought of Blake talking to Dee Porter. *You are in for a rare treat, detective.*

At 11:15, Dee Porter was also still in bed, only she wasn't alone. The 52-year-old designer rolled over and straddled her lover, pressing her hands down on the outstretched palms of the younger woman.

115

She then leaned down and began to bounce her breasts against those of her companion's.

"Patty cake, patty cake, baker's wo-man," said Dee playfully, with each bounce. She could feel the other woman's nipples getting harder each time they touched. She reached down and took the right nipple between her fingers and pinched.

"Not so hard, babe," said Pat Hurly, a pretty 37-year-old bleached blonde with a firm, well-proportioned figure. "I'm not into the rough and tumble trade. Soft and easy."

"Like this?" Dee smiled and licked her lips as she slid down Pat's smooth, slightly rounded stomach and between her thighs. Pat ran her hand over Dee's salt and pepper brush cut, then arched her back as Dee's tongue did its magic, slowly circling, then locking onto its tender target, licking and lapping until she felt the younger woman shudder and squeal under a tidal wave of pleasure.

"God, you're wonderful," said Pat, when the orgasm finally passed.

"Say that again," Dee said as she curled in next to her guest and kissed Pat tenderly on the mouth.

"You're the best," Pat said. "I'm spoiled for anyone else."

"I bet you say that to all your lovers," Dee murmured, kissing Pat's callused painter's hands that felt masculine against Dee's soft lips.

"Give me a minute to catch my breath and I'll try to return the favor," said Pat, her face glistening from the heat of passion.

"Let me take a rain check, doll," said Dee. "I've got to get down to the shop. I should've been open by ten-thirty."

"No problem," Pat said as she rolled to the edge of the bed and picked up her jeans and sweatshirt. Dee admired Pat's body as she watched her get dressed. Where Pat was full-figured, with curvaceous breasts and hips, Dee was petite. At just barely five feet tall, Dee had the hard flat figure of a young boy and the creviced face of a weathered man. She knew she wasn't pretty, that her nose was too big for the rest of her face, and that she had thick eye-brows. But she also knew she had the deepest, darkest, most passionate eyes you could imagine. Eyes that could draw you in with a hypnotic force. Eyes that could penetrate your deepest thoughts and desires. Eyes that could connect and hold until you were under their spell and you would do whatever she wanted. In one look, one glance, she knew if a woman was going to open up for her. She was never wrong. She watched as Pat pulled her sweatshirt over her supple breasts, her nipples still hard beneath the soft fabric.

Dee reached out and touched one and Pat started to remove the shirt but Dee stopped her. "I really can't. But you better go before I change my mind."

Pat shrugged and pulled on her jeans.

"I'll see you out," Dee sighed, draping an elegant silk flowered bathrobe over her shoulders.

At the front door, Dee kissed Pat on the mouth and held her close.

"Will I see you at the Duchess later?" Pat asked as she stood in the doorway of Dee's elegantly decorated Soho loft.

"Not tonight, babe. I'll be on Fire Island. Now get outta here. I got work to do."

Dee closed the door and let out a deep sigh. She walked across the room, sat down at her Art Deco vanity and stared at her face. "You old fool," she said out loud and laughed as she started to apply her make-up and stopped. "You're falling in love all over again. You just can't help it."

She applied one layer to cover the lines that seemed to get deeper each day. Then a second coat for color. The eyes always took the longest. They had to be just right. She then went to her closet and looked at her wardrobe, selecting her most expensive red pants suit and black spike heels. She stood up and looked in the mirror. She blew a kiss at her reflection and left the loft apartment.

At 11:37 a.m., Detective Blake arrived at the cluttered storefront shop, Dee Porter's Interior Design Showroom, on Sullivan Street, south of Houston. He felt as if he had just stepped into his Great Aunt Fanny's furniture store outside of Tampa, Florida.

He paused inside the doorway until Dee Porter looked up from her desk.

Blake walked to the rear of the shop careful not to trip over the cluster of furniture blocking his path and assessed the woman behind the desk. Blake decided she was wearing far too much powder and rouge, and her false eyelashes were not glued down enough at the

the corners of her eyes. He figured her real age to be fifty-something, while her attempted look begged to be forty.

"Excuse me, but I'm looking for Dee Porter," said Blake.

"You got her," said Dee, standing up.

"I'm Detective Blake, homicide division of the Manhattan South Precinct."

"What can I do for you?"

"I'm investigating the Joan Walsh killing," said Blake.

"Oh yeah," said Dee. "I heard about that. She was a client of mine."

"That's why I'm here."

"Of course," said Dee. "It's still a little early for me. Haven't had my coffee yet. Can I get you a cup?"

"No thanks," said Blake.

"You mind if I get one then? You know, I was wondering if anyone was going to show up. Not that I know anything. But, you know. She still owes me some money."

"Who owes you money?," asked Blake.

Dee poured herself a cup of coffee and returned to face the detective.

"Joan Walsh," said Dee. "She owes me about four thousand dollars for the work I did on her apartment."

"I didn't know that," said Blake, making a note in a spiral notebook.

"Why are you writing that down?" asked Dee.

"You never know."

"Never know what?"

"Don't worry Ms. Porter. I'm just conducting an investigation. Every piece of information is helpful."

"But just because she owed me money," said Dee. "That's got nothing to do with her death."

"I'm sure it doesn't," said Blake.

"But now that I've brought it up ..."

"You were Joan Walsh's decorator. How long had you known her?"

"About six or seven months," Dee said, watching Blake suspiciously.

"When was the last time you saw her?" Detective Blake asked next.

"Let's see. I guess it was a week ago Thursday."

"Where was that?" asked Blake.

"We went together to the Design Center at Lexington and Fifty-Eighth Street. You need a decorator to visit the showrooms, at least almost every day of the year, except Designer Saturday."

"I see."

"We went there, from floor to floor, looking for a new cocktail table to go with the sofas, love seat, chairs, and window treatments we had worked out for her living room. We found a wonderful glass table with a white wood trim. Custom made. Oh, my gosh! I'd better see if I can stop the order. She only put down a one-third deposit."

"I've found companies are very understanding in situations like this," Blake volunteered.

"Oh yeah," snapped Dee. "You don't know this business, then."

"Do you have a list of all the people who have worked on Joan's apartment or made furniture deliveries to her in the last six months?"

"I don't have a list per se, but I could make one up," Dee replied.

"I'd appreciate it."

Dee walked over to her desk which was piled high with bills, business cards, fabric samples, and an assortment of books on decorating.

"Ah, here it is," Dee said, pulling an address book out of the center of the pile like a magician yanking a multicolored scarf out of a black top hat.

Suddenly Blake felt a wave of exhaustion. He couldn't put his finger on it, but something was making him tired. Maybe it was just the stuffiness in Dee Porter's store, or maybe it was because he was working on a day he should have been off.

"Do you mind if I sit down?" he asked.

"Not at all," Dee said, clearing off a high-backed wing chair. Blake sat down and closed his eyes. He tried to focus on what was making him feel so groggy. Then it hit him. It was her eyes. There was something in the way she looked at him. It was like they were trying to pull the life out of him. He had never experienced anything like it. And he wanted to spend as little time as possible in this woman's show room. There was an unsettling presence here. If Blake had believed in ghosts, he might have attributed the feeling to some supernatural experience, but he didn't. He did, however, believe in his instincts and his instincts told him something was wrong.

"Here," Dee said, a couple of minutes later, her voice startling Blake into an awake state as she handed him a list of names.

"Great," Blake said, jumping to his feet.

"I think that's everyone," Dee said.

Blake tried not to show his shock at the length of her list.

"Oh yes," Dee said, grabbing the list back. "I forgot to add Juanita and Miguel."

"Who's that?"

"The husband-and-wife team who clean Joan's apartment once a week."

"How would you know that?"

"I'm the one who told her about them. Good people. They've been working for me for two years."

Dee added their names at the bottom of the list and returned it to Blake.

"I really appreciate this," said Blake. He took out a card and was about to hand it to her when Dee grabbed the table to keep her from falling.

"Are you all right?" said Blake, alarmed.

"I'm sorry," said Dee. "You know, it all just kinda hit me."

"What?"

"Joan's death," said Dee. "I'll be fine. Please, don't make too much about what I told you. You know about the money. Hell. I ain't exactly on poverty row here. Besides, you might as well know. Joan wasn't just a client." Dee's eyes filled with tears.

"Oh?"

"She was a friend," she continued, wiping her eyes. "A very close friend. She was an only child, you know. I was like her big-city older sister."

"I see," said Blake as he glanced over the list.

"Mr. Carl Duck, Traditional Seating. Mr. Warren Maggio, Downtown Lighting. A Ms. Lauren Galinsky, Window Visions. Ms.

Roberta West, Midtown Carpet. All those people had dealings with Joan Walsh over the last six months? What are these other names? Mario, George, and Jimmy?"

"Mario is the painter, George did the carpentry work, and Jimmy removed the old junk."

"Do you have their phone numbers?"

Dee took back the list, located their phone numbers in her address book, entered them on the list and returned it to Blake.

"You've been very helpful, Ms. Porter," Blake said, this time handing her his card. "In case you think of anything."

"Right," said Dee, stuffing his card in her shirt pocket without looking at it.

Blake left Dee Porter standing in the doorway of her shop. He opened the door to his Olds and started to get in when he glanced back and found her staring at him. A sensation traveled down Blake's spine like a snake coiled to strike. As he settled in behind the wheel he made a mental note to find out more about this Dee Porter. Kimberly Stone seemed to know something. He looked at his watch. It was just after noon and he realized that he hadn't eaten yet. Looking around at the Soho neighborhood, he remembered he wasn't far from one of his all time favorite hamburger restaurants, the Broome Street Bar, so he headed in that direction.

Across the street, while Blake drove off, the killer sat at a table sipping a coffee and made a list of all the people in whom Joan could have confided. Where to begin? *Sooner or later they're gonna make the decision for you. Is that what you want? Or maybe you want them to take control. Just like they always did. You can't make up your fuckin mind. You might as well just turn yourself in. Or better yet, why don't you just blow your fuckin head off for them? Now get moving asshole. It's killing time.*

CHAPTER FOURTEEN

Kimberly spent the time on the train from Maplewood to New York reading Wayne Clark's letters to Joan. They were embarrassing. Nowhere could Kimberly find the slightest hint of a threat. But then Kimberly knew that love, especially unrequited love, was often enough of a motivation behind some of history's most brutal murders. Perhaps if Wayne believed he could not have Joan, then no one else would either.

Several of the letters contained love poems, mostly simple-minded couplets of uneven and awkward attempts at iambic pentameter, each verse more mundane than the last. But then Kimberly found a poem that seemed to come from a different place, and maybe even a different person, someone a bit more sophisticated than the Wayne Clark she knew. Of course, he may have copied it out of a book, but it wasn't anything Kimberly recognized.

As she looked out the window at the New Jersey countryside, she re-read the one poem that caused her eyes to water.

They promised life would be sweet
But even flowers bloom and die.
I must see the leaves upon the trees
Even though naked branches quiver on
bitter days.
Do I unwittingly scar frail beings
And fear they will never heal?
Ah, but the blame is not mine.
It is life, that fiendish freak,
So unpredictable and, sometimes,
So harsh.

Kimberly was trembling as she finished the poem. Somewhere between the lines, a connection was made, a link between the living and the dead, between the killer and the killed.

Unfortunately the poem was typed, as were many of Wayne's letters, and printed on a laser printer. Computers and laser printers had made matching typefaces impossible.

The paper could still hold a fingerprint or two, along with hers of course. It was then that she wondered if the police had her prints on file. They should have taken her prints at Joan's apartment so they could eliminate hers from the others they might find. Why hadn't they? She would have to ask Blake about that when she brought him the letters.

She looked at her watch. Almost twelve-thirty. He had said he wouldn't be back in his office until four. She looked down at the bag full of stuffed animals on the seat next to her and again felt the familiar tug of remorse, as if someone had switched on the light of sadness somewhere inside her mind and body.

As if by reflex, a collar of sorrow squeezed her throat. Was this the way it was going to be from now on? Maybe she should just leave the animals on the train for some child to find. But she knew she wouldn't do that. In fact, whether she wanted to admit it or not, she was starting to embrace the pain as that feeling which now brought her closest to what once was. There was a comfort in this familiar sadness, as well as a danger in that it created its own reality, one that nearly blocked out all other aspects of living.

She pulled a stuffed rabbit out of the bag and held it to her chest. As she let her head fall back against the seat, she closed her eyes and the Walshes' words rewound through her mind. "You can be our extra eyes and ears. We don't want Joan's murder swept under the rug."

Kimberly walked out of Penn Station and headed toward Seventh Avenue. She hailed a cab and gave her address to the driver. But when the taxi reached Sullivan Street, Kimberly told the driver to pull over in front of Joan's building instead. She paid her fare and got out.

During the ride downtown, an idea had formed. She had plenty of time before she had to meet Blake. Why not put it to some use? Joan had another friend who lived in her building, her neighbor, Karen Eissler, in whom she sometimes confided. Maybe Karen knew what Joan was going to tell Kimberly. She hit the buzzer next to the name Eissler on the outside panel.

A female voice cackled over the intercom. "Who's there?"

"Karen? This is Kimberly Stone. I'm a friend of Joan Walsh's. I think we met once or twice?"

"Yes, I remember," Karen answered. Then her voice changed as she said, "What do you want?"

"I was wondering," said Kimberly, "would it be okay to come up? I'd like to talk to you about Joan?"

"About Joan? I'm just about to leave for work."

"I won't stay long."

Two minutes later, Karen, a tall woman in her early thirties with long nails coated in red luminous polish, opened her door. Kimberly stepped into the apartment, which was next to Joan's.

They sat down in the living room, which was identical in size to Joan's, but not nearly as well-decorated. In fact, besides a sofa and chair, the room was almost empty.

"Joan told me you're an actress," said Kimberly.

"Part-time. I also work at a boutique on Bleecker," said Karen. "That's where I'm supposed to be in five minutes. I just came home to grab lunch."

"I'll be quick. Just before Joan was killed, she left a message on my phone machine saying she had something important to tell me but didn't want to say it to a machine. I was hoping that maybe you might know what she was talking about."

Karen looked away for a second, then back at Kimberly.

"I ... I don't know."

"But you know something," said Kimberly.

"I've really gotta go," said Karen, getting to her feet.

"Please," said Kimberly.

Karen let out a deep sigh. "She had me promise never to tell anyone."

"Joan's dead, Karen. It might help us find who killed her."

Karen sat down again and shook her head.

"The last time she was here, she talked about her boyfriend. Bill? Is that his name?"

"What about him?"

"Well, she was worried about what he wanted her to do."

"What was that?"

"Dress up."

"Dress up?"

"You know, in those expensive lace corsets and four-inch spike heels. Made her look like a hooker."

"And that's what bothered her?"

"She really made me promise."

"Come on, Karen. What else?"

"She said he sometimes liked to hit her."

"What do you mean, hit her?"

"Slap her, spank her, bite her. She said it started out fairly tame. Low-rent S&M stuff. Leather masks, cat-o'-nine tails. But then he bought a whip with those metal spikes on it."

"Good God!" exclaimed Kimberly.

"I told her to get rid of him," said Karen. "What if he got too violent?"

"What did she say?"

"She said it was just a phase he was going through. A phase. I know a girl who's crippled for life because of a phase her boyfriend was going through."

Kimberly felt like someone had punched her in the stomach. Why hadn't Joan told her about this? She immediately knew the answer. Joan was ashamed.

125

"Look," said Karen. "I've really gotta run. Are you going to tell the police what I just told you?"

"No," said Kimberly. "You are."

"Oh, man. Okay," said Karen.

"Thanks for seeing me," said Kimberly. She shook the other woman's hand and walked out the door, still dazed by what she heard.

Kimberly walked the block and a half to her apartment, perplexed that she never even suspected Bill was into that kind of stuff with Joan. She checked her watch. Twelve-forty. Maybe Blake was back early. She punched in the number.

"He's still out of the office," a clerk at the police station said. "Can somebody else help you?"

"No thanks. Just tell him Professor Stone called."

She hung up the phone and suddenly felt lonely and tired. She walked into her bedroom and fell onto the bed. So that's what Bill Gardner was hiding. Oh, Joan. Why didn't you tell me? I would have understood. Or would I? Hell, I don't even understand it now. This just didn't seem like Joan. But neither did the messy drawer. Kimberly started to wonder about her best friend. Maybe the Joan she knew was an act. Maybe Joan had split personalities. A Sybil-type character. But how could that be? She had such a normal childhood. Normal children didn't grow up to be abnormal adults. Or maybe there was something going on in her childhood she never revealed to Kimberly, even though Kimberly had told Joan all about her sexual abuse at the hands of her older brother.

In fact, Joan had been the only friend she told. She hadn't even been able to tell her own sister. She remembered what Joan had said.

"No wonder you're still single."

"What do you mean?"

"What your brother did must make it impossible for you to trust a man completely. And I don't care how much therapy you've had. The ghosts of the past will always haunt you. Believe me, I know."

Joan had been right. After ten years of psychoanalysis and dozens of unsatisfying relationships, Kimberly continued to dwell in a world of guilt and terror over being molested by her brother from the time she was four years old to when she left home for college at age sixteen. But how did Joan know? Did she have a similar secret?

As soon as Kimberly asked herself this question, a recent scene flashed through her mind. It was when she was at Joan's parents' house and Mr. Walsh was starting to write out a check to pay Kimberly for her help in investigating his daughter's death.

At the time, she just shrugged off the gesture, but now she found it odd that she would remember it in connection with a conversation she had with Joan about sexual abuse. Ten years of analysis had given Kimberly an acute insight into how important such connections could be. The key, of course, was in figuring out the meaning behind the connection. What did Brian Walsh's offer to pay for Kimberly's help have to do with some secret from Joan's childhood? Kimberly shuddered at the possibilities.

CHAPTER FIFTEEN

Charlotte Katz had been soaking in the tub for about half an hour, admiring her remodeled bathroom, when she looked at the white alarm clock resting on the edge of the sink. It was nearly 12:30 p.m. and she had a one o'clock class. She closed her eyes and lowered herself into the warm soapy water up to her chin. She could live in this room.

Thank God she had followed Joan Walsh's advice and hired Dee Porter. She made Charlotte's fantasy come true, turning an otherwise common bathroom into a pink marble palace with an oversized heart-shaped Jacuzzi, recessed lighting, and plenty of plants. Too bad she couldn't afford to fix up the rest of her townhouse. This had become her favorite room, and it was where she liked to relax after making love with Richard.

Reluctantly, Charlotte forced herself out of the bubble bath and into a white terry-cloth bathrobe, monogrammed in pink embroidery with her initials. The bathrobe was a present from Dee Porter. That was Dee's trademark. She gave all her bathroom clients a mono-grammed bathrobe. Pink on white for women, brown on brown for men. Charlotte's new bathroom had set her back $5,600, so what was a hundred-dollar bathrobe? She thought it was a nice touch, and Charlotte admired a businesswoman who wasn't afraid to spend a little money to make a lot.

In fact, Charlotte thought that someday she might just take some of her $25,000 in savings and start a business of her own. Get out of academia. Start a consulting company that specialized in security and crime prevention. Maybe Richard would come in as her partner or sales manager.

She stood in front of her new floor-to-ceiling mirror and opened the robe. Not bad for over forty. Now if she wasn't too old to have children, everything would be perfect. She was still having her period, so it was still possible. Richard would want children. But the longer he put off leaving his wife, Charlotte's chances of ever getting pregnant diminished. Of course, they could always adopt or consider egg implantation if she was too old to conceive.

Charlotte picked up a towel and began to dry her hair when she heard a sound. Was that the door? She opened the bathroom door and listened. A knock at the front door. Maybe Richard was returning for a romp at lunch.

Charlotte walked to the front door, licking her lips, smiling brightly. She reached out and opened the door.

"Well, isn't this a sur—"

In the doorway stood a figure wearing a blue knit ski mask with only the eyes, nose, and mouth showing through holes.

"Who are—" Charlotte's eyes widened as she saw the pistol emerge from inside the tan trench coat.

The first bullet hit Charlotte in the stomach just below the navel. The second slug struck her left breast and punctured her heart, knocking her backward into the foyer of her townhouse. The figure in the trench coat put the gun away, turned, and walked back to the sidewalk and down the street.

Next door, Roseanne Donato thought she heard a loud crack, but she wasn't sure what the sound meant. She opened the front door of her townhouse and noticed her neighbor's door was open. She started toward the door but stopped and looked down. She saw Charlotte's bare foot and then the rest of her body lying just inside the open door

129

of her townhouse. Roseanne stepped back and looked around to see if anyone else was nearby, but the street was empty. She rushed back inside her townhouse and dialed 911.

Detective Blake had just returned to his office and was making notes on the Joan Walsh file when the phone on his desk rang.

"Blake. Homicide."

"This is Officer Elliot Brown with the Brighton Police Department in Brighton, New Jersey. My supervisor told me to call you. Are you investigating the murder of a Ferguson College professor?"

"That's me."

"There's been another one," said Officer Brown.

"What do you mean?"

"Another criminal justice professor at Ferguson College."

"You're kidding," Blake said. "What's the victim's name?"

"Charlotte Katz," said Officer Brown. "A neighbor found her. Shot twice at close range."

Blake looked down at the Joan Walsh file and pulled out a page of names. He found Charlotte Katz. She was one of the people Blake had intended to interview. Next to Charlotte's name he had written, "co-worker/friend."

"Think there's a connection between the killings?" asked Officer Brown.

"I don't know," said Blake. "Any signs of robbery? Forced entry?"

"No," said Brown. "Seems the victim opened the door herself. She may have known the assailant."

"I can be out there in less than an hour," said Blake. "What's the address?"

"Spruce Street. Number 246. A townhouse."

"I know this is your jurisdiction, but do you think you could leave the crime scene intact until I get there?"

"I'll try," said Officer Brown. "But our forensics team has already gone over everything."

"I just want to have a look," said Blake. He hung up the phone and started to get up when the thought hit him. Kimberly Stone. He picked up the phone and punched in her number.

Her machine picked up on the third ring.

130

"Dr. Stone. This is Detective Blake. I just received a call that another one of your colleagues, a Charlotte Katz, has been shot and killed in her townhouse in Brighton, New Jersey. I'm getting ready to head out there now and I'd like you to come with me. I'll swing by your apartment just in case you're home. If I miss you, call me as soon as possible and the office will patch you through to my car."

Blake hung up the phone and grabbed his jacket. Two out of the three members of a criminology department in a New Jersey college are murdered within days of each other. What are the chances that this could just be a coincidence? As he ran to his car, Blake thought about Kimberly Stone. Could she be next?

Meanwhile, Kimberly was fast asleep, taking a nap with her bedroom door closed. The cordless phone was in the living room, so she didn't hear the phone ring or Blake's message. Curled up under the blankets on her new king-size bed, she was deep in a dream with a group of resistance fighters, hiding from the enemy. They were unarmed and defenseless against the powerful army rolling by with tanks and cannons. They cowered in the darkness, praying they would not be found. But Kimberly wanted to fight. She tried to organize a war party, but no one would go with her. Fine, she said, I'll go alone. And she opened the door and stepped out on to the battlefield.

Bill Gardner sat in his office trying to concentrate on the case he was preparing on behalf of a group of retired investors. They felt they had been deceived by the broker who sold them a portfolio of what he called "risk free" real estate limited partnerships that had all gone belly-up, taking with them the hard-earned savings of people who needed the money to live on. But each time he began a new brief, his mind kept flashing back to Joan and what could have been. He was determined not to let her death upset the life he had finally built for himself and his son.

Unfortunately, young Peter Gardner had quickly formed an attachment to Joan and her passing was having a greater impact on him than his father. Since Peter had never known his mother, any woman his father became involved with tended to fill the maternal role he so desperately needed. And of all the women Bill Gardner had dated since his wife ran off, Joan was the first to have the potential to become a real mother.

Watching his son's depression over Joan's death just made Bill angrier. He even blamed Joan for abandoning his son in such a cruel way.

Unable to work, Bill stood up and looked outside. It was late afternoon and he needed a drink. He couldn't get the gnawing, nagging feeling out of his head that Joan had been seeing someone else. He had no tangible proof. How could he find out? Kimberly Stone. She'd know. Joan told her everything. She knew he was going to ask Joan to marry him. If anyone knew Joan was seeing someone else, she would.

Gardner shut off his computer, put on his suit jacket, and walked out of the office.

CHAPTER SIXTEEN

Wayne Clark drove his black Saab slowly down Sullivan Street, looking for a place to park. He'd been around the block three times and every legal space was taken. What the hell. What's one more ticket, Wayne thought as he pulled next to the curb in front of the fire hydrant directly across the street from Professor Stone's apartment building.

As he sat staring out the window, he wondered if he was making a mistake. He didn't even know if she was home, or if she'd even see him. There's only one way to find out. Wayne shut off the engine and was about to open the door when he saw him. That sonofabitch. What's *he* doing here? Wayne slid down in the seat so he couldn't be seen as Bill Gardner crossed the street in front of the black Saab and walked up to the doorman standing in front of Kimberly's building.

"Can I help you?" asked Hal, quickly assessing Gardner's appearance. Expensive suit. Expensive shoes. Alcohol on the breath. Trouble, thought Hal.

"I'm here to see Kimberly Stone."

"And who may I say is calling?"

"Bill Gardner. She knows me."

Hal nodded to himself thinking, But will she want to see you? as he rang Kimberly's intercom.

Hal waited a few more seconds, then turned to Gardner.

"She doesn't seem to be home."

But then a "Hello, Hal?"

Hal put the receiver back to his ear.

"Doctor Stone, you have a visitor down here. A Bill Gardner."

In her apartment, Kimberly was barely awake and leaning against the wall next to the intercom when she heard the name. A jolt caused her to jerk away from the wall and stare at the intercom receiver.

"Ah ... ah ... could you put him on?"

Hal handed the receiver to Bill. "She wants to talk to you."

"Kimberly, it's Bill. I need to see you. Would you let me up?"

Kimberly looked around her apartment. She closed her eyes and an image flashed through her mind of Bill with a leather mask over his head, whipping Joan.

"Bill, I'm kind of busy right now."

"I won't be long. It's important. Just let me up," he barked in more of an order than a request.

"Bill, I can't see you right now."

"Why not? I came all the way over here to ..."

"You should have called first."

"Kimberly. I don't like to ... Just let me come up."

Kimberly felt a chill of fear from the tone of Bill's voice.

"I know about you and Joan," she said.

"What are you talking about?"

"The beatings."

"Oh, that. I can explain all that."

"I'm sure you can, Bill. But I just don't want to see you right now, okay?"

"That's it?" said Bill. "You won't let me up?"

"Not now. Go away, Bill."

"I just have one question."

"What?"

"Was she seeing somebody else?"

"If she was, she didn't tell me about it. Good-bye." Kimberly hung up her phone.

Bill Gardner thought about what he just heard. *"If she was, she didn't tell me about it."* What kind of answer was that? Why didn't she just say, 'No Bill. She loved you. Why would she be seeing someone else?' What kind of bullshit is this? She knows something. If she thinks she can keep information from me, then she doesn't know who she's dealing with.

Gardner suddenly realized the doorman was staring at him. Hal nodded toward the phone that Gardner still held in his hand. There was a faint sound of the dial tone emanating from the receiver.

"Oh, sorry," said Gardner, forcing a smile as he handed it back to Hal. "Guess I caught her at a bad time." He then turned around and walked back to the sidewalk. He took in a deep breath of New York City air and walked on down the street.

Kimberly put the intercom phone back on its wall holder and let out a sigh. Could Joan have been seeing someone else? Did Bill Gardner think she was and kill her out of a jealous rage? She needed a cup of coffee. She started to walk to the kitchen when she noticed her answering machine light blinking.

She went over to the machine and hit play. Detective Blake's voice filled the room and Kimberly heard herself gasp. She sat in a chair next to the phone machine and hit the play button again to make sure she heard correctly. Charlotte Katz murdered? That had to be a mistake. This was all too bizarre. She picked up the phone and called Blake's office number but was told he had left office. She asked to be patched through to his car.

"I'm sorry, ma'am," said the relay operator, "but he's not answering his car phone."

"Could you tell him that Professor Stone returned his call?"

Kimberly hung up the phone and stayed seated. This was insane. Charlotte Katz, murdered?

Suddenly, a horrible thought crept into her mind. There were only three professors in the criminal justice department of Ferguson college and now two of them were dead. If they killed Joan and Charlotte, did that mean she was next? But why?

Wait. What was that? Kimberly's eyes searched the wall and then her front door. Something moved. What was it? There. The door knob was turning slightly. But the door was locked. Nobody could get in. Could they?

Kimberly rushed to the door and threw the dead bolt to double-lock with a loud click. The knob stopped turning.

She quietly opened a closet door and pulled out a thick broom handle.

"Who's there?"

She put her ear to the door and thought she could hear footsteps in the hallway. She slowly unlocked the deadbolt and the second lock and swung open the door.

Kimberly reared back and swung the broom handle at the silhouette filling the doorway.

"Hey!" said a familiar voice, as the silhouette leaped back, just out of range of the broom handle.

"Detective Blake?" asked Kimberly, lowering the wooden pole. "Is that you?"

"Yes it's me. What the hell are you doing?"

"I saw the door knob turning. I thought somebody was breaking in."

"Just now?"

"Yes, just now. Somebody was turning the handle."

"I didn't see anybody."

"They could have heard you getting off the elevator and ran down the stairs."

"If they did, they're gone now. Did you get my message?" asked Blake.

"About Charlotte Katz? I don't believe it."

"Yeah, well, it kinda puts a new wrinkle on things doesn't it? I'm on my way there now. I thought you might want to come along."

Before leaving for New Jersey with Kimberly, Blake picked up Hunt, his favorite crime scene photographer, and Cummings, a forensic expert. Traveling between seventy and eighty miles an hour

136

against traffic, they made the trip from Manhattan in just under forty minutes.

On the way to Brighton, Kimberly filled Blake in about the poem in one of Wayne's letters as well as what Karen Eissler had told her about Bill Gardner being into S&M, and finally about Gardner's attempted visit just before Blake arrived. Unfortunately, she couldn't connect any of this new information to Charlotte Katz.

Crime scene signs were posted around the entrance to Charlotte's townhouse. Police officers in the beige and brown uniforms of the Brighton Police Department guarded each entrance. Officer Brown, a trim, still athletic-looking forty-year-old with close-cropped prematurely gray hair, greeted Detective Blake, Kimberly, and the NYPD forensics team as soon as they arrived.

"This is Professor Kimberly Stone," Blake said. "She worked with the victim. Hunt and Cummings make up my forensics group. You said someone thought they heard a shot."

"A neighbor," Officer Brown replied, almost in a whisper. "That's her over there."

Roseanne Donato, a short, slightly over-weight woman in her mid-30s with a round, and mildly pleasant face, was sitting on Charlotte's sofa, squirming from side to side. An associate professor of English who fancied herself a budding novelist, Roseanne was trying to memorize everything she was witnessing as if it was going to be the first chapter in her still-to-be-written book. Every few minutes she would scribble a note to herself on an index card.

"Is it all right if I question her?" Blake asked.

"Be my guest."

Blake walked over to Roseanne and extended his hand. "I'm Detective Alan Blake, NYPD homicide. I understand you found Professor Katz."

Roseanne nodded then looked up, saw Kimberly and recognized her.

"I also understand you worked with the victim. This must be tough for you."

"Yes, it is," Roseanne said, her voice cracking. "She was also a good neighbor. Watered my plants if I went away."

137

"When you came out of your apartment, after you heard the shots, did you see anyone coming out of Professor Katz's townhouse, anyone who looked suspicious?"

"I've already gone over all this a dozen times," said Roseanne.

"I know," said Blake. "I'm sorry. Please. If you don't mind?"

"I heard something. It could have been shots," said Roseanne. "It sounded more like wood cracking. I opened my door and saw that Charlotte's door was open. Then I saw Charlotte. Lying there."

"How long have you lived next to Professor Katz?"

"Six years. That's when I started at Ferguson."

"Did she have a boyfriend?"

"I only saw her with one guy over the last few months. I don't know how serious it was."

"Would you know his name?"

"No. But I've seen him around the campus. I think he sells text-books."

"Any other neighbors who might know?"

"Charlotte was pretty much of a loner. Can't think of anyone. There's a flight attendant down the street. She and Charlotte were pretty chummy at one point. "

"Which house?"

"Right at the end of the street. But she's away now. Her name's Valerie Madison."

Blake made a note of the name.

"When was the last time you saw Professor Katz?"

"Last Friday before I went away for the weekend. I stayed a little longer than I had planned. Just got back last night. This is terrible. Two professors, murdered. And in the same department. I guess that means Professor Stone gets it."

"Gets what?" asked Blake.

Roseanne and Kimberly exchanged a look.

"Tenure. They were all up for it," Roseanne continued as if Kimberly wasn't even there, "but the school charter only allows one tenured professor per department, with the others being associate professors. That's what I am. Associate Professor of English. Priscilla Monsky is the only full tenured professor in our department. Tenure in the criminology department opened up last semester when Dr. Bedell retired. Don't get me wrong. I think Dr. Stone deserves it as much as anyone. But a friend of mine in physics said he overheard Dean Putnam telling someone he was leaning toward Joan Walsh."

"I see," said Blake now looking at Kimberly.

"Joan should have gotten it," said Kimberly.

"You've been most helpful," Blake said to Roseanne, handing her his card. "Call me if you think of anything else."

Blake started to walk away but Kimberly stepped in front of him.

"The answer is no," she said.

"What's the question?"

"I didn't kill two of my closest friends and colleagues to get tenure."

Blake just looked at Kimberly, but he couldn't think of anything to say, so instead he gave his photographer some instructions on how he wanted the pictures of Charlotte taken. Then, he took out a pad and began making rough pencil sketches of the crime scene. He carefully looked over Charlotte's body again, spotting a hair on her monogrammed bathrobe. Blake slipped his tweezers out of his inside jacket pocket, picked up the hair, and gave it to the forensic expert.

Kimberly stood to the side, assessing the scene.

"Any prints?" Blake asked Officer Brown when he returned.

"A couple," said Brown. "We're running them through the computer."

Blake looked down at Charlotte Katz and then at Kimberly.

"Any thoughts, Professor?"

"I don't think it's the same person who killed Joan," said Kimberly.

"Why not? Just because one was hit over the head and this one was shot?

"That's part of it."

"What if the killer obtained a gun after the first killing?"

"It's possible," said Kimberly, "but I'd be amazed if you found any hair and fibers here that matched what you took from Joan's apartment."

Blake and Officer Brown exchanged a look.

Blake nodded to Hunt and Cummings and they all headed for Blake's car. Kimberly stepped outside, looked back at Charlotte's body and shivered.

"Are you coming?" Blake asked Kimberly.

Without answering, she turned from the murder scene and walked silently to the car.

A block away, Wayne Clark sat in his Saab at the end of Spruce Street, watching the police activity in front of Charlotte Katz's townhouse. He had followed Blake after he saw Kimberly get in the car with him. He still had to talk to Professor Stone alone. He was sure she could help him with the police, especially with this Detective Blake, who suspected him in Joan's death. Wayne looked at his watch. It was nearly two-thirty, and he had a three o'clock psychology class. The last thing Wayne wanted to do was go to class, but he was afraid that if he didn't, it would raise even more suspicion.

As he drove toward Ferguson College, Wayne tried to remember what had happened this week. He decided to take a little acid to reconnect with what might have happened. Maybe a little lysergic juice would help bring his memory back.

He remembered he'd been drinking on Tuesday. Actually, the drinking had started on Monday. That was the day he decided to visit Joan and get back all of his letters. He had taken some acid that night.

The acid was like an old friend. Dependable. Wayne had started taking LSD when he was a sophomore in high school. Up until then, his drug of choice had been marijuana, which he started smoking in the eighth grade. After his first trip, he wondered why he ever wasted so much time and money on pot, which just made him feel silly and tired. Acid, on the other hand, opened new portals to other worlds, to other levels of consciousness. Because of its potency, Wayne only took the hallucinogen four or five times a year the first three years. But lately he seemed to be taking it two or three times a week. One of the chemistry students at Ferguson College had started making it, so it was easy to get. Each time he took LSD, the hallucinations could last anywhere from a few hours to three days, depending on how much he ingested and the mood he was in.

On that Monday night, Wayne had been feeling pretty low, so he took more acid than usual. It hadn't kicked in right away. At first Wayne thought maybe he bought a bad batch. So he had taken some more. He was almost ready to give up and return home when he reached Manhattan.

140

It was when he was getting out of his Saab that it happened. Like slow motion. Wayne had reached out to open the door and suddenly his entire body seemed to turn inside out. His blood vessels and muscles were on the outside of his body. He looked down and saw his stomach, throbbing and digesting. He saw his spleen and his liver. And then his penis. It was inside out and looked like a vagina.

That was Monday night.

What about Tuesday? Tuesday was a blur. A sea of colors. The day and night. Swirling colors and lights.

As Wayne pulled into the Ferguson College student parking lot, he saw her. Joan? It can't be. Joan was dead. A student turned and looked at Wayne, and Joan's face was replaced with the student's. The acid had kicked in. He suddenly felt angry. It was a familiar feeling. What had he been angry at recently? Had he been angry at Joan? Why was he angry at Joan?

Wayne looked in the rearview mirror of his car and saw his reflection. He looked closer and noticed that his left eye had moved down the side of his face. This was good shit. So good, in fact, that instead of going to his three o'clock psychology class, he stayed in his Saab and played with the face in the mirror.

Richard Meyer arrived back at his office in the industrial park complex near Princeton by 3:30 p.m. After his morning romp with Charlotte, he stopped off at a fast food restaurant for his favorite breakfast of French toast wedges, hot maple syrup, bacon, orange juice, and light coffee. He wanted to sit there thinking about his wonderful morning, savoring every minute of their passionate time together. He licked the syrup off his fingers as if he were tasting Charlotte's intimate wetness.

After breakfast, Richard spent several hours driving to meetings with bookstore managers. There hadn't been time to phone Charlotte, so he looked forward to putting his feet up on his desk and giving her a call. She should be back from her one o'clock class by now.

Richard's office was a cubicle in the middle of an enormous green-carpeted room with twenty other partitioned desks. He didn't mind since he spent so much time on the road.

Just as Richard was about to enter his office, his sixty-year-old secretary waved him over.

"What is it, Margaret?" Richard said, checking through his phone messages.

"Another Ferguson College professor was murdered."

"No. I was just out there," he said startled.

"I know," said Margaret.

"Who?"

"A Charlotte Katz," said Margaret. "Didn't she do some work for us last semester?"

Richard never heard Margaret's question. His mind and body were suddenly numb. Charlotte? That couldn't be. Not Charlotte. There has to be some mistake.

"Can you imagine," said Margaret. "Shot to death in broad daylight, right inside her front door."

Richard had to grab the side of Margaret's desk to keep from falling.

"Are you all right?"

Richard looked at Margaret and without answering walked to his office. He felt as if someone had dropped a brick on his head. His temples were pulsating. He began to feel as if he couldn't breathe. He opened his tight shirt collar and loosened his tie. The room was spinning.

Richard pulled out the chair behind his desk and slowly lowered himself until he was seated. He then folded his arms on top of his desk and leaned forward until his head rested in the crook of his arm. The sobs came from way down deep, and the tears were hot and burning.

Luis Alvarez stood in front of a mirror and smiled at himself. If only his friends could see him now. Yeah, right. He'd never hear the end of it. A door opened. Somebody was in the outer room. Luis quickly removed his disguise and stuffed the clothing in a box that once held liter bottles of rum. He put the box back in the closet just as his friend Raphael entered the room.

"Luis. You missed your probation officer again. He's real pissed, man, ever since you failed to report. Been here four times."

"Whachu tell him?" asked Luis.

"I ain't seen you, man. Maybe you been kidnapped or something."

"Kidnapped? You told him I been kidnapped. Where'd you come up with that shit?"

"I donno. I figured I had to tell him something."

"You're a fuckin retard, man. Who'd wanta kidnap me?"

"I donno. Some homeboys maybe. Somebody you owe money to."

"I don't owe nobody no money."

"Yeah, but your probation officer don't know that."

"Yeah, right. Whad he say when you told him I been kidnapped."

"That you *might* have been kidnapped."

"Whatever. Whad he say?"

"He say it don't matter. That you're still in violation of your parole and that a warrant has been issued for your arrest."

"Fucking parole board, man. They just don't give you any slack at all."

CHAPTER SEVENTEEN

Detective Blake dropped Hunt and Cummings off at the precinct and headed downtown, toward Greenwich Village. Kimberly stared out the side window in silence as he drove. Where Joan's murder had left her grief-stricken, Charlotte's death left her numb. For Kimberly, the world had entered a nightmare state, where all reason and sanity vanished, to be replaced by an intangible horror. She felt chilled to the center of her being as she battled thoughts of utter vulnerability and helplessness. *If they can kill Joan and Charlotte so easily, they can certainly kill you and there's nothing you can do about it.* She was certain the murders were the work of two different people—two people for whom Joan and Charlotte had both opened their doors. What frightened Kimberly the most was the probability that the killers were people she knew.

"I'm going to assign a uniformed team to watch your apartment," said Blake, breaking the silence. "Or better yet, is there anyone you can stay with? A friend. A relative."

"I'll be okay," said Kimberly.

"Was Charlotte Katz involved in the women's shelter?" asked Blake as he drove down Fifth Avenue.

"Not directly. Why?"

"Well, we still haven't been able to locate Luis Alvarez."

Kimberly thought for a second before she responded.

"Charlotte was working with us on the same overall grant. It's a study of why some abused women left their abusers and why others stayed. Joan and I wrote the original grant proposal, but Putnam wanted everyone in the department to work on it. He said that way the school and the department would get credit for whatever we published. I'm sure he intended on using it as a marketing tool to attract students. Anyway, Charlotte's role was to collate the data Joan and I gathered and keep everything organized. She never went to the shelters."

"So there's no chance Charlotte would have come in contact with Maria Alvarez?"

"There's only one possible link I can think of," said Kimberly. "The number on Joan's business card is the number of the criminal justice department at school. It's possible Luis Alvarez called that number and Charlotte answered it."

"We can't rule him out then, can we?" said Blake as they came to the end of Fifth Avenue and Washington Square Park. He turned right and then left to follow the streets around the park to the south side where Sullivan Street began.

"There's someone else," said Kimberly. "But I still have a hard time believing him capable of this sort of thing."

"Who's that?"

"Charlotte told me she was afraid of Wayne Clark."

"Was he writing to her too? "

"No. She just said that he gave her the creeps."

"I can understand that," said Blake, pulling up in front of Kimberly's building. "He kinda gave me the creeps too."

"That's right. You questioned him. How'd that go?"

"They way you described him, I expected to find someone who was shy, withdrawn anxiety-ridden. Only the Wayne Clark I interviewed was belligerent, overly confident, and expressed a hostile disrespect of authority figures. It's like he was two different people."

145

As soon as Blake said the words, Kimberly felt a shiver ripple down her back. "Maybe that's it," she said.

"Maybe what's it?"

"Maybe there are two Wayne Clarks, with two personalities, which could explain the different ways Joan and Charlotte were murdered."

"But you're the one who didn't think he'd be capable of murder."

"I don't," said Kimberly, "but there may be other factors."

"Such as."

"Drugs, for one. The wrong drug with the right unstable personality and everything changes. People who would normally not hurt a fly become psychopathic killers. But there are lots of reasons personalities shift. Last semester I had one of my classes study a case involving a graduate student who murdered three professors. When they asked him why he did it, he said he didn't like the way they reacted to his oral defense of his thesis."

"I think I read about that case," said Blake. "Didn't that happen in New Jersey too. That wasn't your ...."

"No. Same state, different school," said Kimberly. "Anyway, here was a young man, who'd never been in trouble before. Never prone to violence. No record. Suddenly he snaps and kills three people."

"What was it? PCP? Speed? Crack?"

"Diet."

"Diet pills?"

"They may have been a factor. But we determined the primary change in the young man's life at the time was the fact that in the previous three months he had lost over forty pounds. When he started the diet, he weighed two-hundred and eighty pounds. He was trying to get down to an even two hundred, so he had about forty pounds to go when the breakdown occurred. According to his mother, he had gone into a sort of depression because his weight loss had slowed down. She started noticing a change in his personality when he couldn't get below two-forty. He became obsessed with losing the weight. He started throwing tantrums. The slightest thing would provoke outbursts of anger. No one bothered to tell him that the body will slow its metabolism to battle what it perceives as starvation if weight loss occurs too rapidly."

146

"Why'd he want to lose the weight?" asked Blake.

"I'm getting to that. His mother said her son always had nonchalant attitude toward life. Easy going. Never real happy. Never real sad. Plus he'd been overweight since infancy. So here he is, heading into the hardest, most stressful part of graduate school, and one day a group of school girls tease him about his weight. Calling him names, whatever. It's not important. What is important is that this time he decides to do something about it. Here's someone who's been teased about his weight all his life and it never seems to bother him until now. Why now?"

"He met a girl."

"No."

"A boy?"

"You'd never guess, so I'll tell you. His mother was about to remarry. His father had died when he was ten. For the next seventeen years he lived alone with his mother, who was only nineteen years older than he was. So at forty-six, she meets a man, falls in love and decides to get married. He can keep the apartment, but she's going to go live with her new husband."

"So it was a little more than a diet that set this guy off," said Blake.

"Still, diet was a key factor. All his life he used food as a way to deal with his emotions, to soothe his rage, to keep life stable. Food was his safety net and that fat was the wall around his inner turmoil. The diet took away the net and tore down the wall, letting out the monster inside."

"Anyway," she continued, "the point I'm trying to make is that Wayne Clark, or whoever is responsible for these killings could be somebody who appears outwardly normal ...."

"But who's hiding a monster inside?" Blake said, completing the sentence. "That could be anybody."

"Then we have to get the monster to show."

"How do we do that?"

"That's the tricky part, isn't it?

Blake turned off the engine and looked up at Kimberly's building.

"I'm thinkin' maybe I should come in and give your place the once over. Make sure you don't have any unwanted guests."

"Under the circumstances, I'm not even going to argue with you," said Kimberly, climbing out of the car.

They entered the building and walked toward the elevator.

"Where's your doorman?"

"Hal's part time. He comes on at four."

They rode the elevator to the fourth floor in silence. Kimberly unlocked the door to her apartment, and Blake entered with his gun drawn. She stayed in the hall and watched as he carefully inspected every room and closet, every possible hiding place. As she followed with her eyes, she found herself feeling warm toward this self-appointed protector. She hadn't felt that way toward a man in a long time, and it both scared and pleased her at the same time.

"Everything seems okay," said Blake, as he returned to the doorway. "I'm just gonna call the precinct and order a round the clock surveillance."

While Blake used the phone, Kimberly entered the kitchen to make some coffee. She looked at the clock. Three thirty. It's the middle of the afternoon and everything seems so normal, except there's a homicide detective in the living room and he's asking the NYPD to assign a few of New York's finest to watch the building.

She put some coffee beans in a grinder and pushed a button. Blake entered the kitchen as she poured the ground coffee into a filter basket.

"There should be a car in front by the time I leave," he said taking in a breath of freshly ground beans. "Smells good."

Kimberly filled the glass coffee pot to ten cups and poured the water into the coffee maker. "It'll just take a couple of minutes."

"Maybe one cup. There are a few more people from Joan's address book that I want to talk to this afternoon. What time's the wake?"

"Eight," said Kimberly.

"I don't know if I'll be able to get back here in time to give you a ride. If I can't, I'll send someone else to take you over."

"I can take the train." Blake gave her a look. "Okay. Fine. You know, I've been thinking." As she talked she poured some coffee into a cup. "Black, right?"

Blake nodded yes.

"I'm not a brave person," she continued. "And I'm certainly no heroine, but even an idiot could see the most efficient way to catch the bastard or bastards is to use me as bait."

"I've already thought of that," said Blake. "Too dangerous."

"I'm the next likely target."

"I know. That's why it's too dangerous."

"We could set a trap."

"That we could. But not with you. The procedure here is to disguise a police woman to take your place."

"That's not going to be easy."

"It never is."

"No, I mean, chances are the killer is someone I know and who knows me. A stand-in may not work."

Blake put down his cup and looked out the window. "The car's here. I should be going."

"Joan was my best friend," said Kimberly as she walked Blake to the door. "Let me do it."

"I'll think about it," said Blake. "I'm gonna tell them to come up every hour, just to check on you, okay. Lock the door behind me. If you have to go out, take one of them with you."

"Yes, sir. Go. I'll be fine."

Blake looked at her, made an attempt at a reassuring smile, and went out the door.

After giving instructions to the two officers in the blue and white parked in front of Kimberly's building, Blake went to his own unmarked vehicle and got behind the wheel. He took out his list of people Joan Walsh had seen prior to her death, along with Dee Porter's list of suppliers and trades people involved in decorating or renovating Joan's apartment. He checked an address and realized it was only a couple of blocks away. He turned on the ignition and headed south down Sullivan Street, across Houston and into Soho.

It had turned into one of those warm late spring afternoons that felt more like summer.

At Prince Street, he turned left and drove three blocks until he came to Broadway. Blake turned right and parked his car on the corner of Broadway and Prince Street.

Three doors down Broadway on the left was Warren Maggio's showroom, Downtown Lighting.

Caters to the high-end customers, Blake thought as he entered the showroom. What impressed him most was the sheer quantity of merchandise Maggio was able to pack into his minuscule showroom.

"May I help you?" asked a husky man in his early fifties, wearing a handlebar mustache. He stood over six feet, almost as tall as Blake, but he had a warm, non-threatening face and demeanor.

"I'm looking for Warren Maggio," Blake said.

"That's me."

Blake looked around the elegant showroom. There were no customers in sight.

"I have a few questions to ask you about Professor Walsh," Blake said as he pulled out his identification. "I'm Detective Blake, homicide."

"I've been expecting you. Dee called me."

"When was the last time you saw Professor Walsh?"

"About two weeks ago. She came into the showroom with Dee. They picked out an overhead fixture for her dining room. I installed it later that day, around six, if I recall correctly."

"Don't you have someone doing the installations for you?"

"Yes. But he was booked. Professor Walsh wanted it put in for a dinner party she was giving that night. For her boyfriend, or boss. I don't remember."

"Where were you on Tuesday morning between the hours of eight a.m. and about one p.m.?"

"I was right here. With my assistant, Carla."

"Where is your assistant now?" Blake asked as he walked around the showroom, looking at fixtures, and price tags.

"Out to lunch."

"A little late in the day for lunch isn't it?" Blake nodded to a clock on the wall that said it was nearly four p.m.

"That's the way we schedule it. Normal lunch time is pretty busy, so I prefer her to be here to help with the customers. As you can see, this is a slow period, so she takes her lunch."

Blake couldn't argue with that logic.

"Do you have any idea who might have killed her?"

150

"I've been thinking about it," said Maggio, "but nothing comes to mind. I wish I could be more help. I mean she was a real class act."

"Yeah," said Blake. "Here's my card. Call if you think of something."

"I will, detective."

Blake left Maggio and checked his watch. Almost four-thirty. He still had time to make some more stops, so he drove across town to the Avenue of the Americas. He then headed uptown to Fifty-ninth Street, where he turned left and drove to Central Park West. At Seventy-ninth street, he made another left and drove to Columbus Avenue, parking in front of Laura Galinsky's Window Visions shop. He would have missed the store if he hadn't been searching for it.

The front door was locked, so Blake rang the bell. A brunette in her late thirties who looked like a young Ali McGraw turned around from behind the counter and looked at Blake. She pressed a buzzer near her that opened the front door.

"Well, hello," Laura said somewhat flirtatiously, as she looked over the handsome stranger standing in her doorway.

"I'm Detective Blake, homicide," Blake said as he pulled out his identification. "I'm investigating the Joan Walsh killing."

"It's just awful," Laura said. "Killed in her own apartment. Nobody's safe anymore."

"What can you tell me about her?"

"Joan? I really liked her. She liked to chat, and she wasn't condescending or anything, even though she was a college professor."

"According to her appointment book, she was in your shop the day before she was murdered," said Blake. "Did she seem upset about anything?"

"She was in a hurry," said Laura. "I remember that. We were supposed to pick out some window treatments, but nothing felt right to her. She did seem preoccupied about something, but I wouldn't say she was upset."

"Have any idea what that something might have been?"

"I'd just be guessing."

"I'll take guessing," smiled Blake.

"It was nothing she said. It was the way she acted."

"What way was that?"

"Nervous. Anxious. Like I said she seemed rushed. Like she was running out of time. But when I asked her about it, she said no. But you could tell just by looking at her that something was up. You know how it is when you've over-committed yourself, or realize you're supposed to be in two places at the same time? That's the feeling I was picking up from Joan. She left without buying anything."

"Okay," said Blake. "Just one more question. Did you know a Charlotte Katz?"

"Doesn't ring a bell."

"Here's my card. Just in case."

Out on the street, Blake took in a deep breath. He checked the time again. It was after five. Did he have time for one more interview? And would the person he wanted to see still be there? He could call ahead, but it was his experience that surprise visits always provided the best results. He looked at the list and picked an address at Park Avenue and Seventy-ninth Street, which was only five minutes away by cutting across Central Park

He pulled up in front of a pre-war building with a doorman who looked like he might have fought in the Crimean War.

Blake showed the man his badge and said he was there to interview a carpenter working in one of the apartments.

"That must be Apartment 17-K," the doorman said. "I'll let the housekeeper know you're on the way up."

"Thank you."

As Blake walked through the wood-paneled lobby to the elevator in the back of the building, he detected a familiar scent of so many century-old Park Avenue addresses. It was the smell of old money.

"Seventeen," said Blake to the uniformed elevator operator.

"Seventeen," said the elderly operator when they reached the floor as if there were ten other people in the elevator, all getting off at different floors.

As the door opened, the elevator operator said, "To your right."

"Thanks," said Blake.

The door to 17-K was being held open by a petite Latina, wearing a white apron and black uniform. "May I help you?" asked the housekeeper.

152

"Detective Blake, NYPD. I'm here to talk with the carpenter."

"Ah, si. Come in."

Blake followed her into an enormous pre-war kitchen area that looked like the remains of a bomb strike. Cabinets were torn out and broken pieces of wood were strewn around the floor. The housekeeper nodded toward the rear of the renovation area, where a man in a khaki work shirt and jeans was measuring the wall and making notations in pencil.

"George Stewhalf?" called Blake as he stepped over the rubble.

The carpenter lowered his ruler and pencil and turned around. "Yeah."

"I'm with the police, Mr. Stewhalf. Detective Blake. Homicide."

"What can I do for you?" said George, dusting off his hands.

"I'm investigating the Joan Walsh murder. Talking to everyone who had contact with her over the last few days. I understand you did some carpentry work through Dee Porter."

"Some carpentry work?" smiled George. "I practically rebuilt the interior of her apartment."

"Really?" said Blake. "When was the last time you saw her?"

"The last time. Let me think. What's today? It's been at least a week. Last Thursday. No, Friday. I had to go back to finish some bookcases in her living room. Yeah. Last Friday."

"Was she alone?"

"Alone? Oh yeah. She was alone. I think she was alone. But she wasn't there the whole time. I guess she stayed about half an hour. She told me to let myself out when I finished working."

"You haven't seen her since then?"

"Nope. I've been pretty busy doing other jobs. She was lucky I could squeeze in the time for her bookcases."

"What were you doing this Tuesday morning, between the hours of eight a.m. and one p.m.?"

"This Tuesday? I was working here."

"When did you get here?"

"Around seven-thirty."

"How long did you stay?"

"Around two. Two-thirty maybe."

"Anyone see you?"

"Mrs. Granger, the owner. She was here when I arrived. Oh, yeah, the housekeeper was here."

"The whole time?" said Blake.

"Huh?"

"Was the housekeeper here the whole time?"

"I guess. I was pretty busy, but everytime I stopped for a drink or something, she was here."

"How well did you know Joan Walsh?"

"What do you mean?"

"You said you re-built her apartment. That must have taken quite a while."

"Two months."

"In those two months, did she ever tell you anything that might have some bearing on this case?"

"I kind of doubt it," said George. "We mostly talked about lumber and what she wanted where."

"Did she have any visitors who might have upset her?"

"Detective, have you ever been in an apartment during renovation?"

"Can't say as I have."

"Well, let me put it this way. You don't do much entertaining. I can't remember anybody but Joan or the Super. What's his name?"

"Mr. Fontes."

"Yeah, that guy and his helper. Don't remember his name either. Professor Walsh didn't spend too much time in the apartment while I was working."

"Right. You don't happen to know a Charlotte Katz, by any chance?"

"No. Why?"

"Never heard Joan mention the name?"

"Can't say as I did."

"Okay. Thanks for your time."

"That's it?" asked George.

"Here's my card. Just in case you think of anything."

"Yes, sir."

George returned to his work, ripping out another section of the dry wall.

Blake walked back to the front door. Before he left, the house-keeper reappeared.

"The carpenter says you were here when he was here last Tuesday morning. Is that true?"

"Oh, yes, sir."

"The whole time?"

"I'm not allowed to go out and leave the workmen alone in the apartment."

"Thanks," Blake said as he flipped over his reporter's notebook and walked out the front door.

Back in the car he let out a sigh. It was after six and he still had to get back to the precinct to write up his report for the day. That meant he would not have time to drive back down to Sullivan Street and give Professor Stone a ride to the wake. Maybe that's a good thing. He hated to admit it, but lately he found himself trying to come up with excuses just to see her.

When Richard Meyer looked up, it was already dark outside and the air had turned dank and cold. Everyone else had already left for the day. But Richard felt as if he were tied to his chair. He couldn't move. His limbs were frozen in place and he felt more alone than he had at any time in his life.

No one knew about his affair with Charlotte, so who could he tell? Who could he share the torment he was feeling? He couldn't turn to his wife Belinda. In the last three years, he hadn't been able to talk to her seriously about much of anything. The only time they'd had sex during that time was five months ago, and Belinda got pregnant even though she had assured Richard she was on the pill.

It was around that time that he met Charlotte at an out-of-town sociology convention. Richard was minding the table where his company displayed the new college textbooks it was distributing. Charlotte had stopped by to see what new texts were available.

Initially she resisted having an affair with a married man, but Richard was persistent. Also, knowing he had been faithful to his wife for five years offered some comfort to Charlotte, who had become afraid of having sex with men with unknown or varied sexual histories.

155

Richard got up from behind the desk and walked to the door of his office. He didn't want to go right home. Maybe he'd go for a drive. He'd have to call Belinda and tell her some story. He simply couldn't face her just yet. She might be able to see the pain and start asking questions. Richard didn't think that this time he'd be able to make up any answers.

As soon as Blake returned to his office, he typed up his notes from the last three interviews, along with what he learned from his visit to the Charlotte Katz crime scene. As he compared the information he had from the Joan Walsh killing, he thought about what Kimberly had said—that this could be one person with two personalities.

Then a troubling thought struck him. Where was Professor Stone at the time of Charlotte Katz's murder? She said she was home taking a nap, which was why she didn't hear the phone ring when he called. She also said she had been in New Jersey that morning. Maybe she made quick trip to Brighton, shot Katz and then got home before he showed up. Was she the one hiding the monster inside? What was the name of that movie starring Michael Douglas, where he fell in love with a murder suspect and she turned out to be the real killer? *Basic Instinct.* The woman was played by Sharon Stone. Even their names were the same. Kimberly Stone. Sharon Stone. Was this an omen not to get too close?

Unlike detectives who had reputations for using investigations to bed available, and even some married women, Blake had always kept his distance. He knew how it worked though, how the women would call the detective back, saying they had some information for the case, only to lure him into bed.

So far he had maintained a completely professional relationship with Professor Stone. And she had never given him any sign that it should be otherwise. Still, he couldn't stop thinking about her. Maybe trying to paint her as a possible suspect was his way of tempering his feelings. Unfortunately, it wasn't working. He still couldn't wait to get to the wake just to see her. Let's face it, Blake thought. You know the problem. You've been alone for too long.

Why was it that passive and dependent women turned him off? Why couldn't he find a nice, pretty, dependable woman, who only wanted to take care of him, to please him? Wasn't his mother like that? Dependent on Blake's father? Or was it the other way around? Maybe that was it. All these years, it was really Mom who ruled the roost while Dad just played the role of material provider.

It was Mom who laid down the law, who set the agenda, who made the plans, who directed the family. All Dad did was go to work, come home, hand over his check to Mom, and watch TV, which was where he was when he had his heart attack. Mom thought it was indigestion and went to the store for some bicarbonate of soda. He was dead when she returned.

Blake remembered how hard his father's death was on his mother. Whenever he tried to comfort her, she'd say, "There's nothing you can do, because the one person I want walking through that front door will never walk through it again."

A year later, his mother died in her sleep and Blake remembered actually feeling happy for her, since living had become such a burden. Blake wondered if he would ever feel toward someone the way his mother felt about his father, and as he did, the face of Kimberly Stone filled his mind's eye.

The killer stood in the darkness and felt invisible watching the light come on in the apartment on Sullivan Street. Shadows danced across the ceiling as someone moved around inside.

Dressing for the dead, hey babe. Who are we kidding here? You think Joan cares what you wear? Of course not. You're doing this for yourself, to show the world what a kind caring person you are. What bullshit. You're all fucking hypocrites, every last one of you. Let me ask you this, Professor Stone. Do you think people will dress as nicely for your funeral? We'll just have to see, won't we?

CHAPTER EIGHTEEN

As Kimberly slipped a dark blue dress over head, she tried again to make some kind of sense out of Charlotte Katz's murder. The only problem was that it didn't make any sense. None at all. True, Kimberly, Joan, and Charlotte all worked in the same department at the same college. They were all working on the same study, and yes, they were all candidates for tenure. They even had some of the same students. They both had Wayne Clark. Who else did Charlotte and Joan have in common? Dean Putnam. But what motive would he have? Besides, his reaction to Joan's murder, the possible detrimental effect it might have on future student enrollment, was typical Dean Putnam. His salary was directly tied to tuition, as was hers and every other professor's at Ferguson College. Unless there was another side to Putnam that Kimberly didn't know about.

She checked the time. Seven-fifteen. The wake was scheduled to start in less than an hour at a funeral home just outside Maplewood, New Jersey. Kimberly grabbed her coat and purse and dashed out the door. She could put on her make-up in the back of the police car. She wondered what people were going to think when she arrived in a New

York City blue and white police car. But as soon as she thought of it, she realized she didn't care.

Kimberly arrived at the O'Neil Funeral Home at five minutes to eight. Established in 1925, the home had been run by the O'Neil family for three generations. It could accommodate only one funeral at a time and was attached to the three-story farmhouse, built in 1902, where each generation of O'Neils had lived.

The entrance to the funeral home was right off a curvy country road. Most of the guests parked their cars in the parking lot in back and walked to the front entrance. Some of the older guests were dropped off while their spouses or children parked and met up with them later.

The funeral home was designed very simply. Off the wide, carpeted lobby there was a smaller room where wakes and viewings were held. At the end of the lobby, opposite the front door, was the entrance to the larger room, carpeted in red, where the funeral would take place the next morning.

The mood in the lobby as Kimberly entered was solemn. No one was talking about the way Joan died, just the facts that "it was so senseless" and "she was so young."

The closed casket was at the front of the cool, dark room, already overflowing with scores of relatives, friends, and Ferguson College students and faculty. Kimberly spotted Mr. and Mrs. Walsh. She walked over to them, hugged each one, and moved to the side.

I should go over to the casket, Kimberly thought. It was a betrayal of her friend's spirit to reject her mortal remains at her wake. She also wanted to say good-by to Joan.

Taking a deep breath, Kimberly walked to the casket. It was sealed shut to preserve the memory of Joan before someone put a dent in her forehead. Her picture sat on an easel next to the coffin. Kimberly reached out and touched her friend's face. She was a few years younger in the picture, but Joan had looked much the same in the final days of her life. She had a fresh, vibrant quality that gave off its own energy. She gave new meaning to the phrase "full of life," which made it so hard for Kimberly to accept that her friend was dead.

Kimberly bowed her head and said a prayer asking God to make sure Joan was at peace. She then turned to rejoin the milling guests and saw Detective Blake standing at the side exit, talking to Joan's parents. He nodded, and she walked over to him.

"We're still following a number of leads," Kimberly heard Blake say to Joan's father as she got closer.

"What about that student, Wayne Clark?" asked Mr. Walsh. "Didn't Kimberly give you those letters?"

Blake gave Kimberly a "please help me" look, and she stepped into the conversation.

"I'm sure the detective hasn't had a chance to read them," said Kimberly.

"Why not?" said Mr. Walsh.

"Because I just gave them to him just before he got here," said Kimberly.

"How come you don't have a partner? Don't you guys always have a partner?"

"It varies," explained Blake. "I had a partner, but he got transferred. Right now I'm working with a team of detectives on your daughter's case. But I'm the primary."

"Mark my words," said Mr. Walsh. "That Clark boy is the one who killed our baby."

"I'll be talking to him again," said Blake. "If you'll excuse me, I need to check on the sign-in log. Can I borrow Dr. Stone? I may need some help identifying some of the guests."

Kimberly and Blake walked over to the sign-in book and carefully read through the signatures. There must have been at least one hundred names already. Many were already familiar to Blake— Kimberly Stone, Dean Putnam, George Stewhalf, Dee Porter, Wayne Clark, Associate Professor Roseanne Donato, Dean Putnam, Laura Galinsky, and Warren Maggio. There were also at least twenty names ending in Walsh.

"Who's this?" asked Blake, pointing to a name he didn't recognize.

"Jason Byrd. He's one of her students," said Kimberly, who also looked at the list. "Looks like there's about fifty students here."

"Your friend was very popular."

Kimberly was about to respond when a loud crash on the far side of the room grabbed their attention. Kimberly looked over and saw a crowd of about ten people had formed a circle. She heard what sounded like scuffling coming from the center of the circle. Blake pushed his way through the crowd to find Brian Walsh straddling Wayne Clark, holding him by the collar, and slamming his head into the floor.

"Stop!" Detective Blake shouted as he pulled Mr. Walsh off Wayne.

"He killed my daughter," Mr. Walsh screamed.

"Just calm down, Mr. Walsh," Blake said, keeping himself between Mr. Walsh and Wayne.

"He has no right being here!" exclaimed Mr. Walsh.

Wayne stood up and straightened his sport coat, using his hand to brush his hair to one side, being careful not to catch the earring in his left ear on his sleeve.

"I ... I loved her," said Wayne.

As he heard those words, Mr. Walsh lost control and went after Wayne again but Blake stood between them.

"Get a grip on yourself," Blake said.

"I want him out of here!" Mr. Walsh screamed.

"I came to pay my respects," said Wayne.

"You'll pay all right," threatened Mr. Walsh.

"That's enough," said Blake.

"Enough?" said Mr. Walsh. "This bastard kills my daughter and has the nerve to come in here, and you say that's enough? Do you have any idea how I feel right now?"

"I think I do," said Blake.

"Do you? Do you have a daughter who was murdered? Do you have a hole in your chest where your heart used to be before this scum-sucking lowlife bastard ripped it out?"

"Could someone escort Mr. Clark out to his car?" Blake asked one of the three O'Neil brothers overseeing the funeral.

"I didn't kill her," said Wayne.

As Wayne continued ranting, Detective Blake grabbed him by the collar and walked him out the front door. Along the way, Blake grabbed one of the O'Neils.

"Make sure he gets into his car and leaves," Blake said to the funeral parlor attendant.

Within minutes, the atmosphere in the funeral parlor changed from tension and confusion back to gloom. Kimberly was about to go to the rest room to get some renewed energy when the door to the funeral parlor opened. In walked Bill Gardner and his son, Peter. Bill walked over to Kimberly and reached out to hug her, but she stopped him by extending her hand. He didn't push it. He shook her hand and Kimberly quickly turned her attention to the thin young boy in a pin-striped suit at Gardner's side.

"This must be Peter," Kimberly said, bending down and almost coming to her knees. "Joan told me so much about you and showed me pictures of you."

Peter didn't answer.

"Peter, I was Joan's best friend," Kimberly continued.

Peter looked into Kimberly's eyes as she spoke. As his eyes filled with tears, Kimberly sensed what she was saying was helping him and she should go on.

"Peter," Kimberly said, now holding his frail hand. "Joan told me she loved you very much. She hoped your daddy would ask her to marry him so she could become your new mommy. She wanted that very much."

Peter started to cry quietly. Kimberly held the boy to her.

When Peter finally broke away, Kimberly felt as if some of her strength had been passed on to him.

"I know Joan will always be watching over you from heaven," Kimberly said, tears filling her eyes. She looked up and saw Blake watching her.

She gave Peter another hug and then turned him back over to his father.

"That was nice, what you said," Bill Gardner offered, reaching out to put his hand on Kimberly's shoulder.

She leaned in to whisper in his ear so his son wouldn't hear. "Get your hand off my shoulder. And don't ever touch me again."

Gardner pulled his hand away as Kimberly stood straight. She then turned and walked over to Blake.

"I have to get away from him," she said, taking Blake's arm and guiding him outside to a porch.

"Tell me again what this Eissler woman said."

"It makes me sick just to think about it. Apparently Bill liked to play rough, as in rough sex. He liked to slap Joan around, a friendly whipping now and then. That sort of thing."

162

Blake looked across the room at Gardner, who had one hand on his son's shoulder and the other shaking Mr. Walsh's hand.

"Did Gardner know Charlotte Katz?"

"Of course," said Kimberly. "Joan, Charlotte and I were all pretty close. Bill came to a couple of school functions. Faculty parties. Why? You don't think Gardner could have killed them."

"Until I know for sure, I suspect everyone."

"That means you suspect me, too."

"I wouldn't be a good cop if I didn't."

"I'll accept that. Now, have you thought about my proposal?"

"About using you as bait?"

"About letting me help you flush out the killer."

"I'm still considering it," said Blake, looking at his watch. "I wanted to get back to the office before ten to get the results of Joan's autopsy. But I don't want to leave until everyone else does. Do you need a ride back?"

"You're sure you want to be alone with a suspected killer?"

"I'll chance it," said Blake, smiling. "Did you notice anything strange about Clark tonight?"

"How do you mean?"

"His eyes. They seemed detached. Roving, unable to focus. I think he was tripping on something. I wonder if he even knew where he was. Maybe he was tripping when he killed two of his professors."

"If he was, he may not even remember it," said Kimberly.

"I should have brought him in," said Blake. "Maybe Charlotte Katz would still be alive."

"You even said you wouldn't have been able to hold him."

"We wouldn't have. Unfortunately, we still don't have any hard physical evidence connecting him to either murder. Maybe the final report from the Joan Walsh autopsy will tell us something."

People were starting to leave the wake and head for their cars. As the mourners passed by, Kimberly looked at each one and wondered if the killer was there. Would there be some kind of sign? A look. An expression. An aura. She and Blake waited until everyone but the Walshes had left.

"Well," said Blake. "Any ideas?"

"I'm not sure," responded Kimberly. "If the killer was here to-night, I sure couldn't tell. How about you? Did you see him?"

"What makes you so sure it's a he?" asked Blake

"Good point. Let's go look at that autopsy report."

"Hold on a second. I'll give you a ride home, but I'm afraid I can't let you read the report. That, I'll do by myself."

"But I'll be able to help you with all those big words the patholo-gist throws in just to feel important."

"I think I can manage."

CHAPTER NINETEEN

The entrance to the Duchess was an ordinary, wooden green door on the side of a red-brick building on the east side of Sheridan Square and Seventh Avenue. There was no sign or poster either over or on the door, indicating that behind this amazingly unpretentious portal was the most popular lesbian bar in Greenwich Village.

About the only unusual aspect of the door was that standing next to it was Benson, a human mountain with legs. Benson had played one season of third string tackle with the Jets before his knees gave out and he had to take a job with the money lenders, or as they are sometimes affectionately known, the mob.

Benson owed this particular crime family all of his NFL earnings, and then some, just to pay off his gambling debts. It so happened that this same crime family was the majority investor in the Duchess along with a number of other popular gay bars in the Village. They let Benson work off the remainder of his debt by playing bouncer at their various establishments.

Benson smiled at the steady stream of women lining up to get in the bar. They were mostly regulars tonight, even though Thursdays and especially Fridays brought out the bridge-and-tunnel crowd of lipstick lesbians who played it straight all week. These were the women who came out only on the weekends when they could act out their true desires within the guarded walls and darkened corners of bars like the Duchess, or the Clit Club in the East Village. Then there was Bonnie and Clyde's, which was a mixed gay bar that allowed both men and women.

As a bouncer, Benson liked working at the Duchess the most. Of all the bars owned by his creditors, it gave him the least trouble. Unlike male drunks, gay or straight, women tended to mellow out the more they drank. Every now and then, he'd get an occasional diesel dyke who wanted to show her stuff to impress some pretty young fem. She'd challenge the bouncer to a fight, but that was rare. Most of the time, Benson just played along and let the moment pass.

He'd also get the occasional male, husband or boyfriend, trying to get in, like this man in a navy blue suit and loosened paisley tie coming up the line. As he got closer to Benson, the man looked and smelled like he'd been drinking.

Benson put up his hand to stop him from entering.

"Private party, pal. Women only."

"That's discrimination," replied the man with as much indignation as he could muster. He had trouble standing straight and seemed to lean to the left.

"Oh, yeah? Maybe you oughta call your congressman then," said Benson.

"Come on, man. I think my wife's in there," he said, with a pained expression on his face. "I just want to talk to her."

"Sorry."

"Come on."

"Look, if your wife's in there, that's her business. I ain't letting you in."

"But she's my wife."

"Deal with it when she gets home. Now beat it."

The man moved away as a tall, heavily made-up woman, wearing red high heels, walked right by Benson and into the dark bar. Benson gave her the once-over, but kept his attention on the man in the suit, just to make sure he didn't try to make an end run.

Inside the Duchess, a female disc jockey dressed like Annie Oakley played loud, contemporary music behind a glass-enclosed booth, while several pairs of women danced, bumped, and swayed together on a tiny wooden dance floor. The air was filled with smoke and the faint but unmistakable scent of feminine hygiene spray. In a dimly lit corner, two women kissed passionately, hands under skirts, blouses undone, pressed breast to breast, hardened nipple to nipple. Off to the side, a woman in a plaid shirt was showing another woman in a lace blouse how to shoot pool.

The tall woman in the red high heels walked to the bar and took a seat next to Pat Hurly, who was watching the couple in the corner and sipping a beer. Pat was feeling lonely and horny. With Dee out of town for the weekend, she'd decided that rather than sit home feeling sorry for herself, she would venture out in hopes of finding some temporary comfort in someone else's arms.

Out of the corner of her eye, Pat saw the woman with red shoes take out a cigarette and start to reach for her purse. Pat immediately struck a match and held it out. The woman in red leaned into the flame and touched it with the tip of her cigarette.

"Nice shoes," said Pat looking down and then up at the woman. "Can I buy you a drink?"

"Stoli. Straight, Coke back."

"Sal. Put it on my tab."

Sal the bartender nodded and poured the drink.

"You're new," Pat said, watching the woman drink the vodka in one gulp and then followed with a swig of Coke. She wasn't really Pat's type, but then Pat wasn't looking for a relationship, just a one or two-night stand until Dee got back.

"Better give my lady another one, Sal."

The bartender refilled the glass.

"Thanks," said the tall woman with the red high heels.

"Want to dance?" Pat asked.

The woman drained the second glass and answered, "No thanks. I don't feel much like dancing."

"That's cool."

"Thanks for the drink. I better go."

"But you just got here." Pat nodded for Sal to fill the woman's glass for a third time.

"Are you trying to get me drunk?"

Pat smiled seductively.

"Only if you want me to."

"I was supposed to meet someone, but it looks like she stood me up."

"I find you very attractive," Pat said.

"Maybe you know her."

"Is she a regular?"

"I think so. Joan Walsh?"

Pat and Sal the bartender exchanged a look.

"Oh, honey," Pat began. "I don't know how to tell you this, but Joan was murdered. It was in the papers this morning. Besides, she ain't been in here in over a month. In fact, I heard she'd gone straight. Gonna get married and all that shit."

"Just my luck."

"Here. Maybe you better have another drink."

"I was planning on crashing at Joan's. I gotta find a place to stay tonight."

"Don't worry about that," Pat said as she put her arm around the woman's muscular shoulder. "Any friend of Joan's is a friend of mine. Sal, another Stoli."

An hour and a few more drinks later, Pat said, "Come on. My apartment's just around the corner."

They walked down the street, arm in arm, singing and kissing.

Pat unlocked her top lock and doorknob lock. Together they entered her darkened apartment. Once inside, the woman in the red shoes re-locked the front door.

"I don't want anyone to disturb us," the woman said as her hands reached inside Pat's tight dress, grabbing her left breast. She then unbuttoned the front of her dress and moved to the right, circling her hardened nipple with the tip of her finger.

"That feels so good," Pat said, closing her eyes. Pat lay back on her bed. The other woman reached down and lifted Pat's legs. Pat was wearing cowboy boots.

"Let me help you with those," said the woman. "You just lie back and relax."

Pat smiled as she felt the boot loosen and pull off. She then waited for the other boot to be pulled off and when she didn't feel anything, she sat up, her eyes still closed.

"What about—"

Pat opened her eyes just in time to see the steel-tapped heel of her boot speeding toward her forehead. Thunk! Pat saw a flash of light and then darkness. The boot heel came down again and again, but Pat Hurly was already dead.

Four blocks away, Detective Alan Blake and Kimberly Stone sat in Blake's car in front of her apartment building on Sullivan Street, waiting for another patrol unit to arrive for protective watch.

"You don't have to wait," Kimberly said.

"No problem," said Blake.

"It's way after ten. The autopsy report should be back."

"It won't go anywhere," said Blake, sarcastically.

"Do we have to sit out here?" asked Kimberly. "Why don't we go upstairs? I'll make some coffee."

"You know what? Coffee sounds great."

Once they were inside Kimberly's apartment, Blake used the living room phone to call the office while she went to the kitchen to make coffee. She heard him ask someone to check his desk for an envelope from the medical examiner's office. From the look on his face, she surmised nothing had arrived yet. He gave the office Kimberly's number and started to hang up the phone when he punched in another number. This time, she heard him checking on the patrol unit.

When he was finished, he joined her in the kitchen.

"No autopsy yet?"

"It should be on the way over. The M.E.'s office said I'd have it tonight."

"What about my protectors?"

"Everyone's out on a call. The next available unit will be dispatched forthwith."

"Forthwith. Nobody but cops or soldiers would use a word like *forthwith*."

"If you're going to start insulting the way we talk, I'll wait downstairs."

169

"At least have some coffee first," smiled Kimberly, handing him a hot cup.

He took the cup and then a sip.

"Let's sit in here," she said, leading him into the living room, stepping over a pile of lumber. "Redecorating. It's taking longer than I expected."

"It always does."

Kimberly sat in an easy chair. "Can I ask you a personal question?"

"I suppose," answered Blake, as he sat on the sofa. "I can't promise an answer."

"Why did you become a homicide detective?"

"You doing another study?"

"Maybe."

"You really want to know?"

"I would."

Blake took a sip and thought for a few seconds. He put the cup down and turned toward Kimberly. "Hawaii Five-oh."

"The television show."

"Every week. Same time. Same station. Book 'em Danno. I just loved how they made life safe for those pretty beaches and surfers and knew that's what I wanted to do."

"Forget it."

"Maybe it was *Dragnet*. Just the facts ma'am."

"I said stop. If you don't want to tell me, just say so."

"You gotta promise not to laugh."

"I promise."

"Okay. Straight answer? I wanted to know what was going on. I mean what was really going on. Not just what you read in the papers or see on television. The real story. Some how I got it in my head that by being a cop, I'd know things other people didn't. I'd know the truth. Truth, justice, and the American way. It didn't take me long to realize that being a cop didn't get you any closer to the truth. But it did give me a chance to serve justice every now and then."

"My brother's a cop," said Kimberly.

"What precinct?"

"Coral Gables, Florida."

"Aha."

170

"He went there for spring break fifteen years ago and never came back. We're not real close. But that's another story," she added, then got up and went back to the kitchen. She returned with the coffee pot and re-filled their cups.

"Do you like it, being a cop?" she asked.

"Most of the time. Not the grisly part so much. The dead bodies. That starts to get to you after a while. But the puzzle-solving part. That's the challenge. But yeah. I like it. I still get the rush when I enter a crime scene."

"The rush?"

"I don't know how to explain it, really. It's a feeling. A sensation that just fills me up. I know it sounds like a sick thing. But it's not like that at all. It's not the crime that gives me the rush, but the opportunity to do something about it. It's like by taking this case I've picked up the sword to avenge the fallen and to catch the bad guys in a way the prosecutor can build a solid case. Do you understand what I'm saying?"

"All too well," said Kimberly.

"Really? I was sure only another cop would get understand it."

"I wanted to be a cop once. Detective actually. I don't know if I ever wanted to wear a uniform and walk the streets."

"Why didn't you?"

"I have an aversion to guns."

"I can see where that could be a problem."

"I loved to play cops and robbers when I was a kid. I read the book *Crime and Punishment* when I was fourteen."

"So what's the problem with guns?" Blake asked.

"When I was fifteen a friend of mine was shot and I was there. We were playing in the woods near this lake where my folks had a summer cottage. I heard a shot and the next thing I knew, Jill was lying on the ground, bleeding from her neck. I remember how helpless I felt. I kept staring at the hole and the blood pumping out and I couldn't stop thinking about how powerful and deadly the force of the bullet must have been. I thought about how easy it was to kill someone with a gun and made a decision to never have anything to do with them.

"Anyway, the police thought it was probably a hunter shooting deer out of season. After a couple of days, they stopped looking. So I started my own investigation, asking everyone around the lake if they saw or heard anything. After about two weeks, the sheriff came to see my father to tell him that I was harassing people and that I had to stop asking questions about the shooting. That's when I decided I had to do something. But I couldn't be a cop, because that would mean wearing a gun. So, I chose the next best thing. I would teach police officers how to be better cops."

Blake realized he was staring at Kimberly and not speaking. He stood up and walked over to a window to look outside.

"So, teacher, how do you think I'm doing?"

Kimberly got up and took the empty coffee cups back to the kitchen.

"You want the truth?" she asked, putting the cups in the sink.

Blake joined her in the kitchen.

"Always."

"I think you need help. What Mr. Walsh said was right. You do need a partner. Someone to bounce theories off of. Help with the Q and A's. Collect evidence."

Blake looked at Kimberly. "You have somebody particular in mind?"

"I've served as a consultant on a variety of cases."

Blake shook his head. "Then you must know why you can't be a consultant on this case."

"Why?"

"You're too close to the victims. It's one of the first questions they ask when we assign someone to a case. If Joan had been my best friend, do you think I'd be put in charge of tracking her killer?"

"You always go by the book?"

"In this case I do. I'll keep you posted, okay. If the autopsy report reveals anything significant, I'll tell you. But I can't bring you into the investigation, so do me a favor, okay. Stop asking."

"What are you afraid of?"

"Do you know how it would look to the brass if they knew the victim's best friend was acting as a consultant in this case?"

"Now you're worried about how it would look. I'm offering my expert services to help you solve two homicides, and you're worried about how it would look. You've got yourself a stone-cold murder mystery Blake and you need all the help you can get. You're in over your head and you don't know where to start."

"And you do."

"Maybe if you showed me the evidence gathered at the crime scene, or let me see the autopsy report, I might be able to spot something that you didn't."

"I can't do it. I won't do it."

"You know Blake, you're a perfect example of why I don't date cops."

"Wait a second. How did we get to the subject of dating?"

Kimberly looked out the window. "Did you hear something?"

"No. What do you mean I'm an example of why you don't date cops?"

"Just forget it, okay."

"No. I want to know."

Kimberly turned away from the window and looked at Blake.

"For you, everything is black and white. Right or wrong. Good or bad. The rules say do it this way, so that's the way you do it. No questions asked. The rules say I shouldn't get involved in your homicide investigation because I'm too close to the victim to be objective. But what if my involvement helped catch a killer before he struck again? Did you ever consider that? What if the only way we're going to catch this bastard is if we let him, or her, think they can get to me? I could be your only hope here. But you'd rather stick to the book because it might look bad to your superiors."

Blake shook his head. "Okay, maybe you're right. Maybe I could use some help here. But you gotta do it my way. That means you talk, and I'll listen. It doesn't mean I'm going to share every piece of evidence or information I get. You understand that, then maybe we can work together."

"What if the information is something I might be able to help you with?"

"I'll have to decide that."

"Okay," said Kimberly. "If that's the way it has to be."

Blake was about to say something else when they heard a scratching sound at the front door.

"There it is again. Did you hear it that time?"

Blake nodded and moved slowly toward the door. "Are you expecting someone?" Blake whispered.

"No."

Kimberly followed him to the front door and looked through the peep hole. She shrugged her shoulder.

"Nobody there."

Blake motioned for Kimberly to move away from the door. Then he removed his pistol from his shoulder harness. In an instant, he opened the front door as someone jumped up from a squatting position and ran down the corridor. Kimberly let out a scream and covered her mouth as Blake dashed out the door in a flash, his pistol raised.

"Freeze! Police!"

But the person kept running to the end of the hallway and disappearing down the stairway. Blake aimed but didn't shoot. Instead, he ran down the hallway after the intruder.

Kimberly decided the best strategy was to wait in the doorway. If she ran after them, she might get caught in the crossfire if the intruder was also armed. After five minutes of tense waiting, she heard the elevator ascend. The door opened and out stepped a weary and rumpled Blake.

"Whoever it was got away," he said, still trying to catch his breath. He put his gun back into his holster and tucked his shirt back into his waistband. He noticed Kimberly looking at his spreading mid-section. She was smiling.

"I think it's time to lay off the donuts."

"Yeah. I keep meaning to get back to the gym, but I never seem to have the time."

"Well if you still want to catch the bad guys, you're going to have to make the time."

Blake sat down on the sofa and sighed.

"Don't take this the wrong way, okay, but I think I'd better stay over."

"You really think that's necessary?" Kimberly replied.

"I don't know when a patrol unit's going to show up. Plus whoever that was could always come back. I'd like to be here if that happens."

"I see. So now I *am* the bait."

"You got your wish."

Kimberly let out a deep sigh. She walked over to the hall closet and took out a blanket and some sheets.

"Here," she said, putting the sheets and blanket on top of the living room sofa. "This is a pullout. You can sleep here. There's an extra toothbrush in the bathroom. If you don't mind, I think I'm going to turn in now. This last incident wiped me out too and I didn't even do any running."

"I understand."

"So, I'm going to bed."

"Right. Goodnight."

Kimberly looked around the living room and then back at Blake. She shook her head and went into her bedroom, closing the door behind her."

Blake stared at the door for a few seconds and then looked down at the sofa. An involuntary smile appeared on his face as he started to make up the bed.

He was fluffing the pillow when his beeper went off. Blake turned off the beep, and looked at the words printed out on the small screen: "Your autopsy report has been delayed. Should arrive in the morning."

He quickly called the office and told the desk sergeant he'd be there in the morning to review the report. He was told it would be waiting on his desk.

Outside, the killer stood in the shadows, contemplating the next move when a patrol car arrived and parked in front of Kimberly Stone's apartment.

So this is how they plan to protect the little professor? Don't you idiots know there's a back way in? Wait. Isn't that the detective's car parked over there? He must still be upstairs. Are you getting a little, detective? I think not. Not from the ice queen. Not from Dr. Stone-cold bitch. All the little bitches are gonna get theirs. Oh yes. The flowers have already been picked. A daisy a day keeps the bitches away. There's a flower here for you, my sweet.

CHAPTER TWENTY

Wayne Clark's eight a.m. alarm shattered the Friday morning silence. Even with the alarm clock blaring its obnoxious sound on a table next to his bed, he managed to remain unconscious in a very deep sleep for another twenty minutes. He finally opened his eyes and sat straight up in bed, shaking. He wondered where all the noise was coming from. It took him another couple of minutes to associate the noise with the alarm clock, and when he did, it took him another minute to actually shut it off.

He let his head fall back on the king-size pillow. It had been an exhausting evening. First, the wake for his beloved Joan; then, the incident at the wake; and finally, the fight at the bar where he stopped off afterwards.

Wayne decided he was lucky the other guy didn't tear the earring out of his ear. He had certainly lunged for it often enough. It had started out with a lot of yelling and pushing and then turned into a bloody fist fight, with Wayne's nose and mouth scabbed and swollen. He was sure the other drunk had at least one black eye and a broken finger.

He had no idea how he even made it home. But the bed offered no solace. And as bad as the wake and the fight had been, the restless sleep was ten times worse. The violent nightmares were starting again. How could he make them stop? He'd had nightmares throughout his childhood. When he was very young, they were an excuse to climb into his parents' bed and spend the night there, getting the affection they rarely gave him during the day. His father was not as wealthy in those days, so the boys slept in one bedroom, his sister in another. But after Lisa Murphy's death, the nightmares became more frightening, and they didn't stop until he started writing love letters to Joan. Now, with her death, the nightmares had returned.

The sleep started off pleasant enough. At first, Wayne dreamt about a love triangle. A woman whose face he didn't recognize was in love with him, but another woman, also a stranger, wanted him as well. He thought the first woman might have been Joan because she looked a little like her. But who was the second woman? The situation didn't turn ugly until all three were in bed and the two women simply ignored Wayne and made love to each other. Whenever he tried to join them, they just pushed him away. He was feeling angrier and angrier, until he reached out and pulled one of the women by the hair. Only he yanked so hard, her head came off. He was staring horrified at the head when he realized the head was still alive and the mouth was open. Instead of teeth, the mouth was filled with fangs. A large tongue sprang from the mouth and wrapped around Wayne's wrist, pulling the head and fangs closer. The mouth opened wide to take a bite out of Wayne's wrist when he dropped the head. He then looked down in horror as the head rolled down the bed and between his legs, its mouth open wide, dripping saliva, ready to take a bite out of his penis. The other woman had turned on a chain saw and was about to saw off his legs when he bolted up in bed and heard the buzzing sound. He was relieved to learn it was just his alarm clock.

Still exhausted, his eyes burning and head throbbing, Wayne tried to go back to sleep. He had plenty of time before he had to get ready for Joan's funeral. But what if he had another nightmare? He didn't think he could bear such terror again. Maybe he should stay awake. But as soon as he closed his eyes, the sleep returned, along with the dark tunnel of horror.

Over breakfast in the college cafeteria, Dean William Putnam wondered if someone was trying to destroy the school's criminal justice department. He looked out over the nearly empty dining room that was normally filled to capacity on Friday mornings. Most of the students had left for a long weekend once they heard Friday's classes had been cancelled.

Now that two professors had been murdered, he could no longer argue that the Joan Walsh killing was an isolated act of violence committed in one of the more violent cities in the world. Students, especially the girls, were afraid to go out of their dorm rooms. He sent around a flyer to the faculty, telling them to advise their students to buddy up and not go anywhere alone.

He remembered what Charlotte Katz had said during the faculty meeting. What if the killer was a student? He was Dean of Student Affairs. If a student did kill these women, would he be held responsible for failing to take appropriate action to protect the faculty?

What should be done about the tenure appointment? He was aware of the rumors that the committee intended on giving tenure to Joan Walsh. How did those things start anyway? In fact, he knew the committee hadn't made a decision. Now, they'd probably want to wait until the vacant positions were filled. It wasn't fair to Dr. Stone, but they had to consider the propriety of bestowing such an honor on someone simply because she was the only one left, even if she was the only one who would qualify.

On the Upper West Side of Manhattan, Luis Alvarez stood in the vestibule of the church across the street from the battered women's shelter. His face was a mask of rage as veins throbbed on the sides of his forehead. He opened and closed the switchblade knife he held tightly against his leg so he could feel the cold of the steel through the worn fabric of his jeans every time the deadly point sprang from the handle.

What the fuck did she think she was she doing, putting the cops on him, thought Alvarez?

When Luis had returned to the apartment he shared with Raphael, he found four police cars on the street, blocking off both intersections. He went to a phone booth and called his number. That's when Raphael told him the police had stopped by to serve the arrest warrant and one of the officers mentioned a complaint Maria had filled out and how the judge had signed a restraining order. Luis told Raphael the cops were still outside waiting and that he'd decided to move up his surprise visit to Maria.

"I'll kill the bitch before I go back to prison," he muttered to himself. "She can't stay in there forever. Sooner or later, she's gonna come out, and when she does ...."

He sliced through the air with the blade, swish!

"*Adios,* Maria."

In Westerly, New Jersey, Belinda Meyer prepared breakfast for her husband, Richard, and their two daughters. While she made cheddar cheese omelets, she stroked her belly, as she so often did now, comforting the baby growing inside her. She hoped it was a boy. She had read in one of her women's magazines that couples who had at least one boy were less likely to divorce than those with daughters. The article had said it might be because the father had a closer relationship with his son and because the son would pass on the family name. Belinda did not understand the study, or its results, but it was another explanation for why things had gone wrong with her marriage. A reason that now, if she had a boy, she might be able to change.

She wanted her marriage to work out more than anything else in her life. She loved their daughters, Rosalie, five, and Carol, almost three, but it was Richard whom she really wanted to be with. She had been determined to get Richard to marry her. When he dragged his feet, she let herself get pregnant, knowing he would do the right thing.

To this day, Belinda did not know if Rosalie was Richard's daughter or the daughter of either of the other two men Belinda had been sleeping with at the same time. She knew it was not right to be sleeping with other men when Richard was her steady boyfriend, but he had not proposed yet. She remembered at the time she would have been happy to marry any one of the three men. In fact, she had told each one that she was pregnant, but Richard was the only one who said he would marry her. The other two told her she could have an abortion or have the baby, they didn't care.

Belinda was grateful Richard did not press for a blood test. She had told him that there was nothing she would rather do than stay home and raise their child, and she gave up her waitress job.

It would have been an ideal existence except for one very important detail; Richard did not love or desire Belinda. Her tactic might have worked to get Richard to marry her and support her financially, but she had not been able to win his heart.

"Do you have time for breakfast?' Belinda shouted toward their closed bedroom door.

"I'm not really hungry this morning," Richard said, fixing his navy blue-and-red striped tie as he entered the kitchen, filled with the smell of fresh sizzling bacon and eggs.

Belinda extended her cheek in his direction, but he ignored it.

"Just coffee," he said.

Belinda placed an oversized mug that said "Number 1 Lover" in front of her husband and filled it with steaming hot black coffee.

"You seem tired," Belinda said. "What time did you get in last night, anyway? I fell asleep by ten."

"Eleven or so," Richard said as he added a little milk to his coffee.

"What did you do all night?" Belinda asked. "I called your office and they said you left earlier in the day and that you would call in for messages. I left two messages, but you never called me."

"Listen, Belinda, I had a lot of appointments yesterday, a lot of orders to write up. I went to dinner with one of my biggest clients, and I didn't have time to call. I'm sorry."

"You couldn't find five minutes?" Belinda asked.

"I couldn't find a pay phone that worked." Richard said, unconvincingly.

"What was it? You didn't have time, or you couldn't find a phone that worked? You should at least keep your lies consistent."

Richard stared into the coffee. He must be slipping. He used to be able to lie so well. It was one of the side effects of his five-month romance with Charlotte. But now that she was dead, he didn't seem to care any more if he was caught in a lie. He had actually spent the day and evening before watching *Casablanca* and *East of Eden* at an old revival movie house in Princeton. Sitting in that darkened theater, ignoring what was on the screen, he'd had a chance to relive his romance with Charlotte, minute by minute, day by day. He could rejoice privately in the hot and exciting relationship they'd had together and mourn the tragic way it had ended.

He knew eventually the police would somehow link him to Charlotte no matter how hard he had tried to keep their affair secret. He also knew he had to plan what he would say, to the police and to Belinda. When he left, Charlotte was still alive. They were happy. He was close to promising Charlotte that he would finally leave Belinda. Richard had no motive to hurt Charlotte. He could tell the police the truth about his affair and still not say a word to Belinda. Even if having an extramarital affair was immoral, it certainly was not a crime.

"Did you hear about the second killing?" Belinda asked.

Richard almost spit out the coffee he was sipping.

"It was all over the news last night and this morning. Another Ferguson College professor slain. A Charlotte Katz in the criminal justice department. A customer of yours?"

"I meet hundreds of college professors."

Richard put down his mug so Belinda wouldn't notice it was shaking in his hands.

"I know, but did you ever deal with her?"

"Maybe once or twice."

"So this doesn't affect you personally that much."

Richard opened his mouth, but he couldn't speak.

"According to the radio, the police think the same person might have killed both professors," Belinda said, refilling Carol's cereal bowl with sugar-coated oat flakes. "Can you imagine? A serial killer. I'm sure glad I'm not a professor in the criminal justice department at Ferguson College. Looks like a high-risk occupation."

"I've got to run," Richard said, standing up. He had to get out of there. If Belinda made one more reference to the killings or the criminal justice professors, he was going to lose it and blurt out the truth about his relationship with Charlotte. But there was no reason to do that now. He couldn't bring Charlotte back. He might as well keep his family afloat. Maybe Charlotte's death would bring him closer to his wife.

"Where will you be?" Belinda asked. "I'd like to know in case I need to reach you."

"I'll be at the office," said Richard. "If I'm on the road, just call in and leave a message. This time I promise to call you back."

As Richard slowly walked to his car, he thought again about what life was going to be like without his beloved Charlotte. By the time he opened the car door and sat behind the steering wheel, his eyes were swollen with tears.

Bill Gardner arrived at his office just after nine and wondered where everybody was. The parking lot was empty and the lobby was dark. Was his watch wrong? He even had to let himself in with a key that he kept for emergencies, such as working late or picking something up over the weekend.

He was putting the key away when it hit him why nobody was in the office. He'd told his staff that today was Joan's funeral and that the office would be closed.

He let his briefcase fall to the floor. And then he settled down next to it and started to weep. Wait. Something was wrong with this picture. This isn't Bill Gardner here folks. Bill Gardner does not cry. He makes others cry. This is some pitiful impostor, posing as Bill Gardner. He wiped the water from his eyes and stared at the picture of Joan, smiling up at him from the center of a thick silver frame.

"I hope you don't think these tears are for you," he said, talking to the picture. "What the hell did you do? We could have had such a great life together."

Gardner picked up the frame and smashed the glass against the corner of his desk. He then reached in between the shards and pulled out the photograph. He started to tear the print but stopped. Instead he pushed a switch on the shredder next to his desk and inserted the photo into a slot. The machine made a crunching sound as the photograph slid into the slot whole and came out the other side sliced into thin strips.

CHAPTER TWENTY ONE

Blake was eating a corn muffin and looking out the kitchen window when he saw the blue and white radio car arrive to relieve the car that been parked in front of Kimberly's building for most of the night. His entire body ached from sleeping on the thin pullout mattress that was no more than three inches thick. He could still feel where the steel bar pressed against his lower back.

Kimberly entered the kitchen wearing a sweat shirt and jeans. She don't look any better rested than he did. Blake was about to make a comment, but then decided to keep his mouth shut.

"I know," said Kimberly. "I look like shit. I couldn't sleep." She then gave Blake the once over and smile. "I guess you didn't do much better."

"You could use that pullout sofa in interrogations as a torture device," he said, straightening his back.

"Sorry about that," said Kimberly. "You're actually the first person to sleep on it."

"What makes you think I was able to sleep?"

Kimberly looked up at the clock. "Is it really nine-thirty?"

"It is, and I have to go."

"The autopsy report. Did it arrive?"

"It just came in this morning. Your new baby sitters just arrived, however, so I'm going to the office. There's some fairly fresh coffee there. And another muffin."

"You really know how to spoil a girl," smiled Kimberly.

"I try."

"Are you going to the funeral this afternoon?" asked Kimberly.

"If I can. I'll arrange for someone to escort you, though."

Kimberly started to respond when the intercom buzzed.

"What is it, Hal?"

"A Mrs. Anne Ross to see you," said Hal, over the intercom speaker.

"It's my sister," Kimberly said to Blake. "Send her up," she shouted into the intercom. "What's she doing here?"

"At least you won't be alone," said Blake.

Blake put on his sports jacket and was walking to the front door when the bell rang. Kimberly opened the door to reveal a woman with short, brown hair, oversized eyeglasses, wearing a deep green cotton suit. Anne Ross was two years older than Kimberly and looked nothing like her. Where Kimberly had inherited her mother's good looks, Anne had inherited her father's more masculine features.

"Sis," Kimberly said, throwing her arms around her older sister and giving her a hug while her sister just stood stiff and formal. "What a wonderful surprise."

"When Mom called and told me about Joan, I thought you might need me. Larry said he'd watch the kids if I wanted to fly up for the funeral."

Kimberly pulled Anne in through the door as Anne's eyes met Blake's. "Am I interrupting something?"

"No. Of course not. Anne," Kimberly said, clearing her throat, "This is Detective Alan Blake. He's leading the investigation into Joan's murder. He was just saying he didn't want me to be alone until these murders are cleared up, and here you are."

"Murders?" Anne asked. "There's more than one?"

"I'm afraid so. Charlotte Katz was killed too. You met Charlotte. She was another professor in my department. She was shot to death yesterday."

Anne stared at her sister, then at Detective Blake, without saying a word.

"Are you okay?" Kimberly finally said.

"Good lord," Anne replied. "What's going on, Sis? Two murders in the same department. That's scary stuff. Hey, if you're in danger, then so am I."

"Anne, we'll be fine," Kimberly said, trying to reassure her sister and exchanging a glance with Blake.

"Fine? You think we'll be fine? Are they going to put you in a safe house or something?"

"Sis," said Kimberly. "Look outside."

She did.

"What do you see?"

"A police car," said Anne.

"It's going to be there day and night. No one's going to bother us here."

"Maybe you should come back to Washington with me," said Anne.

"We're safe here, Anne."

"You're sure?"

"I'm sure."

"In that case, let me just use the bathroom to freshen up after my flight."

As soon as Anne closed the bathroom door, Kimberly turned toward Blake.

"Let me know if you find anything interesting in the autopsy."

"I will," said Blake. "Be careful." He opened the front door to the apartment.

"You too," said Kimberly, closing the door behind him. After he'd left, she thought about how she was starting to feel a sense of warmth toward this man, even if he was a cop.

Anne entered the kitchen and raised an eye-brow. "So, tell me. What's he like?"

"What's who like?"

"The hunk who just left."

"It's not like that," said Kimberly.

"Then what's he doing here at nine o'clock in the morning?"

"He slept on the sofa. He was here to protect me. And that's all."

"Protect you. Did somebody threaten you?"

"Somebody's been lurking around. That's why we have the car out front."

"Is that gonna be enough? Don't they have a safe house you could stay in?"

"We're gonna be fine. If you want to leave, be my guest. I'm staying and making breakfast. Want some eggs?"

Blake returned to his office to find the four-page single-spaced autopsy report sitting on his desk. He began reading through it hurriedly, finding everything he already knew now described in detail and language only pathologists understand. Also, as he suspected, Joan had not been raped. There were signs of recent sexual activity, but nothing forced or around the time of death.

He scanned on down the report until one line jumped out at him. He read it again and wiped his eyes. It said "Victim was approximately three months pregnant at the time of death. Fetal death followed by approximately four hours."

Three months pregnant? This puts a little extra wrinkle into the picture. How come no one said anything about this? Could it be that no one knew? Or maybe they did know but didn't want to mention it. But why not?

Blake wondered if the child was Bill Gardner's. Or if it wasn't, did Gardner find out and kill her out of jealousy? He made a note to run a DNA check. He was about to pick up the phone to call Kimberly when the phone rang.

"Blake."

"This is Detective Shields, Seventeenth Precinct."

"What can I do for you?"

"Well, I think I'm supposed to call you. Your name was on the inter-departmental report regarding "special evidence" not released to the press."

"Yes?"

"Well, we found one."

"Found what?"

"One of them plastic daisies."

"Where are you?"

186

"In the village. Jane Street. We're in the victim's apartment right now."

"I'll be there in ten minutes."

Driving with the siren and red bubble on it took Blake only seven minutes to get from Midtown South to Pat Hurly's apartment. When he arrived, the small studio was filled with police officers and forensics personnel.

Detective Shields, an overweight man in his fifties, in a brown suit, his tie loosened around a shirt collar that refused to button, took Blake over to Pat Hurly's body and nodded down.

"She hasn't been dead too long. The exterminator found her when he arrived for the monthly spraying."

Blake pulled on a pair of white plastic gloves and examined the boot-heel shaped dent on the woman's forehead. He then turned her head to the side and saw the plastic daisy in her ear. He removed the flower and compared it to the one he had in a plastic container in his pocket. A match.

"Whaddya think? Some kinda signature?" asked Shields.

"It's something," said Blake. "Whoever killed her wanted us to know it was the same person who killed Joan Walsh."

"Why would they wanta do that?"

"Beats me. We've asked for some help on this from the Behavioral Sciences Division of the F.B.I. in Quantico. Haven't heard anything back yet."

"You might be interested in this," added Shields. "We found the victim's address book. Guess whose number's in it?"

"Whose?"

"Your first victim. Joan Walsh."

"Can I see that?" Blake said, nodding toward the address book in Shields' hands.

"Sure." The detective handed it to him.

Blake looked at Joan's name and then began looking at the other pages. He looked at the K's but could not find Charlotte Katz's number. He skimmed some of the other pages and saw another familiar name. Dee Porter. He then looked at each page but found nothing else until he came to S, and then he stopped and stared. He looked closer to make sure. But there it was. Midway down the page of S's was Stone, Kimberly and her number.

"What is it?" asked Shields.

"Huh?"

"You see something else in there?"

"Huh, oh yeah," said Blake, distracted as he tried to comprehend the significance of his discovery.

Shields looked around the apartment and then at Blake before he spoke. "Since there's an obvious connection between this killing and the Walsh homicide, I've been told to let you be the primary on this one as well."

"Are you okay with that?" asked Blake.

"Hey. My plate's full."

"I know what you mean," said Blake.

"I'll make sure you get a copy of everything my team finds."

"Thanks. Meanwhile, I'd like to hang on to this address book to cross-check some other names we got from Joan Walsh's book."

"Be my guest," said Shields.

"What else have you got?"

"So far, not much. No witnesses. A few prints. Fibers. Forensic shit, but that's it. You notice anything interesting about that address book?"

"Like what?"

"The names."

"What about them?"

"They're all women."

It was nearly two in the afternoon when Kimberly and Anne arrived at the O'Neil Funeral Home. The services were supposed to start at two, but as usual, everything was running about twenty minutes late. There were camera crews from two of the local New York-New Jersey TV stations. One of the field reporters was taping commentary about the murder and the funeral, which was to be run that evening on the six o'clock news. Several still photographers from the local dailies were taking shots of mourners for the late city edition.

Everyone had been advised to send donations to the Joan Walsh Memorial Criminal Justice Scholarship at Ferguson College, which Dean Putnam established immediately with the Walshes' blessing.

There were several oversized bouquets of yellow and purple irises, Joan's favorite flower, at the front of the room near the coffin, as well as two arrangements of roses and a small bouquet of yellow-and-white daisies.

In addition to the full capacity 250-seat-room, about a hundred additional mourners, mostly students, stood in the lobby and outside. They were going to hear the service over loudspeakers.

Mr. and Mrs. Walsh sat in the first row, almost close enough to touch the closed shiny walnut coffin. Behind the casket were huge windows without curtains to block out the sunlight or the view. As Kimberly looked through the windows, she saw several white-bellied squirrels running up and down the branches of soaring maple trees. It was the kind of natural setting Joan would have appreciated. She could even hear Joan, the consummate teacher, explaining to this class gathered here today in her honor how even in death, life still goes on all around us. Kimberly looked away from the window to scan the faces around her.

Kimberly recognized about two dozen representatives from Ferguson College including Bradford Mackenzie, the vice president; Dean William Putnam; Zackary Smith, the chairman of the history department; Linda Wallace, chairperson of the English department, and at least a dozen professors. There were about seventy students from the criminal justice department. Then Kimberly noticed a cluster of familiar faces from other aspects of Joan's life: Warren Maggio, Laura Galinsky, Dee Porter, George Stewhalf, Mario the painter, and even superintendent Fontes. Bill Gardner was sitting with his son. He looked like he hadn't slept since Joan's murder.

She also noticed a number of friends from Joan's childhood such as her bunkmate from a camp she had attended some twenty-five years ago and her closest friend from high school chorus. There were several neighbors from the Sullivan Street apartment building where Joan had lived for the last five years, including Karen Eissler.

Only a handful of the mourners had heard about the tragedy directly from Joan's parents. Most had been told about it over the phone from a relative or a friend of the family, or had read about the murder in one of the city's three newspapers.

As Kimberly moved among the students, greeting the ones she knew, she overheard a number of conversations. They all had to do with the murder of Charlotte Katz. She detected the fear in the students' voices and learned that some of the scholarship students living in the dorms, who had grown up in rough neighborhoods like Harlem, South Philadelphia, and parts of Newark, had started carrying the knives and guns they usually kept hidden in their dorm room or off-campus apartment closets. Security systems, usually only activated after 8 p.m., were now operating twenty-four hours a day, in all major classroom buildings and dormitories.

Dozens of students, especially women, had pledged to go home early for spring break, which was not officially supposed to start for another week, and stay home until the killer was found. If that didn't happen soon, some said they might consider transferring to another college. "My life is more important than whether or not I lose credits for this semester," murmured a twenty-year-old criminal justice major from Boise, Idaho. Kimberly learned that other students were even threatening to go on strike if they had to return to classes without an armed guard posted in front of every classroom building, library, recreation center, and dormitory.

As the ceremony began, Kimberly only half-listened to the words of the priest, who had known Joan and her family for twenty years. Instead, she closed her eyes and let her mind fill with more joyful memories of her friend. There was the time they went water skiing in the Catskills and Kimberly's legs seemed to go in opposite directions. Christmas Eve had become especially memorable for Kimberly since she met Joan. The Walshes had a traditional annual Christmas Eve party for close friends and family and Kimberly had been invited for the last three years. She recalled the smell of fireplace logs burning and the Christmas potpourri spread around the house. It was the first time Kimberly hadn't felt left out on Christmas Eve. Through Joan's friendship, Kimberly felt part of the Christmas spirit even if she did not celebrate the holiday in a religious way. She and Joan had made it a custom for Kimberly to give Joan a Christmas present, and for Joan to bestow a Chanukah gift on Kimberly.

"And now Joan's friend and fellow professor, Dr. Kimberly Stone, would like to say a few words," the priest concluded.

Kimberly realized people were looking at her, and then she saw the priest nodding to her. She quickly stood up, letting go of her sister's hand, and walked to the tall, highly polished walnut podium.

She looked around, searching the faces for Detective Blake, but she couldn't find him. She wondered if he had found anything in the autopsy. She then looked at Joan's parents, who were slightly hunched over, gripping each other's hands. All eyes were on her waiting for her to speak.

"I want to share what Joan Walsh meant to me as a friend and colleague," Kimberly said, her voice starting to crack.

"Joan had an uncanny way of knowing what other people wanted and needed and how to give it to them," she continued. "She didn't have a competitive bone in her body. A successful professor, she loved her work and her students. She loved to teach. She loved life. She had it all. A good job, a man who was about to ask her to marry him. The only thing she didn't have was the one gift to make everything else worthwhile, the gift of time. But those who knew and loved Joan know she did the very best with the years she was given. While I will miss my friend dearly, I will do everything I can to keep her unique spirit and caring voice alive."

Kimberly looked up and for a brief moment she had a vision of Joan. She closed her eyes and imagined Joan's floating image being absorbed into her own body. When she opened her eyes, she saw Joan's parents weeping, as were many others looking up at her.

As Kimberly stepped down from the podium, she glanced out at the audience. You're going to be with me forever, Joannie, thought Kimberly as she returned to her seat.

She also thought about the one person who wasn't at the funeral that she expected to see. Wayne Clark. She actually felt relieved that he hadn't tried to make an appearance. But then she wondered if he wasn't here, where was he?

CHAPTER TWENTY-TWO

After the service, Kimberly rode in one of six black limousines with her sister and two of Joan's cousins to All Souls Cemetery on the border of Maplewood and Newark. There, the priest recited a traditional burial prayer while family and friends said their last good-byes as the coffin was lowered into a freshly dug hole.

Kimberly placed a rose on her friend's casket as it started its descent. She then followed the line of mourners through rows of headstones toward a line of gray and black cars parked on a gravel driveway that ran between the graves. As she neared her limousine, she saw Detective Blake at the end of the caravan. He was waving to her.

Kimberly told her sister to get in the limousine and that she would catch up with her back at the Walshes. She then walked over to Blake, who was leaning against his unmarked car.

"We need to talk," Blake said, an angry edge to his voice.

"What's the matter?" Kimberly asked, sensing the change in his tone since their last conversation. She could almost feel his penetrating stare. "Why are you looking at me like that?"

"Ride with me," said Blake.

As soon as they were in the car, Blake turned toward Kimberly.

"Why didn't you tell me your best friend was pregnant?"

"What?"

"According to the autopsy report, Joan Walsh was three months pregnant."

"That can't be."

"Take a look."

Blake handed Kimberly a folder. She took out the report and read it carefully, until she came to the same words that had stunned Blake. She looked at the detective, then opened her door and hastily scrambled out of the car. She made it to a nearby oak tree before bending over and throwing up whatever food was still in her stomach. Blake got out of the car and went to her. He offered her his handkerchief, which she gladly accepted.

"Are you going to be okay?"

"I don't know," muttered Kimberly. "I feel like I've just been run over by a truck or something."

"I take it you didn't know."

Kimberly shook her head. "No."

"Do you think it's Bill Gardner's?"

"Not likely."

"We're running a DNA check to see if he's the father."

"Don't waste your time. Joan told me Bill had a vasectomy a few years ago. He planned to try to reverse the procedure if and when they got married, but he wasn't sure if it would work."

"Who else was she seeing?"

"Nobody. At least I wasn't aware of anyone."

"No other man, you mean?"

Kimberly saw the look in Blake's face as he asked the question. She felt anger flush her cheeks.

"What's that supposed to mean?" she said.

"Pat Hurly."

"What about her?"

"She was murdered last night."

"Pat? Murdered? Oh, God."

"We found Joan's name in her address book. Want to tell me about it?"

"Not particularly."

"What if I told you that whoever killed Joan also killed Pat Hurly?"

Kimberly felt a tremor slide down her shoulders. She looked at Blake. "Joan and Pat were lovers," she said, looking away.

"What about you?"

She turned to face Blake. "What about me?"

"Your name was in Pat Hurly's book too."

"So?"

Blake just stared at her and she glared back at him.

"Are you getting off on this?" she snapped.

"No. But I am getting a little tired of being jerked around here, professor. You haven't been exactly straight with me, if you'll pardon the pun. I've got three homicides and you knew all three victims. I think it might be helpful to this investigation if the primary detective in two of those murders knew what your involvement was here! Am I making myself clear?"

Kimberly let out a deep sigh.

"We went out. Once. Pat was just trying to make Joan jealous."

"Why?"

"Because of Dee."

"Dee. Dee Porter? The decorator?"

"One night, Pat saw Dee and Joan leave the Duchess together. That's a lesbian bar in Sheridan Square. But all Dee wanted to do was get Joan's business to redecorate her co-op, which she did. We all had a good laugh about it afterward. Pat and Dee got back together, although it's not an exclusive relationship. Dee has a girl-friend on Fire Island.

"Did Wayne Clark know about Joan's girlfriends?"

"I don't know."

"How about Bill Gardner? Or Luis Alvarez?"

"I don't know."

"I thought she was your best friend."

"She was."

"But she didn't tell you she was pregnant?"

"Maybe that's what she meant on the last phone message she left," said Kimberly. "She was going to tell me something the next time we met."

"Your friend led an extremely complicated life, or in her case, several secret lives," said Blake. "Let me try to sort this out. She kept her lesbian relationships secret from her parents and maybe her boyfriend. Meanwhile, she and her boyfriend liked to play secret S&M games. And it appears she kept her pregnancy secret from everyone, even her best friend. So where do we go from here, professor? Help me connect the dots. We have three homicides that appear to be related. What do they all have in common?"

"Me," said Kimberly.

"Exactly. And you know what? I'm the only reason you're not behind bars right now. I'm your alibi. Around the time Pat Hurly was getting her brains bashed in, you were with me. So what I need to know is who, or what, do *you* have in common with the three women who were murdered?"

"I don't know."

"There must be something."

Blake started back toward his car just as Kimberly saw the line of limousines begin to move. She followed him and got in the passenger side. Blake put his car in gear and followed the caravan out of the cemetery. As they reached the main road, Blake noticed the black Saab sitting along the highway with the windows rolled up.

"Come up with anything yet?" asked Blake.

"No."

"What about Wayne Clark? Didn't you, Joan and Charlotte all have him as a student?"

"I thought of that," said Kimberly. "But how do you connect him to Pat Hurly?"

"If he was stalking Joan, he might have seen them together. And if he was on drugs, he'd be capable of anything."

"Okay. Let's say he killed Joan because he couldn't have her. And he killed Pat out of jealousy. Why would he kill Charlotte Katz?" asked Kimberly.

"Maybe we should ask him," said Blake.

"He wasn't at the funeral."

"No, but I think we just passed his car."

Kimberly looked in the side view mirror and saw the black Saab do a U-turn and begin to follow the funeral line. "You're right."

"What's he up to?" asked Blake.

"Can I ask you something?" said Kimberly.

"Sure."

"Do you have to tell the Walshes about Joan's pregnancy or her girlfriends?"

"That depends," said Blake.

"On what?"

"They might know something."

"They won't. Not about that. It would only hurt them more."

"Maybe you can explain something to me, then?" asked Blake.

"I'll try."

"Why?"

"Why what?"

"Why women?"

"You mean you don't buy Woody Allen's explanation about bisexuality, that it doubles your chances of a date on a Saturday night?"

"Should I?"

"No. Actually, it makes things extremely complicated, especially when you're trying to decide what to wear."

"Can we be serious here," said Blake. "I'd really like to understand. Especially if it helps catch a killer."

"Fair enough," said Kimberly. "As long as you understand that what I'm about to tell you is my interpretation of mostly Freudian theory. Any self-respecting feminist would call it all a crock, so here goes—Professor Kimberly Stone's quick course in why women are sexually attracted to other women. Okay. Who was your first love object?"

"Marilyn Monroe."

"Your mother."

"I never wanted to have sex with my mother."

"Are you sure you really want to hear this?"

"Sorry. Continue."

"Your mother, whether you're a son or a daughter, is your first love object. Now men can grow up and marry a woman just like mom and get all the mothering they need. But a woman is supposed to grow up and be a woman just like old mom. But what if she still needs some mothering? What if something happened when she was growing up that left a hole, an empty pit of loneliness because her mother didn't feel like giving her daughter the comfort and nurturing she needed? So now the girl is a woman, but she still has the unfulfilled needs of a child. Where's she gonna look for love? In the arms of some needy male, or the warm soft breasts of another woman? "

Blake just stared at Kimberly.

"Now most gay women I know would probably call me a traitor for expressing that view because they just don't want to deal with it. Plus, Freud was a man, so what could he know about women? I'm kind of in the minority here. And it's a real sensitive topic among lesbian feminists. They'll tell you about how they fought long and hard to feel accepted, and then I come along and talk about how deprived they must have been as children. There's probably a politically correct explanation for lesbianism, like it's the most natural thing in the world, or what difference does it make who you love as long as you love someone, but that'd be no help at all, would it?"

"No."

"Let me ask you another question," said Kimberly. "If you and I were involved, and you learned that I was sleeping with a woman, how would that make you feel?"

"Angry," replied Blake, emphatically.

"Angry enough to kill?"

"Maybe," said Blake.

"Then, that's the real question isn't it?"

CHAPTER TWENTY-THREE

The killer sat in the funeral procession, waiting to leave the cemetery, drifting off in a half-wake, half-sleep. Images flooded into the mind as if a sewer pipe had burst, tortured memories gushed forth of another time, buried deep within a black pit of past horrors. Hands reached out of the darkness.

"Leave me alone. I don't want to play. Don't touch me there. That hurts. You're pinching me. I can't. Don't make me do that."

Fingers probing. Tongues licking. The sound of laughter. Mocking. Teasing.

"Stop! Please. Mommie. Make them stop. Mommie. Don't let them hurt me anymore, Mommie."

The killer awoke with a start. The procession was moving again.

For Blake and Kimberly, the drive from the cemetery back to the Walshes was made mostly in silence as they each pondered the latest developments. Kimberly wrestled with the question of how Pat Hurly was connected to Charlotte Katz. Other than the fact that both women knew Joan, there was no apparent link.

A horrendous image flashed through Kimberly's mind. Suddenly, the killer resembled a contagious disease that destroyed not only the host but anyone with whom the host came in contact. Was someone trying to eliminate everyone Joan knew? Was that even possible?

They pulled up in front of the Walshes' house in Maplewood and Kimberly noticed a number of limousines had already arrived. Their doors were open and people were getting out and starting to walk across the lawn to the house. As she scanned the cars looking for her sister, she saw the black Saab pull up to a curb about one hundred yards behind them.

"He's here."

"Who?" said Blake shutting off the engine.

"Wayne Clark. Back there."

Blake turned and looked down the street.

"He's only sitting there," said Blake. "That's good. I just want to pay my respects to the Walshes, and then I'm going to have another talk with young Mr. Clark."

"Let me make arrangements to have my sister taken back to New York and I'll go with you," said Kimberly.

"I think I should talk to him alone. He may be armed."

"Okay. Maybe you're right. But if you bring him in, I'd still like to watch the interrogation."

"That shouldn't be a problem. Do me a favor. Stay here and keep your eyes on him. If he starts to leave, come get me. I shouldn't be more than five minutes," said Blake.

While Blake went up the walkway toward the house, Kimberly alternated between watching the Saab and looking for her sister. Anne should have been in one of those limousines.

Before he entered the house, Blake looked down the street at the black Saab. He glanced over at Kimberly and wondered for a moment if he should stay outside in case Wayne tried something. He decided that what he had to do shouldn't take that long, so he opened the door and went inside to look for Mr. and Mrs. Walsh.

Meanwhile, Kimberly looked from limousine to limousine, searching for her sister. Where could she be? She hadn't seen her go into the house. Then, out of the corner of her eye, she saw the small black Saab moving slowly down the street behind her, getting closer.

She looked over at the house and hoped Blake would return. The Saab pulled up along side her and a darkened rear window opened.

"Sis, please. Help."

A jolt ran to Kimberly's heart as she turned and saw her sister inside Wayne Clark's car, with Wayne holding a knife to her throat.

"Wayne," said Kimberly. "What are you doing?"

"We have to talk, Professor."

"Put the knife down," pleaded Kimberly.

"We're going to do a little trade, Professor Stone," he said. "You get in. She gets out."

"Okay, Wayne," said Kimberly. "Just take it easy with the knife."

"Hurry up before that cop comes back," said Wayne.

Kimberly looked at the house again but saw no sign of Blake. She opened the back door of the Saab and saw her sister had been crying.

"Are you okay, Sis?"

"Just get me out of here," begged Anne.

"You get in first, Professor," said Wayne. "Right up front with me."

Kimberly opened the passenger door and got in.

"Now let my sister go."

Wayne shifted the knife from Anne to Kimberly. "She can go."

Anne scurried out the back door and turned around as the Saab sped off down the street.

"Help!" screamed Anne. "Please. Somebody! Help!"

Blake was talking to Mr. Walsh when he heard the screams and ran out the door. He saw Kimberly's sister waving frantically next to his car.

Blake ran from the Walshes' porch to the street and took Anne Ross by her shoulders. "What happened?"

"He took her."

"Who took her?"

"Knife," said Anne. "He has a knife."

Blake looked down the line of cars but he did not see Wayne Clark's black Saab.

"Which way did they go?"

Anne pointed down the street.

Blake got in his car, started the engine, and peeled away from the curb. He picked up his cellular phone and punched in a number.

"Officer Brown, this is Detective Alan Blake, Homicide, Manhattan. I'm in Maplewood and I think we may have a hostage situation."

"I don't understand, detective," answered Officer Brown. "I'm in Brighton. That's at least thirty miles from Maplewood."

"I think he's heading your way," said Blake. "Put out an APB for a black Saab, license plate number WC-7. It belongs to a Wayne Clark, a student at Ferguson College. I interviewed him in connection with the Joan Walsh homicide. He lives with his parents in Brighton. He may be heading there or to the college."

"No problem," said Officer Brown. "You have an address?"

"It's a big white Colonial, the only house on Webster Road. Also notify the State Police and Port Authority in case he tries to get across the river into Manhattan?"

"Will do," said Officer Brown. "You said a hostage situation. Could you be more specific?"

"I think he's holding one of his professors at knife-point," said Blake.

"Any other weapons?"

"Can't say," said Blake. "It's possible. He may be involved in the Charlotte Katz murder. That was a shooting death, so he could have a gun."

Blake reached under his seat and pulled out a shotgun, checking the breech to find it loaded.

Wayne Clark, dressed in designer army jungle fatigues, held his speed to just under sixty as he drove with one hand and held his knife to Kimberly's neck with the other.

"You can put the knife down now, Wayne," said Kimberly. "I'm not going to jump out at this speed."

"You think I'm stupid?" said Wayne.

"No Wayne, I don't think you're stupid, or at least I didn't until you did this."

"This is brilliant," said Wayne. "You're my ticket to freedom."

"No, Wayne. You're just going to get us both killed."

"So what? They already think I killed Joan. Now they'll probably try to pin Professor Katz's murder on me, too. What do I have to lose?"

"Why am I your ticket to freedom?"

"Because they'll believe you."

"Believe me about what?"

"You'll tell them I didn't do it."

"Did you?"

"How could you even ask me that question, professor? You know I didn't."

"You loved Joan. Maybe you killed her out of jealousy."

"Jealous of who? That asshole Bill Gardner? She didn't love him."

"Was it you, Wayne?"

"I just said it wasn't."

"I mean, were you the father."

"Father?"

"Joan was pregnant. Three months pregnant. Were you the father?"

"Pregnant? My Joan? Oh Jesus."

"You didn't know?"

"Know. No I, we never ... you know. Oh, God."

"Where are we going, Wayne?"

"I don't know yet."

"I can help you," said Kimberly. "But not like this."

"You've gotta tell them I didn't do it."

"I will, Wayne. But you have to put the knife down."

The first police car that went past did an immediate U-turn behind the Saab and began to follow the black car. Wayne looked in his mirror.

"The cops."

Officer Brown, who was on the driver's side of the car, grabbed the car phone. "In pursuit of a white male driving a black Saab, plate number WC-7, heading toward Route 9W. Suspect may be armed. Proceed with caution."

Two police cars cruising the edge of Brighton received the call to get over to where Route 9W intersected with Main Street and form a roadblock. The town's three other police cars were ordered to join Officer Brown in pursuit of the Saab.

Brown could see Wayne's tail lights about a quarter mile ahead. He looked at the speedometer and saw they were going over a hundred miles an hour.

"Are the cars in place?" asked Brown.

"Not yet," came the response.

"Well, hurry up," said Brown, "or they're gonna miss him."

Wayne reached in his chest pocket and took out a red-and-white capsule which he put it in his mouth. He had already taken four of the pills in the last hour, but the acid still hadn't kicked in. Or had it? Wayne wasn't sure any more.

"What are you doing?" asked Kimberly.

"My medication," said Wayne, grinning.

He looked out the side window and saw the evergreen trees and bushes speeding by. He looked ahead and saw the road weaving back and forth. The road was moving. Cool. The acid was kicking in. In the rearview mirror he could see blinking red lights. They were especially cool, thought Wayne. He just needed some music to fill the void so he pushed his Megadeath tape into the cassette player and pushed the sound up full tilt.

"Pull over, Wayne," pleaded Kimberly.

"If I do, they'll kill me," said Wayne.

"No, they won't."

"They've got guns. I wish I had a gun. I can't let you go. You understand that, don't you?"

"I want to help you, Wayne," said Kimberly. "But I can't as long as you have that knife at my throat."

Wayne sped along Main Street fascinated by the dancing white light on the hood of his car. Where's that light coming from? What's that up ahead, sitting in the road? "Hey, man. Get that car outta the way. I don't think I can stop."

The officers in the cars at the roadblock watched Wayne speeding at them.

"He's not gonna stop," yelled one officer to the other and they leaped from their cars. Wayne gunned his engine and burst through the roadblock, knocking both cars off to the side.

Wayne put his head down as the sound of metal scraping metal blended in perfectly with the heavy metal sound blaring from the car's eight speakers.

"Wayne!" shouted Kimberly. "You've got to listen to me. Your only hope is to give yourself up."

"I can't do that," said Wayne

"Why not?"

"They'll put me in jail."

"Your parents will have you out on bail in no time."

"You don't know my parents."

"Isn't jail better than death?"

"Give me liberty or give me death. Who said that?"

"This isn't a political situation, Wayne. You've kidnapped me, and the police are chasing you. Give up."

Officer Brown, followed by three more police cars, barreled down the highway after Wayne. His phone beeped and he picked it up.

"Detective Blake," said Officer Brown. "I'm chasing the sonofabitch right now. He just busted through a roadblock and he's heading up Route 9W."

Inside the Saab, Wayne was sweating heavily. He felt thirsty and wondered if there was a deli nearby. He needed a beer. LSD always made him thirsty. Then he looked in the rearview mirror again and saw the flashing red and blue lights getting closer.

Where could he get lights like that? He took his foot off the pedal and the Saab slowed down.

"I'm getting tired, man," said Wayne.

All of a sudden a police helicopter appeared overhead, slightly in front of Wayne's car. The police officer said over the loudspeaker: "Stop your car and come out with your hands raised above your head. We don't want to harm you. Stop your car now."

But Wayne could not hear the helicopter. The drug had distorted his hearing as well as his mind, and the loud music muted all external sound.

Wayne looked up at the lights on the chopper.

"Hey, man, is that car flying, or what?"

"Wayne," said Kimberly. "Stop the car."

"Wait," said Wayne. "Where's the flying gear on this thing?" Wayne shifted all over with his stick shift. "I wanta fly too," he whined. He looked up just in time to see the helicopter land in the road about two hundred yards in front of him, completely blocking his path. Wayne hit the brakes and the Saab stopped two feet from the chopper.

Wayne smiled to himself. "Maybe they can show me where the flying gear is." He had lost all connection with reality. He sensed someone in the car with him and turned toward Kimberly. What was she doing here? he wondered. This is great acid, man. Maybe she'd like some. "Hey," he said. "You want some acid?"

Kimberly stared at Wayne, frightened for her life, that this unpredictable self-imposed psychotic was about to do something that would get them both killed. She had to get away from the car.

Within moments, Brown and the three other police cars pulled up behind Wayne, creating a semicircle around Wayne's car. Police officers jumped out and squatted behind their cars, their guns drawn and cocked.

"Get out of the car with your hands up," said Officer Brown, talking into a loudspeaker.

Wayne turned off the engine, and the music died. This time he heard the voice outside the car calling to him.

"Wayne Clark," said Brown into the loudspeaker. "Please step away from the vehicle with your hands above your head."

"Why do they want me to do that?" said Wayne, pondering the directive, wondering what purpose it would serve. He smiled at Kimberly and she could see his eyes had changed. He was completely out of it.

"Maybe they're trying to rob me," he said.

"No one's trying to rob you, Wayne," said Kimberly.

Wayne looked at the police and then at Kimberly. He tried to smile. He then looked at the knife he was holding at her neck and pulled the knife closer to his face and stared at his reflection in the shiny metal blade. Kimberly watched him cautiously.

"Wayne?"

But Wayne was already in a different place, in another world, watching his face melt and stretch in the surface of the knife. His mind was on a solitary trip to lands not of this earth. Kimberly slowly moved her right arm down until her hand found the door latch. Slowly, quietly, she opened the door, watching Wayne to see if he noticed. He didn't. He was somewhere else. It was now or never. Kimberly pushed open the door and fell out onto the hard pavement of the road. Looking back, she saw Wayne still staring at the knife. She started to slowly crawl away and then she stood and ran toward the circle of police cars.

As Kimberly moved away from the car, Blake pulled up behind Officer Brown's car and went to Kimberly.

"Are you okay?"

"I think so." said Kimberly. "He's on something. I think it's LSD."

"What's he doing in there?" asked an officer next to Brown.

"I don't know," said Brown.

"I can take him," said another officer, holding a rifle with a scope.

"Did he have a gun?"

"I didn't see one," said Kimberly.

"Wayne Clark," said Brown over the loudspeaker . "Please get out of the car with your hands over your head. We don't want to hurt you, son."

Hurt me? thought Wayne. Did he say he wanted to hurt me? I didn't do anything. Why does he want to hurt me? That's no fair. I don't wanta play anymore. I'm going home. You boys play too rough.

Suddenly, the rear tires of the Saab started spinning and the black car shot away from the curb, swerving around the helicopter, which rose up and started to follow. Blake took Kimberly by her hand, and they were about to run to his car to resume the chase when Officer Brown gave the order to fire.

"Get ready," said Brown to his sharpshooter. "Aim for a rear tire."

The officer with the rifle got the Saab in his sights and drew down on the right rear tire. He squeezed off a round. The first shot missed, but the second one tore through the thick rubber and steel-belt of the right rear tire, causing the Saab to veer to the left. The rear end of the black car slammed into a metal guard rail, sending sparks flying and causing a screeching sound as metal scraped metal. The passenger door that Kimberly had escaped through had still been open when Wayne sped off so when the car again hit the guard rail on the passenger side, the impact caused the door to snap off like a plastic toy.

Wayne hit the brakes too hard, causing the car to spin left in a 180-degree turn and once again slam into the guardrail on the driver's side where the car came to a smoking, sputter halt..

Police officers jumped in their cars and sped toward the Saab, immediately formed a semi-circle around the smoking, dented wreck pressed up against the guard rail on the driver's side. With the passenger door off, they could see inside. Wayne was still gripping the steering wheel, staring straight ahead.

Blake joined Officer Brown and the sharpshooter behind Brown's car. Every officer had a gun out and pointed at Wayne.

Brown lifted the loudspeaker.

"Wayne Clark. Get out of the car with your hands raised over your head. If you are unable to move, raise your hands over your head and we will assist you. You must, however, do exactly as I say. Any sudden movements, or movements other than what I have instructed, will constitute a hostile action toward a police officer and could result in an armed response. Do you understand these instructions?"

Kimberly joined Blake and Brown and watched as Wayne continued to stare out through the windshield.

"He's tripping," she said.

"Okay," said Brown. "I'm going to approach the vehicle." He turned to the sharpshooter. "I want you to get a clear shot. I'll stay out of your line of fire. If he looks like he's going for a gun, shoot."

Brown donned a vest and bulletproof pants. He also held a shield just in case and started to walk toward the car.

"Wayne," said Officer Brown. "I'm approaching the vehicle to assess the situation. Whatever you do, son, do not move."

Wayne had been watching a crow fly from tree to tree, actually flying with the crow, when he heard something that brought him crashing back to earth and seated behind the wheel of his car. What had he heard? It was a word. Directed toward him. Somebody was talking to him. Who? The word was rising up toward his consciousness. It was getting clearer. Echoing. The word that penetrated the layers of hallucinogenic worlds. The word that now exploded in his head. "Son." Could it be? "Son." Had he heard it right? "Son." Like a shot going off. "Whatever you do, son." There it was. There was the word. "Son." Dad? Is that you? Dad. Wayne started to turn his head toward the word.

From behind his thick shield, Officer Brown could see Wayne's head begin to turn toward him.

"Just sit still, Wayne. Face forward. I'm going to help you. Don't move."

But Wayne had already slid into another place. Dad? You're here? Joan's dead. But look. Look what I have.

Officer Brown was about ten yards from the car when he saw what was happening and couldn't do anything about it except scream. "God! No!!!!"

The sharpshooter took in a deep breath and held it as he watched through his site as Wayne Clark reached across the gear shift and started to open the car's glove compartment. The rifleman breathed out and squeezed the trigger as the compartment opened and Wayne's hand reached in.

The 30-caliber full-metal jacket entered Wayne Clark's head just above his right ear, and exited through his nasal cavity, completely ripping his nose from the front of his face. Gripping something in his right hand, Wayne fell dead across the passenger seat.

Still holding the shield, Brown slowly approached the car. Blake holding his gun out ran up behind Brown and they inched near the open doorway, all eyes locked on the body of Wayne Clark and focusing on the object in his hand.

Carefully, Blake kneeled down to look closely while Brown kept his gun aimed at the still body. Blake wiped the sweat from his eyes as he leaned in closer.

"Is it a gun?" asked Brown.

"I don't think so," said Blake as he reached out under the clutching hand and gripped what appeared to be a bundle of something.

He tugged firmly and the bundle came loose from the clenched fingers. Blake let out a sigh as he looked down at the object he held. There in his hand, wrapped in rubber bands, was a thick stack of letters, smeared with blood. He turned them over and saw that they were all addressed to the same person, Joan Walsh.

CHAPTER TWENTY-FOUR

While police departments from Maplewood, Brighton and two other New Jersey municipalities along the chase route argued over whose jurisdiction was responsible for terminating the hostage situation, Blake drove Kimberly and her sister back to Manhattan.

Anne was still in a state of shock, suffering from post-traumatic stress, having survived the threat of death at the hands of an alleged killer.

"At least he won't be killing any more women," Anne said, trying to put a positive spin on the terrifying experience.

Kimberly and Blake exchanged a look. "Ah sis, we're not really sure Wayne Clark killed anybody."

"Then why did he take us hostage?" asked Anne.

"He may have been scared and confused," said Kimberly.

"Confused?" spat Anne. "Let me tell you something. When he was holding that knife to my throat, I sure as hell thought he was going to kill me. And his eyes. Did you see his eyes? The way they darted around and then stared right through you. If that's not a sign of insanity, I don't know what is."

"He certainly acted guilty enough," said Blake. "Anybody who runs like he did is usually guilty of something."

"Guilty of what, though?" said Kimberly. "That's the question."

"I thought there was evidence linking him to Joan's murder," said Anne.

"We found Clark's fingerprints at Joan's Walsh's apartment," said Blake. "But we don't know when he was there. It could have been any time. We analyzed the scrapings under Joan's fingernails, but we haven't received the DNA report. If it matches Clark, we can wrap up one of the killings. But we still can't connect him physically to Pat Hurly at all. We'll see what the Crime Scene Unit comes up with from Hurly's apartment. And as for Charlotte Katz, that's still unresolved."

Blake pulled up in front of Kimberly's apartment on Sullivan Street just as the sun was setting.

"Are you and your sister going to be okay?" asked Blake.

"We'll be fine."

"I'll check back later," said Blake. He then drove off.

Kimberly watched him drive away and realized her sister was looking at her and almost grinning.

"What are you smiling at?"

"He's kind of cute."

"Cute? He's an over-weight, out-of-shape cop, who probably votes Republican."

"You're not getting any younger," said Anne.

"And life's too short to waste on guys like that. Let me check the mail and phone messages."

"Then let's go shopping," said Anne.

"Shopping? After what we've just been through?"

"Can you think of a better way to put it all behind us?"

"I could, but shopping is probably less harmful. Are any stores still open?"

"Are you kidding? This is New York. It's why people like me like to come here."

"What about your plane?"

"It's the shuttle. They leave for Washington every hour."

By 7:30 that evening, Kimberly and her sister were in one of the many designer dress sections of Loehmann's on Seventh Avenue in Chelsea, that area of Manhattan just north of the West Village.

Kimberly looked closely at the price on a low-cut red Calvin Klein dress.

"Maybe this wasn't such a great idea," asked Kimberly.

"What's the matter?" said Anne.

"Look at these prices. Maybe we should try Macy's, or Bloomingdale's. They're open till nine."

"You think these are expensive? When was the last time you were in Bloomingdale's?"

Two rows away, and behind a double rack of Donna Karen dresses, the killer listened to Kimberly and her sister talking.

Anne picked up a yellow silk dress. "What do you think?"

"Nice," said Kimberly, and then, looking at the price, "but too expensive."

"They're all too expensive," said Anne. "I'm going to try it on anyway. Why don't you try on that red one?"

"I can't afford it," said Kimberly.

"It'll be my treat," said Anne.

"Are you sure? We could get the same dress on Orchard Street for half the price."

"I don't feel like riding all over Manhattan just to save a few bucks on a dress," said Anne. "I'm trying mine on."

Kimberly shook her head and followed her sister to the dressing booths. A woman in her fifties gave them each a numbered plastic tag, color-coded to indicate how many garments they were trying on.

Inside the changing area there were two rows of booths partitioned off by thick curtains.

"There's an empty one over there," said Anne. "You take this one."

As soon as Kimberly and her sister entered their booths, the killer passed by the woman checking dresses, received a plastic tag, entered the changing area, then quickly slipped into a space behind the curtains of the changing booths.

Your patience has been rewarded, my dear. How perfect is this? You are an artist. A master with a palette of death, about to rip open the canvas of life.

Inside one booth, Anne was down to her bra and panties as she held up the yellow dress. She looked again at the price tag, which read $599. She shook her head and started to put the dress over her head.

In another changing booth, Kimberly was having trouble pulling the red dress over her shoulders. Most of the dress was bunched up around her head, covering her face and eyes, while the rest was stuck halfway down her side.

"Damn," Kimberly said, quietly. "Must be the wrong size."

She tried to lift the dress back over her head, but the seams caught under her arms and started to tear.

"I need some help in here," called Kimberly.

With the dress over her head, she couldn't see the curtain behind her begin to move as the point of something sharp began to slice through the fabric. But she could hear the sound of something tearing.

"What's that?" asked Kimberly.

The blade stopped and then started to cut some more.

"Anne? Is that you?"

Kimberly struggled with the dress, pulling with all her might until she heard the seams tear again.

In the other booth, Anne buttoned her blouse when she heard the cry.

"Help!"

Kimberly was still pinned inside her dress, which was now up around her head, shoulders, and arms, binding her arms up over her head. The long sharp blade of a knife sliced through the rear curtain ready to plunge into the bare back.

Anne slid open the front curtain and saw her sister struggling with the red dress. She grabbed the top of the dress and gave a yank, pulling both her sister and the dress out of the booth, just as the killer thrust the knife blade forward into the now empty space where Kimberly had been.

The front curtain closed behind Kimberly as soon as she was clear of it, so neither she nor her sister noticed the knife, nor the tear in the rear curtain. The killer quickly withdrew the knife.

Kimberly shook out her hair and looked at the size on the dress.

"That is *not* a size six." She then looked at her watch. "Hey, Sis, I'm starting to fade. Why don't we head out to the airport? I'll buy you dinner out there."

"You're not going like that are you?" asked Anne.

"Huh?" responded Kimberly, and then realized she was in her bra and panties.

The killer was still behind the changing booth fuming over the near miss when Kimberly re-entered the small enclosure. She quickly pulled on her skirt and was about to button her blouse when she saw the ragged tear in the rear of the booth. She started to reach out to touch the tear when the killer realized she had returned.

You are dead bitch. You just don't know it yet.

The killer brought the knife into striking position, ready to plunge when ...

"Hey sis, look at this," said Kimberly.

Anne pulled back the front curtain and entered the changing booth with her sister.

"What?"

"This rip," said Kimberly nodding toward the tear in the fabric of the changing booth. "It wasn't here before."

"Maybe you just didn't see it."

Kimberly resumed buttoning her blouse while staring at the torn curtain.

"How could I miss it?"

"I don't know, Sis. Can we get going?"

The killer stood frozen, the knife poised and ready to stab, when Kimberly and her sister left the booth.

Why didn't you just kill both of them? You think you're going to get another chance like that? You're an idiot. You deserve to get caught.

The airport restaurant was at the top of the terminal overlooking the take-off area. There were several rows of square tables covered with blue-checkered tablecloths and glass vases holding fresh-cut red roses.

"This is nice," Anne whispered as she removed her napkin and spread it out on her lap.

"I think we deserve it."

Anne forced a smile.

A prolonged silence followed as a bus boy filled their water glasses and placed hard rolls and butter on their gold-trimmed white china plates.

"I found something out today that's very upsetting," Kimberly blurted out.

"What?"

"Joan was three months pregnant."

"That makes her death that much sadder."

"But I didn't know."

"Maybe her boyfriend asked her to keep it secret."

"That's the other part. It's not his. He had a vasectomy."

"Oh."

"I didn't know Joan was having sex with anyone else."

"Couldn't she be your best friend and still want to keep her sex life private? Didn't you have any secrets from Joan?"

"No," Kimberly answered.

"Nothing?"

"No. In fact, she knew something I have never been able to tell you."

"What?"

"I don't even know if I can tell you now," Kimberly said after a long silence.

"Come on, Sis. After what we've just been through?"

"Our brother David."

"What about him? He's a shit. So what else is new?"

"He abused me."

214

"What do you mean, abused you?"

"Sexually. It started when I was four and lasted until I was sixteen. He made me promise not to tell anyone."

"Are you serious?"

"You think I'm making it up?"

"Of course not. But why didn't you tell me?"

"Because I was scared. And ashamed. And I guess because you always shut me out."

"What did he do?"

"You sure you want to know?"

"I don't know. God! Sis. Did he ... you know?

"Go all the way? No. But just about everything else."

Anne just stared at her sister, then she started tapping her fingers on the table.

"Say something," said Kimberly.

"Say something? Okay. At least David showed an interest in you," Anne said emphatically. "He never even knew I existed."

"I would have gladly traded places," said Kimberly.

"I wish you had come to me," Anne said, sadly. "Did you ever tell Mom or Dad?"

"I tried, but they didn't want to hear it. At first they didn't believe it. Then, when they did believe me, they blamed me for going along with him. Anyway, I was eighteen when I finally got up the courage to tell them but the damage had already been done and things have never been the same between us since I told them."

"Wow. No wonder you never come home for the holidays, especially if he's going to be there."

"It hasn't been easy," said Kimberly.

"It was never easy for me either," said Anne. "Always being the virtuous one. You think I liked that role? I would have loved to have done some of the wild things you did."

"Why didn't you?"

"I was scared. I saw the way Mom and Dad punished you. The way Mom would hit you with that belt. I was afraid the same thing would happen to me."

"They thought I was a devil," said Kimberly.

"You weren't a devil, Sis. Just a little free-spirited, that's all. But gosh, sooner or later, you've got to think about settling down. I know this thing with David must have been terrible, but Kim, whatever happened, that's the past. Don't you want to have a family? A couple of kids?"

"I don't know. Sometimes I do, and then other times I panic at the thought of being imprisoned in a house in the suburbs, raising a couple of rug rats, and watching my career rot and turn to dust."

"Don't you get lonely?"

"I do now."

"Now?"

"Now that Joan's gone," said Kimberly, then immediately regretted saying it when she saw the sadness in her sister's eyes. "I don't know if I can explain this the right way," she continued. "But Joan helped show me how to love someone, to trust someone. Not in the romantic, or sexual way. I'm still pretty confused in that area. But just in the way I— "

"Would have liked me to have loved you," said Anne, finishing the sentence for her.

"You said it, not me."

Anne grabbed Kimberly's hand.

"I'm really sorry that I wasn't what you needed in an older sister. But you always seemed so capable. So independent. I was always jealous of you. I never thought you needed anybody. None of us did. If I'd known, I would have been there for you, Kim."

Kimberly put her other hand on top of her sister's.

"I was afraid of you," Kimberly said.

"Afraid. Why?"

"I didn't want to be disappointed. You never seemed to be around when I needed you."

"I'm here now, right?"

"You are." Kimberly squeezed her sister's hand as the ache of a lifetime burned in her throat. "Stay with me tonight."

"What?" said Annie pulling her hand away.

"Get a flight back in the morning."

"I can't sis. I've gotta get back."

And with that Kimberly knew nothing had changed. She looked at her sister and noticed how much more gray hair she had and how much less make-up she wore. Suddenly she felt even more distant from her than ever before. Kimberly had been naive to think Anne

216

could even for a brief instant fill the void left by Joan's death. Her sister could never be Joan. The rapport, the closeness, the psychic connections just weren't there and never could be. The food arrived but Kimberly had lost all desire to eat. She opened her purse and took out some money, placed it next to her plate and stood up from the table.

"Sis," said Anne. "What are you doing?"

"Good-bye Anne. Thanks for coming."

Kimberly walked out of the restaurant with her sister shouting after her.

"Kim. Wait. Look, I'll call you."

Kimberly rushed outside the terminal and walked quickly to a line of taxis waiting for arriving flights. As she opened the rear door of the cab, she again sensed someone was watching her. She quickly climbed in and closed the door behind her.

"Sullivan Street," she said to the driver. "It's in the Village. If you're not sure how to get there, get me to Houston Street and I'll direct you from there."

As the cab pulled away, Kimberly studied the people standing outside the terminal but she didn't recognized anyone. No one seemed to be paying attention to her taxi.

After the cab pulled away, the killer stepped out from behind a column.

You took a foolish chance coming out here. She almost saw you. Why didn't you just wait in her apartment? Now she's going to get there ahead of you. It's time to call it a night. You're not thinking straight.

CHAPTER TWENTY-FIVE

It was a sunny and cool Saturday morning, but instead of enjoying his day off, Detective Alan Blake was back in New Jersey, sitting in the Clarks' living room waiting patiently for Rebecca Clark. He was hoping to gather some evidence that linked Wayne to at least one of the killings.

Brighton Police had obtained a warrant to search the premises, but that search, now long over, had failed to produce a murder weapon or any other evidence connecting Wayne Clark to any of the murders. They did find several capsules of LSD, a bag of stale marijuana, rolling papers, and several pictures of Joan Walsh taken with a telephoto lens.

As Blake waited, an uneasy thought wormed its way through the detective's mind. It was quite possible that Wayne Clark was not responsible for the deaths of Joan Walsh, Charlotte Katz, or Pat Hurly. He was wrestling with this thought when Rebecca Clark finally walked slowly down the spiral staircase, holding on to the banister for support.

When Blake looked up, he couldn't believe the difference in the woman he had met three days before. She had aged twenty years in seventy-two hours. Her vibrant face was now a mask of gloom.

"Detective Blake," said Mrs. Clark. "I'm sorry if I kept you waiting. My husband had to go into town to make the funeral arrangements. That's who I was talking to on the phone. He couldn't decide how much to spend on the coffin. They have such a wide range of prices you know from nine hundred to over twenty-five thousand dollars. Can you imagine? For a coffin."

"No problem, Mrs. Clark," said Blake. "I'm sorry for your loss."

"Let's talk in the library," said Mrs. Clark.

Blake followed her into a wood-paneled room. Two of the walls were lined with floor to ceiling leather-bound books.

"Please," said Mrs. Clark. "Have a seat. Can I have Martha bring us something? Coffee? Tea?"

"Coffee would be fine."

Martha, the housekeeper who had answered the door, was standing close enough to hear the exchange. She went to get the coffee without being asked.

"I'm glad you agreed to see me," said Blake.

"I'm glad you called," said Mrs. Clark. "I thought the phone was out of order."

"Oh?"

"It hasn't rung once since ...." She couldn't finish the sentence. She took a deep breath and took out a handkerchief. Martha returned with a silver tray holding a medium-sized coffee pot and two cups. She poured the coffee and left the room.

"When my mother died," said Mrs. Clark, "the phone rang all the time."

Blake shifted uncomfortably in his chair.

"But I guess this is different," added Mrs. Clark. "People don't know what to say. I wouldn't know what to say."

"I wanted to talk to you a little bit, Mrs. Clark," said Blake. "About what happened."

"You know, at first I thought he might have killed that professor. But now I know he didn't."

"How do you know?"

"I know."

"Then why did he take two women hostage and lead us on a high-speed chase?" asked Blake, putting down his cup and looking at Mrs. Clark.

"My son is, was, a very troubled boy. On drugs most of the time. Ever since the Lisa Murphy incident. He never got over that. I think deep down, he knew he should have been punished for her death. Vehicular manslaughter. Something. But he got off, and the guilt just ate away at him. I think he ran so he could finally be punished for Lisa Murphy's death."

"That's the girl he hit with his car," said Blake.

"That's right," agreed Rebecca Clark. "Anyway, like I said, I now know that he didn't kill Joan Walsh."

"How can you be so sure?"

"This," said Mrs. Clark, as she reached into the pocket of her robe and pulled out an envelope. She handed it to Blake.

Blake looked down and saw the purple post office stamp, "Return to Sender." The date on the envelope was the day after Joan Walsh had been murdered.

"I found it this morning. It came back in yesterday's mail. See the postmark. He mailed it the afternoon she died. Why send a letter to someone if you knew she was already dead?" said Mrs. Clark.

"To confuse the police?" said Blake.

"Wayne's not that clever. You know why as much as I do. He thought she was still alive."

Blake stared at the letter.

"Can I use your phone, Mrs. Clark?"

"Of course."

Blake walked across the room and picked up the phone. As he dialed, he asked over his shoulder, "Did Wayne ever mention someone named Pat Hurly?"

"Hurly? Not that I can remember," said Mrs. Clark. "But he never talked too much about his friends. I don't think he really had any. The only person he ever talked about was Joan Walsh."

Kimberly's machine answered. "I can't come to the phone right now, so please leave a message and I'll return your call as soon as possible."

"It's me. Blake. Call me as soon as you get in."

Blake replaced the phone and turned toward Mrs. Clark.

220

"I miss him," she said. "He wasn't a bad boy. It was the drugs. He became somebody else. I don't share my husband's view on Wayne."

"What's that, Mrs. Clark?"

"That Wayne was a mistake."

Kimberly had been jogging for forty minutes when she rounded the corner of Sullivan and Houston Streets. As she headed up Sullivan Street, she began to slow her pace, and use the final three blocks to cool down. By the time she reached her building, she had slowed to a walk. There were only a few people on the street. A few pushed shopping carts filled with groceries. Something was missing. That's when Kimberly realized the space in front of the building was empty. Her guardians had been withdrawn. Did they really think Wayne Clark's death had closed the case? Even Blake wasn't that stupid. Maybe they were between shifts. She made a mental note to call Blake as soon as she got inside.

She decided to take the stairs instead of the elevator, just to give her midday workout a final aerobic burst. But when she reached her floor, she saw something that made her heart race even faster than the exercise. The door to her apartment was open. It had been locked when she left. She had the keys in her hand.

Kimberly moved quietly toward the door and listened. Someone was definitely inside. She heard a sawing sound and wondered what kind of burglar would be sawing. Knowing better, but angry over the intrusion, Kimberly kicked open the door, slamming it against the inside wall with a loud smack!

"All right," said Kimberly loudly. "What's going on?"

A head covered with sawdust and wearing goggles popped out from the doorway into the living room.

"That you, professor?"

"George?" said Kimberly. "What are you doing here?"

"Finishing up," said George. "I said I'd be back Saturday. I even called to check. Didn't you get the message I left on the machine, to call me if it was a problem? I figured since you didn't call back, it was okay."

Kimberly rolled her eyes. "I'm sorry. I got the message George, but I just forgot all about it."

"You want me to come back some other time?"

"No. That's all right. I just haven't been myself the last couple of days."

"I understand," said George. "It was a shame about Professor Walsh."

"Thank you. I still can't believe it," said Kimberly.

"I never had the chance to thank her for recommending me to you," said George.

"Neither did I," said Kimberly.

"She was a fine woman," said George. "I hope they catch whoever did it and throw the book at him. Who could do such a thing?"

"The police think it may have been one of her students."

"Have they made an arrest?"

"He was killed yesterday in a car chase."

"Wow," said George.

"Are you finished in the bedroom?"

"The platform bed's all done. I'm just finishing the bookcases."

"I'll be in my office then, doing some work," said Kimberly. "Just let me know when you're done. I'd like to look at it before you leave."

"Sure thing, professor. Ah, where's your office?"

"The desk in my bedroom."

"Right. I'll, ah, just get back to the bookcases."

Kimberly watched as George returned to his tool box and began measuring lumber. His muscular shoulders and back pushed against the thin fabric of his t-shirt. Kimberly felt herself mildly attracted and even aroused, but she pushed the temptation away. Now was not the time for a fantasy fling with your carpenter, she thought.

As soon as she entered her bedroom, she saw the message light on the phone machine blinking and played back Blake's message. She picked up her phone and called his number.

The desk sergeant took the call and told her Detective Blake hadn't returned yet. She was getting tired of playing telephone tag with this arrogant detective. Why didn't he just give her his beeper number like any sensible human being? Since he was never in his office, the precinct number was next to useless. Kimberly left a message that she was home and sat on her bed. She looked at the clock. On a normal Saturday, she would start preparing for her Monday classes, but following Charlotte's murder, Dean Putnam had canceled all criminology classes for Monday to give the school time to find interim replacements for the two slain professors. Despite the reprieve, a tidal wave of fatigue pushed her back onto the bed and into the fetal position.

Pulling her knees to her chest, Kimberly shuddered and felt totally alone. She even wished she could have convinced her sister to stay another day. She closed her eyes hoping to relieve the fatigue, but it did little good. A headache was starting to form just as the phone rang.

"Hello," said Kimberly.

"Is this Dr. Stone?" said a female voice.

"Who's calling?" countered Kimberly.

"I'm Samantha Peters, a producer with *Sunday in New York.* We're looking for a criminologist for a segment in tomorrow's show. We got your name out of a directory of experts."

"What's the subject?"

"Crime coloring books."

"I've heard of them."

"They're supposed to be getting real popular."

"Anything to make money, right? What do they do, give them out at prisons?" asked Kimberly, sarcastically.

"No. Actually, they're selling them to school kids. Are you interested?"

"What time?"

"Seven," said the producer. "Do you know where we are?"

"I've been on before," said Kimberly.

"Thanks," said Ms. Peters. "See you tomorrow."

Kimberly hung up the phone. What she had heard about the coloring book was that it glorified violence as well as the violent. Just what the world needs. She was actually looking forward to expressing some healthy rage, and what better target? Just the prospect was starting to make her headache go away.

CHAPTER TWENTY-SIX

Richard Meyer stood in the phone booth, leaning against the cracked glass, staring at the cars passing by. Who was he supposed to call? He couldn't remember. He remembered seeing the phone booth in the service station parking lot. He remembered putting on his directional light and even turning into the parking lot. But the last thing he could recall was stopping the car, turning off the ignition, and getting out. He didn't even remember walking to the phone booth or stepping inside.

As hard as he tried to remember who it was he was supposed to call, all he could think of was Charlotte. Her soft beautiful face. Her voluptuous body. Her lilac scent. She filled his mind, shutting out all other conscious thought. It was almost like a blackout. Only instead of blacking out, he would fall into a semi-unconscious dream state.

These bouts had begun shortly after he heard about Charlotte's murder. He read every story in every paper he could find. He watched every news show and listened to the radio, turning the dial until he found a news report that mentioned her murder.

A shadow appeared in front of the booth. Richard looked up to see a woman, nodding to the phone. Suddenly Richard remembered he was supposed to call his wife. What was he supposed to say? Think.

"Are you going to use the phone?" asked the woman. "I just need to call home."

Home. That's it. He was supposed to tell Belinda that he was coming home so she could prepare dinner.

Richard took out a quarter, dropped it in and punched in his number.

"Meyer residence," said Belinda.

"It's me. I'm coming home."

"That's a nice surprise," Belinda answered. "I've got an idea. Why don't I see if my mother can take the girls for a few hours? It would be nice to spend some time together, just the two of us."

Richard felt a wave of nausea.

"I'm a little tired, hon," Richard said.

"So, we'll just take it easy."

"Okay."

"Hurry home."

Richard hung up the phone and realized he had broken out in a heavy sweat. His face was covered with droplets and his shirt was soaking. He stepped out of the phone booth. The woman stared at him and then wiped off the receiver with a cloth before using it.

Belinda Meyer replaced the kitchen phone and rubbed her hand over her extended stomach. "Daddy's coming home for dinner," she said to her unborn child. "We have to get ready. I know he travels too much. But we need the money, baby cakes. Especially now."

With two, and soon three, kids to support, Belinda was glad Richard had decided to keep his job, even though he'd rather have left to start his own company. The educational book company was very cheap about certain things, such as severance pay if Richard ever got laid off or fired, but they had a generous health insurance policy. With the new baby coming, they needed the insurance to pay the hospital and obstetrician.

Here she was, getting herself worked up again. She wanted to stay calm, if not for herself, for the baby. Unfortunately, Belinda's imagination recently had developed a habit of going to the most negative thoughts. It wasn't unusual for her to work herself into the most incredible frenzies and rages—sometimes at the most inconsequential things, like her daughter dawdling in the morning instead of getting ready for school, or her mother telling her that her house was always dirty and calling her a baby machine.

By the time Richard arrived, Belinda had straightened up the living room, family room, and kitchen, and had gotten her younger daughter off to her mother's. "Mom's picking Rosalie up at a playdate and bringing her home. I told her we'd get the girls later tonight or maybe we'd even let them stay over. I said I'd call by ten, either way."

"Fine."

"What do you want to do this evening?" Belinda asked with a seductive smile.

Richard suddenly realized his mistake. His wife had gotten rid of the children for the evening, but the children were all that really mattered to him.

His marriage wasn't like his relationship with Charlotte, where they could just talk for hours. Besides, Charlotte would never have said, "What do you want to do this evening?" She would have known what to do. Make love. Watch a video. Take a walk and stare at the squirrels. Drive into Manhattan and go to the top of the World Trade Center. He had so much more in common with Charlotte than with his wife.

He forced himself to put his arms around Belinda. Suddenly she started crying.

"Belinda, you're shaking."

"It's just that it's been so long since we've been alone," Belinda sobbed.

Richard stood back and stared right into his wife's deep blue eyes.

"I want to be a better husband and father. I really do."

At that, Belinda broke down and started wailing. She was so upset she grabbed a chair so she wouldn't fall.

"Oh my God," Belinda cried out in a strange voice, deeper than usual. "What have I done?"

226

"What do you mean? What's the matter?"

"It's just that ... I can't stand to think you're acting this way just because she's dead."

"Because *who's* dead?"

"Charlotte Katz."

At the mention of Charlotte's name, Richard's entire body froze.

"What are you talking about?"

"Why couldn't you talk to me like this before?"

"Before what?"

"And now, because *she's* dead, you want me. But it's not me that you want. It's just that you can't have *her*."

"What does Charlotte Katz's death have to do with us?" asked Richard, spacing out each word as he tried to comprehend how she could have known about them.

"Come on, Richard," Belinda said, wiping away her tears, her voice growing stronger. "Don't play games with me. You've been playing games too long. That's what's gotten us into this mess. It's all your fault."

"What's my fault?"

"You know, when I went over there, I just wanted to talk to her," said Belinda. "To tell her to leave you alone. But when I got there, and I saw you coming out of her townhouse, something snapped. I don't even remember what happened after that."

Every part of Richard's body shut down. His throat felt like it was closing off his air supply. He instinctively grabbed on to the kitchen table.

"Belinda, what are you saying?" he asked, hoping against hope that he had misunderstood her.

"I waited until you were gone then drove around for awhile. I almost didn't go back. I didn't think she'd just open the door like that. I thought she'd ask who it was and we'd just talk through the door."

"I don't understand. It was *you*? You killed Charlotte?"

"Yes."

"Oh my God. What ... why? We have to call the police."

"No, no, I can't," Belinda said, biting her lower lip as she looked out the kitchen window at the rusty metal swing set in the backyard. "I just can't. I'm ashamed. It's just too horrible. I can't bear for everyone to know about it."

"Belinda, you shot and killed another human being."

"I didn't kill her," said Belinda. "You killed her. The moment you stuck your cock in her, she was dead."

Richard leaned over the sink and vomited. He felt his legs go numb and held onto the counter for support.

"I can't go to jail, Richard," said Belinda. "Look at me. I'm six months pregnant. You can't keep a baby in jail. And what about Rosalie and Carol? How would they feel visiting their mother in jail? Would they ever understand or forgive us for what we did?"

"We?"

"That's right. You're an accessory."

Richard turned on the faucet and splashed water on his face. He had to think. Right now, according to the radio, the police were trying to connect Charlotte's murder to some student who died following a high-speed chase. Richard looked at his wife. Maybe he should just keep quiet. Not say anything. But then he saw something in his wife's eyes and knew he was in danger.

Richard forced himself to smile.

"Okay. Let's talk about this," said Richard. "You were temporarily insane. You found out that I was having an affair, and in a blind rage of passionate fury, you killed the woman I was cheating with. In some countries, if a husband finds his wife cheating, it's justifiable homicide. It may not be as simple as that here, but if it's a crime of passion, that still counts for something."

Belinda was looking at her husband, but she was having trouble focusing on his words. She knew his mouth was moving and that he was talking, but he wasn't making any sense, or was he?

"Belinda, if you plead guilty, show remorse, and throw yourself on the mercy of the court, maybe you'll get five to ten years. You'll be out in three."

Rage filled Belinda's eyes.

"Three years! I might have to go away for three years?"

"Three years for murder!" Richard shouted back. "Is that so bad?"

"It is if you're the one sitting behind bars. I say we share the sentence."

"But you're the one who pulled the trigger. You killed her, Belinda."

"But you and Charlotte Katz killed our marriage."

"No," Richard said, angrily, "our marriage was dead long before I met Charlotte. In fact, that's the reason I got involved with her. There wasn't anything left for me here. I wanted to stay for the children, and Charlotte helped me do that because at least she was showing me some affection. From you I got nothing. As soon as the new baby was born and I could find a way to support two households, I was going to leave."

Belinda opened her mouth but no words came out.

"Where'd you get the gun?" he asked.

"I just realized something," said Belinda, and then walked into the hallway. She opened a closet, reached up, and pulled out a gun. She turned around and pointed the 38-caliber Smith and Wesson at her husband.

"I shot the wrong person," said Belinda.

"What are you doing?"

"I never should have hurt that woman. She was an innocent victim."

Belinda cocked the gun and aimed at Richard's chest.

"My God, Belinda! Put the gun down," said Richard, backing away.

"You gutless sonofabitch."

"Think of the girls. Think of the baby."

"I am thinking of them."

"Killing me won't solve anything."

"How do you know?"

"Did it help to kill Charlotte? Did it make you feel better?"

Belinda thought for a beat and frowned.

"Do you think killing me will make you feel better?" continued Richard.

Belinda's hands were trembling as she started to lower the gun. Then she suddenly raised the gun, but in the split second before she could steady her aim, Richard grabbed her wrist and wrenched the gun from her hands. The pistol hit the floor and went off in a loud cracking sound that shattered the wall near the ceiling.

Belinda looked at the hole in the wall and fainted. Richard picked up the gun and then let out a deep breath.

He walked up the ten steps to the bedroom level of his split-level house. He went into his bedroom and sat on the bed. He looked at the phone and was about to pick it up. Instead, he went to the door, locked it, then returned to the phone and punched in 911.

In the hallway, at the foot of the stairs, Belinda opened her eyes. She looked up the stairs and heard her husband's muffled voice from behind the bedroom door. She looked around the room and then walked out to the garage, where she found what she needed hanging on the wall. She lifted the ax by its handle and gave it a good swing for practice. Then she returned to the hallway and started up the stairs.

CHAPTER TWENTY-SEVEN

Since Blake was already in New Jersey he decided to take advantage of the Clark's proximity to Ferguson College. Checking his notes, he located Dean Putnam's address in the faculty housing near the school's campus. He called to make sure Putnam was home and asked if he could spare just a few minutes. Putnam said he was about to go out, but that he would meet with Blake briefly if absolutely necessary.

The dean of students lived in a modest, two-story house for which he paid a very low subsidized faculty rent of seven hundred dollars a month, utilities included. Blake arrived ten minutes after he called.

"Sorry to bother you on a Saturday," said Blake, "but I just have a couple more questions."

"Can I offer you some coffee, soda or iced-tea?"

"Coffee would be great."

Once inside, Blake thought that the decor and furnishings made the living room look like an overstocked antique store. He even expected to see little price tags on some of the old wooden chairs and assorted bric-a-brac, along with several shelves of children's wooden toys.

"I'm a collector," said Putnam, returning with the coffee.

"I see. Thanks," said Blake taking a big mug and sipping.

"You can sit on that sofa. It won't break."

Putnam sat in an overstuffed maroon chair as Blake settled down gently on an antique sofa that creaked slightly under his weight.

"Maybe I'll sit over here," Blake suggested, as he found a more sturdy-looking rocking chair.

"Fine. What can I do for you?"

"I understand Professors Walsh, Stone and Katz were all up for tenure this year."

"That's correct. We're in the middle of the review process. Or at least we were. It doesn't seem necessary any more."

"How so?"

"Well, there's only one candidate left. Dr. Stone."

"Will she be granted tenure?"

"It's not my decision. I merely conduct the review, evaluate how the students and other faculty members assess the candidate, and then give my recommendation to the tenure committee. I'm now going to recommend that we wait until other candidates can be found. It's not that I don't think Dr. Stone deserves it, it's just that it might appear inappropriate."

"Who were you going to recommend?"

"That's highly confidential, detective."

"But it may be material to the investigation."

"How?"

"Possible motive."

"You can't be serious."

"Unfortunately, I am. I did a little checking when the tenure question first came up."

"You can't possibly think Dr. Stone killed two of her colleagues to get tenure."

"No. I've already ruled that out."

"Then I'm not sure I know where you're going with this."

"Why aren't you tenured, Dean Putnam?"

"Huh?"

"According to school records, you've been Dean of Student Affairs for the past ten years. That's quite a while."

"Did those records show that under my term as dean, our enrollment has doubled, from one thousand to three thousand students? Did they show how we now supply more parole officers, juvenile delinquency counselors, correction officers and family court investigators than any other college in the country? Even more than John Jay in New York. Did those records show how we get a lot of local, state and federal grant money because we have such a high percentage of minority students? I set all that up. But do you think that matters when it comes to tenure? I guess not."

"You seem a little bitter."

"Do I? I should have been granted tenure years ago. Tenure's a joke. It used to mean something. It used to reflect academic excellence, hard work. Now it's just a Goddamn personality contest. If they like you, they give you tenure. If they don't, you're screwed."

"It seems to me you might be a little jealous of someone receiving tenure before you did."

"It doesn't really matter, since we were deciding on a candidate for the criminal justice department. I wasn't even in the running. So I don't see how——"

"Where were you between eight a.m. and one p.m. last Wednesday?"

"Are you serious?"

"Could you just answer the question?"

"I was here."

"Here. You mean here, at home, or here at the school?"

"I can't believe you're even asking me these questions. Didn't the radio say you guys thought Wayne Clark was the killer? Why are you even here?"

"Just tying up some loose ends. Was anyone here with you?"

"Yes."

"Who?"

"A friend. I was counseling him. He'd just been downsized."

"Downsized?"

"Laid off. Let go. Fired. He had a high-powered job at one of the bigger accounting firms that just announced a restructuring plan that included cutting back twenty percent of its workforce. Since I'm always finding students jobs, he thought I could help in his job search."

"What's his name and phone number?"

"Do you really have to do this?"

"I do."

Blake ripped a piece of paper off a pad and scribbled a name and number of his secret lover.

"That's his temporary work number."

"Do you have his home number?"

"No," Putnam lied.

"Mind if I try to reach him now?"

"It's Saturday. He won't be there."

"How convenient."

"Detective Blake. I liked Joan Walsh. I liked Charlotte Katz. But more importantly, even without tenure, I like this school and my job. And I would never do anything to hurt Ferguson or its reputation," explained Putnam.

"I'm just trying to cover all the bases," said Blake.

"Well, you're way out of line," said Putnam.

"Thanks for the coffee," said Blake, getting up and walking to the door. "I'll be in touch."

Blake let himself out. As soon as he was gone, Putnam sat back into his chair and felt a cold wave flow down his back. Oh God. He's going to find out. They're all going to find out. I'm going to be ruined. Goddamn Joan Walsh.

Putnam closed his eyes, rubbed his temples and remembered the first time he had met the petite woman with flaming red hair. Joan Walsh had arrived for her interview five years ago, wearing a short plaid skirt and silk blouse. She let him know from the start that she found him appealing and he quickly realized the only way to put a stop to her obvious advances was to tell her the truth, that he was gay.

He remembered hating himself for even having to say anything, but he couldn't stand her constantly coming on to him. As soon as he told her, he realized he'd perhaps made a mistake. Then to compound the error he invited Joan to a dinner party, which included his lover as well as some of the gay students he'd been involved with. How stupid could he be? What a disaster that turned out to be. All Joan wanted to know was whether he was practicing safe sex. He assured her that he was. But she couldn't get off the subject. Could she have known then that he was sick? No one knew back then. He didn't even know until he tested positive for HIV last summer. He should never have told her he was gay.

Why was he worried now? Joan Walsh was dead. He should feel relieved. Joan promised not to tell anyone, and she'd kept her promise for the past five years. What's the problem? It's that detective. He's going to dig and dig until he comes up with a suspect and motive. Maybe Joan kept a diary or something. Maybe he was in it. Maybe they'll think he killed her because she knew.

On the drive back to Manhattan, Blake reshuffled his evidence cards in his mind, trying to come up an answer. The image that kept recurring was that of the plastic daisy. The Crime Scene Unit had determined it was a common ornament, easily purchased in any of the thousands of craft stores or five-and-dimes in the metropolitan area. But what did it mean? And why did the killer place it in Joan Walsh and Pat Hurly's ears? He reviewed all the lessons he'd learned over the years about profiling, about how the scene of the crime or the condition of the victim will offer clues to the killer's psychological profile. Why wasn't the procedure working here?

Two women were murdered with blunt objects. The third, two bullets, fired at close range. All three women opened the door for their assailant. All three women were either friends or acquaintances of Kimberly Stone. However, only two of the women had a plastic daisy in their ear. Plus, the third victim had been shot. These cases were giving him a migraine.

When he got back to the precinct he checked his messages and found that Kimberly had returned his call and that he had several messages from Officer Brown. He started to pick up the phone to call Kimberly when the phone rang.

"Blake."

"Hey I got you. It's Officer Brown, out in Brighton."

"I just got back. What's up?"

"Looks like we caught a break in the Charlotte Katz murder."

Blake stopped rubbing. "What is it?"

"We just booked a Mrs. Belinda Meyer for murder," said Brown. "Seems her husband was having an affair with Katz and she popped her. She was getting ready to do the husband too when he called 911 and locked himself in the bathroom of the master bedroom. When we got there, she had just cut through the bedroom door with an ax. A couple more seconds and she might have been charged in two killings. Anyway, I just thought you'd want to know since you thought the Katz murder might have been connected to another killing."

"Two other killings, actually."

"Two huh? Those the ones you wanted that Clark boy for?"

"They were, but it's gotten a little complicated. We're having trouble coming up with any solid physical evidence. There's a good chance he didn't do it."

"Then why'd he run like that?" asked Brown.

"Who knows," said Blake. "Thanks for the call."

Blake hung up the phone and looked down at the two files on his desk. The names on the files were Joan Walsh and Pat Hurly.

He called Kimberly Stone, but got her machine again.

"It's Blake again. We need to have a talk. Call me. It's very important."

He then opened two address books and started to compare names. The only two names in both books were Kimberly Stone and Dee Porter. But then in Pat Hurly's book he found something else. Next to Joan Walsh's name, Pat Hurly had written another name in parenthesis and then erased it. Blake took a pencil and rubbed the graphite over the erased letters. A name began to appear faintly. Bill Gardner? What's this here? he wondered. Were they having a little threesome, maybe?

Blake picked up the phone and punched in Gardner's number. A machine picked up. Blake didn't leave a message. He slammed the phone down, angry at himself for not bringing Gardner in sooner for more questioning.

CHAPTER TWENTY-EIGHT

The sky over Manhattan was turning a dark gray as twilight approached. Kimberly sensed the change in air pressure and knew another spring rain was about to begin. The question was, would she be able to make it back to her apartment, carrying her two bags of groceries, before the downpour came. She had decided to take the opportunity to do some shopping while George the carpenter finished his work, which involved a little more hammering than she could stand. She was halfway down her block on Sullivan Street when thunder rolled and a lightning flash brightened the horizon. She started walking faster when a figure stepped in front of her, blocking her way.

"Aggghhh!" she shrieked, nearly dropping the bags.

But when she realized who it was, anger replaced all feelings of fear.

"Bill, you scared the hell out of me."

Bill Gardner had deep dark circles under his eyes and his face looked drawn and haggard. His shirt was open at the collar and a tuft of chest hair sprouted forth. Kimberly normally found chest hair attractive, but the thickness of what she saw here made the hair look more like fur. There was something else animalistic about him. An odor. Faint but distinctive. A sour scent of male sweat, the kind often found at ringside, or in locker rooms after a football game. The scent of battle. Kimberly backed away.

"We need to talk," he barked.

"I don't think we have anything to talk about," said Kimberly, starting to walk around him, but Bill grabbed her arm.

"Don't walk away from me. I know you must think I'm some kind of monster. But you have to believe me when I tell you the S&M stuff was not my idea."

"Go to hell, Bill," said Kimberly as she pulled away and started to feel the first drops of rain.

"I can prove it to you."

Kimberly stopped and turned. "How?"

"These." He held up a large envelope. "I never intended on showing them to anyone, but it's the only way I'll ever get you to believe me."

Kimberly stared at the envelope, then took it. She stepped under an awning of a Chinese laundry and opened the flap.

Looking inside, she saw a number of color photographs, eight-by-tens. She pulled one out and felt as if someone had kicked her in the stomach. In the photo, striking a fierce pose, was Joan, dressed in leather and spiked heels. One of the heels was stepping on the back of a woman tethered to posts on a floor. Joan held a cat of nine tails in her hand ready to strike. Other pictures showed Joan in various poses in which she was either dominant or submissive. But in either case, it was easy to see by the look on her face and in her eyes that she clearly enjoyed the moment.

Kimberly handed the photos back to Bill. She felt queasy.

"Can we talk now? Just a few minutes," said Bill. "There's a place down the street."

The neighborhood bar was only half-filled this early in the evening as Bill and Kimberly took a table far from the crowd gathered around the television over the bar. They waited for the beers to arrive before talking.

Bill started. "I did love her, you know."

"Do you know who made her pregnant?"

238

"No, and I still can't believe it," said Bill. "We were going be married and she was pregnant with somebody else's kid. Why would she do that? You were her best friend. You must know who she was sleeping with."

"But I don't," said Kimberly, wearily.

"You don't have to protect her anymore," snapped Bill. "She's dead. I want to know who she was fucking. I want to know who was fucking the woman I was going to marry. It wasn't that student, was it? That Wayne Clark?"

The beers arrived, and Bill drained his in one swig.

"I doubt it," said Kimberly. "Who's the other woman in the picture?"

"Pat Hurly," said Bill. "She wasn't really into it though. But she really liked Joan. I think she would have done anything just to stay involved."

"Did that ever make you jealous?"

"What? Pat? Hell no. I kind of got off on it. Watching two women make love. Doesn't get much better than that."

"How come I never knew?" asked Kimberly.

"You mean about the S&M stuff? She wanted to tell you, but she was afraid of how you'd react. You were her best friend. I think she loved you more than all of us. She was afraid you might not understand. I have to tell you, it was a new experience for me. She used to drag me off to the Eulenspiegel Society meetings up on the Upper West Side. She wanted me to meet some of the people who were into S&M. These were normal, average, everyday people. Teachers, bus drivers, doctors, lawyers, CEOs, professors, cops, you name it. And all ages too. Each one had their own sadomasochistic fantasy."

"I have to get going," said Kimberly, standing up.

"I really miss her."

Kimberly saw the tears in his eyes and sat back down.

"I don't know what to do," said Bill. "I don't want to go home. That detective has called about a dozen times. I'm sure he thinks I killed Joan. Don't they always suspect the boyfriend?"

"He suspects everyone," said Kimberly.

"Yeah, well just let him try to pin this on me," snarled Bill. "I'll sue him from here to sundown. I'll own his ass. All they care about is closing the case. Shit, my prints are probably all over her apartment.

239

Now, with her pregnant and all, I've got a motive. I must be at the top of their list."

"There's also Luis Alvarez," said Kimberly.

"Who's that?"

"The husband of one of the women Joan counseled at the battered women's shelter. His wife told me to warn Joan that she might be in danger because Luis might try to get to her through Joan."

"How would he do that?"

"Joan gave his wife her business card and he found it," said Kimberly.

"Have the cops picked him up?"

"They can't find him."

"Oh, man."

"You should go home and get some rest, Bill. If the police call, just talk to them. The more cooperative you are, the less likely they'll consider you a suspect. It's when you try to avoid them that they start to wonder why."

"It's their attitude," said Gardner. "They think they can just say anything they want, push you into some kind of compromising position or statement. I'd like to get them in a courtroom, in a cross-examination, teach them who they're dealing with. Make them sweat a little."

As hard as she tried, Kimberly could feel no compassion for the man who sat across from her. There was something deeply wrong with Bill Gardner and she knew it would take a more experienced person to uncover the inner demons that haunted this troubled soul. She wondered what it was that Joan had found so attractive. But then maybe she hadn't seen how fragile this man really was, or had she?

While Bill and Kimberly were in the neighborhood bar, Blake was pulling up in front of Kimberly's apartment building. He parked his car and walked toward Hal, the doorman.

"Good evening," said Blake. "I'm here to see Dr. Kimberly Stone."

"She went out about two hours ago and hasn't come back yet," said Hal.

"I see," said Blake. "Here's my card. Would you give this to her when she returns and tell her I stopped by. Tell her to call me as soon as possible. It's important that I talk to her."

Hal looked at the card and then at Blake. "Yes sir, detective."

Blake returned to his car and drove off.

Ten minutes later, Kimberly and Bill Gardner walked up to the front of Kimberly's building. The rain had passed and the air smelled clean. Kimberly shifted the weight of her groceries while Bill slumped against a railing.

"I don't suppose I could come up?" said Bill.

"I don't think so, Bill," said Kimberly. "I'm beat. Go home and get some sleep, okay?"

"If you insist," said Bill. He then leaned over and tried to kiss Kimberly on the mouth but she turned so he got her cheek instead.

"Goodnight, Bill."

Kimberly walked to the door which was being held open by Hal the doorman.

"Dr. Stone. You had a visitor while you were out. He gave me his card. Detective Blake. Said you should call him right away."

"Thanks, Hal," said Kimberly taking the card and entering the building. "How about the carpenter. Did he come down?"

"He left about an hour ago."

Kimberly nodded and went inside.

Bill Gardner stayed on the street in front of Kimberly's building wondering what he should do. He looked up to where Kimberly's apartment was and saw a light come on. He didn't really want to go home. But did he really want to force himself on Kimberly Stone? Then he *would* be arrested. He decided a drink was in order to help him plan his future, so he headed back to the bar where he and Kimberly had talked.

As he walked off down the street, he didn't notice someone was standing in the bushes as he walked by.

The killer waited until Bill passed by before stepping out of the shadows, looked up at Kimberly's window and then at Gardner walking down the street.

Eenie, meanie, minie, moe. Catch a victim by the toe. If he hollers, let him go. I don't think so. No no no.

After stopping by Kimberly's building, Detective Blake went home. He turned on the television, muted the sound, grabbed a bag of tortilla chips from the pantry, a can of beer from the refrigerator and sat on his sofa. Sitting on the coffee table staring up at him were two case folders. He stuffed a handful of chips in his mouth and washed them down with a some beer. He tried to relax but too many unanswered questions whirled through his mind. He put down his chips and beer, picked up his phone, and punched in a number.

"Dee Porter's Interior Design," said a female voice. "Our office hours are between 9 a.m. and 5 p.m. If you wish to make an appointment you may leave a message after the tone and we will return your call."

Blake hung up the phone without leaving a message. He looked at the clock over the sink. It was 8:35 on a Saturday night and here you are, in your apartment with a couple of unsolved murders for company. Is this the way it's going to be? Is this your life? Blake finished the beer and was about to get another when he stopped.

Instead, he opened a closet, took out his sport jacket and left the apartment.

Kimberly was lying on her living sofa with some throw pillows under her neck and back trying to get the image of the S&M photos out of her mind. She wondered how she would have reacted if Joan had told her. It was a world Kimberly had never explored. She was sure she could have handled it. Joan might have even been able to explain the attraction. As chilling as some of the pictures were, there was something provocative about both domination and submission. The idea of either taking or losing control struck a primal chord somewhere. What was it about the pain? What role did pain play? Or was it more in the danger that the pain would go too far? That death was lurking just around the corner?

Did Joan take it too far? If she acted this out with Pat Hurly, maybe there was another woman involved. Jealousy was one of the most powerful motives behind murder.

She had reached that conclusion somewhere. It was in a study she did last year in which she surveyed fifty incarcerated murderers. It was around here somewhere. She got up and began looking through a file cabinet until she pulled out a folder.

The survey contained not only statistical data, but letters and in-depth questionnaires from the convicted killers. She retrieved the surveys of only those crimes that seemed similar to Joan's murder. There were twenty-four. In one, a 28-year-old married man killed his best friend over his wife. They had been dating whenever the husband went off on a business trip. He came home a day early and found them in bed together. He beat his friend over the head with his son's bowling ball.

As she lay down on her bed and re-read the letters and answers to the questionnaires, the descriptions of one violent act after another just made her more depressed and weary. Instead of gaining insight, Kimberly drifted off into a restless sleep and began to dream.

The dream was about her brother. He had won the lottery. $100,000. She personally checked each number so he wouldn't get excited for no reason. She handed him the ticket and he smiled at her. Then he reached for her, but she backed away. She called out for her sister, but she didn't come. She looked around for help, but she was all alone. She tried to run, but a hand gripped her ankle and held her back. She thought about Detective Blake, tried to remember his phone or beeper number, but she couldn't. The hand holding her ankle started to pull her into a black bottomless hole. She felt her foot slip over the edge, then her calf and then her thigh. She tried to grab onto something to hold, but there was nothing to hold onto. She felt her hips and stomach and chest slide over the edge of the hole. She was almost entirely in the hole and about to fall when ... the front door buzzed and she opened her eyes.

Dazed and disoriented, Kimberly wiped her eyes and sat up. She looked at her watch. It was after 9 p.m. and she wasn't expecting anyone. She got up and walked to the door. "Who's there?"

She looked out the peephole. The hallway was empty. It must have been part of the dream, she thought. She checked the lock and pushed the thick chain lock into its slip just in case, knowing the chain would never actually stop someone who really wanted to get into her apartment.

Back in her bedroom, she got undressed, walked into the bathroom and turned on the Jacuzzi. She stepped into the tub as the jets turned the water to millions of tiny bubbles. She leaned back into the throbbing, pulsing jets of water. The thick streams felt good on her back and shoulders where the muscles had tightened under the tension of the past week. She picked up a bar of perfumed soap and began to lather herself.

At the far end of the hallway outside Kimberly's apartment, the killer waited in the shadows until the hallway was clear again, then moved quickly to Kimberly's door. A hand reached in a pocket, pulled out a key, and slipped it into the doorknob. The knob turned slowly and then opened, but the chain caught.

Kimberly had lowered herself beneath the water so the jets could massage her shoulders. She was just rising up out of the water when she heard the metal jangle of the chain. Oh God! Adrenaline rushed through her nude body in a burning flash. She looked around the bathroom for a weapon. She climbed out of the tub and pulled on her robe. A curling iron, which had a small blunt semi-sharp point, hung on the wall next to the mirror. She slid the iron off its hanger and slowly opened the door to the bathroom.

She looked into the living room and saw that the door to her apartment was open. This can't be happening. The chain was broken, dangling and useless. She could feel her heart pounding and she took a deep breath hoping to calm her shaking hands. Listening for a sound, she moved quietly and slowly toward the front door, holding the curling iron like a dagger. As she moved, she looked behind her, then to the side, then to the front. If someone was in her apartment, the best thing for her to do would be to leave it.

She was backing toward the front door when it opened wider and she felt the cool air from the hallway on her damp back. Kimberly held the curling iron tightly and whirled around, swinging it down as she turned.

A hand grabbed the wrist that held the curling iron. "Aggghhh!"

"We have to stop meeting like this," said Blake, smiling and holding her wrist.

"Someone's here," whispered Kimberly.

"Not again. You're starting to sound like the little boy who cried wolf."

"Check the chain."

"Huh?"

"The chain on the door."

Blake looked to his immediate left and saw that the chain had been broken in two. He pulled his .38 caliber police special and moved into the apartment.

Kimberly stood in the doorway, holding her robe together as Blake checked every room.

He then returned, put his gun away, and walked over to Kimberly, who was holding the broken chain.

"Whoever it was is gone," said Blake. "Out the window in the kitchen."

"You must have scared him away," said Kimberly. "What are you doing here anyway?"

"Against my better judgment, I've decided to let you help."

"What took you so long?"

"The Brighton police have someone in custody for the Charlotte Katz murder."

"Who?"

"Apparently, she was killed by the wife of some guy she was having an affair with."

"Oh God. Poor Charlotte."

"So you were right. Okay. Here's what I got. The only thing I'm sure of is that whoever killed Joan Walsh also killed Pat Hurly."

"You're sure. Why?"

"This." He reached into his jacket pocket. "We've been keeping this out of the press, but it's the one piece of evidence that connects the Hurly and Walsh murders."

When his hand came out of the pocket, it held a clear envelop containing two plastic daisies. He handed it to Kimberly, who looked at the flowers closely.

"The killer left one of these in an ear of each of the victims," explained Blake.

"And you're just telling me this now?"

"We were keeping it secret. Do they mean anything to you?"

"The flower? I don't know. There's something familiar about it. I've seen it somewhere."

"What else can you tell me about Dee Porter?"

"What else?" Kimberly sat down and put her hand to her head. "Joan hired her to decorate her apartment. Pat Hurly got jealous. She thought Dee had become more than just her decorator."

"Did she?"

Kimberly gave Blake a wide-eyed look.

"What?" asked Blake.

"I just remembered something," said Kimberly. "Dee came on to Joan, and Joan let her spend the night. But then Joan broke it off before anything serious started."

"How'd the decorator take it?"

"She seemed okay," said Kimberly. "It was me she was angry at when I went out with Pat, remember?"

"Unfortunately, I do."

"But Dee and I became friends again when I told her I liked what she'd done to Joan's apartment and asked her to do some interior designs for me as well."

Blake looked at Kimberly closely, and Kimberly realized she was still in her bathrobe.

"If you're wondering if I slept with Dee Porter, the answer is no. She did some designs and I hired her carpenter, who does great work, by the way. He did these bookcases and my bed. Do you mind if I put on some clothes?"

"I'm sorry," said Blake.

"Why don't you make us some drinks while I get dressed? There's some wine in the fridge. I'll just be a couple minutes."

While Kimberly went to her bedroom, Blake took off his jacket and went into the kitchen. He opened the refrigerator and took out an unopened bottle of Chardonney. He found the corkscrew, removed the cork and poured two glasses.

Kimberly slipped into jeans and a white blouse. As she was buttoning the blouse the connection hit. "Oh, God," she said to herself, and then went back to the living room where Blake was waiting.

He handed her a glass of wine.

"We need to talk to Dee Porter, don't we?" said Kimberly.

"I called her too, but I got a machine."

"I think I know where we might be able to find her," said Kimberly.

It was nearly ten-thirty when they pulled up in front of the Duchess. Blake parked the unmarked car on Sheridan Square, about a hundred feet from the entrance. A steady stream of women lined the sidewalk. Some leaned against the redbrick wall talking, while others formed a line to get in. Kimberly looked at Blake and smiled.

"Maybe you oughta wait here."

"I don't think so," said Blake.

"I might be able to get more information," said Kimberly.

"I'm still going in."

"You sure are stubborn. Okay, suit yourself," said Kimberly, getting out of the car. Blake followed her to the entrance, where Benson stood guard. The bouncer took one look at Blake and Kimberly and grinned.

"She's okay, but you're a nay."

"A nay?" said Blake. "What's a nay?"

"As in nay-go-tive. Just beat it, pal."

Blake pulled out his shield and held in front of the bouncer's face.

"This is a homicide investigation. So if you even try to stop me from going in there, I will personally escort you to the Sixteenth Precinct and book you for obstruction of justice."

"Hey," said Benson. "I'm just doing my job."

Blake put his shield away and patted the bouncer on the shoulder. "Keep up the good work." He then took Kimberly's arm and led her into the Duchess.

Inside the dark bar, a Madonna song was playing on the jukebox and women were dancing together. A couple of the women stopped dancing when they saw Blake. Some stared at him as if the wolf had just entered the hen house. There was an overt anger in some of the glares directed at Blake, as well as at Kimberly for bringing a male into female only territory. Blake had an unusual expression on his face as he sniffed the air.

"What that scent?"

"Feminine hygiene spray."

"Huh?"

"Pussy spray," said Kimberly, with a slight smile.

"Oh."

247

They made their way to the bar. Several women got up and moved away leaving several empty stools. They took two seats near the center and tried to get Sal the bartender's attention. After a while, it was obvious he was ignoring them, assuming if he did so long enough, they'd just leave.

Kimberly looked around the room at the women. Some were alone, and some were in pairs or groups. It looked like any other singles bar, only here the customers were all women. Some were very striking in a Hollywood way, while others played down their femininity as much as possible.

A few gave Kimberly the once-over as they passed by.

"Is she here?" asked Blake.

"I don't see her."

Blake turned back toward the Bartender who was now serving a young woman who had followed them in.

"Hey," shouted Blake. "Can we get a couple of drinks down here?"

Sal put a beer in front of the woman, took her money, and then walked slowly toward Blake.

"I don't know how you got in here, slick, but I gotta tell ya, you sure as hell ain't welcome," said Sal.

"No shit," said Blake. "Well I'm sorta used to that."

"Is that so?" said Sal. "Why's that?"

"I'm a cop. Now, why don't you bring my friend here a white wine and get me a club soda?"

Sal shook his head and disappeared into the darkness of the bar to get the drinks.

"I think I recognize someone," said Kimberly. "I'll be right back."

Blake watched as Kimberly got off her stool and walked across the room. An attractive woman wearing a dark purple velvet blouse and almost black lipstick sitting alone at a table smiled as Kimberly approached. Kimberly bent over and whispered something to the other woman, who then stood up and began slow dancing with Kimberly.

Sal returned with the drinks and saw Blake watching the two women dancing, moving together slowly to the music, hips to hips, breasts to breasts. Sal shook his head.

248

"You know, if you're looking for a threesome, you've come to the wrong place. You oughta try the Botany Talk Club over on Twenty-seventh in the flower district."

"We're looking for Dee Porter. Have you seen her?"

"Dee Porter?" said Sal. "I don't know no Dee Porter."

"Is that right. What's your name?"

"Sal."

"Sal. Is this your regular gig?"

"Six nights a week."

"Don't fuck with me Sal. I know Dee's a regular here. It's sweet of you wanting to protect her, but we need to talk to her. She might be in danger. So, I'll ask you again. Has she been in tonight?"

"She never comes in on the weekends. She's got a house on Fire Island. Cherry Grove. She usually comes in on Mondays."

"How about Pat Hurly?"

"Is that what this is all about?"

"You know about what happened, I take it."

"That was a shame about her," said Sal. "Pat was a real sweetheart. Good tipper too."

"Was she in the bar Thursday night?"

"Pat was."

"How about Dee Porter?"

"Let me think," said Sal. "You know, I don't remember seeing her. She was in Monday. But Thursday. I don't think so."

A woman wearing a leather wrist band covered with metal spikes motioned to Sal from the other end of the bar, and he left Blake to take her order. Blake turned back and saw that Kimberly and the other woman were no longer dancing. The other woman had her arm resting on Kimberly's shoulder and was looking at her with a seductive smile on her lips. Blake almost spilled his soda when the woman pulled Kimberly to her and they kissed. Kimberly pulled away and put a hand on the woman's cheek softly, then turned and walked toward Blake.

When she got to the bar stool, she blew out some air and took a long drink of wine. Kimberly realized Blake was staring at her.

"Gloria says Pat Hurly left with someone Thursday night, but it wasn't Dee Porter," said Kimberly. "Some stranger wearing a fur coat, dressed like a New Jersey housewife on the make."

"Gloria says that," said Blake. "And who's Gloria?"

"Detective Blake," said Kimberly, "do I detect a tone of jealousy?"

"Jealousy? What, are you kidding?"

Just then Sal the bartender returned.

"I just remembered something," said Sal. "Pat was talking to a tall redhead Thursday night. I served them."

"A redhead."

"Actually, I think it was probably a wig."

"Did this redhead have a name?"

"I didn't get that. But get this. She said she came in to meet up with Joan Walsh. That college professor who got murdered."

Blake and Kimberly exchanged a glance.

"Who could that be?" asked Blake.

"I don't know any tall redheads," said Kimberly. "With or without a wig."

"Well, apparently Joan did," said Blake. "Come on, let's get out of here."

"What's the hurry?" said Kimberly. "I want to finish my wine." She turned toward Sal. "What else did this woman say about Joan?"

"Let's see. Oh, yeah. She said she was hoping to stay at Joan's that night. She didn't know Joan had been murdered."

"Did Pat and the redhead leave together?" asked Blake.

"I think so."

"Here's my card," said Blake. "If the redhead comes back, call me. Come on let's go."

"I'm not finished yet," said Kimberly, sipping her wine.

"Yeah. Well Gloria just finished her drink and she's headed this way. I think she's gonna put a move on you."

"She already put a move on me while we were dancing."

"You're kidding. What did you say?"

"Some other time."

"Come on. We're outta here." Blake got up and led Kimberly out of the bar.

Once outside, Kimberly started laughing.

"What's so funny?" asked Blake.

"You are."

"What? You think that shit bothers me?"

"You're the one who wanted to go inside," said Kimberly.

"I just realized something," said Blake. "I didn't eat any dinner. Are you hungry?"

"I could go for a little food."

"Chinese?"

"Sounds good to me."

"Hunan? Cantonese? Mandarin?"

"Mandarin is a language."

"You pick."

They got into the car and pulled away, unaware of the person in the alley next to the Duchess.

The killer watched them drive away.

You can run, but you can't hide, pretty baby. It's all a matter of time.

CHAPTER TWENTY-NINE

Luis Alvarez felt invisible. Two policeman walked right up to him, smiled, tipped their hats, and then walked right on by. The plan was working. And tonight was going to be the night. Nothing was going to stop him now. After he finished Maria, he would meet up with Raphael and they would travel together to Atlantic City, do a little gambling, a little craps, some blackjack, and then head south. Lay low for a while till things blew over. Till the cops had other cases to deal with. Till the death of another *punta* whore was yesterday's news and Luis Alvarez could return to walk his streets again.

The Peking Duck House just off Mott Street in Chinatown was nearly empty by the time Kimberly and Blake placed their order of one house specialty, braised string beans, and cold sesame noodles.

While a waiter carved slices off a crisp aromatic duck as if he was a chief surgeon, Kimberly tried to put a face on the tall redhead who was last seen with Pat Hurly. Sal had said the woman told them she was a friend of Joan's. Kimberly pictured all the women Joan had been with. No redheads came to mind. Nobody tall either. Maybe she was wearing a wig. Could it be someone from Joan's past? She could think of only one other person who might know: Dee Porter.

Kimberly poured some green tea into a tiny white ceramic cup while Blake poured himself a tall glass of Chinese beer.

"So, where to next? Want to hit a few S&M bars, see where that takes us?"

"Actually, that's probably not a bad idea. Do you have a particular favorite? I hear the Anvil's a swinging place this time of night."

"Hey, I was just kidding," said Blake.

"I know. But maybe we shouldn't rule them out. Especially if what Bill Gardner claims is true. That the S&M stuff was Joan's idea."

"I'm getting too old for this," said Blake. "Used to be I could run all night and hang with the best of them. Drink 'til dawn and then hit the beach to go surfing out at the Rockaways. Now, all I want to do is eat this fine meal, go home, turn on the TV to some movie channel, and fall asleep."

"How romantic."

"Romantic? You want romance now?"

"This time I was just kidding," said Kimberly, grinning. "I take it you're not married."

"We're getting personal now."

"If we're going to be working together, I'd like to know who I'm dealing with."

"What you see is what you get."

"I suppose I could guess," said Kimberly. "Let's see. You're what? Forty-five. You've been a cop most of your adult life. You got married young, and it lasted less than a year. No children. You've had a number of serious relationships since, but none has lasted longer than one, maybe two years. How am I doing?"

"You're starting to scare me."

"I read your file. Plus I've got friends on the force, remember. Students of mine from when I used to teach at John Jay. Plus I asked around."

"Why didn't you just ask me?"

"Yeah, but you already know everything. Now I can't even make stuff up."

The waiter wrapped four slices of duck in separate pancakes, then added a large scallion and a smear of Hoisin sauce. He bowed and walked away, leaving the carcass and a knife in case they wanted to pick the duck dry. Blake lifted a pancake to his mouth and took a healthy bite and swallowed.

"So what else did you learn about me?" asked Blake, wiping his mouth.

"You run through partners faster than you ran through girl-friends. Nobody likes to work with you because you're too good at what you do. Makes them look bad. You've got a great arrest-conviction ratio. You know how to handle and document evidence. The Crime Scene Unit loves you, but other detectives in your pre-cinct are jealous and can't wait for you to step on your dick big time, is the way somebody put it."

"Who said that?"

"Can't reveal my sources. Anyway, it comes down to this. You're obsessed with your job, which I think is good. You live it/sleep it/wear it. Solving murders is your life. Nothing else matters. And if you weren't assigned to this case, I'd pull all the strings I could to get you here, because if there's one cop in this city who will find the per-son who killed my friend, it's you. But you pay a price for the way you are. You don't have any friends on the force. Now let's eat. I'm starved."

By the time they finished, it was nearly one in the morning. On the way to the car, Kimberly turned to Blake.

"I know how we can catch the killer."

"So do I, but are you willing to do it?"

"You know I am. What about you?"

"If you can handle it, so can I."

"But we have to make it look real," said Kimberly. "We can't have a police car sitting in front of my apartment all night. Whoever it is has to think I'm alone."

"I can get rid of the police car. But how do I get inside without being seen?"

"There's a back door to my building. You drop me off. Drive around the block to Thompson Street, which is one street over and runs parallel to Sullivan. About midway down the block there's an alley on Thompson that ends just behind my building. There's a narrow courtyard in the back and a wall. You'll have to climb over the wall. It's about four feet high. Think you can do that?"

"Just make sure the back door's unlocked."

They got to the car and Blake looked across the roof at Kimberly.

"You know, some of those women I was with for less than one or two years, actually liked me." With that he smiled, unlocked his door, and got inside.

Kimberly waited until her door was unlocked and was about to open her door when she stopped and looked around. Someone was watching her again. She could feel it. She scanned the street and shadows. Then she looked up and saw an elderly Chinese woman sitting in her window, looking down at the street below. Kimberly smiled and climbed into the car.

"What's the matter?" called Blake.

"Nothing," said Kimberly. "Let's go."

After they pulled away, the killer stepped from an alley next to where the car was parked.

Well, well. Setting a trap, are we? Oh, this is going to be so much fun.

On the way to Sullivan Street, Blake canceled his request for radio car protection. He then dropped Kimberly off in front of her building and drove around the block. Ten minutes later, he was in Kimberly's apartment taking off his jacket.

"I just realized something," said Blake.

"What?"

"I should have gone home to get a change of clothes."

"Yeah, and by the time you got back, I could be the next victim. Why don't you use the bathroom to get ready for bed and I'll make up the sofa."

The thought of another night on the sofa bed brought a pained look to his face. "You know, if you don't mind, I'll just nod out in this recliner." He took off his shoulder holster and draped it over the arm of the chair.

"Suit yourself."

"I would like to use the bathroom, though."

"It's all yours."

While Blake entered the bathroom, Kimberly put a pillow and blanket on the recliner. She then picked up the jacket and was about to hang it up when she stopped. Instead, she put the jacket down and kneeled down next to the chair. She reached out to touch the soft leather of the holster, then the cold steel of the standard issue .38 police special. Her finger ran down the barrel to the sight and then back up along the notched revolver that held the bullets. Carefully, she unclipped the leather strap and lifted the gun from its holster. As she expected, the gun felt heavier than it looked. She let it lie in her hand and closed her grip around the handle, her finger sliding through the opening of the guard, pressing lightly against the smooth flat surface of the trigger.

A shadow fell across her shoulder, and she whirled around holding the gun.

"Take it easy," said Blake, reaching out and taking the gun from her. He put the pistol back in the leather holster and helped Kimberly stand up. "This model doesn't have a safety and the trigger doesn't require much pressure."

"Sorry," said Kimberly. "Have you ever had to use it?"

"Every week," said Blake smiling as he sees the look on Kimberly's face. "At the firing range."

"You know what I mean."

"You mean did I ever have to shoot at the bad guys? Never."

"Never?"

"Never had the opportunity. By the time I get involved, it's usually after the fact. The crime's already been committed. Whenever we apprehend a suspect, we go in with a team, fully armed and equipped. The perp rarely puts up a fight."

"That figures," said Kimberly.

"What?"

"Well, I didn't become a cop because I hated the idea of ever having to use a gun and now I find out that one of our city's most decorated homicide detectives has never had to use one."

"I think it's healthy to be afraid of guns. I wish more people felt like you."

"I didn't say I was afraid of them. I just don't like them. We used to have guns around the house all the time. My brother and father used to hunt deer in the woods behind the house. We lived in the country then. I'd hear the shots from my bedroom window and always hoped the deer would get away."

"You know what, professor?"

"What?"

"You would have made a good cop."

"Did I actually hear you pay me a compliment?"

"A moment of weakness. I must be tired."

"Here's your bed," she said nodding toward the chair. "I doubt if anything will happen tonight, but we might as well be prepared, right?"

"You sure you don't want me in there with you?" He nodded toward her bedroom.

"Detective Blake!"

"I mean, just in case he comes in through the bedroom window."

"Then he'd have to be able to fly. You're in greater danger than I am."

"I am?"

"This guy, or girl, comes in through the front door, remember. No forced entries. I'm pretty sure whoever it is, it's someone I know. They'll probably even knock first. I just want you here and ready when they do."

"Okay."

"I've got to get to bed now," said Kimberly. "I promised to appear on a television program tomorrow morning. Very early tomorrow morning. I've got to leave by six."

"I'm with a celebrity," Blake said with a grin.

"We'll see after tomorrow," said Kimberly.

"What's the topic?"

"Crime coloring books," said Kimberly. "It's filled with pages for kids to color depicting a famous killer, the scene of the crime, and the victim. It's aimed at kids aged four to eight. But it's the first coloring book to sell 150,000 copies to adults."

"You're kidding."

"I'm afraid not," said Kimberly. "I'll be on with the publisher, taking the opposing view, of course."

257

"What time is it on?" asked Blake. "I want to make sure I watch."

"Seven o'clock," said Kimberly. "Why don't you just stay here and sleep in. You can tape it for me."

"Seven a.m."

"Okay. You sleep. I'll set the VCR to tape it," she said.

"You can program a VCR?"

"Yes."

"Will you marry me?"

"Good night." She started toward her bedroom.

"I just want to ask you one more question," said Blake.

"What's that?"

"What would you do if Gloria was here?"

Kimberly let out a sigh and looked deep into his the eyes.

Blake reached out and touched her cheek with the back of his hand. Her skin felt warm and soft. Their eyes locked and he pulled her to him, his lips finding hers in a passionate kiss, until she pulled away.

"What are you doing?" she asked.

"I've wanted to do that from the first moment I saw you," said Blake.

"Don't ever do it again."

"Whatever you ..."

But this time it was Kimberly who cut him off with her lips, her tongue filling his mouth, in a surge of desire that ended when she pushed him away again.

"This is a mistake," she said between breaths. "It won't work."

"So what?" said Blake.

"I might break your heart."

"It's been broken before."

"Goddamn you."

He picked her up and carried her into the bedroom. She felt weightless as he lowered her down on to the king sized bed. It had been so long since she had let herself go like this. She felt an animalistic urge to rip his clothes off. But he beat her to it, by reaching down and tearing her blouse open. It was as if he was trying to recapture some kind of ground on a very primal orgasmic level.

She felt his hands and then his tongue on her breasts as he took her left nipple into his mouth, his lips and teeth sucking, then releasing until the nipple sprang erect. She felt a finger push inside her damp opening as she slid down his chest, pulling open his shirt, buttons flying. She unbuckled his belt and pulled open the front of his pants and saw the bulge trying to break though his underwear.

Blake arched his back as she took him in her mouth. She pinched the nipples on his chest with one hand and cupped his buttocks with the other. He felt as if he was about burst when he rolled over and held her down. He then put his head between her legs as his tongue found the moist lips of her opening. She squirmed and jerked as his tongue probed deeper and deeper, licking, tingling, lapping up her juices until she could hold back no longer.

He rose up and entered her deep and hard, moving in rhythm like the waves on a raging sea. She arched up to take him deeper and he could feel the surge of heat as they rode to the precipice, gripping, squeezing, until they melted together in an orgasmic flow.

They lay in each other's arms, their bodies glistening in the light of the night sky that poured in through the window. Neither one wanted to speak, to break the spell that surrounded the moment.

As it turned out, it was an electrical device that invaded their new found world. Blake's beeper cried out from the darkness. He rolled off the bed and turned off the beeping sound. He didn't even have to look at the number to know who it was. The precinct. Kimberly handed him the portable phone and he punched in the number.

"It's Blake. What's up?"

Kimberly looked at him as his face took on a pensive expression.

"Is she okay? How'd he get in? I'll be there in fifteen minutes. Get as many patrol cars in the area as possible, then alert the transit police."

Blake hung up the phone and looked at Kimberly.

"Luis Alvarez broke into the women's shelter. He cut one of the women pretty bad when she tried to stop him."

"What about Maria?"

"She wasn't hurt. But she's pretty shaken up. We're going to cordon off the area. He might still be around. Are you gonna be okay?"

"Maybe I should go with you."

259

"No," said Blake as he pulled on his pants and shirt. He started to button his shirt and realized the buttons had been ripped off. So he just pulled it together and stuffed the tail in his pants.

Kimberly followed him into the living room, where he strapped on his shoulder holster and grabbed his sport coat. When he got to the door he wrote something down on a piece of paper and handed it to Kimberly.

"My beeper number. Double lock the door and get some sleep."

"Sleep. What's that?"

"I'll have a patrol car re-assigned in front of your building, just in case."

"You better get going," she said.

He started for the door, stopped, turned and kissed her softly on the mouth. "I'll be back as soon as I can. Remember. You open the door for nobody but me."

"Be careful," she said.

After Blake left, Kimberly double-locked the door and then wedged a chair under the door knob. She thought about Maria Alvarez. The poor girl. As bad as Kimberly's luck had been with men, at least none had tried to kill her. She thought about what had happened with Blake. It was a moment of weakness for both of them. They were two horny adults. That's all. No need to make more of it than what it was. Yet, it was pretty damned good.

Kimberly looked at the clock. It was after two in the morning. She had to be at the TV studio no later than 6:45, even though she wasn't scheduled to go on until the second segment. She had to get some sleep. But how? The Jacuzzi. She went into her bathroom and turned on the faucets. The tub began filling when the telephone rang.

She let the water run as she walked into the bedroom and picked up the phone. "Hello." No answer. "Is anybody there?" She heard the click as someone hung up.

A tremor ran down Kimberly's spine. The Jacuzzi was no longer the place she wanted to be right now, so she returned to the bathroom and turned off the water. She then went to the front window and looked out. The street looked empty. No one was walking. And there was no sign of a patrol car. She made sure the window was locked and then re-checked all her other windows as well.

At 2:30 a.m, even Soho was winding down. Many of the streets that had been thriving and full of people just two hours earlier were now nearly deserted. A wino looking for a place to crash for the night without being disturbed thought he heard the glass breaking on the rear window of Dee Porter's Interior Design Showroom. He hoped whoever was breaking in wouldn't set off an alarm because then the street would be flooded with cops and he'd never get any sleep.

The door to the showroom opened silently and the intruder entered.

The main room was sectioned off into different sample rooms designed in a variety of interiors. Most of the rooms were dark as the visitor moved silently among the living rooms and kitchens. At the front end were the bedrooms. There it was. The crown jewel in the early Colonial bedroom. A four-poster canopied bed.

The mattress creaked under the weight of the body. Outside on the quiet street, the wino thought he heard someone moaning. Now what? He got up and walked across the street. He put his ear to a window of the decorator's building and listened.

Inside, the bed was creaking loudly now as the sounds of masturbation reached a frenzy, then a climax. The killer sat up and looked around the room. The wino moved away from the window. He didn't need this. He walked on down the street. He didn't see the match being lit and the plush velvet fabric going up in flames.

CHAPTER THIRTY

Blake was speeding up the nearly empty West Side Highway when he called the precinct to have a radio car reassigned to Kimberly's building.

"Sorry, Detective," said the voice on the car speaker-phone. "All available units have been dispatched to assist Manhattan North, at your request I might add. Didn't you order the area around some women's shelter cordoned off?"

"Yes," said Blake, hitting the dash board with his fist. "As soon as one becomes available, send it to Sullivan Street."

"Whatever you say Detective."

Blake hung up the radio phone and pressed down on the gas. He left the Westside Drive at 96th Street and sped through the lights of Broadway, Columbus and Amsterdam until he reached Central Park West. As he drove by, he noticed two patrol cars were parked at each intersection, while others drove slowly up and down the side streets and main avenues.

Even at this late hour, Broadway was busy, as were Columbus and Amsterdam Avenues.

We're never going to find him, thought Blake as he neared the shelter. There are too many places to hide.

Back in the Village, Kimberly sat in her living room, looking out the window, wondering why it was taking so long for a radio car to arrive. Sullivan Street was nearly deserted. A person here and there, walking home, or going somewhere else. Still, every time she heard footsteps, or saw someone walk under a street lamp, she couldn't stop thinking that it was Joan and Pat's killer, coming to eliminate the final connection. But the connection to what? Or to whom? Kimberly looked at her watch. Blake had only left a few minutes ago yet it seemed like hours. What was she so worried about? The door was double-locked. Where was the police car? He had said it would only take a couple of minutes. Maybe she should call and check. She was reaching for the phone when it rang. She grabbed the receiver.

"Hello."

No response.

"Hellooo."

Still nothing. Kimberly listened quietly. She could barely hear it, but the sound was unmistakable. It was the sound of somebody breathing.

"Who's there?"

She then heard a "click" as the line disconnected. She looked at her caller I.D. box but the read-out said "Number Blocked."

Who would be calling her at this hour?

Blake pulled up in front of the shelter and quickly got out of his car. There were a half dozen blue-and-whites on the scene and a curious crowd of local residents and shopkeepers had gathered on the sidewalk near the entrance to the shelter. Blake made his way through the hovering crowd, wondering what he would find, when he saw the body lying on the sidewalk, covered with a black canvas.

A uniformed officer in his early 20s, with short, blond hair and a worried face, saw Blake pushing his way through to the body and intervened.

"Excuse me, sir," said Patrolman Williams, as Blake slipped his shield holder into his jacket pocket.

"Blake, Homicide. What happened?"

263

"Ah, well, ah," the patrolman stammered.

"Who's this?" Blake asked, nodding to the body.

"Luis Alvarez."

"Alvarez? You got him?"

"Ah, we, ah didn't exactly get him."

Blake looked alarmed as he kneeled down next to the still covered body. He lifted the canvas cover and looked at the body of Luis Alvarez covered with blood. Enough of the face was showing along with a pair of lifeless eyes bulging in an expression of surprise and anger. It was then that Blake noticed what Alvarez was wearing. A nun's habit. Blake dropped the cover and stood up. That was when he looked over toward the entrance of the shelter and saw Maria Alvarez talking to a policewoman. Maria was wearing handcuffs.

"What the hell happened here?" asked Blake.

"The place was crawling with police officers," said Patrolman Williams. "We were in cars, in the park, with dogs, we must of had officers from ten precincts searching for that sonofabitch. We tried to keep all the women from the shelter inside, but we thought maybe Mrs. Alvarez could help us spot her husband. We were leading her to one of the cars when this nun walks up. We thought she was with the shelter or something, ya know. These places always have nuns around. But Mrs. Alvarez is the only one who looks at the nun's face and realizes it's her husband.

"But get this. She doesn't scream out or anything. She waits for the nun to get close and whoosh. She pulls out a knife and lunges at the sister of mercy. I was about ten feet away and pulled my gun. I was ready to shoot when the nun's habit fell off and there was this short Latino man with a knife sticking out where his dick used to be. By the time we pulled her away, Mrs. Alvarez had cut off his nuts and gutted him like a fish out of water."

Blake shook his head and walked over to the shelter.

"Take off those cuffs," he said to the policewoman talking to Mrs. Alvarez.

"Who are you?" asked the policewoman, whose name tag read Officer Moriarty.

"Detective Blake. I'll take over from here."

"Be my guest," snarled the policewoman, as she unlocked the handcuffs.

Maria Alvarez looked at Blake with an expression of confusion on her face.

"Aren't you going to arrest me?"

"I'm afraid I have to, but I don't have to make you wear handcuffs unless you pose a threat. Are you going to give me any trouble?"

"No."

"Good. I understand you have children."

"*Si.* They're staying with my mother."

"Okay. We're going to have to take you in and start the process. Do you have a lawyer? Did anyone read you your Miranda rights?"

"Yes. The woman."

"I'll call the D.A.'s office so someone can meet us at Manhattan North. As far as I'm concerned, Mrs. Alvarez, you were acting in self defense. That's going to be my report. Now, I have to ask you some questions about your husband because he's a possible suspect in two other homicides."

"You mean Doctor Walsh?"

"That's one of them. You told Dr. Stone that your husband might try to find you through her."

"Ah, *si,* I remember. But he didn't."

"I'm sorry. What do you mean?"

"He didn't find out where I was through Dr. Walsh."

"How do you know?"

"A girlfriend told me. It was a stupid thing to do, but I told her where I was. Luis threatened her and she told him I was here. I don't think he ever talked to Dr. Walsh."

"Would you excuse me?"

Blake walked over to the policewoman.

"I was going to take Mrs. Alvarez in and start the process. But something's come up. Can I give her back to you?"

"I don't suppose you want me to put the cuffs back on, though, do you?"

"I don't think that's going to be necessary. The guy was going to kill her. She did us all a favor. Take care of her for me, okay, Moriarty? I'll owe you one."

"Shit. You owe me two. You already spoiled my Saturday night."

"Thanks."

Blake walked to his car and got inside. He took out his notebook, crossed another name off his short list of suspects, then let out a deep sigh. He stared at the remaining names on the page of his notebook. None of the people on the list had given him a good alibi for the time of Joan's murder. The name now at the top of the list was Bill Gardner. He checked Gardner's address. He could cut through the park at 96th Street and be at Gardner's building in less than five minutes.

As he started to pull away, Blake saw Officer Moriarty leading Maria Alvarez to a blue-and-white patrol car. Maria turned as he drove past and smiled at him.

Blake thought back to his interview with Gardner. There was something about the guy that didn't seem quite right. As far as Blake was concerned, there were only two truly powerful motives for murder. Love and money. What if Gardner's jealousy had driven him to kill Joan because she was pregnant by another man, and to kill Pat Hurly because she and Joan had been lovers?

The detective was formulating in his mind what he would say to Gardner when his beeper went off. He looked at the message. It read Kimberly. Urgent. Please call.

CHAPTER THIRTY-ONE

Kimberly sat in the dark, staring at the phone as if it was a snake preparing to strike. It had rung eight times since Blake had left, and now that she had beeped him, she prayed this ninth ring would be his.

It wasn't. Kimberly lifted the receiver to her ear, hoping against hope to hear Blake's droll, gravely voice. Instead she heard the sound of silence, the sound of nothing, not even breathing, a black hole of anti-sound sucking all audible life into a deep abyss. She started to hang up when she heard the beep of call waiting. She immediately disconnected the first line and connected with the second.

"Hello."

Again, nothing. Whoever was calling had now effectively tied up her call waiting line which meant even if Blake was trying to call, he couldn't get through.

Blake tried Kimberly's number again. Still busy. He was sitting out in front of Gardner's building trying to decide what to do. He called the precinct and again requested the next available patrol car go to Sullivan Street. The dispatcher said it might take a few minutes. Then Blake considered the worst possible scenario. The killer was taking the bait. Kimberly was alone in her apartment. And he was at least 15 minutes away. He pounded the steering wheel and threw the car in gear, burning rubber away from the curb.

Let's not panic here, thought Kimberly. Even though Blake can't call, he must have received your beep. He's probably on his way. The plan she and Blake had contrived to catch the killer might still work. But what if the killer didn't come? Just because she'd gotten a bunch of nuisance calls, didn't mean someone was on their way over to kill her. Besides, didn't Blake leave to apprehend Luis Alvarez? He may have confessed already. Or maybe he's on his way here.

Kimberly turned off the lights in her living room and moved to the window. She looked down at the street below. No one was there. She let out a sigh, then the intercom buzzed, exploding the silence of the apartment. Kimberly leaped off the sofa and jolted up right. Her hands were shaking. Maybe it's Blake. Calm down, now. Take a breath, let it out. Another one. She had to force her feet to move across the room to push the button on the intercom speaker.

"Who's there?"

Silence, again. She went to the window and looked out but from this angle she could not see the front entrance. Then she heard the faint sound of the buzzer from another apartment. Someone else in the building had buzzed the person in. Maybe the person had hit her buzzer by mistake. Then again, maybe the intruder had hit all the buzzers until someone complied. She knew this was a common trick among apartment building invaders.

A cold chill rippled up her wrists to her neck. The killer was in the building. She knew it. She had never felt such fear. She had to stop the involuntary shaking of her right knee. She pressed her body against a wall of the living room. Oh God! Please, let me get through this. She thought about the self-defense course she was taking. Then she remembered how poorly she had done at her last class. She felt so vulnerable, like a frightened little girl.

She could hear footsteps in the hallway outside her door. If only she had a gun. Suddenly, her fear of firearms seemed ridiculous. If Joan had had protection, she might be alive right now.

A knock. Did someone actually knock? Then she heard it. Her name.

"Kimberly?"

The voice. A familiar voice. But then Kimberly knew it would be. She moved toward the door. An old feeling was coming up. A feeling from childhood whenever she found herself alone in her home with her brother. It was a feeling of numbness, a numbness that pushed the cold tremors or terror so deep within her that she no longer felt any fear at all.

"Kimberly, I need to see you," the voice whispered.

The word "need" echoed in her mind. Need? He needs me? Wasn't that what her brother used to say? He needed to feel her, to kiss her, to touch her, to be touched by her. Kimberly put her hand on the door and pressed her palm into it.

"Please let me in," pleaded the voice.

She watched as her hand slid down the door to the first deadbolt and then slid it unlocked. The hand then twisted open the second lock with a loud "clunk." And finally both hands grabbed the chair that she had wedged under the door knob and pulled it away. This must be what an out-of-body experience feels like thought Kimberly as she watched her hand turn the knob and pull open the door. It was as if her mind had left her body and she was watching from above. Come on Blake. Be on your way. Be here soon.

There in the doorway he stood, with a crooked smile and a day's stubble of beard on his face. Bill Gardner, smelling of old sweat and alcohol. His tie was stained with food spots and his suit was wrinkled in unusual places. It was obvious that he had been sleeping in it. There was a demonic expression on his face, and the whites of his eyes were crimson, making his dark eyes even darker.

"Aren't you going to invite me in?" asked Bill Gardner.

Kimberly watched as she saw herself stand back to let him enter her apartment.

She closed the door behind him and watched as he looked around the living room. He started to lean to the left and then steadied himself.

"Whoa," he said, smiling.

"What do you want?" Kimberly heard herself ask.

"Oh Kimberly," said Bill. "Can I sit down?"

Before she could answer, Bill stumbled toward a sofa, turned and settled onto the couch.

"That's better," he continued. "You have anything to drink?"

"How about some coffee?"

"I was thinking more like vodka."

Kimberly thought for a second and then came to the conclusion that if he was here to kill her, she might have a better chance if he was weaker from more alcohol. She went to the kitchen and took down an unopened bottle of vodka, broke the seal, and poured him a full glass.

She returned to the living room and found Bill standing next to the fireplace, looking at pictures of Kimberly and Joan sitting on the mantel.

"There's my Joannie," he said.

Kimberly handed him the vodka and he took a long drink.

"Let's have a drink to Joannie." He raised his glass and took a long swig and turned toward Kimberly.

"She loved you more than anyone," he said. "Did you know that?"

"She loved you too, Bill."

"Did she? Did she really? I thought she did. I thought I'd finally met someone who could fill that big hole in my life. It hasn't been easy, you know. Raising a son alone. You know that before I met Joan, it had been nearly four years since I'd been with a woman. Four years without getting laid. Without getting touched. Without a warm body beside me. Can you imagine what that's like?"

Kimberly took a seat next to the sofa and wondered if she was supposed to answer that question. Before she could, Gardner went on.

"Something's happening to me Kimberly. I think I'm losing my mind."

"It's called mourning, Bill. You're depressed. The woman you loved is dead. And I do know how that feels."

"No. It's more than that."

"What then?"

"I'm not sure. I'm not a paranoid kinda guy. I'm not even afraid of that detective. What's his name?"

"Blake."

270

"Yeah. So what if he thinks I killed Joan. I know I didn't. And there's no way he can prove otherwise."

"So what's the problem?" asked Kimberly.

"It's a feeling I get. That somebody's watching me. Following me. You know what I'm talking about?"

"I'm not sure."

"No matter where I am. I can feel these eyes on me. I can't even sleep anymore."

"Maybe it's Joan."

"What?"

"Maybe it's guilt you're feeling, Bill."

"Guilt? Guilt about what?"

"What really happened?"

"Happened?"

"Between you and Joan? Did it get out of hand? Did the sex get too rough?"

"What are you talking about?"

"You didn't mean to kill her, did you? It was just an accident."

"What the hell?"

"But why Pat Hurly? Why did you kill her?"

"Kimberly, what are saying?"

"I know. You must think I'm pretty stupid saying these things, when you've come here to kill me, but I'd just like to know the truth. Don't I deserve that?"

"Kill you? I didn't come here to kill you."

Just then a police siren wailed in the distance. Gardner looked at the open window as the sound of the siren got louder.

"The police. Did you call the police?"

"My, my" said Kimberly. "You have gotten paranoid."

"This is some kind of trap. You're wearing a wire."

Bill reached out and tried to tear Kimberly's bathrobe, but she backed away. A boiling rage was building inside him.

"You bitch." He glanced at the window and saw the flashing lights reflecting off the glass. "You set me up."

"Give it up, Bill."

"You're too much. And to think, I thought you and I could, you know, have something."

"Not in this lifetime."

Gardner made it to the front door and whirled around.

"I'll be back," said Bill, looking past Kimberly and at the window. "And you will be sorry."

With that he dashed out the door and Kimberly slumped down on her sofa, and buried her face in a throw pillow. Then it occurred to her that the siren was getting fainter again. She went to the window and looked down the street to see the tail lights of an ambulance disappearing in the distance. While she watched the ambulance fade from sight, she looked down and saw another car pull up in front of her building. The door opened and Blake stepped out. She let out a deep sigh.

Bill Gardner waited in the shadows until the detective had entered the building. Then looking in both directions, he walked off in the shadows. He never did trust that Stone bitch. What was he thinking about? Just because Joan had strong feelings for both of them, did he really expect the ice-queen, Kimberly Stone, to let him into her bed? No wonder she lived alone. He must be really losing it. And now the bitch had tried to trap him. She was going to get hers. Nobody fucks with Bill Gardner like that.

Kimberly was looking through the peephole when she saw Blake step out of the elevator. She opened the door of her apartment and ran to him.

"Kimberly," he said holding her. She was shaking in his arms. "What is it?"

"He was here."

"Who?"

"Gardner. He heard a siren and ran off just as you pulled up."

"I'll put out an all-points."

"Don't leave me alone again tonight," she said.

"I won't."

As they walked back to the apartment he told her about Maria and Luis Alvarez. She closed and locked the door behind them and he called the precinct to request a city-wide bulletin to apprehend Bill Gardner. After he hung up the phone, Kimberly took his hand and led him back to her bedroom, where they fell asleep in each other's arms.

Bill Gardner stumbled along Bleecker Street and hailed a cab. He looked at his watch. It was nearly three a.m. But he was thirsty, and lonely. What was still open? There was a new S&M bar on West Street in the meat-packing district. He gave the taxi driver directions and before he knew it, he was standing in front of a large black building with a huge letter "V" painted on the side. Over the red entrance door was the name of the place. The Vault. A doorman collected the twenty-dollar entrance fee and Bill stepped inside.

The place was packed with an assortment of people. There was the obvious black leather crowd, with men outnumbering women almost five to one. Bill made his way to the bar and ordered a vodka tonic, light on the tonic. He could feel several pairs of eyes on him as he waited for the drink. Maybe this wasn't such a good idea. The blaring heavy metal music was deafening, and the dance floor was filled with body slammers and headbangers. Bill felt immediately old when he realized the average age in this place was twenty something.

Maybe he should go over to the Anvil, which was more his speed. He looked at the people around him and virtually everyone had some part of their body pierced with nipple rings, nose, and lip rings. Arms and elbows clanged with metal rubbing metal. He longed for the old fashioned leather collars and masks, a cat-o-nine tails, a little hot wax.

He finished his drink quickly and was about to leave when she sat down next to him and took out a cigarette. She was tall, almost as tall as Bill, and wore a bright red dress. She looked almost as out of place as Bill felt, and then she held out her cigarette to be lit and he did the honors. Maybe he'd have another drink here after all.

The alarm woke Kimberly at six a.m. Sunday morning and she now regretted making the commitment to do the interview. But it should all be over by 8 a.m. She could come home and get back into bed and sleep as long as she wanted.

At six-thirty, Blake drove her to the *Sunday in New York* studios on East Sixty-seventh Street and Third Avenue.

She wasn't wearing any makeup; the studio had told her their people would take care of that prior to the segment. Even though she still looked attractive, Kimberly felt a little shy in front of Blake. She couldn't remember the last time she'd let anyone see her in such an unprotected state.

"Are you going to be okay?" asked Blake.

"I'll be fine. Are you going to stay and watch?"

"I can't," said Blake.

"What are you going to do?"

"Pick up Bill Gardner."

"Be careful," she said, then kissed him and got out of the car.

"Give 'em hell in there."

"Right, thanks."

Kimberly watched as Blake drove away and then took in a deep breath before entering the studio. Although she felt a little nervous about being on television and in the homes of hundreds of thousands of New Yorkers, she was confident about what she had to say against coloring books that glamorized crime. She just hoped she'd be able to concentrate with everything else going on. She'd much rather be with Blake when he arrested Gardner, just to see the bastard hauled off in handcuffs.

As soon as she stepped inside, a producer's assistant greeted her and led to her to the green room where guests wait to go on. This particular room had absolutely no green in it anywhere, but it was filled with over-sized chairs, a big-screen television and a table covered with pastries, bagels, croissants, muffins and fresh fruit. There were two large coffee urns, along with juice and bottled water.

"Shouldn't I go to make-up first?" asked Kimberly.

"Someone will come and get you about ten minutes before you go on. They'll take care of all that stuff. Just relax and help yourself to the coffee and Danish," said the assistant, who looked like she was still in college.

As soon as she left, Kimberly went directly to the coffee urn and poured a cup. She couldn't stop thinking about Blake. If Gardner was the killer, could he be in danger? He wouldn't go there alone, would he? He'd call for backup if he thought there was chance he'd be in danger. Wouldn't he do that? This *is* what he does for a living you know.

When Blake arrived at Bill Gardner's co-op, he told the doorman not to let Gardner know he was there. He wanted to surprise him. Blake took the elevator to Gardner's floor and then knocked on the door to his apartment. He knew he might be taking a chance here, confronting a possible killer alone, but didn't Kimberly do exactly that the night before? Why would she let him into her apartment? Why was he here now without assistance? What was he trying to prove, and to whom?

The precinct had issued the all-points bulletin and had even dispatched a patrol unit to Gardner's office and address last night. But without a warrant to enter, that was all they could do. The officers who responded reported no one answered the door at either address. He had to be somewhere, and Blake had a feeling that this was where he'd be. He pushed the buzzer on the heavy door.

"Mr. Gardner. It's Detective Blake. I just want to talk."

No answer.

Blake pressed his ear to the door, trying to hear any movement. That's when he realized the door was not locked. When he pushed against it, the door opened and he stepped into the foyer of the dark apartment. He had his gun out and in a firing stance, scanning the room over the tip of the barrel.

"Mr. Gardner? Hello. Is anybody home?"

Blake came to a light switch and turned it on as he stepped into the living room.

"Mr. Gardner?"

Blake stopped when he saw Gardner lying on a leather sofa, his lifeless eyes staring at the ceiling. Moving closer, his gun still at the ready, he saw that Gardner was naked except for one tiny object inserted into his left ear. A white and gold plastic daisy.

CHAPTER THIRTY-TWO

"Count backwards from ten so the sound man can check your level, Dr. Stone," said the stage director.

Kimberly counted backwards.

"That's fine. Now, just stay here. If you get up, your microphone will pull out."

She tried to find a comfortable position as the round-faced anchor of *Sunday in New York* strode out onto the set.

"Professor Stone," said a handsome man with thinning white hair combed straight back as he slid into a chair next to Kimberly. "Roger Homans."

"Pleased to meet you," said Kimberly.

"I want to tell you how grateful we are you agreed to appear on the show," said Homans. Kimberly could feel Homan's eyes roving over her body.

"My pleasure," said Kimberly, remembering the host's reputation as a lady's man.

"If I'd known how attractive you are, I would have asked you sooner," said Homans. Kimberly felt herself blushing through the thick pancake make-up.

Just then Gordon Henry Thomas, the publisher of the *Crime Coloring Book*, arrived and took a seat on the other side of Homans, facing Kimberly. Thomas was a short, round man in his late fifties, nearly bald, with a bushy mustache.

"Mr. Thomas," said Homans. "Glad you could join us."

Thomas counted backward for the sound engineers and the stage manager gave the signal. "On in ten."

"Please stand by," said a voice off-stage. Suddenly hot blinding lights came on and Kimberly had to squint to adjust to the light.

"Good morning, New York," said Homans, reading from a Tele-PrompTer over the camera.

"Fifteen million Americans are robbed, assaulted, raped, or murdered each year," said Homans. "And millions more—relatives, friends of the victims—are also hurt by crime. One of my guests, Dr. Kimberly Stone, a professor of criminology at Ferguson College in New Jersey, has been researching crime for ten years. She is especially opposed to something our other guest, Gordon Henry Thomas, has just published ... a coloring book that depicts famous crimes throughout history.

"Besides publishing coloring books, Thomas has a toy-gun company, which has also drawn some criticism. But nothing has raised the public's ire as much as this coloring book. Professor Stone, what is it about this coloring book that is so harmful, especially to our children?"

Kimberly looked at Homans and Thomas instead of the camera.

"First of all," said Kimberly, "it makes folk heroes out of people who are deranged, deviant, and violent. It glamorizes crime, and studies have shown that children are extremely susceptible to this sort of thing. It tells them that murder is all right. It gives them permission to rape, to rob, to kill."

Homans took in a breath and looked at the publisher.

"Care to respond?"

"What can I say? Dr. Stone has her opinion. I have mine. As far as I know, there's never been any definitive study to support her claims."

"Actually, a criminologist in England studied something quite similar over a ten-year period," said Kimberly. "In fact, I believe a coloring book was even used. They found that children exposed to violent images in coloring books were more likely to see violent crimes as acceptable forms of behavior."

"Very interesting," said Homans.

"Well," said Thomas, "even so, our coloring books are designed to show children how terrible crime is. Besides, don't all those super-hero comic books depict violent crime as well?"

"There's a big difference between those comic books and your coloring book," said Kimberly. "While I don't advocate those comic books either, at least they show good defeating evil. Your books show only the evil. They glorify the criminal."

"Who's in your coloring books, anyway?" said Homans.

"Lizzy Borden, Richard Speck, John Wilkes Booth ..."

"I notice you're only giving the names of the criminals," said Kimberly. "What about the victims?"

"A coloring book of victims wouldn't sell very well, Dr. Stone," said Thomas. "This is what the people want. I can't control that."

"Actually, you're probably the only one who can," said Kimberly. "Unfortunately, all you seem to care about is how many coloring books you can sell."

"I have a responsibility to my business, my investors," countered Thomas.

"You also have a responsibility to society not to promote and provoke the kind of pain, suffering, and victimization your coloring books glorify," said Kimberly.

"I don't have to listen to this," snapped Thomas.

"I'm afraid you do," said Kimberly. "This is, after all, a free country. Whether you do anything about what I say, that's another matter. I have the feeling that the greed in your heart far outweighs any compassion."

"I'm afraid we're going to have to do a commercial," said Homans. "Stay put. We'll be right back."

As soon as the lights in the studio dimmed, Thomas stood up and removed his microphone. "The hell we will," he said and stormed off the set. Homans winked at Kimberly.

"Great stuff," he said, patting her knee.

Kimberly unhooked her microphone and started to stand up.

"Oh, don't go," said Homans. "We still have two minutes left in the segment."

"Run another commercial," said Kimberly. "Besides, what fun would it be without Thomas to malign?"

Blake was still at Bill Gardner's apartment waiting for the medical examiner and Crime Scene Unit to arrive when he got the beep. It was another detective from his office who was assigned to assist him on the Joan Walsh/Pat Hurly homicides. He called the number.

"This might not have any bearing on your case," explained Detective Leo Burns, "but I recognized the address from your Q and A reports. Arson Squad just took a call to inspect a suspicious blaze in Soho at a Dee Porter's Design Studio."

"When?"

"Just now. Thought you might like to get there before the fire boys cart off all the good stuff."

"Thanks," said Blake, looking over at Gardner's body. There wasn't anything else for him to do here. The forensics team would collect any prints or fibers. Besides, his primary suspect was now in the victim category.

After leaving the set of *Sunday in New York* and thanking the producer for giving her a chance to present her views on the crime coloring book controversy, Kimberly suddenly felt hungry. She thought about all the pastries and bagels she didn't eat in the green room. Was it poor form to go back and grab a bite? Probably. She'd stop at a coffee shop on Sullivan Street.

She walked out the front door into the bright morning sun. She covered her eyes to look for a taxi. Nothing on Sixty-seventh, so she turned and was about to head toward Second Avenue when she bumped into someone on the sidewalk. The glare of the sun was in her eyes, so she couldn't see the face of the person standing in front of her as he said, "Professor Stone, I thought you were terrific in there."

Kimberly stepped to the side and into the shade as she focused on the familiar but out-of-place voice.

"George?"

The figure stepped into the shade with her, and Kimberly looked into the smiling face of her handsome carpenter. "You gave that publisher holy hell."

"George," said Kimberly. "What are you doing here?"

"I heard you were going to be on the show so I thought I'd come down and watch. You know. Give you a little cheering on."

"You heard? How?"

"I think I saw it on a commercial or something. They mentioned your name. And I said, wow, I know her."

"That was sweet, George. What did you think?"

"A knockout in the first round."

"Yeah," said Kimberly. "I guess it was pretty one-sided."

"Hey, you want to get a cup of coffee or something?" said George.

Kimberly gave George a warm smile. Maybe he could hear her stomach growling. She was tempted to take him up on the offer, but something stopped her. It didn't feel right. Besides, it might send the wrong message.

"Thanks, George, but I really should get home," she said. "I did-n't get much sleep last night and I'm really beat."

She saw the look of disappointment wash over his face, and it made her feel sorry for him.

"I'm flattered you asked," said Kimberly.

"Can I give you a ride, then," asked George. "My jeep's right over there."

"That's not necessary."

"It's not a problem. I gotta stop by your place anyway. I left one of my tools there."

"Oh," said Kimberly, "well, in that case. Sure. I'd love a ride."

Since the FDR was still under construction with only one lane open to traffic, Blake took Second Avenue downtown to Dee Porter's Design studio. On his way there, he wondered whether he was wasting his time. What could he possibly learn from a torched showroom? What was he looking for? But when he finally arrived, he immediately knew he'd made the right choice.

The street in front of Dee Porter's studio was blocked off with fire trucks and police barriers. Blake pulled over and parked his car.

He walked the rest of the way to what was left of the Dee Porter Design Showroom. He saw a fire detective giving orders so he approached him first.

"Detective Blake, NYPD Homicide. What's the story?"

"Definitely looks like arson," answered the fire detective.

Blake looked inside the broken front window and saw that the showroom was still smoldering as firemen put out the last remaining flames.

"But we didn't report any homicide," said the fire detective. "Far as we can tell, the place was empty. You mind telling me what you're doing here, Detective?"

"I was hoping to question the owner regarding a couple of homicides I'm investigating," said Blake.

"She's on her way here now. She was out on Fire Island when we reached her. Should be here any minute."

"You mind if I take a look?" asked Blake.

"Help yourself," said the fire detective.

Blake walked into the wreckage of smoldering sofas and burned furniture. Not only was the place destroyed, but someone had smashed several chairs, torn some fabric, and spray-painted obscenities on the walls. Somebody was very angry at Dee Porter. He walked among the ruins, holding a handkerchief over his nose, which did little to blot out the stench of smoldering ash. He made his way to what was left of the four-poster bed and then he spotted something lying on the floor next to the charred headboard.

Blake knelt down and used his handkerchief to pick it up. As he rose, he saw a limousine pull up in front of the showroom. Out climbed Dee Porter, dressed in a purple chamois work-shirt and jeans.

She looked at her carnage and shook her head. She was about to enter when Blake stepped through the door.

"Detective Blake. What are you doing here?"

"Morning, Ms. Porter. I have a few more questions, if you don't mind?"

"Can't it wait?" she said. "As you can see, I have a slight problem to deal with."

"Well," said Blake, "I think your problem may be connected to the deaths of Joan Walsh, Pat Hurly, and now a Bill Gardner. In fact, until now, I was starting to suspect you might have had something to do with their murders, at least until I found this. It was left on the floor next to what used to be a four-poster bed."

Blake opened his handkerchief and Dee looked down. It was a yellow plastic daisy, just like the ones found on Joan Walsh, Pat Hurly and Bill Gardner.

All color seemed to drain from Dee Porter's face. A darkness shadowed the pain in her eyes.

"I'll kill him," said Dee Porter, trembling.

"You know who left this?"

Dee Porter looked at Blake with tears and anger in her eyes.

"Know? Goddamn right I know, the little prick. He's gone too far this time. I'm gonna rip his nuts off."

CHAPTER THIRTY-THREE

George parked his black Jeep Wrangler across the street from Kimberly's apartment building. Normally he would never have found a legal parking place, but this was Sunday morning and there were plenty of spots.

On the ride over, he had proudly recapped, in detail, her performance. By the time they pulled up in front of her building, Kimberly was feeling slightly ashamed of her coldness toward him.

"While you're looking for your tool," she said, climbing out of the Jeep, "I'm going to put on some coffee. Would you like some?"

A wide smile formed on George's face. "That would be great," he said, as he hauled his large toolbox from the rear of the Jeep.

"What do you need that for?" asked Kimberly.

"This?" said George, holding up his red tool box. "I don't know. I guess I feel kind of naked without it," he grinned.

Kimberly raised her eyebrow. Okay, she thought. Take it easy. He's just flirting with you. Don't snap the poor kid's head off. Look at him. He's beaming just because you invited him in to have coffee with you. It was an innocent comment. His tool box is probably like his security blanket. You're just feeling a little giddy from your romp with Blake. And now you have this gorgeous man in awe of you because you appeared on television. Let's not complicate things, now. With Blake, things are already tense enough.

As she approached the lobby, she could see George's reflection in the glass of the front door. She did a quick scan over his sturdy build, the wide chest, and muscles rippling over his forearm. She felt like a school girl. And it was all because of Blake. He had opened her up, somehow.

She used to shudder inside when some men looked at her. Especially handsome men, like her brother. She was sure they only wanted one thing. To force her to submit. It was a fear she wore like an old coat. But now, as she watched George walk up behind her, she realized the fear was gone. And it was all because she had let it happen with Alan Blake, and it was okay. It was better than okay. It was great.

"Morning professor," said Hal as he opened the lobby door.

"Morning, Hal," said Kimberly. "You know George, my carpenter."

"Sure," said Hal.

"How's it goin?" said George, nodding to Hal.

"Can't complain," said Hal.

"What are you doing here?" asked Kimberly. "You're not supposed to come on until four."

"Well, I got the landlord to switch my hours. Just for today. It's my mother's birthday and I'm taking her out to dinner."

"That's nice, Hal," said Kimberly, patting him on the shoulder.

"So you have some more work to do?" Hal asked George. "I thought he was finished."

"He is Hal. He's just picking up some tools."

"Ah," said Hal, nodding as they entered the lobby.

In the elevator Kimberly shook her head, "Hal is such a gossip. Has to know everyone's business."

"Really," said George.

Kimberly unlocked the door to her apartment and let them inside.

"I'll put on the coffee," said Kimberly.

"Okay," said George. "I'll start looking for that screwdriver. It's got a special handle. I think I was using it on your bookcases so I'll just look in here if you don't mind."

"Take your time," said Kimberly. "You know, I think you did a terrific job, George, especially with the platform bed. In fact, I'd like to give you a little extra."

"That's not necessary," said George, smiling.

"I insist. Exceptional work should be rewarded," said Kimberly. "Besides, I just remembered. Joan told me how she gave you a, what did she call it, a special tip for the work you did at her place."

"A special tip? Is that what Joan told you?" said George. "What else did Joan tell you?"

"That's all, except that you really did good work. George. You're blushing. You're a great carpenter. That's nothing to be embarrassed about."

Kimberly was reaching for her purse when she saw it. A jolt of electricity ran down Kimberly's arm and bile began rising in her throat. Why hadn't she noticed it before? There it was. Right on the side of the red toolbox. Suddenly, she felt faint and leaned against the wall for support. When she looked up again, she saw George was staring at her.

"Are you all right?" he asked.

"I ... I'm fine," said Kimberly, only she wasn't looking at George when she said it. She was staring at his toolbox and the small plastic daisy glued to the side. She quickly shifted her attention to George, but it was already too late. The awareness was instantaneous. He could see the glimmer of terror in her eyes and knew she had seen the daisy and understood what it meant.

Blake finally found a pay phone that worked and punched in Kimberly's number. His cell phone battery had discharged and he had neglected to recharge it in all the activity of the past few days. Her phone rang and rang until the machine picked up. He hung up the phone and started to leave but then turned and punched in her number again. The machine answered again, but this time the line went dead. Blake looked at the phone, slammed the receiver into the hook, and ran for his car.

George Stewhalf held the disconnected phone line in his hand. He then picked up the answering machine and threw it against the wall, smashing it into a dozen pieces.

"She gave me a special tip, all right," snarled George in a voice now filled with rage.

"Oh, God," thought Kimberly as she started to walk backward toward the kitchen.

George kneeled down and opened the top of his red metal tool-box.

"She said I was the first real man she'd had in over a year."

He reached inside and pulled out a claw hammer.

"You must be in real tight with the police there, professor," said George. "To know about the daisy and all. They kept it out of the newspapers and TV stories. They do that sometimes to make sure they get the right killer. I seen that on *America's Most Wanted.*"

Kimberly made it into the kitchen and looked around. She started pulling open drawers until she found the knives.

"I wish I didn't have to do this," said George from the other room. "I hope you understand that. But I can't take any chances. You were Joannie's best friend. She might have told you. She might have told that woman Pat. Even her boyfriend, Bill. I could never be sure. It's all Joan's fault, you know. None of this ever had to happen. She could have had an abortion. I told her I'd even help. But no. She wanted to keep it. I couldn't let her do that. I mean, my God. What kind of mother would she have made?"

Kimberly grabbed what she wanted and edged back toward the entranceway to the living room. She peeked around the corner and saw George's open toolbox on the floor near the fireplace. But where was George?

"George?"

Kimberly stepped out into the living room and turned around. George was behind her. She whirled around and was about to plunge a knife into his heart when he grabbed her wrist and twisted until the knife fell to the floor. God, he was strong.

He had a hideous grin on his face as he squeezed her wrist even harder until they heard a snap. Kimberly thought she was going to faint from the pain. Still holding her by the wrist, he brought up his other hand. In it was the most gruesome instrument Kimberly had ever seen, a claw hammer, with curved talons, like sharp metal fangs.

"I know you'd rather play with my mommie than me," said George, a wildness in his eyes. "I know all about you, professor. You and Joan and that other pussy-eater, Pat. Man, I had that dyke fooled, didn't I? She thought she'd bagged a live one in the muff bar. And then old Bill. What an asshole he was. I still don't see what Joan ever saw in him. You know what he wanted me to do? Ever heard of golden showers? That's right. Old Bill Gardner, attorney at law, wanted me to piss on him. Of course, he didn't know it was me. You should see me in a red dress, darling, with a little mascara. Oooee. The answer to your dreams, honey. Did you know that Joan liked me to wear a dress when we made love? That really got her hot. She could live out all her fantasies at once. A dress and a dick."

George raised up the claw hammer above Kimberly's head and was about to strike when a searing pain ripped across his stomach. George looked down and saw that in Kimberly's other hand was another knife and it was imbedded in his abdomen. He dropped the hammer and pulled the knife from his stomach.

"You bitch!" he gasped.

Blood was soaking through the front of his shirt. Kimberly started to run for the front door, but George lunged after her, grabbing the back of her dress and pulling her back. He then picked her up from behind and carried her back, away from the front door to the living room. Kimberly tried to kick her way free, but George held on, bleeding all over the back of her dress.

"Please, somebody help!" she screamed.

George tore off a piece of his shirt and shoved it into Kimberly's mouth to muffle her screams. With the bloody knife, he cut another strip of cloth from Kimberly's dress. He tied the strip around her head to hold the gag in her mouth. Kimberly tried to squirm free, but George pressed her into the floor with a knee in her back. He tore off more strips from the dress, pulled her arms behind her, and quickly tied her hands with the strips.

Kimberly tried to crawl away, but George pulled her back and held her down.

Blake got into his car and jammed the key into the ignition. The engine roared to life and he was about to throw the Oldsmobile into reverse when he looked out the back window and then the front. He was completely blocked in by more police cars and fire trucks.

He got out and started running up the street when he saw a patrolman with a portable radio. Shouting over his shoulder as he ran, Blake gave patrolman Kimberly's address and asked him to send two radio cars. "I'll meet them there," he yelled and continued running north toward the Village.

Kimberly tried to shift the gag, but it was no use. George rolled her over and straddled her. She tried to squirm under his weight, but he punched her full in the face and she stopped moving. He stood up and walked over to his toolbox.

Breathing in deeply through her nose, she regained consciousness and saw him across the room. Her vision blurred, she tried to crawl toward the door on her back by pushing with her feet.

George looked over at her and grinned. He snapped open his tool box, reached inside, and pulled out a screwdriver. Discarded it, reached back in, and pulled out a pair of pliers. But he tossed the pliers aside and reached in again. This time his hand came up holding a battery-operated electric drill. He pushed the "on" button and the drill came to life with a loud buzzing sound like a dentist's drill.

Kimberly reached the front door and tried to push herself up, but George just walked over and pulled her back down onto the floor. He again straddled her, then reached down and touched his wound, and brought his hand up covered with blood.

"See this. This is what you did. And now I'm gonna do you." He took his bloody hand and made a cross on her forehead. "A good carpenter always marks his spot before he drills."

This was it. This was how she was going to die. At the hands of a deranged monster. He held the drill above her forehead, its deadly tip spinning viciously about to rip open her skin and flesh and skull, moving lower toward the bloody "x" in the middle of her forehead.

CHAPTER THIRTY-FOUR

Hal the doorman stood outside Professor Stone's door and listened. He hated to do this, but Mrs. Peck, in apartment 3G, just one floor below, had called to complain about the noise. He pressed his ear against the door and heard a strange sound. Then he remembered the carpenter had come up with her and that's probably what it was. He was just drilling some holes for her. Well, he was here, and he promised Mrs. Peck he'd say something, so reluctantly, he knocked on the door.

"Hello, Professor Stone. It's me. Hal."

Inside Kimberly's apartment, the razor sharp tip of the power drill was less than a quarter inch away from Kimberly Stone's forehead when George heard the knock. He pulled up the drill and turned it off.

Somebody knocking on the door.

"Professor. I'm sorry to bother you. Could you please open the door?"

That voice. The doorman. The nosy doorman. George looked down at Kimberly. She must have fainted from fear, thought George.

Okay. Let's not panic here. Think. Should you do the doorman too? Just yank his fat ass in here and finish it? Hey. Why the hell not? George stood up and started to walk to the door, holding the drill down to his side. He was reaching out to open the door when he heard the siren. Faintly at first, but getting louder. The distinct sound of a police siren.

In the hallway, Hal also heard the siren. He started to turn and walk down the hall when, through one of the hallway windows, he saw a police car pull up in front of the building and two uniform officers jump out. Now what? He heard the elevator go down and then come back up. The elevator doors opened and two police officers stepped out with their guns drawn.

"What are you doing here?" asked one of the policemen.

"I'm the doorman. Somebody complained of a loud noise coming from this apartment. I was just checking it out," said Hal.

The policeman pushed past Hal and went to the door.

"This is the police. Open the door."

No response.

"Do you have a key?" asked the second patrolman.

Hal got out his key ring and unlocked both locks.

The first patrolman pushed open the door and they entered, guns in front.

When they reached the living room, they froze. Kimberly was lying on the floor, still gagged, bound and unconscious and covered with blood.

"Oh my God. Professor Stone," said Hal as he knelt down next to her.

The officers immediately started to search the other rooms in the apartment when Blake appeared in the doorway, gasping for breath. He saw Hal kneeling next to Kimberly and went to her. He quickly checked her pulse and then removed her gag.

"She's alive," said Blake. "Kimberly."

She was still out. He untied her hands and examined her for injuries. He realized most of the blood was on the outside of her clothing.

290

There was some blood on the back of her head where it had struck the coffee table.

He turned to Hal. "Why are you here?"

"Like I told the officers. I got a call from someone in 3G. She heard noises," said Hal.

Blake put a cushion under Kimberly's head and his jacket over her upper body to keep her warm. He stood up and looked around the apartment. He noticed drops of blood on the floor. He kneeled down to examine them closely.

Blake looked up when the two patrolmen returned to the living room.

"Nobody else here," said the first patrolman.

"That's impossible," said Hal, and they all turned toward him. "What about the carpenter?"

"Carpenter?"

"That guy George, whatshisname. He came up here with her."

Blake got up and pulled his gun. "Again," he said to the other officers.

One patrolman entered the kitchen, while the other checked the closets. Blake moved toward the bedroom, holding his gun in a two-hand firing position. He pushed open the door and slipped inside. He bent down and looked under the bed but found it was solid from floor to mattress, a platform bed. He cautiously opened the door of a large walk-in closet, and pushed the dresses aside. Satisfied it was empty, he then checked the bathroom and bathtub. Both were empty.

"In here, detective," called one of the patrolmen.

Blake left the bedroom and followed the voice to the kitchen, where the officer was standing next to an open window. Blake looked outside and saw that if someone jumped, he could reach the fire escape from the window. He looked up and down but didn't see anyone.

"One of you take the roof, the other, the street," said Blake. "Although he's probably long gone by now. I'll call an ambulance and a Crime Scene Unit."

The officers left on their chase as Blake made the calls. That done, he got some ice from the freezer and wrapped it in a dish towel. He returned to Kimberly, knelt down with the improvised ice pack and placed it on the back of her head, which had started to swell.

"Oww," she muttered, pulling her head away. Kimberly opened her eyes and looked up at Blake. A single tear rolled down her face.

"It's okay," he said.

"Did they get him?" said Kimberly.

"Not yet," said Blake. "But we will."

Kimberly's eyes focus on Hal the doorman. "Hal?"

"Just lie still," said Blake.

"What's Hal doing here?"

"I think he may have saved your life."

"Where's George?" asked Kimberly.

"He's gone," said Blake.

"Gone?" Kimberly tried to push herself up.

"No," said Blake. "Don't move. The doctor will be here in a minute. You might have a concussion."

"He was going to kill me," said Kimberly.

"I know. Just take it easy," said Blake. "Everything's going to be all right. I'm here now."

"You know? How did you know?"

"Detective," said Hal.

"Yes," said Blake.

"I should get back to my post."

"Go ahead, Hal," said Blake, then turned back to Kimberly.

"I stabbed him in the stomach," she said.

"So that's where all the blood came from."

"I still don't understand something," she said.

"What?"

"How did you know about George?"

"I just had a nice chat with his mother."

CHAPTER THIRTY-FIVE

While a doctor examined Kimberly's wounds, Blake called the precinct to make sure Dee Porter was under full protective watch, with undercover officers stationed around her burned-out showroom and her loft apartment. He then consulted his notes and found the address he needed.

"I've got to go out for a little while," he said to Kimberly.

"Why," she said, brushing the doctor's arm away along with the small flashlight he was using to look in her eyes.

"I just need to check on something. It won't take long. I've assigned an officer to stay here in the bedroom with you, along with a nurse. We have plainclothes officers all over the building, as well as outside, both front and back, just in case he tries to return."

"Do you really have to leave? Can't you send somebody else?"

"I wish I could," said Blake. "But this person could also be in danger."

"Who's that?"

"The housekeeper in an apartment uptown," said Blake. "It's where George Stewhalf was working when I first questioned him."

"I don't understand."

"When I asked George where he was at the time of Joan's murder, he said he was working in the apartment. The housekeeper confirmed his alibi."

"Then why would *she* be in danger? Wouldn't he want to make sure nothing happened to her?"

"Not if she was lying, and we both know she was. I want to find out why and warn her George may try to get to her. You're going to be okay here." He turned to the physician. "How's she doing, Doc?"

"She's tougher than I am," replied the elderly doctor, who looked like he was near retirement. "No concussion, a couple bruises, and she's going to have a pretty little bump on the back of her head for a while. But nothing serious. I'll give her something for the pain, along with a mild tranquilizer."

Kimberly took Blake's hand.

"Promise me you'll come right back," she said.

"I promise."

"I can't believe he's still out there."

"He won't be for long. We'll catch him."

The doctor picked up his bag and prepared to leave. "Make sure she gets plenty of rest."

"I will," said Blake.

"You've got my beeper number," said the doctor. Blake and Kimberly watched the doctor leave. There were still a few forensics personnel dusting window sills and objects the assailant may have touched. Others were gathering fibers and any possible evidence that would link George Stewhalf to the murders of Joan Walsh and Pat Hurly.

After the doctor left, Kimberly closed her eyes and held on to Blake's hand. Then, she opened them and looked up.

"I'm afraid to sleep. Every time I close my eyes, I see him standing there with that drill. It's like he's still here."

"He isn't, and you're safe," said Blake. "I'll have the nurse sit next to you while I'm gone."

"Be careful," she said.

"I'm always careful."

On his way out, Blake checked to make sure police guards were posted at the front and rear doors and in the hallway outside the door to the apartment.

Driving uptown, Blake thought about what Dee Clark had told him about her son, George, the offspring of an accidental pregnancy. Dee had been married briefly, but she had divorced George's father before he was born, never even telling her husband she was pregnant. Raised a Catholic, Dee equated abortion with murder and planned to put the child up for adoption soon after birth.

But when the baby came, Dee was lonely and depressed and decided to keep the child, raising him herself and with whomever she was involved with at the time. This included several girlfriends who would tease and taunt five-year-old George about his little penis. George used to hide in a closet and watch his mother make love with other women. As he got older, he would not only hide in the closet to watch, but he would put on his mother's clothes and masturbate while watching the women reach their own climaxes.

Not your typical American upbringing. The psychologists were going to have a field day sorting out this guy, thought Blake.

He finally arrived at the apartment building on Park and Seventy-ninth and sat in his car, looking up at the building. What if George had gotten here first? What if he was still here? He got out of his car and checked his weapon. Where was the doorman? Blake entered the lobby and looked around.

"Hello? Anybody here?"

Blake removed his gun from his holster and proceeded toward the elevator bank. The elevator was descending. Blake stood off to the side, aiming at the elevator. Drops of sweat had formed on his forehead and were starting to slide down the side of his face. The ancient elevator creaked downward. Blake wiped the wetness from his eyes. The elevator stopped and the thick wooden door began to open.

Blake took his stance, holding the gun with one hand, his gun wrist with the other. He took aim just as a drop of sweat blurred his vision. Out of the elevator came a mountain of white.

"Stop! Police!" yelled Blake.

The mountain of white stopped, then dropped to the floor, revealing a frightened doorman and a wide-eyed woman wearing an apron and black dress. Blake wiped his eyes and blinked. The two people were staring at the detective and his gun, which was pointed at them. Blake looked down and saw that the mountain of white was a pile of laundry, mostly bed sheets and pillow cases. He lowered his weapon and let out a deep breath.

"I'm sorry," said Blake. He pulled out his badge. "I'm looking for someone and I'm a little jumpy." The two people relaxed. "Here," he said, "let me help you with this stuff."

Blake holstered his gun and started stuffing the sheets back into a plastic basket. It was then that he realized the woman in the maid's uniform was the housekeeper he was coming to see.

"I have to get back to the front door," said the doorman.

"That's okay," said Blake. "I'm here to see her."

The housekeeper gave Blake a curious look as she finished re-loading the laundry basket. The doorman tipped his hat and returned to the front door.

"Remember me?" said Blake.

"Of course," said the housekeeper as she picked up the basket and started toward a door labeled "Laundry Room." Blake walked along with her.

"I need to talk to you about the carpenter who was working here," said Blake.

"Which one?" said the housekeeper. "We have workers here all the time."

"George Stewhalf. When I was here the last time, I talked to him and then to you. You said he was in the apartment last Tuesday morning."

"*Si*, I remember."

"I want you to think again about last Tuesday morning. Did he have to go out at some time, or did you?"

"Oh, no. You see, my boss, she's very strict about making sure I'm in the apartment whenever work is being done. She's afraid of being ripped off. One time some guy was working in her bathroom and stole some jewelry. So she makes me stay here."

"So you were both here all that time?"

"Yes."

"Hm. That's interesting. I wonder then how he managed to be at two different places at the same time."

"I don't understand," said the housekeeper.

"Well, last Tuesday morning, you said that George Stewhalf was here, when at about 9:30 that same morning he was about seventy-five blocks away in Greenwich Village murdering a college professor."

The color drained from the woman's face as she fell back against the dryers. Blake reached out and steadied her.

"Are you okay?"

The woman looked away and then back at Blake. This time he could see the fear in her eyes.

"Why did you lie for him?"

"I didn't ... lie for him," said the woman.

Blake was about to counter her statement when she continued.

"If I tell you the truth, will you have to tell my boss?"

"That depends," said Blake. "If you don't tell the truth you could go to jail for obstruction of justice."

The woman's mouth trembled. "Jose, my boyfriend, drives a produce truck," she said reluctantly. "He makes deliveries to markets all over the city. On Tuesdays, he stops at the supermarket across the street. It's the only time we have to see each other except on weekends. So while the store is unloading his truck, we usually go for a walk, or get some coffee. Something like that. I'm only gone a little while. But if my boss knew I was away while a worker was in the apartment, she'd fire me."

"So you left the apartment last Tuesday morning while George was working."

"I wasn't gone too long," she said. "And he was here when I got back."

"How long were you away?"

"An hour and a half maybe. Not too long."

"But long enough for George Stewhalf to leave here, get to the Village, murder a woman and get back before you did."

The housekeeper lowered her head. Tears were in her eyes. "What are you going to do?"

"We still have to catch him."

"Will I have to testify in court?"

"I don't know," said Blake. "Two women and a man were killed by him and I'd like to catch him before he kills again. In fact, he might come after you."

"Why me?"

"Now that he knows we're on to him, he may try to contact you, to see if he can still use you as an alibi. I'm going to assign a police officer to watch out for you until he's in custody."

"This woman. Why did he kill her?"

"She was going to have his baby."

CHAPTER THIRTY-SIX

Back in his car, Blake called in the request for 24-hour surveillance on the housekeeper, both at the Seventy-ninth and Park address as well as her apartment in Queens. He then headed back to Sullivan Street to check on Kimberly.

When he arrived, Blake introduced himself to the uniformed and plainclothes officers guarding the building. In the apartment, he found another uniformed officer and a nurse. Kimberly had finally drifted off to sleep. Blake took off his jacket and sat down in a chair next to her bed.

Where was George Stewhalf? He was bleeding. A stomach wound. He couldn't have gone far. He picked up the phone and punched in a number.

"Hello," said Dee Porter.

"It's Detective Blake. Heard anything?"

"You don't really think the sonofabitch is going to call me, do you?"

"He might. If he does, you can reach me at this number." He gave her Kimberly's number, which she recognized.

"How's she doing?"

"Kimberly? She'll be okay."

"It's my fault Joan was killed, isn't it," said Dee.

"What do you mean, ma'am?"

"I knew how George felt about me, what I am. I never should have let him work for anyone I was involved with. I never thought something like this would ever happen."

"Who would?" said Blake. "We've got a tap on your phone. If he calls, try to keep him on as long as possible. We might be able to locate him."

"I'll try, but like I said, I don't think he'll call."

Blake hung up and phone and noticed that Kimberly was awake.

"Who was that?"

"Dee Porter," said Blake. "We have a trace tap on her phone in case he calls."

"I'm glad you're back," said Kimberly. "I still feel so tired."

"Good," said Blake. "Try to get some more rest."

"Will you stay here?"

"I'll be right here," promised Blake.

Kimberly took Blake's hand and closed her eyes. She had already drifted off when he pulled the chair closer to the bed, and closed his eyes. Every now and then, he would look over and watch her sleeping, a restless worried sleep. Leaning back in his chair, Blake felt a wave of fatigue take over as he started to drift off.

Outside, the moon had moved behind the clouds over Sullivan Street. The streets were quiet now. Across the street from Kimberly's building, two detectives sat in an unmarked car, watching the front entrance.

Another unmarked car was parked across the street from Dee Porter's burned-out showroom, and still another outside Dee's loft.

In the hallway outside Kimberly's apartment, a uniformed officer sat in a chair reading an Ed McBain 87th Precinct novel, hoping to pick up some pointers on proper police procedure.

Next to Kimberly's bed, Blake was still asleep in the chair. Kimberly opened her eyes, a look of fear on her face. But then she saw Blake and she smiled. She pulled herself up in bed and reached over to touch him when, up from below the bed, came a hand out of the darkness. It grabbed Kimberly's wrist.

Her scream awakened Blake who bolted up and grabbed his gun. Kimberly was sitting up in bed, clutching her blanket. Blake put the gun down on the night stand and sat on the bed next to Kimberly.

"There, there," he said, stroking her hair.

"Oh God! I thought he was here. I must have been dreaming," said Kimberly. "It just seemed so real."

"It's probably the drugs they gave you," said Blake. "Besides, you had a traumatic experience. You're bound to have nightmares."

Blake started to get off the bed, when Kimberly reached out and took his arm. He sat back down, leaning back against the headboard. Kimberly smiled and closed her eyes. Slowly, the terror in her heart began to fade as she felt the protectiveness build a wall around her. Detective Blake was here. There was nothing to be afraid of. A slight tremor rippled down her back and then disappeared. She could feel his breathing shift into sleep next to her. Everything was going to be okay.

She felt herself start drifting back into sleep when she sensed something. She reopened her eyes. What was it she felt? A movement? A sensation of moving? Where was it coming from?

Kimberly raised up and looked over the side of her bed. She stared down into the darkness, trying to focus on where she thought the movement had come from. As she stared at the side of her platform bed, she noticed something different. What was it? One of the built-in drawers was slightly open. Just an inch or so. Had she left it like that? She didn't think so. She lowered herself back until her head touched the pillow and stared up at the ceiling.

There was a faint sound. A scraping sound. Could a small animal have gotten under her bed? She peered over the side and then froze. One of the over-sized drawers was sliding open all by itself, as if by magic. Kimberly stared at the incomprehensible sight, when out of the drawer came a hand. Her mouth was open, but she couldn't scream. It was caught in her throat. Another hand appeared and pressed against the platform side, pushing the drawer open wider until a head and shoulder rose up.

In the hallway, the police officer reading the Ed McBain novel put down his book and stood up to stretch. He picked up his soda can and jiggled it. Empty. He looked at the door to the apartment and then up and down the hallway. He looked at his watch. Four a.m. There was a soda machine in the laundry room in the basement. He could be down and back in two minutes. He checked his pocket for change. Just enough for one can. He stretched again and walked to the elevator. He hit the button for down, the door opened, and he got in. The door closed just as Kimberly began to scream.

"No!"

But it was too late.

Before Blake could move, George slammed his metal toolbox down on Blake's head, knocking him off the bed and onto the floor. Blake tried to push himself up, but George swung again, hitting him on the side of the temple with the metal tool box. A sharp burning pain, then blackness. Blake could feel himself slide into unconsciousness, and there wasn't a damn thing he could do about it. He didn't even feel the impact as his cheek smacked against the bedroom floor.

Kimberly slid to the far side of the bed and looked down at Blake lying motionless on the floor.

"You killed him," she whimpered.

"I sure hope so," smiled George. "Look at the dent he put in my tool box."

A surge of terror gripped Kimberly's chest, and she had trouble breathing. George reached out and pulled the sheets and blankets off the bed. He then climbed up on the foot of the bed and stood looking down at her. His face had turned a ghostly gray from loss of blood. He had tied a white pillowcase around his stomach wound and it was now a brownish red from absorbing all the blood. He had the power drill in his hand again. He switched it on and the loud buzzing sound filled the room.

"Remember this?"

It was starting all over again. Where were the guards? Weren't there supposed to be guards outside? Just then, out of the corner of her eye, Kimberly saw something on the night stand. A black metal object. Blake's gun. She started to inch toward that side of the bed when George took a step across the bed and came right up to her, holding the drill to her throat.

"That's far enough."

Kimberly felt the air from the spinning drill on her neck and closed her eyes. Please God. Give me the strength to do this. Her fingers wrapped around the cold metal as George shifted his weight to get a better thrusting angle. She felt his muscles flex. He was going to do it. Now or never.

The explosion filled the room. George stood up straight still holding the drill. He then looked down and saw Kimberly with the smoking gun in her hand. He let the drill fall from his hand and then stared down at his right leg. A small hole had filled with blood just above his knee.

"Kimberly," said Blake's voice.

"Blake? Are you okay?"

"I don't know. What happened?"

"That does it," spat George as he limped around the bed to where Blake was lying.

"What are you doing?" said Kimberly. "Stop or I'll shoot."

George continued moving toward where Blake was struggling to stand up.

"Get away from him!" shouted Kimberly.

But George just smiled, and then he kicked Blake in the head, knocking him out again.

"Stop it!" she cried, tears blurring her vision as she tried to hold George in her line of fire.

George just kicked Blake again but Kimberly's hand was shaking too much to shoot. She might hit Blake by mistake. George bent down and picked up the drill.

"No," said Kimberly.

George held the drill directly over Blake's head with the drill pointed down.

"I'd be careful if I was you. I mean, if you shot me now and I dropped this on his head, it'll make some kinda mess."

Kimberly started to tremble as she held the gun.

"Now put down the gun," he said.

Tears filled Kimberly's eyes. She couldn't believe it. The sonofa-bitch had won. She couldn't shoot George because he'd drop the drill and kill Blake. Checkmate.

"Put it down or he dies."

There was nothing else to do, except surrender. She felt so help-less. She closed her eyes and silently prayed to God. She then let the gun fall to the bed and lowered her head in shame.

Suddenly George pushed Blake aside and lunged across the bed. Kimberly looked up startled and saw the sharp end of the spinning drill bit charging at her face.

There was no way to reach the gun in time. She'd made a fatal mistake and was going to pay for it. Or was she? A memory flashed. Something from self-defense class about leverage and speed.

Kimberly dropped to her knees on the bed and reached up as George flew at her. She could feel the breeze on her cheek from the deadly spinning metal as she gripped George's wrist, then twisted and pulled at the same time.

For an instant, George wasn't sure what was happening. And when he realized what was going on, it was too late.

Still gripping the wrist holding the drill, Kimberly yanked with all her might and flipped George over her shoulder. As he landed on his back, she twisted his wrist again and pushed down with all her might.

The scream that poured from George's mouth was the most hor-rible sound she had ever heard. But then she saw something that made her scream just as loud.

She stood up and stepped back in horror as George held the drill up to his face. Something was on the spinning tip. It was large and round and mostly white with red and blue nerve endings whirling around like tentacles.

George turned toward Kimberly and she covered her mouth. Where his left eye had been, was now a hollow, bloody socket sur-rounded by ragged pieces of flesh dangling under what was left of the eyelid.

Kimberly thought she was going to vomit, but she held one hand over her mouth and knocked the drill to the floor with the back of her other hand. But the spinning drill continued to drone on as it chewed up the floor. George looked up at her with his one good eye glaring. She picked up the gun and pointed it at him.

"Finish me," George pleaded

Kimberly started to shake.

"Come on. I know you want to. Put me out of my misery."

Her eyes filled with tears.

"Just think. I could still get off. You know, maybe cop an insanity plea. Get one of those country club hospital prisons."

Behind her, Kimberly heard a banging on the front door.

"Are you all right in there? Open up."

She turned toward the door, but George reached out, and with one hand grabbed her leg. The other hand held the bloody drill.

"Either do it, or kiss this beautiful leg goodbye."

Kimberly cocked the hammer back.

"That's a good girl," said George.

The front door came crashing in as Kimberly pulled the trigger.

The explosion from the shot filled the room as the police guard burst into the bedroom, his gun out and pointing at Kimberly. With his left hand he flicked on the light switch.

"Freeze!"

Wisps of gun smoke floated around Kimberly as she looked down.

"Drop the gun."

She let the weapon slide from her hand as the policeman moved toward her. He held the gun on Kimberly as he moved closer to see what she was looking down at.

As his eyes followed hers, his mouth opened when he saw the still smoking bullet hole piercing the now silent drill.

CHAPTER THIRTY-SEVEN

The sun was starting to rise on this mild spring morning as Kimberly watched two police officers carry George Stewhalf out of her building and to a waiting ambulance. Emergency medical personnel had bandaged his wounds and one had even made a make-shift patch for his eye. They started to secure him in the back of the ambulance when Kimberly walked up to them.

"Could I have a moment alone," she asked.

The officers looked at each other. One checked George's bindings and nodded. "He ain't goin' anywhere. Don't take too long."

Blake was watching from a sofa in the lobby as Kimberly backed out of the ambulance and let the officers close the doors. The ambulance pulled away and Kimberly walked back into the building.

It had been less than an hour since Blake had regained consciousness and his head was covered with bandages. He still got dizzy when he tried to stand up, as he did when Kimberly walked across the lobby.

"Hey, take it easy," she said, helping him lie back down.

"What was that all about?" asked Blake.

"I had to know."

"Know what?"

"About the daisy."

"Well?"

"Guess what 'Dee' stands for?"

"What?"

"She was born Daisy Porter, but she hated the name so much she had it legally changed about five years ago. Whenever George wanted to get her really mad, he'd call her Daisy."

Blake started to laugh but stopped. "It hurts too much."

"Come on," said Kimberly. "I think we should have a check-up. I feel like I've got two heads. In fact, here comes our ride now."

Just then another ambulance pulled up, and the paramedics jumped out.

As they started to climb inside, Kimberly turned to Blake.

"Well, you know," said Kimberly, "a bit of history was made today."

"What's that?" asked Blake.

"One of us got to use your gun."

She waited about a week and then asked Blake to drive her out to Maplewood, New Jersey. At first, she wasn't sure he would go with her, but when she threatened to start getting involved in all his other cases, he gave in.

They walked toward the mound of dirt at the end of a long row toward the rear of the cemetery. The stone had not been put in place yet, but Kimberly remembered the spot where her best friend had been buried.

She held one long-stemmed red rose in her left hand and gently placed the flower on top of the dirt mound.

"Rest in peace, dear friend," said Kimberly, tears running down her face. "Joan, I know that death is a natural state. That whoever is born must one day die. We just hope that death will come gently and that the struggles of our youth will somehow be rewarded by a long and fruitful life.

"Unfortunately, you and hundreds of thousands of others had to suffer untimely deaths, your lives snuffed out because of violence. I may never really understand completely why you did some of the things you did. But I think I now comprehend some of it. It took awhile, but then I remembered what you had said, about how much you wanted a baby before it was too late. It must have been a shock to learn the man you wanted to marry was no longer able to have children. But then along came an opportunity. A good looking opportunity, too. A little fling. An accidental pregnancy. And suddenly, it looked like you just might be able to have it all. The baby, the husband, the dream. How could you have known that behind the dream lurked a nightmare? You took a chance, dear friend. And while you lived out your dream, you died in love. Maybe we can't ask for much more than that.

"Meanwhile," she continued, her voice beginning to crack. "I want to introduce you to somebody special. This is Detective Alan Blake. I know, he's a cop, and you know how I feel about cops. But he's different. And you would have liked him, even though almost nobody else does."

Blake gave her a nudge and she nudged him back. She then took his hand and squeezed it as tears started to roll down her cheeks. As she leaned back until her head pressed against his chest, she silently mourned the loss of one friend while letting herself feel the warmth and comfort of another.

That same afternoon, in the hospital ward at Riker's Island, a man in an orange prison jumpsuit sat in a wheelchair and stared out at the high walls and barbed wire. He wore leg irons that had been welded to the chair and a black patch covering his left eye socket.

He reached down and pulled a tiny flower from the grass. Looking at the real daisy in his hand, a smile formed on his lips as he pulled off a petal.

"Mommie loves me."

Then he pulled off another.

"She loves me not."